Praise for *That's Just Perfect*

'I love everything Nicola writes. I'm a real fan girl! Her
books are full of heart, real characters and hope and are a
fantastic read – and *That's Just Perfect* is no exception!'
Olivia Beime, author of *Three Nights in Italy*

'Laughter, tears, and a whole lot of life lesions – this
book has everything'
Gillian Harvey, author of *The Bordeaux Club*

'A heart-rending book that's very funny and poignant'
Victoria Dowd, author of *Murder Most Cold*

'Three generations, three brilliantly-drawn characters, three
lives unravelling in different ways – Nicola Gill brings her
beautifully drawn characters together with warmth and wit.
Laugh out loud funny yet poignant at heart, this is
feelgood fiction at its best'
Frances Quinn, author of *That Bonesetter Woman*

'*That's Just Perfect* is a gorgeous tale of mess-ups, second
chances and being perfectly imperfect. So relatable, real,
and uplifting. Another gem from Nicola Gill'
Jessica Ryn, author of *The Imperfect Art of Caring*

'*That's Just Perfect* has all the elements readers have come to
expect from Nicola Gill's novels: warm, loveable and relatable

characters facing tangible dilemmas, written with heart and humour on every page. The messaging about authenticity is beautifully executed, and the ending deeply satisfying. It's a gorgeous book which left me feeling all is well with the world'
Kate Storey, author of *The Memory Library*

'Nicola Gill has done it again. This wonderful story about Emily, her father Ed and their mutual life regrets is very funny, uplifting but also moving. Nicola places her flawed-but-lovable characters in impossible situations, and the ensuing story is always credible and a delight. A real treat of a book. Buy it'
Eleni Kyriacou, author of
The Unspeakable Acts of Zina Pavlou

'Nicola Gill has a rare talent for skilfully conjuring wonderfully complex, relatable characters which her readers are routing for all the way, despite, or perhaps because of, all their imperfections. I loved this book so much, and just had to know what was going to happen, so that my plan to read just one chapter became one more, then one more after that each time I picked up the book. *That's Just Perfect* is full of humour, warmth and I admit, a few happy tears at the end. A perfect holiday, weekend, or indeed, anytime, read!'
Louise Fein, author of *The London Bookshop Affair*

'A cautionary tale about the lies that can so easily fester within fractured families. Hugely readable, utterly relatable and packed with appealing characters, both major and minor'
Sue Teddern, author of *The Pre-Loved Club*

Also by Nicola Gill

We Are Family
The Neighbours
Swimming for Beginners

NICOLA GILL

THAT'S JUST PERFECT

Bedford
Square
Publishers

First published in the UK in 2024 by Bedford Square Publishers Ltd,
London, UK

bedfordsquarepublishers.co.uk
@bedfordsq.publishers

ISBN
978-1-83501-053-2 (Paperback)
978-1-83501-054-9 (eBook)

2 4 6 8 10 9 7 5 3 1

Typeset in Garamond MT Std by Palimpsest Book Production Ltd,
Falkirk, Stirlingshire

Printed in Great Britain by CPI Group (UK) Ltd, Croydon CR0 4YY

MIX
Paper | Supporting
responsible forestry
FSC
www.fsc.org
FSC® C171272

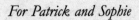

For Patrick and Sophie

Monday

Chapter One

Until last Friday, I had the perfect life. Now I am crying over a packet of fig rolls.

To be fair to me, they are an entirely pointless biscuit. Squidgy. But they haven't upset me for rational reasons, they've upset me because they're Mark's favourite biscuit and I have picked them up on autopilot.

I stand in the middle of the supermarket aisle trying to get a hold of myself. But this is not the sort of genteel weeping that makes men melt in the movies, it's full-on sobbing. With snot. And there's a chaser of molten rage.

It's all very un-Emily.

'Miss Baxter! Miss Baxter!'

I look around to see one of the kids from my reception class. *Marvellous.* 'Hello, Callum.'

'Why are you crying?'

'Umm… I'm not crying. I've got hay fever.'

Callum sucks his gappy teeth like the world's smallest builder. 'I thought people get hay fever in summer?'

'Umm…'

'Oh, there you are, Callum,' says his harassed-looking mum, rounding the corner with a heavily laden trolley in which a red-faced baby sits gnawing at the soggy stump of a breadstick. 'What have I told you about running off?

'Miss Baxter,' she adds, drawing level. 'I didn't recognise you.'

I glance down at my 'outfit' – an ancient pair of joggers with a hole in the bum and a big baggy sweatshirt Mark left behind (along with me). I have worn the latter on repeat because it smelled of Mark and am pretty sure now it just smells. There are food stains all down the front too, which is a nice touch.

'You're a bit dirty,' Callum volunteers.

'*Callum!*' his mother says. 'That's very rude.' She turns back to me. 'Are you okay?'

I wipe my eyes and nose with my sleeve. What was I thinking leaving the flat? 'Fine. Just hay fever. Well, allergies really. Like a sort of autumn hay fever.'

Even the red-faced baby stops gumming its breadstick to eye me sceptically.

Callum's mother's eyes have flickered downwards, and I see her register the large pack of incontinence pads sitting at the top of my basket.

'They're for my elderly neighbour,' I say quickly.

Callum's mother gives me a small sad smile and pats me on the shoulder before leaning towards me conspiratorially. 'Don't be embarrassed. My pelvic floor is shot to pieces since the kids.'

On a different day, I might summon up the energy to insist my pelvic floor is just fine thank you.

Callum's mother leans even closer and I can smell the coffee on her breath. 'Are you crying because of what happened with Tommy Cassidy?'

My stomach lurches. How does she know about that? It only happened this morning, for God's sake. After spending the whole weekend as a shuddering mess in the flat, I managed to put on a happy face and make it into work, where I was just about holding it together until Tommy Cassidy started whistling every time I turned my back.

'I wouldn't blame you if you did shout at him,' she says. 'He's a right little sod. We invited him to Callum's birthday party because we didn't want to leave anyone out and he nearly ruined it.' She holds her thumb and forefinger a few inches apart. 'He had his tongue this close to the motor of the bouncy castle at one point.' She shakes her head. 'If I hadn't got to him.'

My mind cartwheels. Maybe I should have talked to my head of department or even Tommy's mother about what happened? But it's not as if I *shouted* shouted. And I had already asked him to stop three times. 'It was nothing.'

Callum's mum puts her hand on my arm. 'I'm sure.'

'Callum's doing very well with his reading.' Goodness knows why I've decided to hold an impromptu parents' evening right here by the custard creams, but it sure as hell beats talking about my life.

'Can I get some chocolate biscuits, Mum?' Callum pipes up. 'Because Miss Baxter says I've been good with my reading?'

Callum's mum enters into negotiations. He can get some chocolate biscuits, but he can't have one until after his tea and then only if he's eaten his broccoli. At least four florets.

'Three?' Callum says, holding up his grubby digits.

I see my chance to get away. 'See you tomorrow, Callum.' *Assuming I can drag myself in to work.*

I back away so my pupil and his family don't see the hole in the bum of my joggers. It's hard to imagine being any more humiliated, mind you. I *never* cry in public. Even when my mum died, I kept my misery firmly behind closed doors.

By the time I reach the relative safety of Foods of the World, my heart is thudding in my chest. There cannot be problems at work. Not on top of *everything*. It will be even worse now too. For all her head-tilting faux sympathy, Callum's mum is not the type to keep things to herself. *The state of her when we bumped into her in the supermarket. She'd definitely been crying and she smelled, for goodness' sake. What happened with Tommy must have been even worse than we thought. And did you know she's incontinent too? I expect it's the stress.*

I force myself to breathe. In and out. In and out.

I *hate* this place. How have I never noticed that before? Too many people, too much noise, too much cruel, buzzing fluorescent light. And that's before you even get to the assault on your senses that is *so much stuff*.

I tell you how I've never noticed it. It's because I come here with Mark on a Sunday afternoon around 4 o'clock because he's worked out that's one of the quietest times to come. We have a list that's in the order of items in the shop.

Today, there's no list. And no Mark.

I force myself to keep moving down the aisle. Someone has dropped a jar of pasta sauce, and it is lying shattered and forlorn, its blood-red contents splattered far and wide. It has been cordoned off like a crime scene.

I think about Mark's pasta surprise, an emergency dish that comprises a jar of tomato sauce and whatever vegetables he can find hanging around in the salad drawer. Turns out he had much bigger surprises up his sleeve though.

I pick up the soy sauce Mrs Desmond asked for, guiltily registering that I haven't called my own grandma in nearly a week, despite the fact that she recently broke her shoulder and has had to temporarily go into a care home. It's not as if she's got any other family either. My father lives in Florida and, even if he didn't, he's about as reliable as Network Rail in bad weather. I normally talk to Grandma every few days but I just can't face telling her about Mark. She loves Mark.

I head for the alcohol section. However much I want to get out of here, I cannot leave without wine. But blocking my path is a huge display of the champagne Mark and I drank to celebrate our engagement. I feel like one of those cartoon characters with a pressure valve on their head. Why didn't I realise that all Mark's beautiful words and promises meant nothing?

Breathe, Emily, breathe.

Slowly, I manage to get myself past the champagne and throw a bottle of red into my basket. Just cat food now and I can go home and fall apart in private.

In the pet food aisle, I glance down and am surprised to see the fig rolls sitting in my basket. I have no recollection of putting them in there but guess it must have happened during the humiliating exchange with Callum and his mother. I stare at the red packet reproachfully as if it and it alone is responsible for how I feel right now.

There's a plethora of different cat meals — casseroles, pâtés, even soups. (Who serves their cat pâté or soup? Are they main meals or just appetisers?). I have always bought Pebbles the same kibble on repeat. Maybe if I'd been a bit more adventurous on his behalf, he'd like me more? I shake the thought from my brain. Pebbles likes me well enough, of course he does.

I put an 'Oh So Meaty' cat casserole in my basket and stuff the fig rolls in its place on the shelf. I have always taken a very dim view of people who put things back in random places in supermarkets, but I am desperate to get out of here.

I join the queue for self-checkout, digging my nails into my palms. An image forces its way into my consciousness: the fig rolls among the cat food. 'Excuse me,' I say to a sharp-featured woman just ahead of me in the queue. 'Would you mind keeping an eye on my basket? I've, err, forgotten, something.'

The woman glances up from scrolling on her phone and gives an uninterested nod.

I sprint through the crowded supermarket, one hand over the hole in my jogging bottoms. A man who isn't looking where he's going barrels into me, and I apologise to him.

Panting, I reach the pet food aisle, my eyes scanning the shelves until I see the bright red packet. I pick it up and run towards the biscuit aisle, where I place it back with its squidgy pointless friends.

I rock back on my heels, my breath catching in my throat. This time last week, I was everything a woman is meant to be: calm, easy-going and, most importantly, nice.

Now look at me.

Chapter Two

Ed

Ed never wanted to see another fancy dress costume in his whole goddam life. The condo was littered with them: dinosaurs piled on the sofa, fairies hanging from the back of the door, pirates and their flaccid cutlasses all over the table.

Sunlight streamed through the windows, bouncing off the fairies' glittery wings. Ed had lived in Tampa for eighteen years. Long enough to say trash and trunk and closet (though he still pronounced 'tomato' the English way). One of the things he most loved about his adopted homeland was how the weather lifted your mood. Usually.

A few months back, a friend of Shona's told Ed she was making great money reselling things on the internet. It sounded like Ed's perfect job. No set hours, no going into an office and, best of all, no dick boss.

Ed decided he'd start reselling watches. Why not? He'd always had an eye for a nice watch. He went on the internet and found some that were made in China and looked great. They were unbelievably cheap too. He was going to make a killing. Flushed with excitement, he ordered five hundred. When they arrived, the watches didn't look quite how they did in the photos. In fact, if truth be told, they were more like something you'd find in a Christmas cracker. Ed cursed himself for not doing the online reseller course Shona's friend had recommended or at least ordering samples. No point crying over spilt milk though. He bought some fancy boxes, told himself great presentation covers a multitude of sins and set up his online store. The watches started to sell and the complaints and return requests quickly followed.

Laughter drifted through the paper-thin walls. The little girl and her dad who lived in the neighbouring condo. Ed's gut twisted. There was a time when Emily was captivated by him. Back when he used to magic ten-pence pieces from behind her ear. Now she was twenty-nine and not one bit captivated. You reap what you sow, as his mother was so fond of saying.

Ed ran his fingers absent-mindedly across a pirate costume, the static-y fabric giving him a small electric shock. He'd been shopping for groceries one day when he'd seen a kid dressed as Spiderman. He decided there and then that he'd ditch selling watches and sell fancy dress costumes instead. He'd pivot (a dick term his old boss at the car dealership had loved). He got home and had a quick Google of the most popular kids' fancy dress costumes. This time, he did order samples and they looked just like they did in the photos, better even. Ed ordered several different characters in several different sizes. It was a big outlay, but it was cheaper to buy in bulk. Plus, everyone knows you have to speculate to accumulate, right? Ed got three new credit cards to cover the costs. He told Shona his business was going to be big. He'd treat her to that pricey new couch they'd seen in town. Or a meditation retreat. Or both.

Then Ed tried to list his costumes and found he couldn't sell them in the US because they didn't meet the appropriate safety standards. Some bullshit about fire retardancy. Ed tried to send them back but discovered he had no right of return. Which is how he came to be here surrounded by what felt like about five hundred tonnes of nylon.

Ed stared at a tiny T-Rex atop a pile. Its face was set in a sort of rictus grin as if it was laughing at Ed. As one might, quite frankly. He was, however you cut it, royally screwed. Not only had he racked up considerable credit-card debt, but he'd failed to tell Shona these costumes were going nowhere fast (she was under the impression a big order was pending). Worse still, Ed had taken out a loan against the condo that she had no idea about.

Shona was undoubtedly the easiest-going woman Ed had ever been in a relationship with. Whether it was because of all the yoga or the meditation or the huge amount of drugs she'd taken in her youth, she didn't nag Ed about anything – not to get a job, or empty the trash, or be out of bed by the time she got home from work in the evenings. The only thing she wasn't so laissez-faire about was cheating. Her ex had slept with her then best friend, and Ed had a reputation that preceded him. This meant, when they'd first got together, Shona was paranoid if Ed so much as looked at another woman. Two years in, he'd earned her trust, though, and she'd stopped grilling him about where he'd been and who with.

But, for all Shona's easiness, Ed knew she'd go ballistic if she found out they were about to lose the condo, and that Ed had risked it without so much as telling her. Firstly, because who wouldn't (she was placid, but she wasn't a saint) and secondly because she bloody loved this place. It might not be in the best part of Tampa or have the hardwood floors realtors were so obsessed with, but to Shona, who'd grown up in a trailer park and then lived in her car for three years when she was battling addiction, it was a palace.

Ed stared at one of the needlepoint cushions Shona had lovingly stitched. *I plan on being with you until forever ends.*

Yeah, unless he lost their home.

He gave himself a mental shake. He wasn't going to lose their home. He reached for his phone. It would be four o'clock in the afternoon in England now.

'Edward,' his mother said. 'Well, this is a surprise.'

Ed ignored the jibe. 'How are you doing, Mum? How's your shoulder?'

'Painful.'

Ed stared at dust motes dancing through the air. She was obviously pissed at him. No change there. And he supposed he should have called her at least once since she'd got out of hospital, but he'd been busy. Kind of. 'Sorry to hear that. And what have you been up to?'

A loud tssk made its way from Broadstairs to Tampa. 'What do you think I've been up to? I've got a broken shoulder. I've had to put myself in a care home for a bit while it gets better.'

'A care home?'

'Yes,' his mother snapped. 'I had all kinds of plans before I fell over, and now I do nothing but eat and sleep and watch rubbish on telly. Honestly, I've never felt so old. Anyway, enough of me moaning, have you spoken to Emily recently?'

'Not in a while.'

Another tssk.

'She's busy.'

'Right.'

There was a world of disapproval in that one word, but Ed chose to ignore it. He soldiered through a few minutes of attempting small talk. It was something of an irony that he could charm almost anybody except his own mother or daughter.

'I was going to ask a small favour,' he said.

'You want money.'

Ed dabbed at his sweaty brow with his sleeve. 'Just a small loan. I've started up my own business and things are going really well.' He looked at the massive pile of princess dresses. 'But, well, there are some start-up costs.'

'I'll stop you there, Edward. I won't be giving you any more *loans*.'

Ed felt as if someone had punched him in the stomach. His mother always bailed him out. Not graciously, but she still did it. 'But Mum—'

'Please don't try to change my mind. You're fifty-four years old and it's about time you stood on your own two feet.'

'But—'

'No buts. My answer is no.'

Ed hung up the call despondent and spent the afternoon pacing around the small living room. He'd only intended to borrow a small amount against the condo, just enough to tide him over while he wasn't working and fund his fledgling business. But somehow months had passed, costs had spiralled and the debt had got bigger and bigger. 'Just stick to the repayment schedule,' the thick-necked kid at the bank told him. Like there was any 'just' about that.

Ed would have to go to that loan shark on Boulevard. This wasn't a prospect he relished. His mate Donny had got money from him once and then been hospitalised after the 'reminder' to pay up. The interest on the debt was more than double the original sum too.

Maybe there was something Ed could do to change his mother's mind? He might have a slightly better chance if he could talk to her face to face, but she was a stubborn old mare, and it was a long way to go on the off chance. What he really needed was some way of getting into her good books.

Yeah, good luck with that. Ed could count on one hand the number of times his mother had seemed pleased with him. She'd taken particular umbrage at him leaving his marriage eighteen years earlier. You might have thought that if his own mother was going to take any side, it would have been his, but that was to underestimate both her love for Catherine, who was like the daughter she'd never had, and her disgust at Ed for 'taking up with a twenty-four-year-old cruise ship floozy'. The damage was cemented in the years that followed when his mother constantly berated him for 'totally forgetting his responsibilities as a father'.

A lump rose in Ed's throat. He might have an uncanny ability to shrug off most criticism but even he knew that one was a fair cop.

He looked around the living room. This condo meant everything to Shona. She was houseproud in a way that would put Martha Stewart to shame, forever mopping, scrubbing or polishing. She'd made curtains, tended houseplants, and stitched so many needlepoint cushions, Ed teased her they needed a bedroom of their own.

He put his head in his hands and groaned.

But then suddenly inspiration struck. The way to please his mother was to repair the rift between him and Emily.

He leapt to his feet, optimism surging around his body. Okay, he'd tried and failed to do this in the past, but that was before he'd learned making amends from the 12-Step Program – how it's about so much more than just saying sorry.

Ed would fly to England and harness his new-found wisdom.

He'd have to scrape together the plane fare, but he could go to the loan shark for that. Assuming his mother shelled out, Ed would be able to pay it back as early as next week. Which meant he could avoid both crazy amounts of interest and death threats (always good).

As he lifted a pile of pirates to look for his keys, Ed felt the muscles in his shoulders start to loosen. He'd wanted to make things right with Emily for a long time, so this was the very definition of a win-win.

It was only as he was putting on his flip-flops that he realised that the meeting he'd just arranged with the loan shark was at the exact time he was supposed to be at yoga with Shona (the loan shark having a diary slightly more booked up than George Clooney's). Shona may be the laid-back sort but the two of them going to Monday afternoon kundalini yoga mattered to her a lot. Ed stared at his phone, wondering what sort of excuse he could dream up to explain his last-minute absence. *So sorry, babe,* he tapped out eventually. *Got a killer migraine so going to miss yoga x*

Poor baby! Shona replied. *Take some feverfew and rest up xx*

Ed felt a twinge of guilt. He was doing this for Shona though.

He stepped out into the pulsing sunshine and headed to the Boulevard, turning over his plan in his mind. What if he flew all the way to England and got a frosty reception just as he had in the past?

This time would be different, though.

Ed literally could not afford for it not to be.

Tuesday

Chapter Three

Ninety-six hours and twenty-three minutes and not so much as a WhatsApp from the man I thought was my whole life. I shut the door to my flat behind me, sink to my haunches and burst into the tears I had to hold back at work. Somehow, I managed to sleepwalk my way through another day. I wasn't, it has to be said, the kind of teacher I like to think of myself as. No inspiring the next generation. Instead, I found myself looking at the clock from ten o'clock, the kids' endless questions made me feel like screaming, and I told Nisha that not all stories have happy endings. But I didn't shout at anyone (and went out of my way to be nice to Tommy Cassidy); lessons, albeit lacklustre ones, were provided and everyone including me made it to pick-up time without crying.

Pebbles appears in the hallway and surveys me from a distance. Today, more than ever, I wish he would come to me. I know cats are not dogs, of course. I can't expect a wagging tail or excited barking, but I've seen other people's cats offer up a bit of a welcome – weaving themselves around legs, allowing themselves to be stroked, doing a bit of polite meowing.

Of course, Pebbles was once another person's cat: he was my mum's. In my more paranoid moments, I wonder if that's why he doesn't like me – because he knows I wasn't the perfect daughter I somehow fooled the rest of the world into thinking I was.

'I keep replaying last Friday evening over and over in my head,' I say. 'Me getting home burbling about how I really deserved my takeaway. The kids had been feral little buggers all day, probably not helped by the fact that it was bucketing down at break time, so I'd had to keep them all in the classroom. Hannah Marshall got a satsuma pip stuck in her ear. Did Mark know how lucky he was to work with people who didn't put fruit pips in their ear just because they were bored? But then I stopped mid-sentence because Mark was sitting there on the sofa totally silent, his face ashen.'

Pebbles makes no comment.

'He said we had to talk, and my stomach flipped because everyone knows what that means. Except that couldn't be right because this was Mark. My Mark. The boy next door but one who I'd grown up with it. The Ant to my Dec. The person who pulled me through when Mum died.'

Pebbles says nothing.

'Then he said he'd been headhunted for a job in Manchester and my whole body flooded with relief. I made a lame joke about how when I'd said I wanted to travel, I'd been thinking more in terms of Australia. Mark didn't laugh.' My voice cracks. 'Which is when I knew this wasn't about Manchester. Mark picked at a thread on his cuff and told me neither of us had ever dated other people. Like that was news to me. He said every time he thought about our upcoming wedding, he felt scared.'

Pebbles doesn't reply.

'Why did he leave? It can't have been something he did on impulse, right? It must have gradually dawned on him that he didn't want to marry me. Which means there must have been signs. Signs I was completely oblivious to.'

Pebbles doesn't offer up an opinion.

'I suppose I shouldn't be surprised by a man having a deep-seated fear of commitment. Hell, I've got my very own Peter Pan of a father. I thought Mark was different though.'

Pebbles remains silent.

'Did he know he was going to dump me when we celebrated my birthday last month? When we bickered about the recycling? Did he already know what he was going to do when we went to Sal and William's for dinner last Saturday night? We had a great evening, for God's sake. And when we got home, we had sex. Really good sex. Or at least I thought it was. I keep exhuming memories and examining them with a new lens.'

Pebbles watches me, his expression impassive.

'Is he telling me the truth when he says there's no one else? Is he really frightened of marriage or is he just frightened of marriage to me? What's wrong with *me*?' I wipe my eyes with the remnants of a soggy, balled-up tissue. 'I haven't told a single person about the break-up. I just can't. Telling people would make it real.'

Pebbles has no answer.

'Today, in the staffroom, Rachel asked me what my fiancé and I were up to this evening and I just mumbled something about having a quiet one. But who knows what Mark is doing? Downloading Tinder, probably. Of course, I wouldn't get away with keeping the break-up to myself if Mum was still alive. One look at me on FaceTime and she'd know something was up.' A sob escapes from somewhere deep within my chest. 'I must be the only twenty-nine-year-old in the world who has never experienced a break-up. Where's the bloody instruction manual?'

Pebbles yawns expansively.

'I don't know if I can get through this.'

Pebbles stands up and I wonder if he's moving towards me. Perhaps he can sense how sad I am and is going to make an exception to his 'no petting' rule. I imagine my fingers sinking into his soft, smooth fur.

Pebbles stalks off with his tail in the air, not giving me so much as a backward glance.

I sigh and wipe my eyes. I have just poured my heart out to a cat, asked it questions, for God's sake. And as if that isn't already certifiable enough behaviour, it's not even a cat who likes me that much.

I drag myself to my feet.

Every inch of this flat reminds me of Mark. The previous owners had a penchant for sludgy colours and 'unusual' paint effects such as rag rolling and stippling. Mark and I spent hour after hour repainting it. We didn't mind, though. It was actually quite fun working side by side while listening to cheesy pop music. Plus, this was our forever home.

Back when we had a forever.

A sharp pain blooms in my chest. I remember the first time in my life I discovered heartbreak can actually be something you feel physically. It was back when I was eleven and my dad left. Best not to dwell on that now though. One abandonment issue at a time. (Although maybe I should be looking at the pattern here? Examining what it is about me that makes people want to leave?).

The doorbell rings and my heart leaps. Mark! He has realised he's made a crazy mistake and he's back.

I bolt towards the door almost tripping on the edge of the rug.

I fling open the door. There before me is not Mark, but my

father. I imagine my soul as a deflating balloon. 'What are *you* doing here?'

'I thought I'd pay my little girl a surprise visit.'

'All the way from Florida?'

'Yup. Aren't you going to invite me in?'

I can think of few things I'd like to do less. I move aside and let my father pass, the bitter disappointment fizzing around my body. I really thought it was Mark. But, of course, Mark has keys. Which is the least of why I'm an idiot for thinking it was him.

My father and I stand facing each other in the small living room. He looks much older than when I last saw him a few years ago, and he is wearing some sort of ridiculous yoga gear that is way too clingy.

'So why are you in London?' An irrational thought flits into my mind: did I somehow summon up my father by thinking about him a few minutes ago, like some kind of unwelcome genie who has sod all power to grant wishes?

'I told you I came to see you.'

'You came four thousand miles to see me? And didn't think to give me any warning?'

'Yes and yes. I wanted it to be a surprise.'

'Well, it's certainly that.'

If my father notices my vinegary tone, he ignores it. 'Shall I pop the kettle on?'

'I'll do it,' I snap. The nerve of him acting as if I am failing in my duties as a hostess.

'Where's Mark?' my father says over the sound of the kettle.

My stomach lurches. What the hell am I going to say?

'Where have all the decent mugs gone?' I say, burying my face in the cupboard and playing for time.

If I don't feel ready to tell the world about my split with Mark, the person I least want to know about it is my father. It has been a point of pride on my part to show him that my life is a success *despite* him. Plus, unlike everyone else, he has always seemed annoyingly lukewarm about Mark, even asking me if I was sure that's what I wanted when we got engaged.

Now I imagine the words *Mark has left me* coming out of my mouth. The inevitable tears. My father will look at me with pity. Poor little Emily. Humiliation floods my body.

I can't. I won't.

'Mark is away on business.'

'Oh, cool,' my father says, plonking himself down on the sofa. 'Where?'

For a second, I can't think of a single place, but then the obvious answer floats into my consciousness. 'Manchester.'

'Oh, cool.' He takes a swig of tea. 'How's work?'

'Great.' Another lie.

'Cool.'

How many times is my father going to say 'cool'? And is he actually putting his feet up on the coffee table? (The glass table that shows every little speck of dirt.) I hope he doesn't think he's staying for long. I fiddle with the engagement ring I haven't yet been able to bring myself to remove.

'You not having a cup of tea?' he says.

I shake my head. 'So are you still with Shona?'

'Yup. Shona's the one.'

I have to force myself not to roll my eyes. My father has a long history of women who were 'the one'. That said, he does seem to have been with Shona a while now. What a bloody world it is when he's the one in a stable relationship and I'm the one having to pretend I'm still engaged. 'Listen, you really should have told me you were coming.'

'Like I said, I wanted it to be a surprise.'

He's doing his puppy dog eyes thing, and it's all I can do not to scream that it may have worked on God knows how many unsuspecting women over the years, but it most certainly will not work on me. 'Right. How long are you staying?'

'My flight back to Tampa is next Monday evening.'

Oh, God, six whole days away! 'And where are you staying?'

'Well...'

Oh, no, no, no. My father cannot expect me to drop everything the moment he clicks his fingers. He waived those sort of privileges by deciding he'd spend the last eighteen years playing nothing more than a walk-on part in my life. 'It's just I've got a lot on right now. Work is crazy busy at the moment. We're taking the whole reception year on a trip to the Science Museum this Friday. And then at the weekend, I have loads of plans.' My father's eyes are fixed on mine. Does he somehow know I'm lying? That my weekend 'plans' involve nothing more than shuttling between fridge and sofa while wallowing in self-pity. 'I'm going to look at some wedding venues on Sunday afternoon.' This is sort of true in the sense that I have appointments booked. For obvious reasons, I have been meaning to cancel them though.

My father nods. 'So Mark will be back by the weekend?'

Sweat prickles my armpits. 'Err, no.' When had he said his flight was? 'Not until Tuesday.'

'Oh, so you're going to look at wedding venues without him?'

I feel myself start to flush. 'Yes, without him. Mark trusts me completely. He's happy for me to go ahead and book somewhere if I like it.'

Why did I say that? Good liars, which I most certainly am not, don't feel the need to over-explain like this.

'Well, that's great,' my father says, smiling. 'I'll come with you.'

Tears prick the backs of my eyes. I choke them back, hoping my father hasn't noticed them.

'Look,' he says. 'I know me turning up out of the blue like this must come as something of a surprise, but I've been thinking about you a lot recently and all the mistakes I've made in the past.'

Mistakes? He buggered off to the other side of the world when I was eleven and pretty much forgot he even had a kid.

'Good to see Pebbles is still alive,' my father continues as the cat appears in the living room.

Yup, alive and unwillingly playing the role of my confidant.

'The thing is, Em, I really want to make amends. I know I've said this before, but I've changed. I learned from the 12-Step Program.'

My mouth opens and closes like a fish. I had no idea that my father was an alcoholic. He has a thousand other things wrong with him, but I've never thought of him as a particularly big drinker. I suppose it's good he's getting clean.

It doesn't mean I'm going to let him stay though.

Chapter Four

Ed

If Ed had a mantra in life, and really mantras were more Shona's thing, it was 'Make life easy on yourself'.

This mission he was on, however, was looking far from easy. Emily could scarcely have been less delighted to see him. Forget her face dropping when she opened the door, her whole body sagged.

Ed sat on the toilet, too knackered and fed up for a standing-up pee.

Was his plan doomed? Sitting in the condo in Florida, making things right with Emily and then demonstrating that reconciliation to his mother had seemed doable. But cold, grey London had served up a hefty dose of reality.

Ed knew he was an idiot to be surprised by Emily's less than effusive welcome. He was all too aware of his shortcomings as a father and didn't need Emily, his mother, or anyone else to remind him of them. Generally, he prided himself on going full Edith Piaf when it came to regret, but even he couldn't fail to wish he'd done things differently with his daughter.

To this day, it brought a lump to his throat when he pictured eleven-year-old Emily's confused little face when he and Catherine

27

told her they were splitting up (a generous way for Catherine to frame the situation given that Ed was leaving her for a twenty-four-year-old cruise ship singer). Ed put his arms around his daughter's scrawny, shaking body. 'This is nothing to do with you, Twiglet. Nothing is going to change between us. I'll always be your dad, always love you.'

He'd meant every word. But suddenly there was none of the easy intimacy of living under the same roof. Overnight, Ed became the sort of father who couldn't tell you the names of his kid's friends at school, or what her favourite breakfast cereal was or whether she still liked Furbys. It didn't help that he didn't have a flat and crashed on friends' couches when he wasn't working on cruises. This meant he and Emily were reduced to spending 'quality' time together in service station cafés, greasy spoons or McDonalds. They would eke out warm Cokes and stilted conversation.

Over the months, Emily grew more and more hostile. Why hadn't Ed told her the truth about why he'd left? Did he know her mum cried herself to sleep most nights, that she thought Emily couldn't hear her, but she could? Did he know how much Emily longed to go to her mum in those moments but that she couldn't because her mum would have hated Emily seeing her so upset? 'What do you do?' Ed asked. Emily's eyes filled with tears. She stayed in her bed, placed a hand on the wall between her and her mum and whispered that she was there, and it would be okay. But it wasn't okay, was it?

The gaps between Ed and Emily's meetups started to stretch. There were all kinds of excuses. Ed was travelling a lot, he was in a volatile new relationship, he had money worries. The main reason was guilt though. When Ed was away from Emily and her mother, he could be Ed the Good Guy, but around them he couldn't hide from his own shittiness.

Ed stood up. He had a stiff neck from sleeping in an awkward position on the plane and a whisper of a headache was starting to pulse behind his eyes.

Before he left for England, Shona had stuffed one of her sage bundles into Ed's suitcase. She was a great believer in 'smudging' any new environment to cleanse it of negative energy. Ed had laughed and told Shona that you could get locked up for engaging in any of that woo-woo stuff in England. Now he was wondering if it might be useful to smudge after all. He could clearly do with all the help he could get.

He stared at his reflection in the bathroom mirror, pulling at the pouchy skin under his eyes. How had he got so fucking old? How had he let two decades slip by without playing a meaningful part in his daughter's life? How had he let himself lose the one thing in his life he could actually have been proud of?

If there was one shred of hope, it was that Mark was out of the way. Mark had never been anything but polite to Ed, but he was fairly sure the younger man wasn't keen on him. Hardly surprising when you considered Mark's family had lived down the road from them. Mark had had a ringside seat when Ed walked out on his family and had been there to see the trail of devastation he'd left in his wake. He'd also been dating Emily when her mum had been diagnosed with cancer so knew exactly how Ed had handled that one.

Ed turned the tap and water spluttered out. Emily clearly didn't want him to stay. He had to somehow change her mind though. He didn't want to fritter away money on a hotel but, more importantly, if he had any chance of connecting with Emily they had to spend lots of time together.

He had noticed she had teared up when he offered to go to look at wedding venues with her. She was obviously surprised and touched that he'd bother. The one silver cloud to being a useless parent was that when you got the smallest thing 'right', it was noticed. Ed knew he hadn't taken as much interest in Emily and Mark's engagement as he could have. He also knew, at the risk of being sexist, that women lost their shit over weddings. Even sensible women like Emily.

A surge of optimism flooded Ed's weary body. The wedding was his golden ticket. If he could show Emily he cared about the wedding, that would show her he cared about her.

He squirted handwash into his palms. His nostrils twitched. He picked up the bottle and read the label: lavender and sage.

The universe was telling him not to give up.

Chapter Five

Liz

Liz didn't know why this place served supper at six o'clock. Like they were babies.

She was sitting next to a woman called Sonia. In the week that Liz had been here, Sonia had hooked on to her. She was nice enough, but she smelled aggressively of lavender and she talked at you relentlessly. Lonely probably.

Liz's phone bleeped with a message from Peter. *Love you to the moon and back xxxx*. He was such a romantic. Not to mention good-looking, funny, kind and successful. She was one very lucky woman.

'How's your shoulder today?' Sonia said.

Liz reflexively glanced down at the sling. 'Still a bit sore but I can't complain.'

'My friend Philippa broke her shoulder, and it took over a year to heal properly. Doctors said it was a bad one. Tell me again how you had a fall?'

Liz didn't like the phrase 'had a fall'. They'd used it all the time at the hospital. There was a world of difference between 'had a fall' and 'fell over' and the former was definitely for *old* people. There was no way her shoulder was going to take a year to heal either. She'd be better and back home within a few weeks. 'The pavements were wet and slippery, and it was getting dark. One minute, I was zipping along, the next I was flat on my back like a beetle.'

'Oh dear,' Sonia said.

Liz looked around the room. It was nice enough, she supposed. There were big vases of faux flowers and heavy brocade curtains and lots of the sort of prints that no one could hate and no one could love.

Apart from her and Sonia there were eight other people at the dining table. One youngish woman with cerebral palsy, a bunch of women with exactly the same hairstyle (perhaps they had a regulation care home haircut – like the army) and two men who were talking about football. Tottenham were rubbish this season. That manager of theirs ought to be ashamed of himself. Especially when you thought what they were paying him.

One of the carers asked Liz if she'd like a glass of wine. The manager had made a huge thing of how residents were offered a glass of wine with their supper. As if that was so extraordinary. Frankly, with the prices they charged they ought to be serving vintage Bollinger, not Blossom Hill.

There were people who ate in their rooms. The woman next door to Liz never seemed to come out, but then she needed to be fed. Liz had seen one of the carers shovelling soup into her mouth when she walked past. Scraping the spoon across her chin like you do when you're feeding a baby. It made her feel so sorry for the woman. She couldn't even bear the thought of someone having to cut up her food for her. That was why she'd chosen cottage pie tonight even though she'd never been keen on cottage pie. *Take me to Switzerland if I ever get that bad,* she messaged Peter. *Never,* he replied. *I don't even want to imagine a world without you in it.*

'It's your anniversary' Sonia said.

What?

'One week!' Sonia said, laughing and raising her glass.

She meant her anniversary of being *here*. Like that was something to be celebrated. Liz forced a smile.

It wasn't anti-ageing creams or Botox or fillers that kept you young, it was good health. Before she *fell over*, Liz was driving a car, working two days a week at the Oxfam bookshop and doing her elderly neighbour's food shopping (oh, the irony). Now she was in a care home. Not for long though. She didn't live here like Sonia and most of the others. As soon as her shoulder healed, she'd be back in her own home. Even better, Peter would be living there with her. The thought made her whole body thrum with pleasure.

Sonia was prattling away. Her chicken had a nice flavour but it was a little dry. Not too bad if you doused it with enough gravy, she supposed. She had this annoying way of using a laugh in place of a full stop.

Be kind, Liz admonished herself inside her head. 'So you said last night you have three granddaughters?'

'Yes,' Sonia said, beaming. 'Hope, Faith and Charity.'

Dear God.

'Hope is getting married next year.'

'Oh?' Liz said, taking a gulp of the horrible wine. 'So is my granddaughter, Emily.'

Sonia clapped her hands together in delight. 'Isn't that a coincidence?'

It wasn't that much of a coincidence. Liz had read once that there were over 85,000 weddings every year in the UK. She nodded dutifully though.

Sonia had launched into a stream of chatter about Hope's upcoming nuptials and how excited she was about them.

Liz adored her granddaughter. Some of the happiest times of her life were when Emily had come to stay with them when she was a child. Liz could still picture her standing on the bridge over the river wearing her red ladybird wellie boots, her small face lit up with delight as the two of them chucked sticks into the water to see which one emerged the other side of the bridge first – Pooh Sticks. Years later, when Emily was seventeen and her mum died of cancer, she moved in with Liz and, even though the circumstances could hardly have been worse, Emily never gave in to self-pity or let her grief diminish her innate instinct to put others first. She had a wise head on young shoulders too.

Not like Ed. Liz loved him, of course, but he was something of a chocolate fireguard as a son. Not to mention as a father. Liz had never really forgiven him for walking out on Catherine. She supposed she might have got past that. You can never really know someone else's marriage from the outside (even if Liz was pretty sure she laid the blame for the failure of this one firmly at her son's feet). But what had been truly unconscionable was how after the split Ed had shirked his responsibilities as a father. Dipping in and out of Emily's life as and when he felt like it.

Liz did wonder if she'd been a little harsh with Ed when he'd called the other day. She was annoyed he hadn't picked up the phone since she'd come out of hospital though. She knew he was in America but really. Also, she couldn't help noticing that, when he did call, it was often because he wanted money. Like some kind of eternal and infernal teenager.

'Shall I take your plate? Have you finished?'

Liz looked up to see Domenica, who was probably her favourite of all the carers here.

'You haven't eaten much?' Domenica said, sounding concerned.

'Not much of an appetite today,' Liz said, smiling. Domenica was kind. The people with dementia lived upstairs behind a double set of key-coded doors but they were brought downstairs for the entertainment and activities and Domenica was lovely with them. There was one man who seemed to wear a permanently vacant expression, but the other day, when the dogs had been brought in, Domenica had picked up a Jack Russell, put it on the man's lap and gently placed his gnarled hand on the dog's back, at which point his whole face became animated.

'Hope is having seven bridesmaids,' Sonia said, laughing. 'Seven! They're going to be wearing royal blue, which isn't a colour I would have picked. I had my colours done years ago and the woman told me it's a shade that doesn't do much for anyone regardless of where they are on the colour wheel. You can be a winter, spring, summer or autumn and still not look good in royal blue. What colour has your granddaughter chosen for her brides-maids?'

'I'm not sure,' Liz said. 'I don't think she has even got her own dress yet.' She made a mental note to ask Emily about it when they next spoke. It hurt her heart to think of Emily having to plan this wedding without her mum around. Especially as Ed was distant in every sense of the word. Still, at least Emily was marrying a good man. She and Mark were perfect for one another – soulmates.

Just like her and Peter.

Chapter Six

'So what's your wedding dress like?' my father says, reappearing in the sitting room, stinking so much of sage and lavender handwash it's as if he's doused himself in it.

My stomach knots. 'I haven't bought one yet.'

'Really? With the wedding seven months away. That's not like you.'

How dare he tell me what is and isn't like me? He doesn't know me. He happens to be right in this instance but that's hardly the point.

He plops himself back down on the couch. He doesn't seem like a man who is in any hurry to leave. It's awkward. Much as I want to get rid of him, I feel as if I have to spend a bit of time with him first. I'm still trying to process the news that he's an alcoholic and, although neither that, nor the fact that he lives on the other side of the world, is my fault, it does make it harder to give him his marching orders. I don't believe for a second he's come all the way to England just to see me, though. He's very good at schmooze, but I have learned the hard way that his words are often empty ones.

He adjusts the waistband of the God-awful yoga trousers. 'Are you waiting for a sale or something?'

'I've just been busy.' I'm not about to explain that the mere thought of shopping for a wedding dress without Mum is too painful to contemplate. It's a rite of passage that you and your mum shop for a wedding dress together, that she is there to burst into tears when you come out of the changing room, to tell you that you look so beautiful, and she can hardly believe it because surely – surely – it was just two minutes ago that you were starting nursery.

I stare at a pair of Mark's running shoes that are lying forlornly by the door. Normally, I would have put them in the shoe cupboard by now, bemoaning Mark's untidiness, but I just haven't had the heart. I get up and pour myself a glass of water, raising an empty glass in the direction of my father, who shakes his head. 'Are you still working for the telesales company?'

'No, that, err, came to an end. I've started an online reselling business.'

'A what?'

'An online reselling business. Basically, I buy stuff wholesale and then resell it online at a marked-up price.'

'What do you sell?'

'I started with watches. That reminds me, I brought a couple of them over with me as gifts for you and Mark.' He rummages in his rucksack and pulls out two rather smart-looking boxes. 'This one is for you.'

I open the box to see a watch that looks as if it belongs in a kid's dressing-up box. It's the thought that counts, I suppose. 'Thanks.'

'You're welcome. Shall I leave Mark's here on the coffee table for him for when he gets back?'

'Err, yeah.' I force a smile. 'So you're selling watches?'

'Not anymore. I've moved on to fancy dress costumes.'

'Fancy dress costumes?'

'Yeah. But I'm going to move into something else. Pivot, as I believe the young people say. I haven't decided what yet.'

'Riiiiight.' My father has had many different 'careers' over the years, and this one sounds particularly hokey. How can he not even know what he is going to be selling?

'Do you have a particular style of wedding dress in mind?'

And we're back there.

'Princessy? Sleek and simple? I know you could pull off whatever look takes your fancy.'

When did he suddenly become a wedding dress aficionado? Despite a lifetime of womanising, my father has only actually had one wedding and I know from the photos that my mum didn't go for a 'proper' wedding dress. ('You can't really when you're six months pregnant.')

'I don't know. I need to try some on.' *Well, I would do if there was actually going to be a wedding.* I feel the tears start to rise and choke them back.

My father picks up his mug before realising it's empty and putting it back down. 'We could go to a few stores together at the weekend if you like?'

I almost spit out my water. It's as if I've been dropped into some kind of nightmare. 'Err… I don't think…'

'C'mon,' my father says. 'It will be fun.'

'Any decent bridal boutique has appointments booked up months in advance,' I say, grateful for the excuse dropping into my mind.

'Maybe I could persuade them? Explain I'm over here from the US and that I'm only around until Monday and would just love to see my little girl in a wedding dress?'

The nerve of the man! As always, he's convinced his charm is a superpower. 'Don't be so ridiculous.'

My father looks genuinely wounded and I feel a small stab of guilt.

'Are you leaving?' I say as he stands. I've wanted nothing more than for him to go, but I'd rather it wasn't under a cloud. What if he's heading to the pub, his recovery forgotten? I don't want that on my conscience.

He gives me one of his megawatt smiles. In all his years in the States, he has never got himself 'American teeth', I imagine because he can't afford them. Somehow though, despite the wonkiness of his smile, it's definitely of the movie-star variety. 'I thought I could grab us a takeout?'

There are so many things I want to say. I can't deal with you at the moment. I don't want you to stay here. We call it takeaway. Instead, I just nod. I'll let my dad stay one night and then send him packing.

Wednesday

Chapter Seven

Ed

Ed had known that a bridal boutique called Love Shack would be achingly hip. So he wasn't surprised to open the door to a space that looked more like a contemporary art gallery than a store. The room was long, double height and aggressively lit, resulting in a stark and clinical aesthetic. Sombre-looking sales consultants in sharply cut black trouser suits hovered with iPads.

He'd started shortlisting bridal boutiques the second Emily had left for school that morning. He knew he could just phone around and would certainly be able to talk to more people that way. But he had taken the view that he had way more chance of securing an appointment in person than he would have done over the phone. Although Ed had been good at his job in telesales, it had cemented his belief in the importance of face-to-face inter-actions. You can't build a rapport in the same way with a disembodied voice. There's no eye contact, no smiles, no tiny non-verbal signals.

Ed assessed the three sales consultants. They only seemed marginally more human than their iPads.

'Excuse me,' he said, selecting one at random and giving her his most beaming smile. 'I wonder if you could help me with a little problem I have?'

The woman cocked her head to one side.

'My daughter is getting married next May. I live in the States and I'm over here visiting just until next Monday. We'd planned to go wedding dress shopping together. Her mother passed away, very sadly. I was supposed to book up some appointments for her to try on dresses this weekend, but I totally forgot.' He gave his best self-deprecating laugh. 'Men just aren't great at this stuff.'

The woman looked him up and down. 'We don't have any appointments available this weekend.'

'I understand,' Ed said. 'But I was wondering if there was any chance you could squeeze us in? Just because I don't live in the UK, which means this is the only chance we have.' He paused, taking in the woman's impassive expression. 'As I mentioned, my daughter's mum isn't around anymore. We lost her to cancer. As I'm sure you can imagine, the whole wedding dress shopping thing is quite hard for my daughter. I mean, every woman wants her mum by her side for that, right?'

'We don't have any appointments for this weekend.'

Jeez, had the woman not heard everything Ed had just said? He'd almost made himself cry.

Seconds later, Ed stepped back into the rain. He mustn't be discouraged. He still had three shops left on his list and, assuming they were staffed by actual humans, he'd definitely be able to sweet-talk someone into giving him an appointment.

Ed had selected the shops on his list on the basis of them looking decent and being within a small radius of each other. It was a myth that lazy people aren't organised. Ed planned lots of things with military precision. Organisation was the best weapon he knew against expending any extraneous effort or energy.

The second bridal shop had a very different feel to the first. It was stuffed with baroque furniture, huge, ornate gold mirrors, and flower arrangements the size of a small child. A gaggle of women were clustering around a bride-to-be trying on a big, puffy dress and their laughter and squeals of delight bounced off the pale pink walls.

It was only now Ed realised he hadn't seen a single customer in Love Shack. Perhaps they were too messy for the shop floor?

He had a much higher chance of success here. He picked out an assistant who he reckoned was about his age. She had a friendly, open face. 'Hi, I wonder if you can help me get out of a very deep hole?'

The woman laughed. Great start!

'My daughter is getting married next May.'

'Congratulations,' the woman said. 'So is mine actually.'

'Aww, lovely.' This was going better than Ed could possibly have imagined. 'I bet you'll be a radiant mother of the bride.' For a second, he wondered if the compliment had been too much, but the woman grinned and rolled her eyes before telling him that flattery would get him everywhere but to tell her what he wanted.

He gave her a sheepish smile and made his eyes go very wide. 'My daughter's mum died of cancer. Emily was only seventeen at the time and it was a devastating blow to her. She and her mum were so close. Although Emily's obviously very excited about the wedding, well, as you can imagine, it's bittersweet.'

'Poor thing,' the woman said, looking genuinely upset. 'I hate to imagine my daughter having to organise her wedding without me. I go with her to everything, from menu tastings to make-up try-outs. I love it, but honestly, it's taken over my whole life.'

The bride-to-be who was trying on the dress yelped in protest as one of her friends jammed an ornate jewelled hair clip into her hair.

'Yeah,' Ed said. 'So when it comes to shopping for wedding dresses, well, I'm all the poor kid has got. Which isn't ideal. I mean, I do my best, but blokes aren't great at this sort of thing, are they?'

'Oh, no. My husband wouldn't be able to tell you what a fish-tail skirt was if his life depended on it.'

'Me neither,' Ed said. 'But that's not the worst of it. You see, I was supposed to book up appointments for this weekend. I live in the States and I'm just over here until Monday night. Anyway, I'm ashamed to say, I messed up and didn't book a single appointment.'

The woman's face scrunched. 'Oh.'

'So I was wondering if there was any chance you could save my life and squeeze us in on Saturday?'

The woman shook her head. 'I'd really like to help you but there's no way, I'm afraid. We're absolutely booked solid.'

'We wouldn't need that long,' Ed said. 'My daughter is the decisive type. And we could come in very early or very late. Whenever really.'

'I'm sorry,' the woman said. 'Our whole ethos here at Hearts & Flowers is making sure every bride gets the time and attention she deserves. Choosing a wedding dress is a big moment. You only do it once. Or, at least, that's what we all hope. It wouldn't be fair to give your daughter an appointment if we can't give her the service we pride ourselves on. I'd love to help her, though. It must be terrible to lose your mum when you're so young. Maybe we can book your daughter an appointment in a few weeks' time, and I'll make sure I look after her myself?'

'But I won't be here in a few weeks' time.'

The woman nodded. 'I'm so sorry.'

And just like that, Ed was back out in the cold.

Chapter Eight

I can hardly believe that, on top of *everything else*, my father turned up on my doorstep last night. And, as if that wasn't bad enough in itself, I'm supposed to feel sorry for him because he's got a drink problem. We shared a tense and stilted evening and, even though I don't normally think of myself as a big drinker, I had to fight the powerful urge to stow a bottle of wine under my jumper and nip off to the bedroom to swig it back. (My father, to be fair, asked me a couple of times if I fancied a 'snifter' but I could hardly say yes, could I?).

Today has done nothing to lift my spirits. At 11.40, the head-teacher received an email to say that Felstead Infants is being inspected by Ofsted tomorrow. *Tomorrow.* As in less than twenty-four hours away. The whole establishment has been catapulted into panic.

And now it's home time and Tommy Cassidy's mother has assaulted me with the five words no teacher wants to hear: Can I have a word?

'Of course,' I say, my legs suddenly gelatinous. 'Mrs Glover,' I say, turning to my teaching assistant. 'Would you mind keeping an eye on Tommy for five minutes please? Mrs Cassidy and I are just going to have a quick chat.'

'Sure,' Maggie Glover says, shooting me a sympathetic look.

I lead Mrs Cassidy into the classroom, which smells of paint and playdough with top notes of urine (there were two accidents today, one of which genuinely made me wonder how such a small person's body could hold that amount of pee).

We sit down opposite each other in two of the child-sized plastic chairs. I might be a passionate advocate of body positivity, but I can never sit in one of these chairs without feeling elephantine.

'Tommy says you shouted at him,' Mrs Cassidy says without preamble. 'On Monday morning.'

I squirm in my seat. 'We have to maintain discipline, Mrs Cassidy—'

'By shouting?'

'No,' I say, my palms growing damp. 'By asking the children to modify their behaviour where necessary.' Why am I talking in this weirdly formal way all of a sudden? 'Tommy kept whistling, you see, and it was a bit distracting, so I asked him to stop.'

'He has just learned to whistle. His father taught him.'

I'm not quite sure what to say to this, so I keep quiet and force a smile. I glance at the friendship tree on the wall. All the leaves have photographs of the children in the class plus the things they came out with when I asked them what makes a good friend: Plays with me, is kind, shares toys. I thought Mark was my best friend. I stuff the thought down. I have enough to deal with in the moment.

Mrs Cassidy leans forward. 'So you're saying you didn't shout at Tommy?'

The question is direct and unambiguous, and I know it's my moment to come clean. Tommy's mother might even be sympathetic if I do the whole 'mea culpa' thing; we might share a laugh about how trying small children can be. 'Certainly not.'

The other woman narrows her eyes. 'Hmm. So Tommy is lying?'

'Err… I wouldn't say lying,' I stammer. 'More that he's mistaken. Children can be oversensitive.'

Mrs Cassidy says nothing, and I stare at the paper plate self-portraits the children made. Emma's pipe cleaner smile has slipped down onto the top of Jaydon's head.

'Well,' Mrs Cassidy says. 'I suppose I have little choice but to take your word for it.'

I let out the breath I didn't realise I was holding.

The other woman scratches her neck. 'It's just you do seem to have a bit of a problem with Tommy. You've called me in a couple of times to talk about his behaviour.'

'I can assure you I don't have a "problem with him". In fact, only today I gave him a good-behaviour sticker.' Thank God for Tommy managing to be vaguely passable for two hours straight and thank God for my need to overcompensate for the incident I have just vigorously denied even happened.

'Right,' Mrs Cassidy says, standing and smoothing down her skirt. 'Well, I'm glad to hear that.'

I stand and follow her outside to where Tommy is busily stripping petals off a daisy, watched over by a weary-looking Maggie.

'What was all that about?' Maggie says as Tommy and his mother walk away.

For a second I'm tempted to confide in Maggie, who wasn't in the classroom at the time of the incident. She has over twenty years of experience and I trust her completely. But I'm not sure I want my unfailingly patient colleague to know I snapped. 'Nothing,' I say. 'Nothing at all.'

*

Maggie and I walk back into the classroom.

'Blimey,' she says. 'It looks like a bomb's gone off in here. And I'm guessing with Ofsted coming tomorrow, you're going to be even fussier than usual about leaving the place immaculate?'

'Umm…'

Maggie laughs. 'Yep, that's what I thought. And here's me hoping to get away on the early side.'

I get down on my hands and knees and start picking up wooden trains and track. I put them in the plastic box with the picture of a train on the front. 'I can always finish up on my own. I'm in no rush.' That's certainly true. I am dreading getting home and giving my father his marching orders, even if I do know that is exactly what I have to do. Last night was *a lot*. The treble whammy of my father's completely unexpected arrival, his sudden desire to atone for sins of the past and then, just when I couldn't be much more discombobulated, the discovery that he is an alcoholic.

Maggie gets a cloth and starts to wipe down the paint splattered easels. 'I'm not leaving you to do all this on your own.'

'It's probably not as bad as it looks.'

Maggie raises her eyebrows and I laugh. I pick up the plastic washing-up bowl and empty the soapy water into the sink.

'I can't believe you agreed to wash Meghan's feet every time she'd been in the sandpit,' Maggie says.

'Her mother said the sand really irritates her feet.'

Maggie makes a pfftt sound. 'You know what irritates me? Parents who have no clue that their little darlings are just one of twenty-six kids in the class.'

'I know. But it doesn't take me that long. And Meghan is such a sweetie.'

'She is,' Maggie says, rinsing a paintbrush under the tap. 'But she's a sweetie with a penchant for the sandpit, which meant you had to do your whole washing Jesus's feet routine about five hundred times today.'

I laugh. 'I think it was more like four.'

'And isn't she the same mother who asked you if you could heat up Meghan's soup in the microwave?'

'Yes, but that was only one time.'

Maggie shakes her head. 'You're too nice, Emily.'

Not so nice I'm not planning to kick out my alcoholic father. Not so nice I didn't shout at Tommy. Not so nice I'm not lying about everything from that to the break-up with Mark.

Maggie places the cleaned paintbrushes in a pot. 'I can't believe Ofsted are coming tomorrow. Why can't the buggers give you a bit of warning?'

'Hmm,' I say, retrieving a board book from inside the toy oven. Ofsted are far from the only buggers to have given me no warning recently.

Maggie and I work on in silence, my mind straying to whether I ought to talk to my department head about the conversation I had with Tommy's mother. Get ahead of any issues and nip them in the bud? But Tommy's mother had seemed mollified, hadn't she? And anyway, I'm not entirely confident I can get through another stressful conversation without bursting into tears. Whatever else I'm doing at the moment and however hard I try to concentrate on it, the break-up with Mark and the thought of life without him is always *there*, and sometimes it overwhelms me to the point I struggle to remember how to breathe.

I glance at my watch. 'Goodness, Maggie, it's gone four. You go.'

'I can do th—'

'Please,' I say, placing a hand on her arm. 'It's mostly done now and I'm happy to finish up on my own.'

'Sure?'

I nod.

'Okay, thank you,' Maggie says, shrugging on her jacket. 'Just promise me you won't start cleaning the windows or washing the walls?'

I poke my tongue out at her. 'See you tomorrow.'

'See you tomorrow. And have a nice evening.'

Unlikely.

The classroom seems quiet with Maggie gone and I have to fight to squash down the thoughts that are jostling for position in my mind. If only they were as easy to put in order as the classroom.

I survey the shelves in the book corner and decide to pull all the books off them and place them back in their proper height order.

I'm halfway through the task when Tara pokes her head around the classroom door. 'I might have known you'd still be here.'

'Yeah, for reasons best known to myself I decided I should start rearranging the bookshelves.'

'Good idea,' Tara says. 'It's not as if the kids will undo all your efforts in about five minutes flat.'

I smile.

'I was wondering if I could ask you a favour actually.'

'Shoot.'

'Well, you know I run cookery club after school on Thursdays?'

I do know because Tara talks about it constantly. Says how it's the biggest pain ever and she has no idea why she ever agreed to do it. 'Yeah.'

'Well, I was just wondering if there was any chance at all you could cover it tomorrow for me? I've got my best friend's hen do this weekend and I'd really like to get my highlights done.'

I hesitate. Normally, I'd say yes in an instant even though I already run two after-school clubs of my own. But at the moment it's hard enough dragging myself through the working day, let alone extending that day. Especially a day that includes an Ofsted inspection. It isn't even as if Tara needs to do something like go to the doctor either. 'Er...'

'They're making pizzas so it will be dead easy. Plus, I've already printed out the recipe sheets.'

'Well, okay.'

Tara's face splits into a huge smile. 'Thank you, I owe you one.'

Tara blags favours all the time, so she owes me considerably more than one. Still, who's counting?

'See you tomorrow,' she says, disappearing with a cheery wave.

I pick up a book and place it on the shelf.

You're too nice.

I'm not, though. I'm really not.

Chapter Nine

Ed

Ed walked out of the penultimate bridal store on his list deflated. He'd been in there for less than two minutes. A snub-nosed child of a woman had practically laughed in his face when he said he was after an appointment for the weekend.

He headed towards the final store on his list. He was trying hard to remind himself that making amends with Emily was not entirely dependent on getting this appointment. But he couldn't shake the visceral feeling that it mattered. Emily was normally ultra-organised, so the fact that she hadn't chosen a dress yet told Ed she hadn't been able to bear to shop for one without her mum. That broke Ed's heart. And told him he absolutely had to step in and step up.

He turned into a pretty cobbled street. Shona would have called it 'darling' and taken about a zillion pictures for her Instagram. She was a rabid Anglophile who talked constantly about her cockney heritage (a great-grandmother who hailed from Clapton). Ed reckoned her love of all things Brit was a large part of her attraction to him. He was like Marmite or M&S or proper tea.

He click-clacked across the cobbles, the expression 'nothing worth having comes easily' floating into his mind. It was an adage he'd always been slightly dismissive of. He'd spent a lifetime getting all sorts of things he wanted with minimal effort on his part. He'd been both clever and popular at school and good at just about any sport he turned his hand to. Later, he discovered dating to be a breeze and he was constantly surprised by just how grateful women were to any man who behaved with a semblance of decency or even just let them finish a sentence.

Maybe getting this appointment would prove impossible, though? Ed shook such negative thoughts from his brain. Shona was a big believer in both positive thinking and manifesting. 'You gotta tell the universe what you want.' She encouraged Ed to set intentions and voice them out loud. Normally he was resistant, but desperate times called for desperate measures. 'I will get this appointment,' he muttered to himself. 'I will make things up with Emily. I will get my mother to help me out of the financial hole I'm in.'

His intention setting was interrupted by a notification pinging on his phone and for one mad second Ed wondered if the universe was responding immediately? Perhaps it was the woman from the last store saying she'd had a cancellation? Or, better still, his mother saying of course she'd give him a loan.

In fact, it was job alerts from one of the recruiters. That could be the universe: solve your financial problems by taking a job. But Ed was a business owner now, and okay that business had had a few teething problems, but he'd find something he could resell. He'd been a bit unlucky with the watches and the fancy dress costumes, but there was definitely easy money to be made flogging stuff online.

Ed was outside Helen Yately Brides now. He decided he'd have a quick peek at the jobs, purely out of curiosity. Right at the top was a telesales role at Spectrum. Ed's old job. If he'd been in any doubt before, this made up his mind. He'd rather be a dog food taster (real job: Ed had met a guy at the gym who did it) than go back to Spectrum. He'd liked working there at first. He was a natural when it came to getting people talking and got way fewer people hanging up on him than anyone else in the team. He'd often get into long interesting chats with people he called. One guy had worked for NASA, for God's sake, another had seven kids. Seven! But everything changed at Spectrum when a new manager called Brad joined. Brad was a stickler for process and liked to micromanage. Why wasn't Ed sticking to the script when he phoned people? Why was he twelve minutes late last Tuesday? Within a couple of weeks, Ed had walked out.

Ed opened the door to the shop. The ceiling was carpeted in what he assumed were fake pink flowers and there were zebra print rugs and exposed brick walls, creating a fancy cocktail bar vibe.

Two brides-to-be were twirling this way and that in front of long mirrors. One had a single friend with her but the other had a huge entourage complete with a couple of token men.

A sales assistant with a mass of dark curls was picking her way across the shop floor carrying a big stack of shoeboxes. The boxes wobbled before crashing to the floor like a stack of Jenga bricks.

Ed was across the room in an instant, helping to retrieve various ivory, gold and silver shoes and putting them back in their boxes.

'Thank you so much,' the assistant said. 'That serves me right for trying to carry too many in one go.'

Ed handed her a jewelled stiletto and smiled. 'You nearly made it.'

The woman laughed.

Ed gave her a full-beam smile. 'I'm hoping you can help me make a mission impossible possible.'

'Oh?'

'Yeah, you see the thing is I've messed up. Like not just a little bit but spectacularly.' In Ed's experience, few things endeared you more to women than honesty (even fake honesty). He told her about the wedding and Emily's mum no longer being around. He said he was only over here until Monday and was supposed to have booked up appointments at bridal boutiques for next Saturday but had forgotten.

The assistant raked her hands through her curls. 'I'd like to help you, but we're booked solid at weekends. We don't even get breaks. Last Saturday, I actually thought I might wet myself.'

Sweat prickled Ed's armpits. If he didn't win over Emily, he had zero chance with his mother. The thought of his mother caused a switch to flip in his brain. 'I think maybe the reason I forgot to book up the appointments is that my head is all over the place right now. My mum is dying, you see. We're all in bits about it, particularly my poor daughter. She adores her grandma, and she's been more like a mum to her since Catherine died.' He hung his head low. 'We're having to move the wedding forward.'

The assistant chewed on her bottom lip. 'Listen,' she said, lowering her voice to a whisper, 'come in at midday on Saturday and I'll just pretend there was a mess-up with the bookings and fit you in.'

It was all Ed could do to not start dancing a little jig. 'You're a superstar!'

The assistant smiled. 'Just don't tell anyone the truth.'

Ed tapped the side of his nose and gave her a beaming smile. 'See you on Saturday.'

He stepped out into the rain. A small stab of guilt punctured his elation. He probably shouldn't have told the assistant that his mother was dying.

Then again, it was kind of true. We're all dying.

Chapter Ten

I walk up the steps to my front door with a steely sense of resolve. I am going to tell my father he has to leave. I know he will charm and wheedle and do all the things he does so well, but I will stand firm. I cannot deal with him right now. And, yes, I feel bad that he is struggling with addiction and has apparently travelled all this way just to see me (if that is even true), but neither of those things are my problem. He didn't even warn me he was coming, for God's sake.

But I open the door to the flat to discover my father is nowhere to be seen. For a second, I wonder if he has left for good and I'll find some hastily scribbled note. That certainly wouldn't be out of character. But then I see a jumble of his clothes strewn across the sofa and his book next to a dirty mug on the coffee table. He is just out.

I wander into the bedroom and throw myself face down on the bed. Mark's empty side taunts me, and I fancy I can still detect a faint whiff of the citrusy aftershave he has worn since he graduated from Lynx Africa. Maybe the smell isn't there, though, but just haunting me like a phantom limb.

Eventually, I heave myself up, change out of my work clothes and go into the kitchen, where I pour some kibble into a bowl.

(Pebbles firmly rejected the cat casserole.) The sound summons up the hitherto invisible feline.

'Hey,' I say. 'How's your day been? Mine has been Grim with a capital "G". We're going to be inspected by Ofsted tomorrow and I've somehow agreed to do cookery club for Tara. Plus, Tommy Cassidy's mother cornered me at home time and said Tommy had told her I shouted at him, and I know I should have come clean, but I couldn't bring myself to.'

Pebbles has nothing to say about this turn of events.

'Also, I have to get rid of my dad. I just can't cope with him right now. Not on top of everything.' Hot tears roll down my cheeks and I wipe them away roughly with my sleeve. 'I can't believe Mark is gone.'

Pebbles offers no wisdom or advice.

'I'm kind of shocked at how easily I lied to my dad when I told him Mark was away on business. And I lied to Tommy Cassidy's mother. I don't think of myself as a liar. What were my choices in either situation, though? I can't let one mistake ruin my reputation as a teacher and I don't feel ready to talk to anyone about me and Mark, let alone my father. Hey, Dad, my relationship has failed; I've failed. I'm staring into this cavernous black hole of aloneness and, unless I want to die alone and for my body to be eaten by cats...' I trail off and stare at Pebbles. I don't *think* he'd eat me. 'Neighbours would eventually alert the authorities about the smell. How tragic is that?'

Pebbles doesn't comment.

'I'm going to need to navigate some sort of future without him. I'll have to go on dating apps even though I'm the only person under thirty who has zero experience of them. Until Jasmine explained it to me a couple of months ago, I thought breadcrumbing was the thing in "Hansel and Gretel".'

I bend down. 'Come here, Pebbles.'

The cat's ears flatten.

I move towards him, reaching out for a stroke. Pebbles runs away, a blur of grey fur.

I sit down on the kitchen floor, engulfed by fresh tears. I can't even get a cat to like me.

Where the hell is my father? It's so typical of him to just disappear without explanation like this. Now you see him, now you don't.

I was eleven years old the day my father left. I had been in trouble at school, having forged my mum's signature on a detention slip I'd received for talking in class. The teacher had immediately known the signature was penned by me and had phoned my parents. I dawdled on my way home from school, nausea churning in my belly as I prepared myself for a huge telling off. But when I got home, everything was weird. No one so much as mentioned my crime and there was a battered red suitcase in the hall, which was odd because my dad didn't have a cruise ship job that week. Mum and Dad asked me to take a seat on the sofa (sofas it seems are dangerous places for me) and I braced myself. The telling off was coming, I just needed to be sitting down for it. I'd watched enough TV programmes to know this was bad. My parents didn't mention the forgery, though. Instead, they told me they were splitting up. I knew two things with absolute certainty in that moment: my life would never be the same again and this was my fault. My dad had always called me his 'perfect little angel' but recently, in a wholly unsuccessful attempt to get in with the cool girls at school, I had started being naughty. My dad was leaving because of me.

*

Where has Pebbles gone? He loves his food but would clearly rather go without dinner if access to it means having to endure being stroked by me. If memory serves me correctly, he was a pretty friendly cat when Mum was still alive. But during the ten years I've had him, I can count on one hand the number of times he has tolerated my affections. I have tried everything from cat treats to toys, even shelling out for a book called *Feline Feelings: All You Need to Know*. That's £8.99 I'll never get back.

I wonder if my father is in the pub right now. I am sorry about his problems, but the truth is my dad hasn't been much of a parent. It was Mum who was the main family breadwinner, Mum who helped me with my homework and Mum who put a coat over her pyjamas to pick me up from sleepovers I'd decided I didn't want to stay at. My father, meanwhile, was a shadowy figure in my life, albeit one who could be a whole lot of fun when he did show up. He has never been someone I could rely on; he had missed everything from my fourteenth birthday to my burst appendix to my graduation. And then of course there was his performance when Mum was sick.

'Hello,' my father calls from the doorway now.

I rise to my feet. 'Hi.'

'How was your day?'

'Horrible,' I say, before I can stop myself.

'Oh?' Dad shrugs off his jacket. 'Why?'

'Oh, nothing. Just the school is being inspected by Ofsted tomorrow.'

'Ah,' he says, swiping his hand through the air. 'It'll be fine.'

It'll be fine is my father's signature phrase. He trots it out without taking in whatever it is you're worrying about. It was a wonder he didn't wheel it out when Mum was diagnosed with cancer. 'Where were you, anyway?'

'On a mission,' he says, grinning.

'What do you mean?'

'All will be revealed,' he says, winking. He rummages in his rucksack and pulls out a bottle of champagne. 'I thought we'd celebrate.'

The last thing I need is to get sucked into my father's problems, but I can't in all conscience let him drink right in front of my eyes. 'No!' I say, prising the chilled bottle from his hands.

His brow furrows. 'What's the problem?' He breaks into a smile. 'Oh, because I talked about the 12-Step Program, right? I'm not an alcoholic.'

'*What?*'

'Yeah, I like a nice beer as much as the next man, but I've never had a problem with booze, thank God. I don't think I've got any addictions actually. I did wonder at one stage if I was addicted to sex, but I think I just really, really like it.'

I shake my head. 'First of all, eww, and secondly, if you're not an alcoholic, then what was all the talk about the 12-Step Program?'

'Shona has taught me that there is so much wisdom in the 12 Steps. You know she's an ex-addict, right? Well, she's been clean for nearly nine years, but she still follows the principles of the Program. She says there's so much we can all learn from it, regardless of whether we're addicts. She's particularly evangelical about the concept of making amends. Which is something I know I need to do when it comes to you.'

My brain is struggling to catch up. I can't believe I let myself be suckered in by my father yet again. That, despite myself, I felt sorry for him: bravely battling his demons. Committing himself to his recovery. But he isn't an alcoholic and he isn't doing the 12-Step Program. Which calls into question what the hell else he is lying about. 'Why are you actually in England? And don't tell me you came all the way here to see me. I want the truth.'

He raises his palms. 'I did come over to see you, but it wasn't the only reason. I also want to visit your grandma. I haven't seen nearly as much of her as I should have done over the last few years and, not to sound maudlin, but her fall has made me realise that she's not getting any younger.'

I stare at him. It's painful to think about my grandma not being around anymore. I love my mum's parents, but it's Grandma Liz who has been most like a mum to me since mine died. She's the one I went to live with aged seventeen and while, of course, no one can ever replace Mum, she's the person I turn to when I need mothering. She'll inevitably be the first person I go to when I'm ready to start discussing the split with Mark.

Dad presses his thumbs into the bridge of his nose. 'It's not just about seeing you and seeing Mum, though. It's about the connection between those two things. You and I both know how much my mum adores you, and we also know that, quite rightly, she doesn't think I've been the father I should have been. She has made no secret of her disappointment in me or how sad it makes her that things aren't better between us. And I suddenly realised that I can't let any more time pass with her thinking I haven't fixed things. I've wanted to do that for years and this has given me the kick up the bum I needed.'

'I see,' I say, my mouth dry. At least my father is being honest with me now. There is so much to take in, though.

'I thought maybe we could go and visit Mum together while I'm over here? I think it would mean a lot to her.'

'I think it would,' I admit. I picture Grandma Liz coming over a few months after mum dying and quietly and calmly starting to box up her things which I sobbed and fussed over letting so much as a half-used pack of dental floss be thrown out.

'We could go on Sunday afternoon,' Dad says. 'We'll be in that neck of the woods looking at wedding venues.'

Ah, yes, *that*.

'Shall we have a glass of champagne?' Dad says.

Ten minutes ago, I thought he was an alcoholic. And that I was about to throw him out. 'Yeah, I suppose so.' I get two champagne flutes out of the cupboard. 'Why are we having champagne anyway?'

'Because I have a surprise.'

'Not another one?'

Dad laughs. 'Touché. But this is one I know you'll like. I've managed to get us an appointment at Helen Yately Brides for this Saturday.'

'You've what?' I squeak.

'Yep. Midday Saturday. Time for you to pick out that dress.'

I feel as if all the air has been knocked out of my lungs. This is like some kind of awful nightmare. I cannot go and try on wedding dresses like a tragic little Miss Havisham. But how on earth can I get out of it without telling Dad I've been lying about Mark's whereabouts and that he's actually dumped me?

Dad pops the champagne cork. 'I thought their dresses were very you.'

I nod mutely. Although I haven't ever physically gone shopping for a wedding dress, I have been assiduously compiling mood boards of dresses I like and a great many of them are by Helen Yately. There is one stretch crêpe and lace gown with a sweetheart neckline and an open back that I've become a little obsessed by. My dad is either very in tune with my tastes or very lucky.

He hands me a glass of champagne. 'Here's to a successful trip and finding you the perfect dress. Cheers!'

'Cheers,' I mumble.

Chapter Eleven

Liz

Liz wasn't one for self-pity but damn that slippery pavement. She was used to being the person who dashed around at a thousand miles an hour. The person who got things done and looked after others. Not some frail old thing in a care home who was tucked up in bed at 7.30. Someone who had to have help getting dressed.

She was watching a sappy movie, the sort she normally had no truck with. The man and the woman had just met. She was a journalist (because the law states that all female leads in romcoms must work in the media) and he was her interviewee. Right now, they hated each other with a visceral passion, although in about seven scenes' time they'd be madly in love (cue the montage).

Liz wished she was at home. She hated this place with its constant cacophony of competing noise, its hall lights that were never extinguished and the overwhelming smell of artificial pine that failed to mask even less pleasant odours underneath it.

What are you up to? Peter messaged.

Liz smiled. It was as if he somehow knew when she was feeling a bit glum.

Watching a movie.

Wish I was there with you. Snuggled up and cosy.

Me too.

Hope you're not in too much pain? Remember the doctors said you shouldn't hesitate to ask for the stronger painkillers if you need them.

Liz loved that Peter was so caring. Especially since he was dealing with so many things in his own life at the moment.

Not too bad, she messaged back. Her shoulder was throbbing like hell, but no one likes a whinger, do they?

Glad to hear it. And talking of pains, how's Sonia? I hope you're not being driven too mad by all the talk of Hope's wedding?

Liz laughed. She'd only mentioned Sonia once, so was amazed Peter had logged her name let alone her granddaughter's. She'd never known anyone who listened like he did, especially a bloke.

I'm looking forward to a full rundown of the floral decorations. Maybe a blow-by-blow description of the wedding cake recipe? 😂😂😂 Btw I've been thinking about what we should do for your birthday. Maybe I can take you away for the weekend? San Sebastian? Puglia? Lisbon?

Bless him!

Think you've got enough on your plate right now without worrying about my birthday, especially as it's still four months away.

It's a priority! Anyway, have a think. I'm signing off now but chat again tomorrow. Love you more than anything else in the world xxxxx

A huge smile spread across Liz's face. Anyone walking past would think the movie was a lot better than it actually was. Well, either that or that she was a loon. *Love you too xxx.* She opened her photos app. Her favourite picture of Peter was one of him sitting by the pool playing backgammon. He had a beer in his hand and his head thrown back in laughter. Not only did he look what Emily would call hot, but it perfectly captured his zest for life. She ran the fingers of her good hand across the screen, inwardly rolling her eyes at what a soppy old thing she'd turned into.

Smooth Radio played insistently from the room across the hall. She turned up the volume on the TV. If her shoulder wasn't so sore, she'd have got up to close the door. She was always asking the carers to do it but not many of them did. One had explained it was best if they could easily keep an eye on people. The impertinence! She didn't need to be babysat.

The lead actors in the movie were both young and beautiful, of course, but love wasn't just for the young. Peter had taught her that. Before they found each other, Liz had thought that part of her life was over. She hadn't even been especially sad about that. She had friends, hobbies and a part-time job. She wasn't one of those poor old souls who are desperately grateful when someone turns up to read their electricity meter. In fact, Emily often teased her that she had a better social life than she did.

Looking back now though, Liz wondered if, despite that, she may have been a little lonely. There's no getting away from the fact that if you live alone you spend a lot of time, well, alone. A funny programme is less funny when there's no one to laugh with you; an interesting story about your day doesn't keep indefinitely and there is something ineffably sad about the scrape and chink of a solitary knife and fork (although Liz might swap that for another dinner listening to Sonia).

The woman in the movie had a head cold but was still managing to look adorable in her ditzy print pyjamas. No doubt the man would turn up having swapped his suit jacket for a chunky cardigan. He'd bring flowers, Lemsip and chicken soup. This would be a prelude to a grander romantic gesture such as standing outside the woman's building with a boombox, or turning up at her workplace and declaring his love in front of a gaggle of shocked co-workers. Behaviour that was dangerously close to stalking.

Peter didn't indulge in any such questionable tactics, thank goodness. He did show Liz he cared in a million tiny ways though. She couldn't quite believe the universe had delivered her such a wonderful, self-assured and sensitive man. Probably the love of her life, if she was honest, although she felt a bit guilty towards her late husband for thinking that.

Cookie cutter romcom man was rushing to the airport to declare his love before the woman got on a plane to leave the country forever. There were no taxis to be found in the whole of New York City, of course, so, by the time he got to the airport, the woman had gone through security. Luckily, our hero's winsome charm made the security staff let him through. Like that would happen.

Liz hadn't told many people about her and Peter yet. Judith knew about him, of course. In fact it was her oldest friend who'd talked her into going on the dating app. (Judith's horrible husband Martin knew too but that was only because he was the world's biggest eavesdropper.) For the moment, Liz was enjoying the fact that she and Peter were in their own delicious little bubble. They'd go public soon, though, and certainly before he moved in with her. Liz was particularly excited about telling Emily because she knew how much her granddaughter worried about her. Ed would be pleased for her too, of course, although with Ed it was pretty much always about him.

The romcom couple were on the airport tarmac now. He declared his love and they fell into each other's arms and kissed passionately, oblivious to the torrential rain.

Liz had never understood this particular movie trope. She didn't think she'd stand kissing anyone in the pouring rain. You'd both catch your death of cold, your hair would frizz uncontrollably, and your clothes would end up smelling like a wet dog.

No, not even Peter would get kisses in the rain. That was about the only time she could imagine herself saying no to him, though.

Chapter Twelve

As we drain the last of the bottle of wine that followed the champagne, Dad and I have somehow got on to the subject of robot vacuum cleaners.

'My mate Donny bought one,' he says. 'His husband Matthew is something of a neat-freak and is always calling out Donny for not doing his share of the housework. So Donny bought this robot vacuum and got into the habit of leaving it to clean the downstairs when they were getting ready for work. What he didn't factor in was they have a Great Dane, Napoleon, and one morning poor Napoleon got a bad case of the squits.'

'Noooo!' I say, laughing and clamping my hand to my mouth.

'Yup. Donny and Matthew went downstairs to find the whole kitchen looking as if there had been a dirty protest.'

'Eww, that is so horrible.' I'd forgotten what good company my dad can be. It doesn't make him any less useless, but credit where credit's due. It's a welcome, if temporary, distraction from the fact that my life has imploded. 'We need tequila!' I announce, jumping up.

'What? On a school night?'

'Yeah,' I say, rummaging through the cupboard. 'Why not?' I pour us both a shot and raise my glass. 'Here's to you *not* being an alcoholic!'

'I'll drink to that,' he says, knocking back his drink. 'Tequila always reminds me of your mum.'

'Really? I never had Mum down as a tequila woman.'

'She wasn't really but we ended up in this Mexican restaurant on our first date and I persuaded her frozen margaritas were a good idea. You might not be here today if it wasn't for margaritas.'

'Ha,' I say. 'She only fell for you because she had her beer goggles on.'

'Hey,' he says, pretending to be offended. 'That and the fact I was a great kisser. Have I ever told you—'

'That actual fireworks went off when you first kissed her? Yes, you have, but only about eleven billion times.'

He laughs. 'Well, it was amazing. We were walking back through the park, and we kissed and, at that exact moment, fireworks went off in the distance. To this day, I don't know what they were for. It wasn't as if it was new year or anything.'

Pain stabs at my guts. Actual fireworks didn't go off the night Mark and I first kissed, but it was pretty special.

Suddenly, I realise with a flash of clarity that I haven't fought hard enough for Mark. WE ARE MEANT TO BE TOGETHER. And, yeah, he'd got a few pre-wedding jitters, but that was all it was, and I have to fight for him. 'Let's have one more tequila.'

'Okay,' Dad says. 'What are we drinking to this time?'

'Courage.'

Chapter Thirteen

Ed

For someone lying in the world's most uncomfortable sofa bed, Ed was pretty happy. He and Emily had had an unexpectedly lovely evening together and, for the first time since he had set foot inside this flat, the idea of being able to repair the damage to their relationship seemed possible.

True, the whole misunderstanding about him being an alcoholic had been awkward, but his 'honesty' about why he'd really come to England had saved the day. Ed did feel a little guilty about that, of course he did, but nothing he'd told Emily was a lie, he just hadn't mentioned anything about needing money from his mother.

By contrast, telling the woman in the wedding dress boutique that Liz was dying was an out and out whopper, but it had secured the appointment for this Saturday, so Ed couldn't say he regretted it.

He rolled over, wondering if there was any position he could lie in where he wouldn't have a metal bar poking through the wafer-thin mattress and digging into some part of his anatomy.

Emily hadn't seemed as excited as he might have hoped when he'd told her about Saturday's appointment. She'd love it when they got there, though. It was one seriously swanky store and, although Ed didn't claim to be any sort of expert when it came to wedding dresses, he reckoned the ones in there were some of the nicest he'd ever seen. (As well they might be at those prices. Ed had to stifle a gasp when he glanced at one of the tickets. How could any dress be worth that unless the sparkles it was covered in were real diamonds?).

A message from Shona flashed up on his phone: *Miss you so much Big Teddy Eddy xxxx*

Ed smiled to himself. As long as he could persuade his mother to give him that loan, Shona wouldn't lose her home or even find out it had ever been at risk. And he'd managed to find a position on the sofa bed that was verging on comfortable. A sleepy contentment washed over him.

But then, just as he was drifting off, an unwelcome thought floated into his consciousness: it wasn't enough to look at wedding dresses with Emily on Saturday, Ed was going to have to buy her one. Of course he was – he was the father of the bride. He sat up in bed and groaned.

All his credit cards, and he had every single one he could get, were maxed out. Of the $1,000 he'd borrowed from the loan shark, he still had $400 ($600 having gone on his flights). He'd felt quite smug about it. It was enough to enjoy his time in London, buy Emily a nice dinner out and still have money left in his pocket when he went back to Tampa. But now the maths (or math as they called it in his adopted homeland) looked rather different. The wedding dresses each cost around £2,000 (the equivalent of approximately $2,500).

Ed got out of bed. There was no way he was sleeping now.

Maybe he didn't need to buy the wedding dress? Emily had never been the greedy sort and, if Ed didn't suggest he paid, he doubted she would. He couldn't shake the thought that he ought to, though.

He headed towards the kitchen, tripping over his rucksack and stubbing his toe on the coffee table Emily was forever cleaning. 'Ouch, ouch,' he yelped, hopping around, hoping the noise hadn't woken her. He retrieved his scattered possessions, stopping to run his fingers over the leather bookmark that had fallen out of his book. Emily had given it to him for Father's Day when she was about six or seven. Her drawings had been printed on the front and, on the back, there was a printed message in gold type that Ed knew off by heart: *Thank you for being the best daddy in the whole world. I love you, Emily xx*

If only she still thought he was the best daddy in the whole world. Ed limped into the kitchen, took a bottle of milk from the fridge and poured some into a pan. He used to make hot milk for Emily when she was little and couldn't sleep. Back then, he was a rock star in her eyes. He could still picture her running to the door to greet him when he got back from a cruise, her eyes shining with delight: 'Daddy! Daddy!'

Buying the dress on Saturday would be a 'proper dad' thing to do and, while Ed was under no illusions that it would reinstate his rock star status, it would definitely show Emily he cared.

He took his mug and sat down on the edge of the sofa bed, rubbing his sore toe with his spare hand. He took a sip of the warm milk, which wasn't nearly as delicious in reality as it had been in his mind. He set the mug down, went to the window and pulled back the blind. A woman emerged from her house carrying a suit bag and a holdall. Ed wondered idly if she was going on holiday, or, more dramatically, walking out on a relationship.

He really wanted to be able to buy Emily a wedding dress, but how? He supposed he could try to go to another loan shark here in London, but he couldn't see them paying out when he had nothing of value to offer as security.

Pebbles slunk into the living room and eyed Ed warily.

'Hey,' Ed said. 'Any idea how I can magic up two grand?'

The cat didn't answer, and Ed turned back to look out onto the dark street. A man in a baseball cap was hurrying along the pavement, head down. Maybe he was up to no good? Then again, perhaps he was on his way to work?

Maybe Ed could sell the fancy dress costumes here? The UK might have less stringent fire retardancy regulations? He would have to take a hit on the shipping, of course, but needs must. Optimism surged through his body.

He was being an idiot though. Even if the UK safety regulations were looser (a big if) and Ed could sell every costume he had within the next few days (a huge if), it wouldn't generate enough dosh to pay for one of those wedding dresses. The fairies and dinosaurs and pirates were not going to come to the rescue.

Ed turned around to see that Pebbles had curled up on the sofa bed. His mind flashed back to the cat lying on the end of Catherine's bed when she was desperately ill. Even after she was moved to the hospice, Pebbles would still park himself in exactly the same spot, barely seeming to leave it.

One evening, when Emily was still at the hospice, Ed had tried to coax Pebbles off the bed and towards his untouched food. He couldn't do much for Catherine now, but he could at least make sure her beloved pet didn't pine to death.

The cat was more stubborn than Ed was patient, though. Ed had given up and went out, ending up blind drunk in a seedy-looking casino playing poker with a hotchpotch of people who were very friendly until Ed started winning.

A piece clunked into place in Ed's brain. He suddenly knew exactly how he was going to get the money for Emily's dress.

Thursday

Chapter Fourteen

I come to, a dull ache pulsing behind my temples. I glance at my phone and see it's 7.45.

Seven forty-five! I am normally at school by now. And it's an Ofsted inspection day too. Of all the days to be late.

I throw myself out of bed, ignoring my head and a wave of nausea. If I skip a shower, I can be at school well before the kids are dropped off at 8.50. The only problem with that plan is that I am pretty sure the smell of tequila is emanating from my every pore. Not a great look for anyone, let alone a primary school teacher. I am going to have to wear a lot of perfume.

'Morning,' my dad says brightly as I stumble into the kitchen. A memory crashes into my consciousness: my father has booked us an appointment to look at wedding dresses this Saturday. How the hell am I going to get out of that one?

'Coffee?' he says. 'Breakfast?'

'No time,' I mumble, pulling on my boots. 'I'm very late.'

'Really?' School doesn't start until nine, does it?'

'Eight fifty,' I say through gritted teeth. 'And we have to get there well before the kids.'

'Oh, I didn't realise that.'

'Right,' I say, wrestling my arm into my jacket. 'And I bet you think teachers finish work by four o'clock every day and spend most of the year on holiday.' I know I am being a grumpy cow, but I don't care. It's my father's fault I am in this state. I never forget to set my alarm. If he hadn't turned up with the champagne and his emotional landmines, this never would have happened.

'Where's my rucksack?'

'Maybe your bedroom?'

I race back towards the bedroom, passing Pebbles, who shoots me a look of naked feline disgust. Pebbles never overdoes it on the tequila.

'Yup,' I mutter. 'I hate myself too.' And with those words comes a clear and sickening memory. I sent Mark a stream of messages last night. They started out wheedling and needy and then, when Mark didn't reply, they became aggressive and nasty. Because that always works when you're trying to get someone to come back to you.

Molten shame washes through my body. I can't afford to dwell on Mark or the messages, though. That is a treat for later. Right now, the only thing I can focus on is getting to school before the kids and the Ofsted inspectors. And managing not to throw up.

My father is standing at the door with a keep cup, a foil-wrapped packet and a blister pack of paracetamol.

'I don't feel like eating anything,' I say, snatching the pack of painkillers and the keep cup.

'You might do later. Just pop the toast in your bag.'

'Fine,' I say, ungraciously.

'Have a nice day,' my father calls after me.

'Yeah, right,' I mutter, running down the front steps. It is pouring with rain. 'Bloody hell,' I say, unlocking my bike. I get on it and cycle as fast as my legs will take me. I just want twenty minutes or so to collect myself before the kids are dropped off. That will do fine, especially since I left the classroom in such good shape last night. There is still the small matter of the Ofsted inspection, of course, but hopefully that will go smoothly. I am certainly going to do everything in my power to demonstrate my mastery of the early years foundation stage curriculum.

The school looms into view and I pedal harder. I may even have time to drink that coffee my dad made me. If ever there was a day that calls for industrial quantities of caffeine, it's today.

All thoughts of EYFS and caffeine are wiped from my mind as I register a small flash of light and then a car door being swung open in front of me. Like *right* in front of me. Fear courses through my body as I slam on my brakes. I avoid the slab of vehicle by a whisper, swerving into the path of the car behind and prompting the angry blare of the horn.

Trembling, I manage to right my bike, stop, and pull up onto the pavement. 'WHAT IN THE HELL DO YOU THINK YOU'RE DOING?' I shout at the driver who opened his car door in my path.

The driver, a sharp-featured man in a badly fitting grey suit, looks me up and down. 'Yeah, sorry about that. No need to shout, though.'

'NO NEED TO SHOUT?' I scream. 'YOU COULD HAVE KILLED ME!'

'Riiight,' the man says, shaking his head.

It's all I can do not to slap him across his pointed little face. Instead, I turn and wheel away my bike. There is no point wasting a second's more breath or emotion on this guy. I hope he might think twice about dooring another unsuspecting cyclist in the future, but his unrepentant tone doesn't exactly instil confidence. He's not my problem, though.

Chapter Fifteen

Liz

Liz just wanted someone to help her get dressed. Was that too much to ask at nearly ten o'clock in the morning? That was why she was here, wasn't it? Apparently, they were short-staffed. Again.

It didn't matter, she told herself.

The day hadn't started well. She'd had a text message from her bank saying she'd exceeded her overdraft limit. Panic coursed around her body. Up until a couple of months ago, she'd never been in debt. Never even failed to clear her credit card balance each month.

These financial problems were temporary, though. An injection of funds was due any day now. Peter reckoned within the next few weeks.

'Knock, knock,' Judith said, appearing in the open doorway. 'Oh, good, you're having a lazy morning. That'll do you the world of good.'

'No, just no one has bothered to help me get dressed yet. Sorry, didn't mean to snap. I just hate being so useless.'

As if on cue, a ruddy-faced woman with multiple piercings arrived. She introduced herself as Anna and told Liz she was here to get her ready for the day.

'Thank you,' Liz said. 'Do you want to wait for me in the lounge, Judith? Or even in the garden if it's as warm as it looks?'

'Oh, a cup of tea in the garden would be lovely,' Judith said. She reached into her handbag and pulled out a wodge of letters. 'I brought your post, by the way.'

As Anna chatted away about what Liz wanted to wear today and how she advised layers because it was warm one minute and cold the next, Liz focused on the pile of letters. Most of them would be the usual rubbish no doubt, but one of them looked as if it was the letter she had been waiting for.

'Could you please open that letter for me?' Liz said. 'The one in the brown envelope.'

'You sure?' Anna said, laughing. 'I do my best to ignore those.' She opened the envelope and handed the letter to Liz.

Liz skimmed the text. *We're sorry to have to tell you your application for a loan has been unsuccessful.*

What? Why?

'Bad news?' Anna said.

'No, no.' Liz opened the top drawer of the bedside table with her good hand. She felt as if she was going to be sick. It simply hadn't crossed her mind that the loan application would be turned down.

Anna was standing in front of the open wardrobe. 'Skirt or trousers?'

'Umm…' All Liz cared about was that letter. And what the hell she was going to tell Peter.

Liz couldn't believe it was a sunny day and yet she and Judith were the only two people in the care home garden. You'd have thought the inmates would be desperate to get out.

She'd resolved to put the rejected bank loan application out of her mind for now. She'd find a way around things.

'How are you coping?' Judith said, picking up her cup of tea. 'Is this place truly awful?'

'S'okay.' Liz said with a one-shouldered shrug. 'It was so kind of you to offer to have me to stay but I wouldn't have wanted to put you out.' Or spend more than a few hours under the same roof as that maddening husband of yours.

'I wouldn't have minded,' Judith said. 'I was thinking, by the way, you should give me your laundry and I'll wash it and bring it back. When my mum was in a care home, they lost everything. Well, either that or shrank it to doll-sized.'

'I can't give you a bag of my dirty pants and nighties.'

'Why ever not? You had to clear up my vomit on more than one occasion when we went travelling.'

Liz laughed. 'That was nearly sixty years ago.'

'Just give me the washing. It's no bother to bung it in the machine.'

'Thank you, that's so kind. Honestly, I think you, Peter and Emily are the only people who have kept me sane since I *fell over*.'

'Hmm.'

'What does "hmm" mean?'

'Nothing. Well, just I wish Peter was here looking after you.'

The custard cream Liz was eating turned to sand in her throat. 'You know he can't be. He has to be in the States right now. His grandson is in intensive care fighting for his life.'

Judith nodded and the silence stretched between them until Liz could bear it no longer. 'If you've got something to say, just spit it out.'

Judith stared at her nails. 'Well… umm… it's all going so fast with you and Peter.'

Liz felt as if someone had punched her in the guts. 'You were the one who persuaded me to go on the dating apps in the first place. Don't you remember how reluctant I was, how worried that everyone would swipe left on me? Or that I'd find a match but then discover he thought Covid had been invented by the "mainstream media". Or have a nickname for his penis or belch loudly after meals and say proudly that in some countries that's taken as a sign you appreciated the food. But you kept *on and on* at me about giving the apps a try. Told me that life is short and there was nothing to lose. You created my profile, for goodness' sake.' Liz was aware she was raising her voice, but she didn't care. 'And now I've met this wonderful man. This kind, handsome, funny man who makes me feel things I thought only existed in books and movies and you're all, *it's going so fast.*'

Judith stared into her tea. 'I'm just saying you should be a little careful.'

Where had *this* come from? Judith had been even more excited than Liz when the two of them had first pored over Peter's photos on the dating app. Judith kept going on about how young he looked. Maybe it was the full head of hair? She said he reminded her of Harrison Ford. And he looked such fun too – laughing or smiling in every single shot.

Now Judith sucked in her lips. 'I'm happy that you've met someone you like.'

'*Are you?* Because it sure as hell doesn't sound like it. And I don't like him, by the way, I love him.'

'But—'

Liz silenced her friend with a look. If she was fair, she couldn't entirely blame Judith. If someone had told her six months ago that they'd fallen in love with someone they'd met online she'd have thought they were bonkers. She and Peter had this deep connection, though. They'd spent hours and hours chatting and messaging and talked about anything and everything, from their previous relationships to their deepest fears, to Peter's property developing business (Liz was in awe of how calm he stayed while negotiating deals worth millions).

'Look,' Judith said. 'I don't want us to fight. We never fight.'

Liz smiled tightly. Someone should deadhead those roses. If she had her secateurs with her, she'd do it herself. Well, her secateurs and a functional right arm.

'You're not giving him money, are you?' Judith said.

Liz felt sure her mouth must have literally dropped open. 'What kind of question is *that*? I'll have you know that Peter is a very successful businessman. He owns properties all over Spain. His company is worth millions—'

'Sometimes these people aren't who they say they are. I read a newspaper article once—'

'Do you think I'm some kind of idiot?' Liz said, slamming her cup down with so much force she was surprised it didn't crack the saucer. 'I've obviously googled him.' She'd only done this out of curiosity but she was glad she could bring it out now.

'Oh… well… that's good.' Judith had the good grace to look a little embarrassed. 'Please don't let's fight. We never fight. I was just looking out for you.'

'I can look out for myself. And Peter is the best thing that has ever happened to me.'

Chapter Sixteen

Ed

Ed blinked, his eyes adjusting to the low lighting. It felt a little weird to walk into a casino at eleven in the morning, especially one that had such a nightclubby vibe. It had six floors, an atrium of what must be about sixty feet and seemingly endless amounts of black, glass and chrome.

Ed walked past a middle-aged man in a mobility scooter who was sitting slack-jawed in front of a slot machine.

The casino was slap bang in the centre of London but normal life felt a million miles away. This place had its own little ecosystem with bars, restaurants and even a medical centre (the mind boggled).

'Excuse me,' Ed said to a uniformed woman walking past with a tray of pints. (Ed didn't know whether he was appalled or impressed by people necking beers at this time of day. Maybe a little of both?). 'Where are the poker tables?'

'On the lower ground floor. But poker doesn't start until midday.'

That was annoying. He should have checked before he left Emily's. Still, no matter, he'd warm up with something else. He looked around the green baize gaming tables. Maybe roulette?

Nah, roulette was a game for losers. Literally. He'd go for black-jack.

Ed sat down at one of the tables, smiling at the other players. There was a group of youngish guys in suits who, by the looks of them, could well have been there all night, an older man who you'd cast as a serial killer in a movie and a solitary woman of about Ed's age.

The dealer, who didn't look old enough to be in a casino, let alone work in one, and had fingernails that were bitten to the quick, shuffled the cards and then offered it to serial killer guy to cut the pack.

Ed placed his bet. He'd start small with just £20, ease in.

The dealer placed two cards in each box and dealt one to himself.

Ed looked at his cards. A king and a ten. Pretty goddam good. He should have been braver with his bet.

The dealer looked from player to player to see whether they wanted to stick or twist. Then he drew his cards. 'Pay seventeen and above.'

Yes!

The woman dropped a couple of her chips and Ed bent to retrieve them from the plush scarlet carpet.

'Thanks,' she said, smiling at him. 'Good start for you.'

'Yup,' Ed said, smiling back at her. 'Long may the luck continue.'

Chapter Seventeen

I feel a little guilty about car door guy. Admittedly the man could have killed me, but it isn't like me to lose my temper like that. Then again, rocking up at work with a monster hangover isn't my normal modus operandi either. Next thing I know I'll be sending an email that doesn't start: Sorry to bother you.

I look around the classroom, grateful the paracetamol are finally making an impact on my headache, the kids are happy and engaged in what they're doing, and no one has wet themselves. The word going around is that the Ofsted inspection seems to be going okay too, and I'm not even that nervous about them observing one of my lessons. I do wish I didn't smell of sweat and tequila but, as long the inspectors don't get too close, I'll be fine.

'How many dinosaurs have you got there, Callum?' I say. 'Shall we count them?'

'One, two, three, four…' Callum says, his sausagey fingers moving each dinosaur as he counts it.

How many messages did you send to Mark last night? I shove down the thought.

'…five, six, seven, eight, nine, ten…' Callum pauses. 'Eleven,' he says, triumphantly.

'Very good,' I say.

'My mummy's got a hairy bottom,' Callum announces apropos of nothing.

I force myself not to laugh. Parents would be horrified if they knew the things their offspring share about them. 'W' is for the wine that's Mummy's medicine, 'C' is for Dad's chicken farts. I pick up one of the dinosaurs. 'How many dinosaurs are left if we take this one away?'

'The ankylosaurus?'

'Yes,' I say, smiling. Callum's dinosaur knowledge and the earnestness with which he shares it never ceases to make my heart swell.

'Ten.'

'That's right.'

The classroom door opens, and I look up to see Fiona the school manager. 'Miss Baxter, the Ofsted inspectors would like to sit in on your lesson now.'

'No problem,' I say, telling myself I have no reason to be nervous. I'm not certain of much in my life right now, but I do know I'm a good teacher.

Fiona stands aside and a woman with a mass of red hair and a big lopsided smile walks into the classroom.

See, I tell myself, that's not someone looking to trip you up. And then I see the person behind the redhead. A man in a badly fitting grey suit.

Car door guy.

Chapter Eighteen

Ed

The luck had continued. By the time Ed left the blackjack table, he'd won £320, and now, after just under an hour playing poker, it was £1,600. In fact, he was starting to wonder if maybe he should forget about online reselling and become a professional gambler? All very James Bond.

Pretty hard to make a consistent living from it, though. And Donny, who had worked for ten years as a croupier in Vegas, had plenty of stories about high rollers who rolled right into disaster.

Ed looked around at his fellow poker players, all male and none of them what you'd call friendly. Not like Geraldine, the woman whose chips he'd retrieved from under the blackjack table. She was a right laugh. They'd talked about all sorts, and she'd even given Ed her business card when he left, offering him mates' rates from her design studio if Emily needed wedding invitations or orders of service. Ed hadn't quite plucked up the courage to ask her what he really wanted to know, which was what a well-dressed, respectable-looking woman with her own design company was doing in a casino on a Thursday lunchtime, but maybe it was just her way of letting off steam.

Ed matched the previous player's bet to stay in the game. His hand was good, not amazing, but good enough to want to keep going, especially as he was sure the man who looked like a catalogue model was bluffing. Maybe the 'I've got a good hand' pose wasn't one he'd been taught?

Ed won the pot. Another £300. He was only a hundred quid away from being able to buy one of those dresses. Adrenaline and endorphins surged around his body. This had been the best idea ever.

'Another game?' the dealer asked.

Ed hesitated. He'd won an awful lot of money in a very short space of time and, even though he'd like to think some of that was down to skill, he had to acknowledge he'd also had luck on his side. Which meant he probably ought to quit while he was ahead.

He was still £100 short of what he needed for a dress, though. Plus, it would be lovely to have a little extra – enough to buy a few treats for him and Emily. Maybe he could even get Shona a present. She'd go mad for a Fortnum & Mason hamper. So British!

He could even keep going until he won enough for Monday's repayment on the condo. Take his fate out of his mother's hands.

'One more game,' Ed said.

Chapter Nineteen

Liz

Well, this was just marvellous. Liz's oldest friend, one of the people who knew her best in the whole world, was treating her as if she was some kind of idiot. Like she wasn't already feeling a bit old and useless since she *fell over*. Not being able to put on a pair of socks or wash her hair without help.

Sometimes these people aren't who they say they are.

'Ready for some lunch?' Anna said, appearing in front of Liz. She had a sheen of sweat across her face.

Liz shook her head. 'I'm not very hungry. I think I'll stay out here in the garden for a bit.'

Anna looked as if she was about to argue but then thought better of it.

You'd have thought Judith would have a bit more faith in her. Treat her like the sensible, level-headed seventy-nine-year-old woman she was, instead of some silly, love-struck teenager.

She reached for her iPad and used her left hand to clumsily type in the website address of Peter's property company. The one she'd googled just after they'd matched. She wasn't sure why she was looking for it now. To convince herself it was really there, that she wasn't crazy?

There it was, right in front of her eyes. *Casas Marga. The family real estate agents in Spain.* It had been named after Peter's late wife.

Casas Marga was set up in 2010 by husband and wife team Marga (Spanish) and Peter (English but a hispanophile!) Curran. Our mission is to provide the best possible service to every client we meet. Whether you're buying or selling, and whatever your budget, we want to make the whole process a pleasure.

Liz could almost hear Peter talking.

She flicked through the properties, lingering on the modern apartment block in Lomas de Campoamor with the gorgeous communal pool and gardens. When she'd visited the website before, the apartment block was just another swanky-looking white building. But over the ensuing months Peter had talked a lot about the various teething problems. Liz knew all about the marble tiles that has got stuck in customs and the air-conditioning system that Peter said had 'a mind of its own'. She hadn't realised three of the apartments had now sold, though. That was great news.

She looked up from the screen and watched a blue tit who was pecking away at the bird feeder. Why was she even doing this? She trusted Peter. Of course she did.

She went back to reading the website.

The Spanish way of life is the envy of the world. The sun is always shining, and people take their time to enjoy themselves whether that's playing a round of golf, swimming in the sea or lingering over a meal of fresh fish washed down by a glass — or two! — of local wine.

Again, she could almost hear Peter.

She clicked on 'Contact Us'. Saw Peter's name and there underneath it the name of his personal assistant Alba Perez. When Liz had looked at the website before, Alba's name had meant nothing to her, but now she knew that Alba was a woman who'd kept Peter sane when his wife died, how, even though she was young enough to be his daughter, she'd acted more like his mum. Liz smiled as she thought of Peter telling her that Alba was so organised, he was surprised she didn't file herself under the letter 'A'.

She looked up from the screen and stared at the flowerbeds. Someone should really deal with those weeds before they took over completely.

It was good to see the website again. Good to have proof Peter was exactly who he said he was.

Chapter Twenty

I shut the cubicle door behind me, sit down on the toilet and put my head in my hands. I didn't completely flunk the observed lesson, but it didn't go well. From the second I saw car door guy, I was jittery and off my game and the kids, as ever, sensed the change in mood and became fractious and unsettled.

But I am probably being paranoid to think car door guy was patronising me when he looked at my assessments and said there was 'no prescribed way of recording them'. And the woman probably hadn't frowned when she'd looked at the risk assessment I'd prepared for tomorrow's trip to the Science Museum. Any more than car door guy can have winced when I asked Meghan to put the 'doggy' back in the animal box. He must know that the kids will be exposed to a more accurate use of language over time – that they are babies still?

I pee and flush. I am half tempted go straight to the head-teacher and say my observed lesson didn't go well. Better Clare Wood hear it from me than them. But Clare is already stressed today and, anyway, I have other, equally unappealing, fish to fry.

I pull my phone out of my pocket and stare at it. I often feel jealous that my friends with office jobs are able to look at their phones throughout the day. They don't know how lucky they are they can make a doctor's appointment or book a plumber or even have a quick doom scroll of the news. Today, though, I've been grateful to have had a morning where I've had no chance to look at my phone. Because on my phone live last night's messages to Mark and, while I can't remember the detail, I know they aren't going to be pretty.

My fingers hover over the keypad and, before I can chicken out, I open WhatsApp. There before me are a sea of messages from me, all of them opened and none of them replied to. Sweating, I start to read them.

Hey, just wondering how you are?

That's okay. We were together for thirteen years and we've known each other since we were two. I can ask him how he is.

I miss you and I know you miss me to

The wrong 'too'! Mortifying!

I reckon you just got scared. Well, guess what, we're all scared. But you and me are MEANT TO BE TOGETHER!!!!! I love you and you love me.

Not awful apart from the multiple exclamation marks.

Unless you're lying to me and there's someone else?

That's it, isn't it? You're lying to me.

You're a fucking liar and a coward and I thought you were different but you're just like all the rest

You're like my father

You know the worst thing about you, Mark? You're a phoney and a fake. You're not really a nice guy after all

I have to stop looking for a minute and take a few deep breaths. A new message flashes up on my phone.

I'll do dinner for us tonight. What do you fancy? Roast chicken?

What I fancy is telling my father to take a hike. Roast chicken is all very lovely, but it's about fifteen years too late. I don't have the energy to get rid of my father tonight, though. That conversation will have to be a treat for tomorrow.

I flick back to my messages to Mark.

You're just like all the rest

You probably even send dick pics

I groan. I am never drinking again.

Good riddance Mr Fake. Sayonara Mr Phoney.

That was nice. Mature.

I blink back tears. My lunch break is nearly over, and I have to get out of this cubicle. Getting my life out of the toilet looks a whole lot more difficult.

Chapter Twenty-One

Ed

Ed hadn't won his 'one more game'. So he'd played another. And another. And another.

Now he ached all over from sitting for hours on end, a headache pulsed behind his eyes and he was harbouring murderous thoughts towards catalogue man.

'I've got to pee,' he said, as he failed to win another game.

He walked up the huge sweeping staircase. He mustn't feel despondent. He still had £1,000 more than when he'd walked into this place six hours earlier, shaking the rain off his jacket. (Rain? Daylight? Such things felt like a distant memory.) For a lot of people, winning a grand would constitute a good day. Hell, who was Ed kidding? He wasn't exactly used to making that kind of dosh in a day.

It was just bloody annoying that earlier he'd had nearly double that. But now he didn't have enough to buy Emily a wedding dress on Saturday.

The men's toilets smelled of pee and artificial jasmine. Lift muzak pumped from the speakers and there was a uniformed man providing the wholly unnecessary service of handing you a towel that was sitting right in front of you.

It was tempting to try to win back the money he'd lost. But he wanted to be there when Emily got home from work, cook her a nice dinner and look after her a bit. Anyway, he was tired now. He'd come back tomorrow when he was feeling sharp again.

Tomorrow was another day.

Chapter Twenty-Two

The pizza making is not, of course, 'dead easy'. In fact, as I stand in the classroom, in which almost every surface is dusted with flour and pepperoni, peppers and shreds of cheese are scattered far and wide, it is hard not to feel a little murderous towards Tara, who is now presumably sipping a cappuccino and flicking through a magazine while she waits for her highlights to develop.

I pull my phone out of my pocket. After much deliberation, I sent Mark a message apologising for last night's messages and saying it was the tequila talking. Mark replied with a curt, *No worries*, which made me feel about two foot tall.

Car door guy pokes his head around the door. 'I didn't leave my pen in here, did I? It's a Mont Blanc.'

Tosser. 'I haven't seen it.'

'Mind if I have a quick look?'

'Sure.' *Because I could do with having you in my face right now on top of everything else.* I stuff my phone back in my pocket before getting a broom and starting to sweep the floor. Several of the kids in cookery club were quite feral but, with the Tommy Cassidy thing still fresh in my mind, I was too nervous to be even vaguely strict.

I had to pretend not to see when Gemma and Abigail started putting passata in each other's hair.

'It's quite a mess in here,' car door guy says. As if I might not have noticed.

'We've been doing cookery club. Making pizzas.'

He nods. 'Don't you do that in the kitchen?'

I shake my head. 'Health and safety.' *You should know that.* 'The kids assemble the pizzas here and then cook them at home.'

'Right. I can't see my pen anywhere.' He heads towards the door, stopping to pick up a small red plastic rolling pin from the floor. He hands it to me, his nose wrinkling slightly but unmistakably. Surely, I can't still smell of tequila? He flashes me the briefest of smiles. 'Night then.'

'Night.'

Forty minutes and one back-to-normal classroom later, I wearily cycle home in the driving rain. At least the weather has done me the courtesy of reflecting my mood, I suppose.

I come to a stop outside my house, park up my bike and wipe the dripping rain from my face with my palms. My headache is back with a vengeance.

It's hard to imagine that little over a week ago I still had a perfect life. Now I've been dumped by the only man I've ever loved, am screwing up left, right and centre at work, and am planning a fake wedding with my estranged father. Oh, and I have also started pouring my heart out to a cat who hates me.

I guess the only positive one can draw is that it's hard to imagine things getting any worse.

'Hello,' my father calls from the living room as I put my key in the lock. 'In here.'

I walk in to see Pebbles sitting on my father's lap being stroked.

'*What?*' I say.

'What?' my father says.

'Nothing.' I shake my head and peel off my wet cycle jacket. 'Nothing.'

Pebbles purrs.

Friday

Chapter Twenty-Three

Liz

The bedside clock read four in the morning. Liz lay in the half-light, her heart pounding. Looking at Peter's website earlier had quashed any prickle of anxiety Judith had caused. But then, a couple of hours later, she had been chatting away to Peter on the phone and had let something slip about it being great he'd sold three of the apartments in Lomas de Campoamor. She immediately realised what she'd done and felt herself flush. It was no big deal though, right? Everyone googled each other. Peter had almost certainly looked her up.

'Eek,' she said, laughing. 'Busted. I was just curious—'

Silence buzzed down the line. 'What are you doing checking up on me?' Peter's voice was icy.

'I wasn't checking up on—'

'You obviously were.'

Panic coursed through Liz's veins. Why was he angry? What did he have to hide? What if Judith was right?

Of course she wasn't right, Liz told herself firmly now. She ought to put all this nonsense out of her head, get some sleep. There was nothing odd at Peter being upset that she'd felt the need to check up on him. No one wants to think they're not trusted. Especially by someone they love.

And yet.

No! She loved Peter and Peter loved her.

Shadows danced in the half-light, and nausea churned in Liz's belly.

When Judith had asked if she was giving Peter money, the lie had been instant and reflexive. Because it wasn't an innocent question, was it? The subtext was as clear as it was ugly: *He's only interested in your money. You're an idiot.*

She wasn't an idiot. Yes, she'd lent Peter some money and she'd done it without hesitation. There was some problem with his grandson's medical insurance. 'I'd pay for everything in a heart-beat,' Peter had explained to her. 'But you know I've just bought all those new properties. None of my assets are liquid right now.' He was paying her back when his deal was finalised and that was in just a few weeks' time. He'd even offered to pay her interest, for goodness' sake.

Liz felt as if she was struggling to get her breath suddenly.

Had everything about the last four months been a lie? That meant there was no soulmate, no future, no happy ending. Worse still, it cut to the core of how Liz saw herself. How could she think of herself as sensible or smart or level-headed? How could she ever trust her own judgement again, let alone another human being?

Hot tears rolled down her cheeks onto the pillow. She'd seen the website. Black and white proof of everything Peter had said about himself.

And yet.

The woman in the next room was snoring like a freight train, two carers were talking in loud whispers and somewhere a radio burbled, but Liz felt utterly and completely alone.

If Peter didn't pay her back, she would lose her home of fifty-eight years. The home she'd returned to as a giddy young bride, the one where she'd taken her infant son back to from hospital and where her husband had died.

Her life savings were gone too, of course. She and John hadn't been spectacularly rich people, but they'd been financially prudent, and Liz had always had enough to top up her state pension and buy a few luxuries.

She could live without savings or even her house, though. The heartbreak too maybe, even if it felt as if it might kill her.

But even that was nothing – nothing – compared with the humiliation of other people knowing what had happened. Knowing she was a pathetic, stupid, deluded old fool.

She might have got away with being able to lick her wounds in private if it wasn't for Judith's husband. Liz had been over at Judith's one night and the two of them had been chatting about Peter (this was back when Judith still thought Peter was the best thing ever) and not realised that Martin was lurking around in the hallway eavesdropping.

He would tell everyone about this. It would be a juicy titbit to be produced at every turn. (Liz very much disagreed with the notion that men don't gossip. Martin may as well carry around a white picket fence.)

A small sob escaped from her mouth as she imagined people stopping talking when she walked into a room, or looking at her with contempt or, worse still, pity. And was there anything more humiliating than everyone laughing at you behind your back? *Did you hear what happened to poor old Liz? She actually thought the guy was in love with her – that they had a future together. Silly old thing.*

Liz couldn't live with that.

Chapter Twenty-Four

As soon as I get into school on Friday morning, Fiona calls me into the office and tells me that Maggie has food poisoning and isn't going to be able to go on the trip to the Science Museum. 'For fuck's sake... Like this week hasn't been bad enough with those Ofsted idiots in our face.'

Fiona shoots me a horrified look, which confuses me as, when there are no kids in the vicinity, she's quite the potty mouth herself, but then I hear someone clearing their throat behind me and I spin round to see the world's least charming and least cycle-aware Ofsted inspector.

'Morning,' I squeak.

'Morning,' he says, flashing me the thinnest of smiles and then turning to Fiona. 'Miss Cooper and I are going to start in 1H today.'

'Poor 1H,' I say as soon as he is out of earshot.

'I know,' Fiona agrees. 'He's got a bit of a stick up his bum, hasn't he? Anyway, what are we going to do about today?'

Ah, yes, today. The thing that prompted my string of expletives. And made me think the universe must have it in for me.

'You're a woman down,' Fiona says.

'Yup. And not just any woman either, but Maggie.'

'Right,' Fiona says. 'I know the other two reception class teachers and TAs will do their best to help you out, but they'll already have their hands full, so I wonder if we should try to get another of the parents from your class to step in?'

'Hmm, I already have the two most useful ones. I suppose we should try to find one more though. Otherwise, the child to adult ratio just isn't great. If I take one kid to the loo, that leaves just two parents in charge of twenty-seven kids.' I already woke up with nerves clawing at my stomach like a trapped rat. Whatever else is and isn't negotiable as a teacher, you are very much expected to keep all the children alive and that becomes considerably more challenging when you take them off-site.

Fiona and I divide up a list of possible parents who might step into the breach and start making calls.

Think positive, I tell myself, dialling Meghan's mother. Someone will be able to help.

But Meghan's mother is not able to help and nor is Callum's.

'I've drawn a blank,' Fiona says.

'Morning!' Tara says, walking past and giving a cheery smile. I squash down a wave of annoyance. It's all right for her with her non-food-poisoned TA and her immaculately highlighted swooshy hair. I bet she didn't find a piece of pepperoni in her bra when she took it off last night.

Focus, Emily, *focus*. I look back down at my list. Only George's dad can save me now.

'Hello,' he says.

'Hi, it's Emily Baxter here from Felstead Infants. No problem at all but I was just wondering if you could help us out of a tricky situation? As you know, we're taking the kids on a trip to the Science Museum today.'

'Yes, George is very excited about it.'

'Err… me too. But the thing is Mrs Glover, our wonderful teaching assistant, isn't very well, which means we're an adult down. So I was just wondering if there was any way you could help out?'

'I'd love to,' George's dad says.

My heart lifts.

'But unfortunately, I'm working today. It was all a bit last minute, but I guess that's the nature of freelance, right?'

I mutter a garbled goodbye and put the phone down.

'That's everyone,' Fiona says. 'There's no one else we can ask.'

I sigh. 'Actually, there is one more person.'

Chapter Twenty-Five

Liz

Liz felt like an absolute heel. She couldn't believe how much of a state she'd worked herself into in the middle of the night. That she'd allowed herself to entertain any doubt about Peter.

Because here he was now full of apology. And not just on the phone either, but a video call. They'd never video called before because where Peter lived in Spain the Wi-Fi was rubbish. But now here he was and the picture was terrible, but Liz couldn't have cared less because it was almost as if he was right here in the room with her.

'I'm so sorry about being shirty with you last night, my darling.' He ran his hands through his hair. 'I think I was just a bit upset to think you don't trust me. I completely overreacted though. I'm just so tired from being at the hospital night and day and so worried about Michael.'

Tears sprang to Liz's eyes. 'Of course. And I'm sorry I made you feel as if I was checking up on you.'

Peter laughed. 'Check away, my darling. God, it's lovely to see you on video.'

'You too. Your hair has got so long.'

Peter laughed. 'I know. With everything that's been going on, I haven't had a chance to get to the barber. I look like an ageing hippy, don't I?'

'A little,' Liz said grinning. 'But a very handsome ageing hippy.'

They chatted a little after that, but Liz could barely concentrate because all she could think about was the relief. After they'd said goodbye, she practically floated towards the dining room, sat down next to Sonia and gave her a beaming smile, which didn't even slip as Sonia started wittering on about Hope's wedding. She was so pleased they were going to book a live band and not have one of those disc jockeys. The band would be sure to play all the old favourites. You can't have a wedding without 'That Ole Devil Called Love'.

Liz was almost giddy with joy. She wolfed down a piece of cold toast that had been slathered with some unpleasant faux butter.

She looked up to see Anna moving towards her with a huge bunch of cellophane-wrapped flowers.

'Ooh,' Sonia said. 'Looks like someone's got a secret admirer.'

Liz's heart felt as if it was too big for her chest. She'd mentioned to Peter once in passing that peonies were her favourite flower and he'd remembered, bless him.

'Want me to open the card for you?' Anna said. She handed it to Liz.

Love you to the moon and back, P xxxxx

Liz smiled. She was never going to doubt him again.

Chapter Twenty-Six

It isn't fair of me to be irritated by my father. He is helping me out, and very graciously at that. He even obeyed my instruction not to wear the yoga trousers.

And yet. Before we'd even got out of sight of the school, he'd told the other teaching staff on the coach that he and I were going wedding dress shopping tomorrow and then venue hunting on Sunday. Which had prompted a load of excitement and questions and made me almost relieved when I had to rush down the coach with a sick bucket for Nisha.

By the time we arrived at the Science Museum, I was pretty sure that every single person on that coach, young or old, knew Ed was my dad (a concept that blew many of the children's minds: how could teachers have parents?) and that he and I were going to spend the weekend planning my wedding. Meghan wanted to know if I was going to have a dress like a princess, Kate asked if she could be a bridesmaid and Tommy said he hoped my fiancé was an Arsenal fan.

The wedding mania died down a little when we arrived at the museum's hands-on gallery and a couple of very young, very enthusiastic members of staff from the museum talked us through the four zones. Many hands shot up.

'Can we build whatever we like in the construction bit?' Meghan asked.

'When are we having our packed lunch?' Ralph said.

'What happens if my clothes get wet playing with the water?' Callum wanted to know.

'I need a wee,' Nisha said.

Once enquiries and bodily needs were dealt with, the children began to explore. My class started in the building zone and quickly got into the rhythm of loading blocks into wheelbarrows and using the bucket hoist and snake chute.

I watch as my father helps Tommy to pile bricks into a tower. I hate to admit it, but I have never seen Tommy as well-behaved as he is today and a lot of that is down to my dad. The two of them bonded talking about football on the coach and Tommy has been glued to Dad's side, and a model child, ever since.

'What's the best thing that's ever happened to you?' Dad says to Tommy.

'Rocky road ice cream,' Tommy says without missing a beat.

Dad smiles. 'Solid choice.'

'What's the best thing that's ever happened to you?' Tommy says, wiping his nose on his sleeve.

'Emily,' Dad says, putting a red brick on top of the teetering tower.

A lump rises in my throat.

'Miss Baxter, Miss Baxter,' Kate says, tugging at my sleeve. 'When are we going to play with the water?'

'Soon,' I say. 'When Mrs Redland's class have finished there. Aren't you enjoying the construction zone?'

Kate shakes her head so hard her bunches hit her across the face. 'No, Robert keeps putting too many bricks in the chute and they get stuck.'

'Hmm,' I say. 'Let me see if I can help.' I glance back towards my father just as the tower he and Tommy made crashes to the floor, making them both burst out laughing.

What he said to Tommy was lovely. But words are cheap.

My relief when the last kid from my class is safely collected proves short-lived.

'May I have a quick word?' Clare Wood says, appearing out of nowhere.

My stomach flips. Clare's tone is amiable enough, but the head doesn't ask for a quick word to chat about the weather. Especially at 4.40 on the Friday afternoon before half-term.

'Of course,' I say, trying to ignore the hammering in my chest. The menace to cyclists must have told Clare my observed lesson was terrible and that I have single-handedly jeopardised the school's Ofsted report.

I follow Clare down the corridor, passing my father, who is on his way back from the toilet. 'I'll just be a minute,' I say to him.

Clare stops in her tracks. 'You must be Emily's dad. Thanks so much for stepping into the breach today.' She extends a hand. 'Clare Wood.'

'Lovely to meet you,' he says, giving her his most winning smile. 'Are you joining us in the pub?'

My stomach lurches. I can't believe my dad just invited Clare Wood to the pub. For that matter, I didn't even know we were going to the pub. No one asked me.

Clare smiles. 'I'd love to, but I've got to shoot off, I'm afraid. I won't keep Emily long.'

'No worries,' Dad says. 'I'll wait for you in the staffroom, Em.'

'Do you know where it is?' I ask.

'Yeah, Rachel showed me.'

119

Of course she did. Rachel, like all my other colleagues who've come into any sort of contact with my father, seems very taken with him.

'Marvellous your dad could help out today,' Clare says as we resume walking. 'I hear he was great with the kids.'

I smile tightly. I know I should be pleased.

'Do take a seat,' Clare says, shutting her office door behind us. 'I'm sorry to have to tell you Tommy Cassidy's mother has written a letter of complaint about you.'

'*What?*' I squeak, my stomach plummeting as if I was on a rollercoaster.

Clare nods. 'She alleges you shouted at Tommy and that this is part of a wider problem. She believes you are – her word, not mine – bullying Tommy.'

Nausea swirls in my belly. Never in my life have I been called a bully. Suddenly I can see myself losing the job I love so much. A failed career to go with a failed relationship.

'Of course, I know that's not true,' Clare says. 'You're an excellent teacher, Emily, one of our best.'

'I… I…' My brain can't form a coherent thought.

'We'll deal with this,' Clare says firmly. 'But I need the weekend to think about how best to respond. Mrs Cassidy is, well, tricky and it's important not to give a knee-jerk response. I'd like for you and me to meet again on Monday and discuss our response. I hate to ask you to come into school on the first day of half-term, but I don't think we can let this fester. Is that okay?'

'Fine,' I mumble.

'Great,' Clare says, standing. 'And, in the meantime, try not to worry.'

Chapter Twenty-Seven

Ed

Nothing about the staffroom was luxurious but Ed was just grateful to be sitting down. And not have anybody asking him 'why' questions. Or vomiting. Or telling him they needed the toilet, and it was *urgent*.

'So how did you find today?' Rachel asked.

'Exhausting,' Ed said.

Rachel grinned. 'Well, you did very well.'

'Yeah,' Tara added. 'I was particularly impressed at how quick you were to get Liam to spit out those bits of brown paper bag before he swallowed them.'

'Yeah, why was he eating a paper bag?' Ed said.

Tara shrugged. 'Because he could.'

Ed laughed. He'd been about to leave for the casino this morning when Emily called, and now he was itching to log on to one of their online poker games to try to make up the shortfall in his finances. He couldn't exactly start playing poker on his phone in front of Emily's colleagues, though. Not a good look.

'Do you really have to check your class reading records now?' Rachel said to Tara. 'I want to get to the pub.'

'Yeah,' Tara said, stamping one of the yellow booklets with

her reading owl stamp. 'My plan is to see tonight as a warm-up for the hen do I'm going on tomorrow and get trolleyed. I don't want to take these home with me, in case I end up leaving them in the pub. I'll only be another ten minutes max.'

'O-kay,' Rachel said, smiling and doing a stagey sigh, 'Who wants a quick cuppa?'

'Yes, please,' Ed and Tara choroused.

Ed really wanted to be able to buy Emily a dress tomorrow. Earlier on the coach, when he'd been talking about the trip to the bridal store, Rachel had gone all misty-eyed and talked about how she'd never forget the day her mum bought her wedding dress.

Bought. It cemented the idea in Ed's mind that he had to pay for Emily's dress tomorrow. It was expected, de rigueur, the right thing to do. Which meant he had to get his hands on another grand. By tomorrow.

Rachel handed Ed a mug with 'World's Best Teacher' emblazoned on it.

'We could have a slice of cake too,' Tara said, abandoning the pile of yellow booklets. 'I could do with some sustenance before looking at Chloe's reading record. Her mother always writes an absolute essay. Perhaps she thinks it's me who needs reading practice?' She opened a large Tupperware container that was sitting on the counter. 'Eww, maybe not. Looks like one of Jeff's sugar-free numbers. No wonder there's some left over. Avocado does *not* taste like chocolate just because you whizz it up with a bit of cocoa powder.'

'I wonder what Clare needed to talk to Emily about,' Rachel said, blowing on the surface of her tea. 'It must be important if she's doing it now. Maybe I'll quiz Penny later.'

'Clare's secretary,' Tara explained to Ed. 'Otherwise known as Megaphone Mouth.'

'I hope Em's not in any kind of trouble,' Ed said.

'She won't be,' Tara said, bringing her owl stamp down on another reading record. 'She's the golden girl.'

'Yup,' Rachel agreed.

Ed smiled. There had been a little girl on the trip today who'd really reminded him of Emily when she was little. She was first to line up when asked to, never needed to be told to shush and had even picked up a discarded juice carton from the floor to put in the bin along with the rubbish from her own lunch box.

Ed guessed he could always play online poker after Emily had gone to bed. Hell, he'd stay up all night if he had to.

'Last few,' Tara said, closing another yellow booklet and placing it on top of the pile.

Anxiety bubbled in Ed's stomach. It was weird to think about blowing two grand on a dress when he didn't even have the money he needed for Monday's repayment to the bank.

His mother would give him the loan, though. Of course she would.

Chapter Twenty-Eight

I sit in the pub, my mind churning. Is there anything worse than being called a bully, especially when the person you are allegedly bullying is twenty-four years younger than you and supposed to be in your care?

My father is regaling the table with the story of Donny and the Great Dane and the robot vacuum. I'd forgotten how he always repeats his anecdotes, although to be fair no one but me has heard it before and it is a good story. Tara is laughing so hard, her gin and tonic comes out of her nose.

'Sorry to hear about your problems,' Rachel whispers to me.

My heart lurches. How the hell did Rachel find out about me and Mark? And how humiliating is it when just this morning I allowed my dad to talk about wedding dress shopping and venue hunting?

But then a piece clunks into place in my brain. Rachel isn't talking about the break-up with Mark, she's talking about the letter of complaint from Tommy Cassidy's mother. Clare's secretary Penny isn't exactly the model of discretion. 'Yeah, it's not great.' I catch sight of my dad looking over, all inquisitive now his story is finished. 'Can we not talk about it now, though.'

'Of course,' Rachel says. 'Let's grab a coffee tomorrow morning, just the two of us. Oh no, wait, you're wedding dress shopping.'

'Not until twelve.' I take a large swig of my wine. 'We can meet before.' It will be good to talk to Rachel about the Tommy Cassidy thing. I can be honest with her – say I would never bully a child, but I did lose my cool that day. It wasn't *shouting* shouting but I'm still ashamed of myself.

It will be helpful to get Rachel's take on what to do next. And good to have one hour of the weekend when I'm not forced into planning every detail of my fake wedding.

Chapter Twenty-Nine

Ed

Ed had sort of hoped today might have won him a few brownie points with Emily, but she had been quiet in the pub and was now cleaning out the fridge in a way that could only be described as ragey.

'Why are you doing that now?' he said. 'It's eleven o'clock at night.'

'It needs doing,' Emily snapped, opening a jar of marmalade and wrinkling her nose. 'Oh, look at this.' She tipped the jar towards Ed to show him the greenish-grey fur covering the surface of the preserve.

'Hmm,' he said, going back to his online poker.

Emily put the jar down on the counter with rather more force than was necessary. Whatever was the matter with her? Was she annoyed he wasn't helping?

She rummaged under the sink. 'What's happened to all the food waste bags?'

'I could buy some tomorrow?' Ed offered.

Emily tipped the marmalade into the bin.

'Are you okay?' Ed said.

'I'm fine,' Emily said, pulling a slimy-looking bag of salad leaves out of the fridge and making loud tssking noises.

'You seem…' Ed paused. 'Angry.'

'I'm not angry.'

For someone who wasn't angry, Emily was giving off signals of being absolutely bloody murderous. Even Pebbles had abandoned his kibble and scarpered.

Ed looked back down at his phone screen. He had a half-decent hand.

'Oh, for goodness' sake,' Emily said. 'What's this chicken carcass doing in here?'

'Umm… we had roast chicken last night.'

'Well, I know that. But I mean, what's the stripped carcass doing back in the fridge? I don't imagine you're going to be making stock, are you?'

Her voice dripped sarcasm and, for one moment, Ed felt like styling it out and saying he was indeed planning some stock-making. 'I used the last of the chicken this morning to make us a couple of sandwiches for the trip. I was rushing and didn't realise there was no meat left on the carcass.'

Emily gave a sigh that could shake the room and chucked the chicken carcass into the bin. 'Right,' she said, shoving the plate into the dishwasher. 'I'm going to bed.'

'Good idea,' Ed said. 'Big day tomorrow.'

Emily looked at him, her expression unreadable. Surely, she couldn't have forgotten? 'Going to buy you a wedding dress.'

'Oh, yeah,' Emily said.

Was it Ed's imagination or did she even sound a bit fed up about that? No, of course she didn't.

Saturday

Chapter Thirty

I lie in bed. I can hardly believe that in just over four hours I am going to be trying on dresses for a wedding that isn't happening. It's typical that my father managed to get a last-minute appointment. He always wheedles the impossible out of people. Once, when I was at primary school, he wanted to take me on a cruise during term time. He somehow managed to convince the headmistress, not known for being a pushover, that this was a good idea. I can still hear the woman simpering about travel 'broadening the mind' and how 'education didn't just take place in the classroom'. As if I was going to be helping my father save the world's rainforests rather than watch him be a B-tech Elvis on a ship full of retired Americans. The only things I learned were the words to 'Are You Lonesome Tonight' and that you can in fact get motion sickness on a cruise liner.

I pull the duvet over my head. Surely I can't go through with the wedding dress shopping? It's the sort of thing you read about in the tabloids: *The jilted fiancée who won't stop planning the wedding.*

There is no way I am telling my father I've been dumped though. Quite apart from the pact I made with myself years ago that I would prove that my life is perfect *despite* him, I've rather missed the opportunity to come clean by spending four whole days pretending everything is fine and Mark is just away on a work trip. I can hardly nonchalantly drop in a mention that there is no wedding. Especially since I have lectured my father many a time on his casual relationship with the truth.

Dad will have to know about me and Mark eventually, of course, but I will tell him when I have had a chance to come to terms with it myself (a time I struggle to envisage). The conversation with my dad certainly won't be face to face either, a phone call at most, more likely a WhatsApp.

The sheets are a tangled, sweaty mess. A largely sleepless night was punctuated by nightmares when I did finally manage to drift off. To make matters worse, I kept waking with a raging thirst but didn't want to venture out of my bedroom because I could hear my father prowling about.

I poke my head out from under the duvet. There is no choice but to grit my teeth and get through today. It will be hard seeing myself in wedding dresses but there are tougher challenges ahead. The situation at work for one. I can hardly believe I am the subject of a letter of complaint that labels me a bully. *A letter.* It is so formal, so serious. And while Clare made supportive noises, there wasn't even a flicker of 'we'll just ignore this neurotic mother'. Is this going to blow up into something big? Go on my record? Cost me my job? People tease me about being Clare's favourite but, at the very least, this will surely change that, especially if she finds out I also shouted at one of the Ofsted inspectors (admittedly before I knew who he was and not without justification, but still) and messed up my observed lesson.

The problems at work pale in comparison to me and Mark being over, though. And we are over. Until his icy response to my drunken messages, there was a little part of me that thought him walking out on me had been a moment of madness, some bad dream I'd wake up from. Now I am faced with the stark reality. The person who knows me better than anyone in the world and has been there for *everything* (I still have a visceral memory of his hand clutching mine as my mum's coffin was lowered into the ground) is gone. I am alone.

What happened to me and Mark? We've been best friends since we were kids. I still get goosebumps when I remember the first time we kissed. It was at Karen Howarth's sixteenth birthday party. There seemed to be a wonderful inevitability to the kiss, as if it was pre-ordained by the universe. We'd been inseparable ever since, choosing the same uni, going interrailing together afterwards (the happiest three months of my whole life), and then moving to London when Mark was offered his dream job here.

I force myself out of bed. My father is still snoring away in the sofa bed. He is lying on his back in a starfish position that looks strangely childlike (perfectly on brand, now I come to think of it).

I tiptoe past as quietly as I possibly can. I need a bucket of tea before I can deal with my father. But as I walk into the kitchen, all thoughts of keeping quiet vanish from my mind as I scream 'PEBBLES!' in a voice I don't even recognise as my own.

My dad and I are on our hands and knees on the kitchen floor scrabbling through the contents of the bin to piece together the chicken carcass in an attempt to see what is missing.

'What the hell was I thinking, throwing chicken bones into the bin?' I say. 'I know Pebbles can get in there.'

'Em, stop. It was a mistake. And Pebbles is fine.'

I glance over at Pebbles, who glares from the cat carrier. 'But Google said there's a risk of an intestinal blockage or tear. That he could need surgery.' A sob escapes from my throat. 'It could even be life-threatening.'

My father places a greasy hand on my arm. 'Everyone knows that googling anything is a recipe for panic. And don't forget it also said that more often than not cats can digest chicken bones no problem at all.' He digs through a pile of soggy salad leaves. 'Look, here's the other leg bone. I don't even think Pebbles ate much, if anything. You clearly interrupted him before he had a chance to get going.'

'Maybe.' I desperately want to believe my father. He always says everything is fine, though.

I pick up a rib and add it to the pile of chicken bones. Callum once brought a dinosaur fossil digging kit in for Show and Tell. 'You have to use the chisel to get to the bones and build the whole dinosaur,' he explained.

'Cats are carnivores,' my father says. 'Just think of all the things they eat in the wild.'

'But he's not in the wild, he's in South London.'

'Close.'

'This isn't funny,' I snap, retrieving another bone from under a blob of mouldy marmalade.

'Even most domestic cats eat all sorts,' my father says. 'Do you remember Tigger? She loved nothing more than chowing down on small birds. Upset the hell out of your mother but never did Tigger any damage whatsoever. She lived to a ripe old age.'

'True,' I say, rocking back on my heels. I glance over at Pebbles, who is looking out from the cat carrier. 'Maybe I should call the vet just in case, though?'

My father shakes his head. 'Nah, go and have a shower and I'll clear up all this mess and then let Pebbles out. One thing I do know is that he does *not* appreciate the incarceration.'

'No, he hates the cat carrier.' I wash my hands in the kitchen sink. 'I still can't believe I was so stupid.'

My father snaps a new bin bag off the roll. 'Anyone ever tell you that you're pretty hard on yourself? Now, go and have a nice shower and stop worrying. This is your day, remember.'

Chapter Thirty-One

Liz

Liz read Peter's latest message, a smile spreading across her face. She couldn't believe she'd doubted him (what is it about the middle of the night that can make the teeniest flicker of worry mushroom into something uncontrollable?). Now things between them were better than ever. His grandson was out of intensive care too, and they'd started to tentatively talk about Peter's move to England.

'Cup of tea?' Anna said, appearing in the doorway.

'Please.' Liz wanted to say, 'and don't slosh half a pint of milk in it like you did last time' but bit her tongue.

Nothing had got to her in the last twenty-four hours. She'd listened patiently to Sonia's prattling, not rolled her eyes at the seven-year-old of a doctor who'd insisted on talking to her veeeeeeeeeeery slowly (Liz had hurt her shoulder not her brain), and not got wound up when she'd looked into getting a bank loan elsewhere and discovered that it was unlikely to be successful. (Apparently, even making multiple loan applications can adversely affect your credit rating.) Middle-of-the-night Liz would have panicked about that, but now she just told herself she'd find another way to get the money.

For all this equanimity, Liz was finding it very hard to forgive Judith, and they hadn't exchanged so much as a message since that awkward conversation in the garden.

Anna placed the mug of tea in front of her and Liz waited until she was out of the way before she made a clumsy left-handed attempt to drink. She knew Anna would have seen worse, of course, but she still had some pride left.

She looked around the small peach-coloured bedroom. The whole place could do with a damn good clean.

Liz had tried to tell herself that Judith was just being her usual worrywart self. God knows, the woman could find the downsides to a lottery win. But she also had a nagging feeling that there was something else going on too. That Judith might be – and Liz hated to use the word even in her own head – jealous. She was, after all, stuck in a miserable, loveless marriage to a man who was an absolute pill. It must be hard watching someone else fall head over heels.

A woman with a world-weary expression and straw-like hair appeared in the doorway. 'Laundry?'

Liz shook her head. 'I'm fine thanks. My friend took it for me.'

The woman disappeared and Liz sat staring at a cobweb in the corner of the room. It had been kind of Judith to insist on doing her washing. And offering to have her to stay. And running back and forth getting clothes and toiletries and books and goodness knows what else. So she was a little jealous – there were worse things.

Liz opened the message app and used the fingers on her good hand to type out a message to Judith.

Chapter Thirty-Two

When I go back into the kitchen, everything has been tidied up and my dad is clattering around making pancakes. As if we are in some American sitcom. He is even wearing an apron, for goodness' sake.

I stoop down next to Pebbles' basket and he immediately runs away. Nothing unusual about that, to be fair. 'How does he seem?'

'A hundred per cent. Stop worrying. Would you like a coffee? Oh, listen to me, all American. You'd probably prefer tea?'

'Yeah, tea. I'll make it.'

'Don't you dare,' my dad says, waving his spatula at me. 'Sit down over there and I'll bring it to you. This is your day.'

I sit on the sofa, avoiding the side Mark sat on when he dumped me. I chew my lower lip and concentrate on not crying.

My father hands me a cup of tea. 'Thanks. By the way, I'm meeting Rachel for a quick coffee this morning.'

Is it my imagination or does my father look a bit put out? He pins the smile back on his face pretty quickly though. 'That will be nice. Just don't be late for our appointment at twelve. Do you have a particular kind of dress in mind?'

'Umm, not really.' I stare at a photo on the wall. It's of me and Mark standing on the Ponte Vecchio when we went inter-railing. We look very young and very happy. I remember the day as if it was yesterday. The Uffizi, the Duomo, the Accademia (you can't go to Florence and not see David). Over the best pizza I have ever had in my life, we fizzed with how this trip was going to be the first of many adventures. We wanted to see Japan, Morocco, Australia – definitely Australia.

'I expect you need to see what things look like on,' Dad says, taking a pancake out of the frying pan and putting it on a plate.

'What? Hmm, yes. Do you really think Pebbles is okay? I'll never forgive myself if he isn't.'

'He's fine. Just look at him.' My dad puts the plate in front of me. 'You didn't have any maple syrup so I've improvised with honey.'

I take a mouthful of pancake. 'Delicious.'

'Don't sound so surprised,' my dad says, laughing. 'I haven't lived in America for eighteen years without learning how to knock up decent pancakes.'

I force a smile. I wasn't being polite about the pancakes, they are pillowy light and fluffy and their sweetness is cut nicely by the berries Dad has served alongside them. I'm struggling to force them down, though. I take a large mouthful of tea, hoping to wash down the wodge of pancake that seems stuck in my throat.

Despite our promises to ourselves that day in the Florence pizzeria, Mark and I hadn't gone travelling since the interrailing. Well, unless you count holidays, which I most definitely don't. A two-week beach break is wonderful, but it isn't Travel with a capital T. The truth is, once we'd got jobs and a mortgage, it wasn't quite so simple. 'Maybe when we retire,' Mark said.

Except, of course, now we won't be retiring together.

'I can see you in a very sleek and simple dress,' Dad says, sawing off a large piece of pancake. 'Unfussy and elegant.'

'Hmm? Oh, yeah.'

'So,' he says. 'I want today to be perfect for you, but I know it can't be.'

Oh, you have no idea.

'It's bound to be painful not having your mum there.'

Yep, that too.

Dad takes a sip of his coffee. 'And although I know I can never take her place and I wouldn't even want to try, it means a lot to me to be able to go with you. Especially, since things haven't always been… y'know… easy. And, while we're on the subject of the past, although I very much want us to have a lovely weekend together, Shona told me I mustn't be afraid to have difficult conversations too. She said if I want to make amends, I've got to hear you. I've got to do the work.'

'Riiight,' I say, taking a mouthful of tea. Shona sounds like a walking self-help manual. And, frankly, there is so much for my father to 'hear', I wouldn't know where to start. I can't deal with it. Not ever really, but especially not now.

Justin Bieber's 'Baby' starts up. Who sets that as their ringtone for God's sake?

Dad fishes his phone out of his pocket. 'Talk of the devil – Shona's FaceTiming me now.' He jabs at the screen. 'Hey, baby. Isn't it like five a.m. there? What are you doing up?'

Shona's voice rings out loud and clear as she explains that she hasn't been able to sleep a wink. The bed is just way too big without her 'Big Teddy Eddy'.

I almost sick up what I managed to eat of the pancakes.

'Would you like to meet Emily?' Dad says.

'I would love to!' Shona says.

He shoves the phone into my hand. A tiny blonde bird-woman in yoga gear is grinning from the screen. 'Emileeeeee! I've heard so much about you.'

'Nice to meet you.'

'Your pop tells me you're going shopping today and y'all are gonna look for a wedding dress. How exciting is that?'

'Yup,' I say, forcing a smile.

'That sounds like a blast!' Shona says, clapping her tiny hands together. 'I wish I was there with you. Did your pop tell you that I'm a little English too? My great-grandma was from Clapton. I never got to meet her, sadly, but I love all things British. Including your pop, of course.' She lets out a throaty chuckle. 'I will be manifesting a day of peace and happiness for you both. I practise daily Qigong…'

As Shona keeps talking and talking, I feel my mind drift. I wonder what Mark is doing today. He sure as hell isn't trying on wedding outfits.

I tune back into Shona's monologue. She has somehow segued into the right to bear arms and I am reminded of my father describing her as a 'curious combination of hippy and redneck'.

'I hate to interrupt,' Dad says. 'But I know Emily has to go.'

'Of course,' Shona says. 'Y'know what I'm like when I get talking!' She blows a kiss through the screen. 'Wonderful to meet you, Emileeeeee. Have a fantastic day and don't forget to tell me all about that gown you pick out.'

I hand the phone back to my dad and listen as Shona tells him she really misses her Big Teddy Eddy and the two of them say a goodbye that seems to go on for about seven and a half hours.

'I can't believe I put a chicken carcass in the bin,' I say when Dad finally ends the call. 'I know Pebbles can get into it. How stupid and irresponsible can you get?'

'Emily,' he says, putting his hand on my arm. 'Stop beating yourself up. The cat is fine.'

I glance across at Pebbles, who is happily licking his paws. 'He does seem okay.'

'So pleased you and Shona got to meet,' Dad says. 'Next time, we'll have to make sure it's in person. Right, you go and get yourself ready and I'll clear up.' He picks up the plates from the coffee table and shakes his head. 'I just can't believe my little girl is getting married.'

Chapter Thirty-Three

Ed

When Ed had somehow managed to win the shortfall in what he needed to buy Emily a wedding dress, he'd been ecstatic. He hadn't cared that it was nearly five in the morning and he was jittery from too much caffeine and gritty-eyed with exhaustion – all that mattered was that he'd only gone and bloody done it.

But this morning's FaceTime with Shona had punctured his bubble. The painful irony of her being so excited about the dress when she had no idea it could cost her her home. Because although Ed had stayed up most of the night with one thing and one thing only in mind, and that was being able to buy a dress for his daughter, it was hard not to think about the fact that the money might be better spent as part of the repayment due to the bank the day after tomorrow. What if his mother didn't change her mind about giving him a loan? How would he then feel about having spent so much on a dress? All his life people had called him reckless and, although he preferred brave, right now there was a not so little voice inside his own head screaming: reckless, reckless, reckless.

Ed scraped the remnants of Emily's pancakes into the bin (she couldn't have eaten more than two mouthfuls) before remembering her saying that all food waste must be taken straight to the outdoor bins from now on. God, she'd been upset about Pebbles getting hold of that chicken carcass. Ed glanced over at the cat sitting in his bed looking happy as Larry. 'You're all right, mate, aren't you? No harm done.'

Ed fished around in the bin, pulled out the discarded pancakes and put them on a plate with the eggshells left lying on the counter in their own little snail trails.

Maybe just going with Emily to look at wedding dresses would be a bonding activity in itself and he didn't need to actually buy one? He could dissuade Emily from buying a dress today, reminding her this was the first time she'd tried dresses on and urging caution. It was kind of a dick move though.

Ed stepped outside to gorgeous sunshine and clear blue sky. Hopefully, the weather would lift everyone's mood. He so wanted today to be perfect, but he was tying himself up in knots about whether or not to shell out for the dress and Emily, despite his reassurances, still seemed to be fretting about the cat, not to mention beating herself up about it being her fault. It was almost impossible to imagine that in just a couple of hours' time, she'd be behaving like the other brides-to-be he'd seen in the boutiques. He couldn't picture her delightedly oohing and aahing over dresses, laughing as assistants clipped the back with bulldog clips, and beaming as she alighted on The One.

Back in the kitchen, Ed couldn't help but notice that he'd created quite a lot of mess for someone who'd made breakfast for two people. He was reminded of Catherine, who had always discouraged him from cooking, saying she couldn't bear the chaos he created. Emily was just as much of a neat-freak. Everything in the kitchen cupboards sat in serried ranks with labels facing forward. You could feel her eyes boring into you if you didn't hang up your jacket within a minute of removing it and, in the four days Ed had been here, he reckoned he'd seen her clean that glass coffee table at least seven times.

He filled the sink with hot water and squirted in some washing-up liquid, filling the air with a distinctly artificial although not unpleasant smell of apple. It was so tricky knowing what to do. On the one hand, buying Emily a wedding dress felt like the least she deserved, but on the other it was hard not to think it was crazy spending that kind of money on a cloud of silk and tulle when his home was at risk. *Shona's home.*

Ed wished Shona was here in London with him. He couldn't talk to her about the dilemma he was facing, of course, but for all her woo-woo stuff with healing crystals, incanting ancient enchantments and goodness knows what else, she grounded Ed, kept him on track.

He scrubbed at the frying pan. The look Emily had given him when he'd said he wasn't afraid to have difficult conversations or do the work was pure Catherine. Really, it said, you sure about that? To be fair, she wasn't wrong. Ed had been far from convinced about the words coming from his own mouth (words he was only saying because Shona had told him he must). Work was something he generally tried to keep to a minimum and his ideal work – life balance was about 80/20 in favour of life. He was also a great believer in leaving the past in the past and not crying over spilt milk. So he'd been relieved when, just after saying he was happy to discuss anything, Shona's call had meant he didn't have to.

A car alarm started up outside, loud and shrill.

His mother would surely change her mind about the loan when he saw her face to face tomorrow, right? Especially if he turned up with Emily and she could see he was trying to make amends? So maybe it wasn't reckless to buy the dress today?

Ed stared at the washing-up water. Globules of grease and bits of pancake floated on the surface of the murky water like some disgusting version of a lava lamp. He pulled the plug and watched the water swirl away. When he was about seventeen, his late dad, who would have been the age Ed was now, told him that the years went quicker as you got older. At the time, Ed thought this ludicrous. A year was 365 days long. Now, though, he could see exactly what his dad had meant. Time had sped up. One minute Emily was a chubby baby with two teeth, the next a ten-year-old with a laugh bigger than her, and then here she was now, a grown woman on the cusp of marriage.

Ed picked up the butter and milk and put them back in the fridge, stopping as he closed it to look at the photographs stuck to the front with magnets. There was a picture of Emily and Mark laughing as they did the obligatory lean in front of the leaning tower of Pisa; one of Catherine taken before she got sick and one of Emily and Mark at their graduation. Ed hadn't made it back to England. He'd made some excuse about not being able to get the time off work, but the truth was he couldn't scrape together the cash.

Guilt stabbed at his guts. He should have been at his daughter's graduation. Especially as her mum had died just a few years earlier. He'd allowed Emily to graduate without a parent there to clap and cheer and celebrate her achievements. How had she felt as she watched all her peers have their photos taken with their proud mums and dads? Ed had let her down because he didn't have the money.

And now he did have the money. There wasn't really a choice to make.

Chapter Thirty-Four

Liz

Have I ever told you that you're as brilliant as you are beautiful?
Liz smiled. She'd been so excited to tell Peter about her plan. She'd known he'd be relieved. His deal was still a few weeks off being finalised and his grandson's medical bills were mounting by the day.

I'll pay you back every penny. With interest.

No interest, Liz typed back. *We're a team.*

The BEST team! Love you so, so much.

Love you too.

Liz was pleased with herself. For a moment, she'd wondered if she was going to have to admit defeat in getting the extra cash. It was clear she wasn't going to get a bank loan and she'd already used up all her savings and taken out a reverse equity deal on the house. She'd toyed with the idea of borrowing the money from family or friends but that would bring its own complications.

What are you up to today?

Liz looked around her peach-coloured cell. *Nothing much. What about you?*

Will be at the hospital all day.

How is Michael?

Doing better thank God.

That's good to hear, Liz typed.

Counting the minutes until we can be together.

Me too, Liz wrote, her stomach flipping.

It was hard to imagine she and Peter had yet to meet in real life. He'd been due to come to England just before Michael was in the car accident. Liz had been beside herself with excitement. She'd booked appointments for waxing and high-lights and a facial. She'd cleaned the house from top to bottom, bought an expensive set of new bed linen and batch-cooked meals for the freezer. 'I feel like a teenager again,' she said to Peter. But she had never got to run into his arms at the airport (for all her criticisms of romcoms, it's hard not to absorb their ideas).

A woman down the corridor was calling repeatedly for her mummy. Surely she ought to be upstairs in the dementia bit? Liz felt sorry for her, of course, but it was hard to listen to.

Did I ever tell you that I'm the luckiest man in the whole world? And that you're the love of my life.

A warmth spread through Liz's body. Peter had told her that before, in fact he said things like that all the time. He was such a romantic.

Did I ever tell you that you're a soppy old thing? ☺

As soon as she pressed send, Liz felt guilty. Peter was romantic, not soppy. Why couldn't she make him feel as special as he made her feel? Did he even know how desperate she was for them to be together? That she was consumed by wanting to know what his hair smelled like and his skin. Whether they fitted together when they cuddled. If he even was a cuddler.

When are you going to come? I don't think I can wait much longer.

She watched the dots that showed Peter was typing. And then they stopped. After what seemed like forever, they started up again.

My grandson is still very sick. That's all I can think about just now.

Liz felt as if someone had punched her in the gut. She had meant to sound romantic, but she had just come off as selfish and callous.

I'm so sorry, she typed. *Of course you need to focus on being with Michael right now.*

She waited for the dots. But no dots came.

149

Chapter Thirty-Five

Ishut my front door behind me, relieved at the respite from my dad and his incessant wedding chatter.

I am not looking forward to the conversation I am about to have with Rachel, though. In fact, the words 'frying pan' and 'fire' spring to mind.

It is sunny and unseasonably warm out, and happy, laughing people are carrying children or coffees or yoga mats and looking as if they have dropped out of a TV commercial. Even the dogs seem to be smiling.

I go over what I am going to say: So the thing is, I am not a bully but I *did* shout at Tommy Cassidy. And then, when his mother confronted me about it, I panicked and said I hadn't. Oh, and, side note, I also yelled at one of the Ofsted inspectors when he doored me on my bike. And messed up my observed lesson.

Maybe Rachel will take all this information completely in her stride? Say the Ofsted inspector deserved a strip chewing off him and my observed lesson went better than I thought. As for the Tommy Cassidy thing, well, every teacher loses their cool from time to time. It's inevitable when you consider the pressures of the job. Had she ever told me the funny story about when she...

Or maybe Rachel will be shocked and appalled?

That's how I'd be if the roles were reversed. I feel a stab of guilt as I think about all the times in the past colleagues have told me about a mistake they'd made, whether it was inadequate lesson planning or missing a problem that later seemed obvious. I'd listened and made the right noises but inside there was always a judge-y little voice shouting: *Try harder, do better.*

The café looms into view and, for a second, I am tempted to keep walking. And walking. And walking.

I'll take myself far away from awkward, embarrassing admissions to colleagues; far away from planning a fake wedding and choosing a dress I am never going to wear.

Instead, I'll go somewhere I can be completely alone. Maybe another café where no one knows me, and I can sit undisturbed and cry into a humongous slice of chocolate fudge cake.

'Hey,' Rachel says, getting up and wrapping me into a hug. 'You poor thing. What a horrible situation.'

I extricate myself from the hug and sit. 'Yeah, look—'

I am interrupted by the arrival of a waiter asking what he can get us. We order drinks and then I take a breath. 'Before we even get on to the letter, there's something else I need to tell you about.'

Rachel listens as I tell her about Ofsted guy. 'God,' she says, when I've finished. 'I'm not surprised you shouted at him. You could have been seriously hurt. Plus, it doesn't sound as if he was particularly sorry. And don't worry about your observed lesson. I'm sure it went better than you think.'

I nod gratefully. Rachel said just what I wanted to hear. 'As for this whole thing with Tommy—'

Rachel reaches across the table and puts her hand over mine. 'It's awful. Honestly, I *hate* parents like the Cassidys. The ones who are never satisfied and believe every word that comes out of their "little darlings'" mouths.'

Yeah, except this time their little darling was telling the truth. 'I sh—'

'It's parents like that who drive good teachers like you out of the profession.'

The waiter reappears with our tea. I look around the café. It must surely be my imagination but, just as it had outside, it seems as though everyone is preternaturally, stagily happy. The couple over at the next table with supermarket carrier bags at their feet (what about the frozen items?) who are laughing with their heads thrown back, the mother who is breastfeeding her baby with a beatific look of contentment, the staff behind the counter who are trading jokes.

Rachel's voice snaps me back into the present. '…I told Tara straight away that you'd never shout at a kid. That's not you at all.'

People change. Do things you think are totally out of character. Like tell you they'll love you forever and then just up and leave you.

I reach for my tea with trembling hands. Suddenly, the mug is on its side and what seems like a bucket of tea has flooded the table and dripped onto my leg, soaking through my jeans.

'Did it scald you?' Rachel says, rescuing her purse from the puddle and shaking it.

I shake my head and swallow the tears that are rising. Luckily, I'd added a fair bit of cold milk to my tea, but my thigh is still stinging in protest. 'I'm fine,' I say, plucking at the wet denim.

Rachel mops at the table with a napkin and the waiter appears with a cloth.

'Sorry,' I say, once everything is dried off.

'Don't apologise,' Rachel and the waiter say in unison.

'I wish you'd told me what was going on,' Rachel says, as soon as we are alone again. 'I knew something wasn't right with you all week – you've been so quiet.'

Is this the moment to cut in and tell Rachel about me and Mark? No, one big revelation is quite enough for one morning. Besides, Rachel was one of the people my father told all about the weekend of wedding planning that lies ahead.

The waiter brings over a fresh cup of tea.

'Please don't worry about the conversation with Clare on Monday,' Rachel says, raising her voice over the clank and hiss of the coffee machine. 'I mean, apart from the fact you have to go into school during half-term, which is a bloody nuisance. I've worked with Clare for years and I know she'll back you one hundred per cent. And talking of people supporting you, I thought it might be a good idea to have a chat with Natasha. As our union rep, she ought to know if we come up against any problems.'

A wave of panic washes over me. I have to put a stop to this before it spirals completely out of control.

My phone rings. 'My dad,' I say to Rachel. 'What's the matter? Is Pebbles okay?'

'Pebbles is fine. What shoes are you wearing?'

'Sorry?'

'What shoes?'

'Why?'

'Shona just phoned me back. She wanted to check you'd remembered to take the right shoes with you to try on with the dresses.'

I glance down at my heavily buckled black biker boots.

'I think you were wearing boots?' my dad says. 'And you only had that tiny bag. So, I'm guessing that means you don't have shoes…'

'Umm. No. But—'

'If you tell me where they are, I can bring some with me.'

I am about to tell my dad it doesn't matter but decide it's quicker and easier to go along with this. 'There are some rose gold sandals in my wardrobe. Mine's the one on the left.' My stomach clenches as I realise that both wardrobes are now mine. Mark still has some things hanging in the right-hand one but only because he was in too much of a hurry to get away the night he left. No doubt soon he'll send a message asking when would be convenient to collect the rest of his stuff. 'Convenient' will be a polite way of asking when I'm out.

I glance across at Rachel, who is jabbing away at her phone.

'The ones with the wedge heel?' my dad says.

'No, those are gold, not rose gold.'

'Ah, okay, found them. Great, see you at Helen Yately Brides. Looking forward to it.'

I end the call and see Rachel is looking at me quizzically. 'My dad just checking I've got some shoes for when I try on the wedding dresses.' I gesture towards the biker boots. 'These not being very bride-y.'

'Bless him!' Rachel says. 'He's such a love.'

'Yeah,' I say, picking at my cuticle.

'Is this the first time you've looked for dresses?'

'Yeah, well I've had a look online but it's the first time I'll have physically gone to a wedding dress shop.'

'And it's so different when you see stuff on,' Rachel says. 'Where are you going?'

'Helen Yately.'

Rachel claps her hands together. 'Oh, they have gorgeous stuff. What sort of thing do you have in mind?'

I stare at the floor. 'Umm, I'm not too sure yet. Look, about talking to Natasha.'

'Yup, you're right to get me back on task,' Rachel says, laughing. 'I could talk about weddings all day. I've already messaged Natasha. I did it while you were on the phone to your dad.'

Terrific.

I take a sip of my tea, which is cold and bitter. I can still tell Rachel the truth about Tommy. It will be awkward, and she will inevitably question why I didn't do it earlier, but it is still possible.

'Natasha is a great person to have on your side with things like this,' Rachel says. 'You wouldn't think it to look at her but she's something of a Rottweiler when she needs to be. She'll even sit in on your meeting with Clare if you want her to.'

My palms are sweating. If I don't tell Rachel the truth now, it commits me to also lying to Natasha and, more seriously still, Clare. Surely I can't do that? It goes against everything I believe in.

Rachel reaches across the table and puts her hand on my arm. 'Please don't look so worried. This will all be over very soon, I promise.'

'Umm... well... thank you.'

'You're welcome,' Rachel says, smiling. 'And, in the meantime, try to forget about it all and enjoy the wedding dress shopping. I'd hate to think of the Cassidys spoiling that for you.'

There is an obscene amount of happiness in this room. Smiling, hugging, laughter.

I stare at the zebra print rug and try not to scream.

I can do this. Pretend I still need a wedding dress. Pretend to be happy.

A woman called Harriet with lots of dark curly hair is fussing around me and Dad, telling me she wants to make today special for me 'despite the circumstances'.

For one awful second, I think Harriet is referring to me being a fake bride-to-be. But, of course, she must be talking about Mum. My father will have played the sympathy card to wheedle an appointment.

'Why don't you start picking out some things you like?' Harriet says. 'And while you do that, I'll get you both a drink. Tea? Coffee? Fizz?'

'Tea please,' I say.

'Sure you don't want a glass of fizz?' my father says. He nods towards a multi-generational group of women in the corner who are clinking glasses.

I glance across at the women, my heart pounding as I see Tommy Cassidy's mother. I blink and look again, to see the woman bears no more than a passing resemblance to Tommy's mother. *Get a grip, Emily. There's plenty to deal with today without letting your mind play tricks on you.* 'Just tea, thanks.'

Harriet disappears and I start to poke half-heartedly through the rails. I am determined not to like anything, but it's hard. Buttery soft satin caresses my fingers, immaculately cut lines seduce my eyes and subtle shimmer lures my senses. It is just my luck that my dad stumbled upon one of the best bridal stores in London. Why couldn't he have chosen somewhere tacky where huge pink puffballs rub oversized shoulders with OTT jewel-encrusted columns?

'Seen anything you like yet?' Dad asks. He has made himself very comfortable on the big squashy sofas in the middle of the room.

'Not yet.' And that's when I have a genius idea. The way to get through this is to try on dresses I don't like. It won't completely kill the pain, of course. I am still going to put on a wedding dress and see myself in the mirror knowing there is no wedding, but I don't have to make it worse by being in a dress I might actually have worn.

'Have you seen the flowers on the celling?' Dad says.

'Yeah,' I say, going through the rails. 'For Instagram.'

'Oh, right. Weird.'

I don't reply. There are lots of things weird about today, but the fake pink flowers carpeting the ceiling barely make the B list.

Harriet comes back with the tea, apologising for the delay. She squeezes my father's arm and asks if he is okay. She knows today must be bittersweet.

Christ, he must have really laid it on thick about Mum. He obviously failed to mention they'd been divorced for six years before she died. I'm not a bit surprised. Grieving widower is very much in his wheelhouse.

'Found anything you like yet?' Harriet asks me.

Everything unfortunately. But then I see what I am looking for. It has huge puffy sleeves and a square neckline, and it looks more like a costume for a period drama than a wedding dress. 'This one.'

Do Harriet's eyes register a tiny flicker of surprise? She pulls the dress off the rail and takes it towards the changing room.

I am in luck too because almost immediately afterwards I find two more 'horrible' dresses. A heavily beaded number in a shade of oyster that looks dirty and an empire-line dress that carries more than a whiff of milkmaid.

'Can't wait to see you in them,' Dad says, breaking off from the conversation he has struck up with a couple of women from another party.

Harriet ushers me into the changing room. 'Must be stressful for you having to move the wedding forward.'

She has clearly confused me with another bride-to-be. Well, either that or the rush wedding was another one of my father's lies.

I make non-committal noises. I am hardly about to admit that I'd kill to have organisational logistics at the top of my worry list.

Harriet says she'll wait outside until I am ready to be done up. I push my fingers into my temples. Within an hour this will all be over. Well, not *all*, but at least this awful game of dress up. I pull off my sweatshirt and step out of my jeans. I'll try the beaded dress first. 'Ready,' I mumble.

Harriet is by my side within a second. This one has loads of buttons so it will take a minute or so to do up. Harriet knows it is a little big, but I should try to see past that. Do I know the bodice is hand-beaded?

I step out of the changing room with Harriet trailing behind like a kind of de facto bridesmaid.

Dad is flanked on the sofa by two women. They are both laughing loudly at something he has said and seem to have entirely forgotten the bride-to-be they are here with.

'Wow,' Dad says, breaking off his conversation. 'It's so weird seeing you in a wedding dress, Em.'

I look at myself in the huge gilt-framed mirror. The pretend bride. I dig my nails into my palms and bite the inside of my cheek.

Harriet is fiddling around with the hem. 'This dress looks nice with quite a simple veil—'

'I don't like it,' I say, immediately feeling bad about cutting Harriet off so rudely. 'It's just not me,' I say more softly.

Back in the changing room on my own, I try to calm my breathing. I keep picturing an alternate reality. One where I am still marrying Mark and I am bubbling with excitement right now. And, hell, if we're fantasising about an ideal world, of course my mum would still be here too. I can picture her now, sitting in the chair in the corner of the changing room, her pale blue eyes blazing with love. She'd tell me off for being abrupt with Harriet, though; say there is never any need to be rude. Of course, I wouldn't have been rude in that reality because I'd be happy.

I pull on the dress with the huge sleeves and am relieved to see it looks even worse on than off. 'Ready,' I say to Harriet.

Dad is exchanging effusive goodbyes with his two new friends. 'Oh,' he says, spinning around to see me. 'Do you like that one?'

Despite my mood, I nearly laugh out loud. For someone who is a consummate liar, my dad isn't half transparent at times.

'No,' I say. 'I really don't.'

'Never mind,' Harriet says. 'Plenty more dresses in the sea.'

'Just one more to try on,' I say, trudging back towards the changing room. I pull the door behind me. This is nearly over. Just the milkmaid dress to go.

I put on the dress. It's perfectly hideous on me. 'Ready.'

'That one is… nice,' Dad ventures.

I shake my head. 'I don't think it's for me. I probably need to do a bit more research first.'

'Bear with me a second,' Harriet says.

Before I have a chance to realise what's happening, she is swooping through the shop like a tiny dervish, pulling dress after dress off the rails.

'How about this one?' she says, showing me an exquisite silk column.

'Er, I don't want strapless.'

'Isn't it worth trying on?' Dad says.

'No thank you,' I say.

Harriet shows me two more dresses, both beautiful. I find something that isn't quite right about each of them.

And then Harriet shows me something that makes me let out an involuntary gasp.

It's the dress from my mood board. Right there in front of my eyes in all its simple, bias-cut perfection.

'Oh, that one is gorgeous,' Dad says.

'It's, it's—' I can't find a single thing wrong with it.

'You have to try it on,' Dad says.

'I think it would look lovely on you,' Harriet adds.

I take a deep breath. It's just a dress.

Back in the changing room, I try to avoid looking at myself. No mean feat when you're in a room with mirrors on every wall.

'Ready,' I say, flatly.

'Oh, wow,' Harriet says, stepping into the room. 'That looks amazing!'

I trail out of the changing room.

Dad looks up and breaks into a huge grin. 'That's just perfect,' he says, his voice cracking.

I can't help but glance at myself in the mirror. I love the dress. Mark would have loved it. My mum would have loved it. I start to cry.

My dad must misread the tears as happy ones because he says he'd known we were going to find my perfect dress today, he'd just known it and he can't believe how beautiful I look.

I swipe away the tears with my palms.

'Your mum would have loved it,' Dad says. 'And she would be so incredibly proud of you and the woman you've become.'

Naturally, this makes me start crying all over again. Even Harriet is looking a bit misty-eyed.

Back in the changing room, I rip off the dress as fast as I can and stand sobbing in my bra and pants. Seeing myself in that dress – my dress – was tough, but my dad saying my mum would be proud of the woman I've become annihilated me.

Why would Mum be proud of me? I have failed in my

relationship with Mark (a man Mum loved like the son she never had) and I am failing at work. On top of all that, I'm a liar.

Mum was a fervent believer in honesty. She worked for a kitchen company but could never give people sales patter. If someone asked her if that pan was worth the money, she'd tell them some people thought it was, but others didn't. Had they considered this one at half the price? After a few weeks of being there, she'd been moved from sales to the customer complaints department, where she'd soothed and cajoled until weeks before she died.

I dry my eyes and blow my nose. I need to get out of this shop. To never have to see that perfect dress again.

I step out of the changing room to see my dad standing by the till laughing with Harriet. In his hand is a huge white and gold bag.

My heart feels as if it is about to hammer its way out of my chest. Surely this can't be happening?

My dad walks towards me. 'Your dress.'

'You've bought it?' I squeak.

'Yup,' he says, with a grin that splits his face in two.

'Paid for it?'

'Yup,' he says, laughing. 'You love it, right?'

Chapter Thirty-Six

Ed

Ed and Emily walked along in the sunshine, the huge Helen Yately Brides bag dangling from his hand. He knew the dress wasn't going to be a magic wand – ta-da, this makes up for me being MIA for the best part of eighteen years – but it was something. A gesture to show how much he cared. And Emily had clearly been moved in the shop.

'You look fantastic in that dress,' Ed said. 'It's just perfect.'

'Thanks,' Emily said. 'And thanks for buying it for me. I know it wasn't cheap.'

'Don't worry about it,' Ed said, trying not to think about the fact that he'd just spent money he could have given to the bank. *The day after tomorrow.*

'I think Harriet must have got me mixed up with someone else who had an appointment today,' Emily said. 'She kept going on about us having to move the wedding forward and how stressful that must be.'

'Hmm?' Ed said. He was thinking about how Shona was going to react if she found out her home was about to be repossessed. He wasn't going to let that happen, though. He'd persuade his mother to give him a loan. He was also going to hedge his

162

bets – pun intended – by playing a bit more online poker and placing several bets. Most of the bets would be on the weekend's Premier League games (Ed might have spent eighteen years in a country that called it soccer, but he knew his football), and then a few on the horse racing. He didn't know as much about horse racing as he did the footie, but he reckoned he'd do all right. The favourite in the 5.15 at Aintree was called The Cat's Whiskers and the second Ed had clicked on his name, Pebbles had weaved around his legs, which must surely be a good omen?

'I said Harriet must have thought I was another customer. Some poor person who has to move their wedding forward because of "tragic circumstances—".' Emily stopped in the middle of the street. 'Wait a minute, you didn't make up some sort of sob story to get an appointment, did you?'

'Well, obviously I mentioned your mum not being around anymore.'

'Right,' Emily said, her brow furrowing. 'Your grieving widower act. But why would that mean I had to move the wedding forward?'

'Umm… well, like you said, she must have got you confused with someone else.' Ed scratched the back of his neck. 'Gorgeous day, isn't it? Hard to believe this is London in October, especially as I spend so much of the time I'm in Florida telling people I had to move there for the sunshine.'

'Don't try to change the subject.' Emily was still standing stock-still in the middle of the pavement and had an expression on her face that reminded Ed of when she was a little girl and you told her she couldn't watch TV or have an ice cream. 'Did you tell Harriet some terrible lie to get her to give us an appointment? I don't know – like I had cancer or something.'

'*Emily,* I'd never say a thing like that.'

'Hmm,' Emily said, starting to walk again.

Ed could feel the sweat beading on his brow and not just because it was warm. That had been one very close shave.

'I don't believe you,' Emily blurted out suddenly. 'Despite your many years of practice, you're not actually that good a liar. I think you did tell Harriet some story.'

'Okay,' Ed said. 'I admit it. I was desperate to get us an appointment. Is that really so bad?'

'What did you tell her?'

'Does it matter?'

Emily's eyes widened.

Ed scratched his chin. 'I may have said Grandma wasn't well.'

'As in dying?'

Ed stared at the pavement. 'Yeah, maybe.'

Emily shook her head. 'How could you, Dad?'

'Look, just because I said it, it doesn't mean to say it's going to happen.'

Emily laughed mirthlessly. 'You really are a complete moral vacuum, aren't you?' She stared at the pavement. 'I'll see you back at the flat.'

'But where are you going?'

'For a walk.'

'I'll come with you.'

Emily shook her head. 'I don't think so.'

Ed lay on the sofa staring at a crack in the ceiling. He prided himself on being an optimist. Many would say to a fault; an ex referred to him as Polly-fucking-Anna. Right now, he was decidedly pessimistic, though. He'd just lost three games of poker in a row, only a couple of the football games he'd bet on were going his way and The Cat's Whiskers had failed to live up to his name.

Not to mention the fact that Emily had placed him firmly in his familiar domicile, the doghouse. It seemed hard to imagine him making things right with her, let alone demonstrating that rapprochement to his mother, all within the next twenty-four hours.

He reached for his phone to FaceTime Shona. She was his person. Well, unless he couldn't get any money out of his mother tomorrow and he had to tell her her home was going to be repossessed. That was *not* going to happen, though.

'Hey, baby.'

Shona's voice instantly made Ed feel a little calmer.

'How y'all doing? Did Emily find her perfect dress?'

Ed pressed his thumbs into his aching temples. 'She did and we bought it. But things aren't great.' He considered telling Shona that Emily was annoyed with him for pretending his mother was dying but, now he came to think of it, he didn't come out of that story brilliantly. 'I feel like I was naive to ever think I can rebuild a relationship with Emily. That maybe too much has happened and nothing I can do will change that.'

Shona's brow furrowed and she sat up a little straighter. 'Now, Big Teddy Eddy, it's not like y'all to be so negative. Let me do some reiki on you.'

Ed would like nothing more than Shona to place her hands on him right now although admittedly reiki was not what he had in mind. 'But I'm here and you're there.'

Shona let out a throaty chuckle. God, he loved the sound of her laugh.

'I can send healing energy across space and time. I just need to evoke the universal life force.' She reached out her tiny arms with her palms facing each other but not quite touching. 'Now I want you to lie back and close your eyes. I'm going to connect with your energetic essence.'

If Ed was honest, he wasn't totally sold on reiki despite Shona's unfettered enthusiasm for it. But it certainly didn't do any harm. He lay back on the sofa and closed his eyes.

He listened as Shona murmured about life force and higher good. It was almost as if she was singing him a lullaby and he felt his eyes grow heavier.

'Hey,' Shona said, pulling him from his half-slumber. 'How y'all doing?'

Ed wrenched his eyes open. 'A little better,' he said truthfully. He may not believe in reiki, but he definitely believed in Shona. 'Oh, I can hear Emily at the door. Want to say hello?'

'No, baby, I gotta get to my meditative dance session. But say hi from me and, remember, stay positive.'

'Hi,' Emily said, putting down her handbag.

'Hi.' Was Ed imagining it or were her eyes red and swollen? 'Look, I'm sorry about before. I probably shouldn't have said that Grandma was dying.'

'Y'think?'

'It's just I really wanted to get us an appointment and I was runn—'

Emily held up her palm. 'I don't want to talk about it anymore.'

'You okay?'

'Fine.'

'I've booked us a table for dinner at a place called Cici. It gets incredible reviews and it's just down the road. Do you know it?'

Emily nodded. 'Umm… yeah.'

'Don't you like it?'

Emily shrugged off her jacket. 'I like it.'

'Great. Well, our reservation is for eight o'clock. And it's my treat.'

'Hi.' Was Ed imagining it or were her eyes red and swollen?

She'd been out for ages too. 'Look, I'm sorry about before. I probably shouldn't have said that Grandma was dying.'

Emily looked about as excited as if he'd told her he'd booked them in for colonic irrigation. 'I'm kind of tired and you must be jet-lagged. Why don't we just stay here, and I can knock us up some pasta or something?'

'Absolutely not. It's Saturday night, we don't see each other very often and I want to spoil my little girl.'

Emily opened her mouth, closed it again and then said she'd go and get changed.

Ed sat on the sofa panicking about Shona. She was so good and kind and true, and she trusted him completely.

Pebbles wandered into the sitting room and it crossed Ed's mind that he looked a bit listless. No, of course he didn't. He was just an old cat. Ed scratched him behind the ears. 'You're okay, aren't you, fella? And I'm going to be too.'

Shona was FaceTiming him again. 'Hey,' he said. 'I thought you were at a meditative dance?'

'Where were you on Monday afternoon when you missed yoga?'

Ed's stomach lurched. 'What do you mean? I told you I had a migraine—'

'Don't lie to me, Edward.'

Edward. Not Ed or Eddy or Big Teddy Eddy.

'I just put down the phone to Lillian,' Shona said. 'She said she was driving down Boulevard on Monday afternoon on the way to get her chakras cleansed and she saw you walking along the sidewalk. Said she tooted her horn, but you were in your own little dream world, and you didn't even see her.'

Fuck. Fuckety-fuck.

'I popped out to get some migraine tablets,' he said.

'Really? You can't bear to even have the blinds open when you've got a migraine. Don't tell me you went out in the blazing sunshine?'

Ed could feel the sweat running down his back. 'I was desperate.'

'Right,' Shona said, sounding anything but convinced.

'Baby, you know you can trust me.'

'I hope so, Edward. I really hope so.'

And with that, Shona was gone, and Ed was left staring at his phone, his heart racing.

'Ready,' Emily said, reappearing. She was wearing a black velvet dress, which was pretty if slightly funereal.

Ed forced thoughts of Shona from his mind. Surely she'd buy the migraine tablet thing? There was a time when she was paranoid about him cheating but those days were behind them now.

He pinned a smile to his face. 'Right, let's go.'

He and Emily stepped outside, where it felt like the warmth of the day had completely evaporated. 'Brr,' he said. 'I need a thicker jacket.'

'It's mild,' Emily said. 'Do you really think Pebbles is okay? It's not like him not to eat.'

'Yeah, but you said you put out the kibble a little earlier than normal, right?'

Emily nodded.

'Maybe he's just not that hungry yet?'

'I guess.'

Ed stuffed his hands deeper into his pockets. Leaves fluttered across the darkening skies. 'You didn't tell me much about your coffee with Rachel earlier – was it fun?'

'It was fine.' Emily burrowed deeper into her scarf, making Ed think she was in fact cold.

'I liked her very much. I liked all your colleagues actually. And the kids are great too. That Meghan reminds me of you when you were little. And me and Tommy were best buddies.'

'I'd rather not talk about work. It's the weekend.'

Normally she loved talking about teaching. You couldn't get her to stop. They walked on in silence.

The maître-d' of the restaurant greeted Emily effusively, asking her where Mark was tonight.

'Away on business,' Emily said. 'This is my father, Ed. Dad, this is James.'

Ed shook the man's hand and then he and Emily were shown to their table.

The place had a cosy, intimate feel; it was the epitome of a neighbourhood joint. Bottle-green walls were adorned with large charcoal landscapes and there was a mishmash of tables and chairs that were squished so close they were almost touching. A tiny open kitchen was populated by just two chefs.

'What an amazing smell,' Ed said to James.

James grinned. 'Isn't it? Tamara has just taken out a batch of garlic and rosemary focaccia. We bake all our own bread here.' He handed Emily and Ed menus. 'Can I bring you a drink to get you started?'

'Gin and tonic please,' Emily said.

'I'll have the same,' Ed said. He'd looked at the prices before booking and just about had enough money left to cover tonight. Stupidly, he'd factored in wine but forgotten about aperitifs. It was fine though. He'd just say he was too full for pudding and didn't fancy a coffee. Oh, and they could definitely get tap water for 'eco reasons'.

Ed's mind drifted to his earlier conversation with Shona. He wasn't sure she was a hundred per cent convinced he was telling her the truth about Monday (which, of course, he wasn't – it just wasn't for the reasons Shona had assumed). Ed couldn't worry about it, though. Right now, his daughter was the only woman he needed to concentrate on.

'That bread really does smell incredible,' he said. 'Do you remember when you and I tried our hand at breadmaking? I think you were only about nine. You loved the whole kneading process, and you had eyes like saucers when our dough doubled in size. Do you remember?'

'Vaguely,' Emily said, not even looking up from the menu.

Okay, so she wasn't interested in taking a walk down memory lane. Ed concentrated on the menu. There were only four or five things in each section but every one of them sounded delicious.

Ed's attention was diverted from reading about the pork collar with butter beans and salsa verde, by the guy at the next table knocking over his water glass. 'Sorry,' he said to the woman he was with, 'sorry.' He mopped frantically at the puddle with his napkin.

'Happens to the best of us,' Ed said, smiling. No wonder the poor kid had knocked over his glass. His hands were shaking violently. Maybe this was a first date?

James returned with two huge gin and tonics and a basket of the freshly baked focaccia.

'What's vadouvan?' Ed asked.

'A French spice blend that's similar to an Indian curry powder. It pairs beautifully with the cod.'

'Sounds delicious,' Ed said. 'I'll get that as my entrée please and the scallops to start.'

'I'll have the sea trout please,' Emily said. 'With the goat's cheese and beetroot to start.'

'So do you and Mark come to this place a lot then?' Ed asked as James disappeared.

Emily nodded. 'It's our favourite restaurant.'

'Great! How lucky was I that it was the one I picked?'

Emily took a large gulp of her gin and tonic. 'Very lucky.'

Ed wasn't trying to listen in to the conversation at the next table, but the tables were so close it was almost impossible not to. He felt bad for the water spiller, who was sitting in terrified near silence while his companion talked. The only time he became animated was when she said she didn't want a dessert and he protested, saying she absolutely had to have one. He said he'd heard the salted chocolate tart was incredible.

'Wow,' Ed said. 'This focaccia tastes every bit as good as it smells.'

'It's pretty amazing,' Emily agreed. 'That's odd,' she added, nodding towards James, who was carrying a plate covered in a large silver cloche. 'I've never seen them do that with any of the food in here.'

Before Ed could answer, the water spiller at the next table had dropped to one knee and James had removed the cloche to reveal not only a slice of salted chocolate tart but a glittering diamond engagement ring.

The whole dining room fell into a hush as it collectively held its breath.

Water spiller stammered out a proposal and the woman started to cry before throwing her arms around him and saying yes, yes she would definitely marry him!

The dining room erupted into applause.

'Aww,' Ed said to Emily. 'Cute.'

'Yeah.' She gestured to James. 'Can I get another gin and tonic please?'

'Of course.' James turned to Ed. 'How about you?'

'I'm good thanks.' Ed was mentally adding another £10.60 to

his bill. 'Is it too late to cancel my side of new potatoes? I think I was being a bit greedy.'

James said he was sure that would be fine and went to say goodbye and congratulations again to the newly engaged couple. Water spiller was looking much more relaxed now.

'Not sure about the whole hiding the ring in the pudding thing,' Emily said. 'If you ask me, it's a little too sickly sweet.'

'Really?' Ed said. 'That's not like you.'

'Jeez, it was a joke. You're king of jokes, no?' Emily got up, balled her napkin and flung it onto the table. 'I'm just going to the loo.'

And with that, Ed was left at the table on his own. Wondering why it hadn't sounded more like a joke. And what on earth was up with his daughter.

Chapter Thirty-Seven

Liz

Liz was sitting in the care home lounge forcing down tears. There had been radio silence from Peter since lunchtime.

She'd sent him multiple messages since then, none of which he'd replied to. The blue ticks told her he'd read them too. What was the expression Emily had taught her? Ghosting.

Sonia had applied a slash of bright fuchsia lipstick, which was bleeding outwards into the fine lines around her mouth. She was delivering another monologue about Hope's wedding. They were having eighty people. Sonia thought that was the perfect number. Big enough to make a proper party of it but not so big it would be chaotic and overwhelming.

Liz nodded vaguely. How she wished she could just unsend that initial message. She'd said sorry a hundred times over, of course, but the damage had already been done.

Two of the regulation haircut women were locked in a dispute about a thriller they'd recently read. Sonia paused her wedding chatter to chime in. 'I don't like that kind of book. There's enough misery in the world without reading something all dark and scary. Me, I like a nice romance.'

Regulation haircut number one looked personally affronted by this and said she didn't like romance *at all*. It wasn't clear if she meant as a literary genre or a life experience.

Sonia turned back to Liz. 'Look at you, checking your phone every two minutes,' she said, laughing. 'Like a young person.'

Liz experienced the very real fear that she might use her one good arm to thump Sonia squarely on her fuchsia-coloured mouth.

'Faith and Charity are Hope's joint maids of honour,' Sonia said. 'Isn't that lovely?'

'Hmm.'

Liz's phone had pinged just before dinner, and she'd felt a surge of relief. But it was just a message from Ed saying he hoped her shoulder wasn't giving her too much bother. Trust him to pick now as the time to communicate more.

'Would you like a biscuit with your tea?' Anna said, appearing at Liz's side. 'You hardly touched your dinner. And you skipped lunch.'

Liz forced a smile. 'Just tea thanks.'

'Are you sure you don't want a biscuit?' Anna said.

I'd like Peter to message me. Liz shook her head. 'No thanks.' She glanced across at the two women who'd been arguing about the book and were now sitting in stony silence.

'And Robin is having two best men,' Sonia said, laughing.

Liz had once watched a programme that talked about how chimpanzees could die of a broken heart. Maybe that would happen to her? Peter would dump her and she would die here waiting for the dots that never came and listening to Sonia?

Chapter Thirty-Eight

I once read that there are over 35,000 restaurants in London. Yet my father picked this one – mine and Mark's favourite.

I flush the loo.

It isn't that surprising, of course. Cici is very close to the flat and its rave reviews in many a newspaper means it comes high up in any Google search.

It is still tough being here, though. As was sitting next to love's young dream as the guy launched into his oh-so-romantic proposal. I'd feared that may unravel me completely. I was that happy once, I wanted to scream. Don't think for a minute it can't all be ripped away from you.

I wash my hands and tell myself to get a grip. My father is leaving on Monday evening and, while his departure won't be an end to my problems, it will at least relieve me of having to keep up this ridiculous facade.

I can still hardly believe that 1,950 quid's worth of wedding dress is sitting at home in my wardrobe. If ever there had been a moment when I'd thought of coming clean with my dad, that had evaporated when he bought the dress.

My plan is to return it to the shop when my father is safely back in America and then set aside the money ready to transfer to him when I finally feel able to tell him there is no wedding.

All that is a problem for later though. Right now, I have to pin on a big, fake smile and go back to the table.

My father is deep in conversation with James, who is laughing uproariously at something he's saying. How charmed people are by my father. I have witnessed it my whole life. Traffic wardens ripping up tickets they would normally claim they couldn't, shop assistants falling over themselves to help him, airport staff upgrading him on flights. He definitely has the 'it factor'. Unless, of course, he happens to be someone you rely on.

I sit back down at the table and force myself to smile. Over the starters, Dad works hard at making conversation and I knock back the wine and do my best to seem upbeat.

'Whatever happened to your dream of going travelling?' Dad says.

I pause, a forkful of beetroot and goat's cheese hovering above my plate. 'There's just never been a right moment to go.'

'What do you mean?'

'I mean exactly that. We've got jobs and a mortgage. We can't just up sticks and head off to go travelling.'

Dad is looking at me sceptically and it's all I can do not to chuck my Viognier in his face. 'This may come as a surprise to you, but some of us actually care about our jobs. I love teaching. Mark is passionate about what he does.'

'But doesn't the charity he works for have offices all over the world? And isn't the beauty of teaching that you can take time out and go back to it? You could even teach English abroad for a bit if you wanted to?'

'It's not that simple,' I snap, the thought flashing through my mind that maybe it is. 'If we were to go travelling now, we'd miss several rungs on the career ladder. We need to concentrate on building a life here.' As I speak, I hear Mark's voice saying these things. See also 'we don't want to end up like your dad', 'we had our interrailing adventure' and 'we've literally been there and got the postcard'. But I believe those things too, don't I? 'It would be crazy to go now,' I say firmly. 'If the worst comes to the worst, we can always travel when we retire and, in the meantime, we can visit lots of interesting places on holiday.'

I squash the thought that I don't want to wait. That, if Mum's death taught me anything, it's that life is short, and I don't want to go to Australia when I am too old to hike up Uluru or the jet lag knocks me out for most of the trip.

'Riiight.' Dad takes a mouthful of scallop.

'What?' I say. '*What?*'

'Nothing.'

Irritation fizzes through my veins. 'Just spit it out.'

Dad puts down his knife and fork, looks me straight in the eye. 'I wondered if it's Mark who's stopping you from going travelling? He has always seemed a little less adventurous than you.'

'You don't even know Mark.' I drain what is left of the wine in my glass.

'No, but I know you, and you've talked about going travelling since you were a little girl.'

'People grow up, Dad. Well, some people.'

It's a low blow, but my father doesn't rise to it. Just sits there saying nothing with an infuriating look on his face.

'Mark and I *both* love the idea of travelling.' My voice is firm but there's another one inside my head whispering all kinds of treacherous thoughts. In the last few years, it has always seemed to be me banging on about driving around the outback, or the underwater splendour of the Great Barrier Reef, or seeing Sydney Opera House. Mark, meanwhile, has been the person to bring me firmly back down to earth. That doesn't mean he doesn't want to go to Australia, though, or that I don't want to be reminded why it isn't a good idea to go now. 'The two of us are on the same page.'

'Great,' Dad says, taking a sip of his wine. 'It's just... oh, nothing.'

'*Just what?*'

Dad looks at me. 'Someone can be a great person but not be your person.'

I can feel the heat rising through my cheeks but there is no way I am going to let myself cry. 'Mark is my person.'

The absurdity of what I have just said makes my guts twist.

Chapter Thirty-Nine

Ed

Ed's main course was beautifully cooked, but the chef may as well have anointed his cod with sawdust as the much discussed vadouvan.

He could bite off his tongue for bringing up the travelling. At the very least, he should have backed off when Emily started to get defensive. And he certainly shouldn't have suggested that Mark was holding her back. What had he been thinking?

'How's your sea trout?' he said.

'Good. How's the cod?'

'Good.'

There was a huge crash as a young waitress dropped a stack of plates and cutlery.

'I bet that guy who spilled the water is relieved right now,' Ed said.

'Hmm?' Emily said, scratching at a red patch on her neck. 'Yeah.'

'How did Mark propose to you? You never told me.'

Emily stared at him, her expression unreadable. 'He took me back to the spot where we first kissed. In Karen Howarth's parents' garden. I think it was quite hard to organise, especially as the Howarths don't live there anymore.'

'That's romantic.'

'Yeah.'

Why wasn't Emily being more forthcoming? She must still be angry about the travelling conversation.

James collected the plates, asking if they'd like to see the dessert menu. They were out of the sticky toffee pudding with Darjeeling ice cream, he was afraid.

'Just the bill please,' Emily said.

Ed's phone pinged with a message from Shona: *Call me.*

No 'baby' or 'honey', no kisses. Ed was in trouble. He stuffed the phone into his pocket.

James reappeared with the bill. Ed handed over his debit card without even looking at it.

'Oh,' James said. 'Would you mind trying again? It says the payment has been declined. These card readers can be very temperamental.'

Ed could feel himself break into a sweat. He'd been sure he had enough money left to cover the bill. They hadn't even had dessert. He swiped his card against the card reader and offered up a silent prayer for some of that positive energy from Shona's reiki. This had been notably absent from the evening so far.

'I'm so sorry,' James said. 'It's saying declined again. Do you have another card?'

'Umm...' Ed had several credit cards. All of which were maxed out.

'I'll get it,' Emily said, slapping down her credit card.

'Sorry about that,' Ed said, as they walked out of the restaurant and into the chill night air. 'I'll pay you back.'

'Forget it,' Emily said, burrowing her head into her woolly scarf. 'Just forget it.'

*

When they got back to Emily's building, Ed told her he fancied a walk.

In reality, he was tired, cold and desperate to get to bed. But he needed to FaceTime Shona and, given the increasingly irate timbre of her messages, didn't want to do that from his daughter's paper-thin-walled apartment.

'Finally,' Shona said by way of a greeting.

'I'm sorry,' Ed said. 'I was having dinner with Emily, and she was talking about all kinds of big stuff so I couldn't really look at my ph—'

Shona cut him off. 'Right, and where are you now?'

'Taking a walk.'

'Hmm,' Shona said, as if that in itself was dubious behaviour.

Ed passed a woman pushing a buggy. It seemed very late for a baby to be out but then he remembered how, when Emily was tiny and he and Catherine couldn't get her to go to sleep, they'd strap her in her pushchair and take her out. Catherine always used to say you couldn't slow down, not even for a minute, until Emily was fast asleep.

'I've been thinking about last Monday,' Shona said. 'You told me you were out getting migraine tablets when Lillian saw you, but I just don't buy it. Like I said before, you can't stand light when you've got a migraine.'

'Babe. I was desperate. I didn't have a choi—'

'There's more,' Shona said.

Ed huddled by the entrance to a pub. It had an ornate and traditional exterior and normally by now Shona would be demanding he pull the camera back so she could get a better view and calling it quaint and darling and so British.

'I've felt things have been a bit off for a while,' Shona said. 'You've seemed very stressed and distracted.'

'*Babe.*'

'And there have been several times when you haven't been interested in intimacy.'

'That's not true. We had sex the day I left. Great sex.'

Shona shook her head. 'I didn't say you were never interested, but there have definitely been a few times when you haven't been in the mood – and that's not like you.'

Ed stared at a young couple who'd come out of the pub arm in arm and laughing. How carefree they looked. 'Everyone gets tired sometimes.'

'Yeah,' Shona said. 'They do. But sometimes when someone acts stressed all the time or stops wanting sex with their partner, it's because they're cheating.'

Emily was trying to call him now for some reason. Ed hit decline. 'Shona,' he said, pressing his thumb into the bridge of his nose. 'I'm not cheating on you.'

'There have been other signs too.'

'What *signs*?' Ed fought to squash the exasperation in his voice. Shona's eyes were red and puffy and, even though he knew he was telling the truth (well, the truth about the cheating at least), she didn't.

A group emerged from the pub and lit up cigarettes.

'A couple of weeks ago, when you went to the bathroom, you took your phone with you.'

Ed's brain struggled to catch up and then the memory clunked into place. He'd been expecting a call from the bank and didn't want to take it within Shona's earshot. He could hardly tell her that though. 'I wanted to play a game on my phone.'

A waft of tobacco floated in the chill night air.

'What game?' Shona shot back.

'Babe, don't do this.'

'See,' Shona said, jumping up from where she'd been sitting. 'You can't even tell me.'

'I thought we were past all this?' Ed said. 'I thought you'd learned to trust me?'

Shona paced around the condo and its various piles of unusable fancy dress costumes. 'I did trust you, and that was real, real hard for me given everything that's happened to me in the past and everything I know about your reputation. And now I'm wondering if I'm the biggest sucker there is. 'Cos right now I've got loads of questions and you don't have any answers.'

Ed sighed. He did have answers. They just weren't ones he could give Shona.

Chapter Forty

Liz

Liz lay in bed, the light from her phone casting a glow across her face. She was euphoric. She didn't care that the woman down the corridor was still calling for her mother and was likely to keep it up all night long. Nor did she mind that it was insanely hot in here, or even that the stupid plastic mattress cover made a scritch-scratching noise every time she moved (the plastic cover of which she had no need – it was her shoulder that was broken, not her bladder).

Nothing could bring down Liz's mood, though, because Peter had messaged.

Liz was a different person to that miserable, scared little woman who'd checked her phone obsessively all day long. She was no longer the pathetic creature who'd had to choke back tears as she listened to Sonia drone on in the lounge.

Even her shoulder seemed less painful suddenly.

Tomorrow morning, she was going to wake up early and find someone to help her dress even if that meant physically hunting them down. She was going to do all the exercises the hospital physio had given her, however much they hurt. If there was a better incentive to work at her recovery than being able to hug Peter, she didn't know what that was.

And she would be able to hug Peter because, while he was naturally completely focused on his grandson at the moment, if Michael's next operation went well, and the doctors seemed confident it would, he would be on the road to recovery.

'Mummy. *Mummy!*'

God, poor woman. Liz wished someone would go to her. She was half-tempted to go herself. That was probably against all the rules though.

She eased herself out of bed and pulled open the curtains. She was way too wired to sleep so why not look at the stars instead of the slubby peach fabric?

Her old life felt as if it was in touching distance suddenly. When she *fell over*, everything had changed the minute her bones collided with the pavement. In an instant, she'd become an old lady. And she supposed she was an old lady but that wasn't how she thought of herself.

Now she saw that her shoulder would heal. She would go home, where she would sleep in a bed that didn't sound as if you were lying on a stack of carrier bags. Instead of being the person who needed help putting socks on, she'd once again be doing her neighbour's food shopping. She would no longer be in the dismal dining room eating lukewarm soft foods while listening to Sonia, but sitting in light airy restaurants with Judith watching young attractive people eat at the bar (never Liz and Judith – far too uncomfortable).

And it wasn't even just her old life she was going to get back either – it was an even better one. Peter's grandson would recover, and Peter would be free to come to England. He and Liz would build a life together, just as they had talked about. Even though most of the properties Peter owned were in Spain, he was confident he could run his business from here. As he said, it was a global world now and a great many meetings took place on Zoom. Of course, he'd still need to visit the properties in person sometimes, but what was so bad about the two of them having to go to Spain a few times a year? They could swim in the sea, linger over long lunches and sip ice-cold glasses of Verdejo as they watched the sun go down from the terrace of their finca. How wonderful did that sound?

Liz loved to travel. When they were fresh out of uni, she and Judith had driven the west coast of America. At the time, the idea of two young women travelling alone had been quite outré but that had only made it more enticing. Later in life, Liz and her late husband had taken all kinds of trips, from trekking in Nepal to tours of India and China. Emily had definitely inherited the travel bug and, as a little girl, had liked nothing better than sitting with Liz looking at all her photos of far-flung places. 'Tell me about riding an elephant, Grandma.'

'Mummy. *Mummy!*'

Why was no one going to her? She sounded more upset by the minute.

As soon as Peter knew for sure when he was going to come to England, Liz was going to make their relationship official.

Judith's words popped unbidden into Liz's head: Just be careful.

Silly old bat. Peter was one of the best things to ever happen to Liz. She'd had a glimpse this afternoon and evening of what it was like not to have him in her life, and she hadn't liked it one bit.

Liz was now firmly convinced that Judith was jealous. She'd been married to boring old Martin for over forty years, so seeing someone else in the throes of so much excitement and passion must be bittersweet. Judith was an all-round good egg but even they have their own stuff.

The person Liz was most excited to tell about Peter was Emily. She knew her granddaughter would be delighted for her. Liz loved the idea of having Peter on her arm at Emily and Mark's wedding. She'd have someone to hug her when the inevitable tears arrived, someone to dance with and someone to rescue her when she gave their secret signal to indicate she'd got trapped talking to someone dull.

'Mummy. *Mummy!*'

Oh, why wasn't anyone going to her? Liz pulled her dressing gown over her one good shoulder and tied the slippery satin belt, leaving the empty right sleeve flapping from her waist.

She scrunched her eyes against the harsh fluorescent light of the hallway. Two young women she didn't recognise were sitting chatting at the nurses' station.

'Do you think someone should go to the lady down the hall?' Liz said.

The two women stared at her as if she had suggested they paraglide naked from the top of the building. One of them had comically huge eyelashes. They looked like drag queen lashes, although Liz was aware she probably wasn't allowed to think such a thing (although it was hard to police one's thoughts even when they didn't align with modern sensibilities).

'MUMMY, MUMMY.'

'Not much we can do,' the woman with the eyelashes said eventually.

'You could try to comfort her?' Liz offered. 'Maybe sit with her for a bit?'

The woman exchanged glances with her colleague and then

heaved herself to her feet before making her way slowly down the corridor.

Liz went back to her room. She sat down on the edge of the bed, looked out at the stars and daydreamed more about the life she and Peter would share. At seventy-nine and seventy-two respectively (yes, he was a toyboy!) they may not have a lifetime together, but they could certainly make the most of every minute they did have.

The woman had stopped calling for her mother. Eyelashes had clearly brought some comfort.

Liz smiled to herself. Sometimes, one person really can change everything.

Chapter Forty-One

'I'm afraid the X-ray does show a blockage.' The vet is probably around my age, with wiry dark hair that is trying to break free of her ponytail. She is wearing the exact same shade of aquamarine scrubs as the doctor who sent me home to rest the night my mum died. 'He's going to need surgery.'

As soon as I got back from Cici, I knew something was very wrong. Pebbles was listless and floppy and his stomach looked distended. His kibble meanwhile had still not been touched. Just as I was dialling the out-of-hours number for the vet, Pebbles started vomiting violently.

'He's going to be okay, though?' my father says now.

I flash him a look. He was the one who told me Pebbles was fine. Made me feel as if I was panicking. You'd have thought I'd have learned not to listen to him.

The vet smooths back a coil of hair. 'It's a big surgery.'

I look at my father. Stupid man didn't even have the decency to pick up his mobile when I called him to tell him what was going on. And, yes, he phoned me back fairly promptly and got to the flat just as I was loading the cat carrier into the taxi, but it would have been nice if just for once he'd been there when I needed him.

I swallow a lump that has risen in my throat and address the vet. 'He's not going to die?'

The vet looks down at the bumble bee charms on her baby pink Crocs. 'We're going to do everything we can, but I need to be honest with you. Intestinal blockages can be life-threatening and Pebbles is not a young cat.'

I stare at the display of brightly coloured pet toys, the over-whelming scent of antiseptic suddenly making me nauseous.

'If you'll excuse me a minute, I'll just go and get the consent forms,' the vet says.

I sit down and put my head in my hands. 'Mum loved that cat so much.'

'Don't do this to yourself, Em. This isn't your fault.'

Tears prick the backs of my eyes. 'Of course it is. God, you'd think I could keep her cat safe for her. I mean, that's the very least I owe Mum. Especially since I wasn't even that good to her when she was still alive.'

'What are you talking about?'

I shake my head but then the words spew out of my mouth like vomit. 'I wasn't very nice to be around. I snapped at Mum when she nagged me about my homework, told her she was horrible when she wouldn't let me go to that new nightclub in town and called her tight when she wouldn't buy me new trainers.'

'You were just a normal kid.'

'She always wanted to spend time with me, but I acted like she was some kind of nuisance. Do you know what I'd do for just one minute with her now?'

'Oh, Em,' Dad says, putting his hand on my back.

I wipe my eyes with my sleeve. 'Months before her diagnosis, she complained about feeling tired all the time and do you know what I said? That she was "just old". I should have made her go to the doctor.'

'No. *No.* You couldn't possibly have known.'

We are interrupted by the vet coming back with the consent forms.

'It's likely to be a long surgery,' she says as I hand her back the signed forms. 'So the best thing you can do is go home and get some rest.'

'I'd rather stay,' I say. What was I even doing the moment Mum was taking her last breaths? Having a shower? Forcing down a sandwich I didn't want? Lying on my bed staring at the wall? I had all the time in the world to do those things, but the minutes with my mum were ticking away.

'Emily,' Dad says, putting his hand on my arm.

'There really is little point in you staying.' The vet's voice is kind but firm. 'We'll call you the second we have any news.'

A lacklustre whiny barking starts up in the next room. For a second, I'd forgotten there was any other animal or person here.

'We'll look after Pebbles,' the vet says.

I nod. It's exactly what the doctors said about my mum.

In the universe's cruellest coincidence, the Uber smells exactly like Mark's parents' car did the night my mum died. I guess it's not that odd. The little green air freshener tree that hangs from the rear-view mirror is hardly uncommon.

The car is silent but for the unwelcome strains of Magic FM. The driver made a few attempts at conversation when we first got in – could we believe the new traffic calming measures, isn't it warm for October, he doesn't think much of this mayor – but quickly gave up.

I feel a bit sorry for him really. My father is usually the king of chit-chat and I'm normally far too worried about losing my 4.9 star rating to not make an effort. (I'm still aggrieved about the driver who didn't give me a full five stars. Why?)

My father reaches across and puts his hand on my arm. 'Pebbles will be okay.'

'You don't know that.'

'Are you going to tell Mark?'

'No.'

'Yeah, I guess there's no point in worrying him. Look, the things you said earlier about your mum—'

'I don't want to talk about it.'

'Okay. But you were a brilliant daughter. The best.'

I stare out of the car window. A couple are having a row outside a kebab shop. Mark and I hardly ever argued. 'What adult puts bumble bee charms on their shoes? As if baby pink Crocs aren't infantilising enough.'

'What?'

'The vet,' I say, wiping my eyes with my sleeve. 'I can't believe I was so stupid.'

'You need to stop blaming yourself.'

'Why? I put the chicken bones into the bin, didn't I? When I know full well that Pebbles can get into it—'

'There's no po—'

'Sometimes you've got to take responsibility for your actions.' It's a cheap jibe, but I don't care.

A memory floats into my consciousness: Pebbles following my mum around the house, waiting outside the bathroom if she had the temerity to close the door on him. I can picture Mum's face as she scooped the cat up, nuzzling her cheek into his soft, grey fur and saying she hadn't gone anywhere, and that he was such a silly thing.

The car pulls up outside the house. I'll be lucky if this driver gives me four stars.

My father and I walk up the steps. 'Pebbles is going to be fine,' he says.

My fists clench. 'Stop saying that, will you? You told me he was fine this morning. And this evening when he hadn't eaten his kibble.'

'Yeah, well—'

I raise my palm as if quieting kids in the classroom. 'You're going to tell me it's not your fault and you're right. I didn't have to listen to you – I'm a grown woman, not a kid, and I could have called the vet. So that's on me. Just please stop fucking telling me everything is going to be fine.'

Chapter Forty-Two

Ed

Emily was on her hands and knees dealing with a pile of pink-tinged watery cat vomit. She was scrubbing so hard, Ed feared she'd make a hole in the carpet. 'Why are you just hovering around?' she snapped. 'What Grandma would refer to as neither use nor ornament.'

'Umm… I'd be happy to clean up.'

'Like you'd do it properly,' she said, scrubbing even harder.

'Shall I make us a cup of tea then?'

'If you want.'

Ed didn't really want, but at least it gave him something to do. He filled the kettle and got two mugs out of the cupboard.

'Why did you disappear when Mum was dying?'

Ed's shoulders stiffened. 'Let's not rake up the past, love.'

'But I thought you said you were prepared to have difficult conversations?'

He had said that. 'But it's already been such an emotional evening.'

Emily scrubbed harder at the carpet. 'Then we've nothing to lose, have we?'

There was no escaping this. Ed cleared his throat. 'It wasn't so much that I disappeared, more that I had to work.'

Emily gave a mirthless laugh. 'Right, as a cruise ship entertainer.'

'Listen, I know it's not the most serious or worthy of occupations, but I needed the money.'

'You knew Mum had a matter of weeks, days even, but you couldn't wait?'

Ed pulled at his collar, which suddenly felt like a noose. 'Like I said, I needed the money. And no one knew exactly how long your mum had left. The doctors said these things are hard to predict with any degree of accuracy. Look, I came back to England when she was diagnosed, didn't I? We'd been divorced for six years by then, but I still dropped everything and came back to England.'

'*Dropped everything*? You came back to England because it suited you. From what I can remember, you didn't have a job or anywhere to live at the time.'

Ed flinched, but it was the truth. He had wanted to help, though, and for the first couple of weeks he'd felt genuinely useful. He cooked endless lasagnes and casseroles, drove Catherine to hospital appointments and made everyone laugh despite the bleakness of the situation. He and Catherine even slept together a few times, something that he didn't think Emily knew about.

He poured hot water into the mugs. 'Listen, your mum was my first love. I don't think I ever stopped loving her actually.' *I just thought I had when I met someone who hadn't heard all my stories, laughed harder at my jokes, and didn't nag me to not leave wet towels on the floor.*

Emily rolled her eyes. 'Yup, nothing says love like ditching someone for a replacement model who's ten years younger.'

'Denise was a mistake.'

'Oh, that's all right then. As long as it was a mistake.'

Ed steeled himself to ignore the bitterness in his daughter's tone. He took out the teabags and added milk to the tea. 'I tried my best when your mum was ill, but I'm sure there are things I could have done better—'

'Y'think?' Emily said, wringing out the cloth. 'Like not buggering off the moment the going got tough?'

After a couple of weeks of Ed being back in England, Catherine's health had taken a steep turn for the worse. She was moved to a hospice. Ed couldn't bear the realisation that he could no longer do anything. There were no hospital appointments to drive Catherine to, no dinners to cook (Emily seemed to eat every meal at Mark's parents' house) and no one was in any mood to laugh. He hated seeing Catherine like that too. A husk of the person she was. She'd tried to hide how much she was suffering, but you could see the pain etched all over her beautiful face.

When he was offered a job on a cruise ship, he decided to take it. Catherine died two days before he was due back in England.

Ed puffed out his cheeks. 'What do you want me to say?'

'What do I want you to say?' Emily's voice went up an octave. 'I want you to say that you're sorry you were sunning yourself in the Mediterranean when Mum was dying—'

'That's not fair. I was working.'

'Pah. You were knocking out Elvis covers and schmoozing retired Americans. It's not exactly vital humanitarian work. The truth is you couldn't wait to get away. Which meant you weren't there for Mum and you weren't there for me.' Tears were streaming down her cheeks now and Ed desperately wanted to go to her but didn't dare. 'In those last few awful days when Mum started breathing like Darth Vader and I was convinced I was going to die too because surely – surely – I could not possibly survive on this earth without her, you were nowhere to be bloody seen. *As usual.*'

Ed stared at the floor. 'Nothing I could have said or done would have made it any better.'

'No, but you could have bloody tried.' Emily snapped off her rubber gloves and poured the soapy water from the bucket into the sink. 'I'm going to bed.'

'Your tea,' Ed said.

'Yeah, I don't really fancy it.'

Emily's face was all splotchy from crying and Ed felt a sharp stab of guilt. 'I am sorry I wasn't there for you.'

'Great. And what about screwing Mum when you knew she was dying? Are you sorry about that? Do you feel you may have been taking advantage – just a teeny bit?'

'I... I... I...'

'You what, Dad? Didn't think I knew about that?'

Ed was normally pretty good with words. He'd talked himself into and out of all kinds of things over the years but, on this occasion, he had nothing.

Emily looked at him and shook her head before turning on her heel and slamming the door behind her.

Ed slumped down on the sofa and put his head in his hands. How had he so completely underestimated the scale of Emily's anger towards him? This wasn't going to be fixed by having a bit of a laugh together or helping out with a school trip or buying a wedding dress. In fact, short of getting himself a time machine, Ed wasn't sure how he'd ever be able to make things right with Emily. He just had to hope that somehow tomorrow was a better day. Starting with Pebbles pulling through. Please, God, let that cat be okay.

Sunday

Chapter Forty-Three

I didn't think I'd slept but am woken by the phone.

'This is Marsha Lane from Hilltop Vets. I'm calling to let you know that Pebbles is out of surgery, and it went well.'

'So he's going to be okay?'

'It's early days but I'm hopeful.'

I rub my eyes. 'Can I pick him up?'

'I'd like to keep him with us until tomorrow so we can keep an eye on him. But that's just precautionary. As I said, I'm hopeful he'll be fine.'

'Thank you,' I say, my voice cracking. I end the call and look at the time: 5.15. I can hear my father moving about in the next room. I pull on my dressing gown.

Dad is in the kitchen making coffee. He is still dressed, and the sofa hasn't been turned into a sofa bed.

'The vet just called,' I say. 'Pebbles is out of surgery, and it went well. They're going to keep him for another day, but it looks as if he's going to be okay.'

'That's fantastic news.'

My father looks old and tired, and a wave of shame washes over me. I said some terrible things last night; went for the jugular. Why did you disappear when Mum was ill? Why weren't you there when she died? Why did you take advantage of her and sleep with her?

In some ways they're legitimate questions, but there's no denying that me blurting them out in the way I had was nothing to do with Dad. Just like me raising my voice at Tommy Cassidy was little to do with him.

My father holds up a mug. 'Coffee?'

I shake my head. 'I'm going to try to get a few hours' sleep. You should do the same.'

'Yeah.' He pours himself a mug of coffee.

I hover in the doorway wondering if I should apologise. But somehow I can't make the words form on my lips.

Once again, I'm woken by the phone. I scramble to reach it, wondering if it's the vet again, but it's my colleague Natasha's name that flashes up on screen.

Her voice is loud and piercing. Rachel has filled her in on everything that has happened. She is furious about it all. (I guessed she must be worked up to be calling on a Sunday, but this is next level.) How dare the Cassidys behave like this? The entitlement! Natasha is heartily sick of parents complaining about ridiculous things. Do I know a parent complained the other day because the coach was late back after the school outing to the city farm? And another one complained her kid is tired after school every day? And another said there were too many girls in the class (sixteen to fourteen) and his son felt outnumbered. These people!

My mind cartwheels and a headache starts to pulse behind my eyes.

'Well, guess what?' Natasha says. 'I've got great news for you. And not just the "I'm your union rep and I'm here to support you" type of news.'

'Oh?' I say weakly.

'Yeah, you see it turns out the Cassidys have form. I remembered they have an older kid at Harris Academy, so I contacted a mate of mine who teaches there. There's documented evidence of the Cassidys making an unfair complaint about a teacher.'

Only this time they weren't being unfair.

Natasha hasn't finished though. 'There's written evidence to show they were aggressive and bullying towards a teacher. Was Tommy's mother aggressive when she spoke to you?'

'Well, not really. I mean, she was upset—'

'Angry?'

'I guess—'

'You shouldn't have to put up with that, Emily.'

And, before I know it, I am saying goodbye and wondering how I have become the victim.

My thoughts are interrupted by a knock at the door. My dad appears with a mug of tea. 'Was that the vet again? Is there more news?'

I shake my head. 'No, it was someone from work.' I take the mug from him with shaking hands. 'Thanks.'

'Want some breakfast?'

'Yeah, but I'll get it.'

Dad pats my leg through the duvet. 'Stay right there and I'll bring it to you. Last night was rough. Toast okay?'

'Yeah, great.' I blow on the surface of my tea and take a sip. When I was in the vet's waiting room, I made a silent deal with the God I don't believe in. Please, please just let Pebbles be okay and I won't ask for anything else. But now, of course, I want more. Like the problems at work to magically disappear. And for Mark to come back saying I am the love of his life and he has made a terrible, terrible mistake.

Neither of those things look to be on the cards, though. Mark hasn't even called. What is he doing right now and how does he feel? Does him being the instigator of the break-up inure him to any kind of hurt? He cried even more than I did when he told me, but maybe that was just guilt? Maybe now he feels nothing more than a tinge of sadness and his overwhelming emotion is relief? He is free.

'Here we go,' Dad says, reappearing with some toast and handing it to me. He sits on the edge of the bed. 'We're seeing the first venue at three o'clock, right?'

For a short time, all the drama with Pebbles achieved the seemingly impossible and made me forget about today's plans. But here we are. As if buying a wedding dress for a pretend wedding wasn't insane enough, I am now going to spend the afternoon schlepping around wedding venues with my father. I am going to discuss catering, music permits and nice places to have photographs taken. 'Yep.'

'Cool. I've been thinking about what we could do before that.'

I brace myself for my father to suggest some wedding-related activity. Getting to grips with the table plan perhaps, or hunting down the best bonbonnière? For someone who has previously shown zero interest in my forthcoming nuptials, Dad now seems to have an unbridled (pun intended) enthusiasm for the event.

'I thought we could go to Botany Bay.'

'I don't know. We've got our surprise visit to Grandma, and three wedding venues to look around before that.'

'Right,' Dad says, raking his hands through his hair. 'But the first appointment isn't until three and Botany Bay is on the door-step. Plus, you know how you love a trip to the beach.'

'Yeah, when I was like eight.' Why am I behaving as if I am still eight? Why do I feel the need to make this petty snipe: you don't know me. Especially since I do still love the beach. 'I'm kind of knackered.'

'It's a beautiful day.'

I look out at the clear blue sky. It is a beautiful day. And I really was a cow last night. 'I suppose we could.'

'Brilliant,' Dad says, clapping his hands together. He reminds me of the kids in my class when I tell them they are to have double playtime. 'We might even have a dip.'

'What? It's October. And you spent most of yesterday evening telling me how cold you were.'

Dad shrugs. 'Yeah, but today the sun is shining. And you know I never miss a chance to swim in the sea.'

'I think if I swim in the sea today, it might actually kill me.'

Dad laughs. 'Nonsense!' He rakes his hands through his hair. 'I'm sorry you ended up footing the bill last night, by the way. I'll pay you back.'

'Don't worry about it.' I wonder if I should say I am also sorry. But it's complicated.

A car alarm starts up outside, loud and insistent, every one of its shrill shouts piercing my skull. 'I don't know why anyone bothers to have a car alarm in London,' I grumble. 'No one takes the slightest bit of notice of them.'

'Same in Tampa.'

I eat the toast. My father has travelled 4,000 miles to see me and then bought me a very expensive wedding dress (not his fault it's never going to be worn). Maybe he really has changed this time? And maybe I should make an effort to be a whole lot nicer?

Chapter Forty-Four

Ed

Ed ought to have been happy as he and Emily picked their way across the scrubby dunes, sand seeping into their trainers. The cat was going to be okay and Emily had agreed to come to the beach with him. His trademark optimism seemed to have gone MIA, though. He couldn't even force himself to trot out his line about there being two types of people in the world: people who love beaches and people who have no soul.

It was now less than six hours until he and Emily went to visit his mother and his idea of that being a wonderful demonstration of the new-found peace between them seemed increasingly ludicrous. 'Who'd have thought you'd get this weather in England in October?' he said, looking up at the cloudless blue sky, and forcing himself to sound cheery.

Emily grunted by way of a response.

A young couple were making their way across the sand holding a buggy aloft. In addition to this chariot, they were both laden with an almost inconceivable amount of detritus, from a cool box to bags to a large old-fashioned windbreak.

'Nothing beats the smell of the sea, right?' Ed said.

'Yeah. Let's set up here.'

'Shall we get a bit closer to the water?'

'Here's good,' Emily said, already plopping herself down on the sand.

Ed sat next to her, fighting the urge to say 'oof' as he did so. What was it about getting older that made you want to make that sound every time you sit? It was like some kind of biological imperative.

'Are you excited about seeing the wedding venues this afternoon?' Ed said. 'Do you have a frontrunner?'

'Hmm, not really. I think I might close my eyes for a bit.' Emily rolled up one of the towels as a makeshift pillow and lay down.

Ed stared out at the grey-green sea. He had started to message Shona this morning but then given up. This wasn't something you could deal with from a different continent. He'd have to talk to her when he got back to the US.

A child of about four and his dad were splashing around in the shallows, the child squealing every time the cold water got further up his body. Ed's chest hurt as he observed the way the little boy was looking at his dad. It made him think of a four-year-old Emily who'd watched him enchanted as he did all the voices reading her bedtime story.

Ed wondered if his mother would be pleased to see him. Shona's parents cooed over her as if she was as cute as a chubby-cheeked baby. But Ed's parents had never been like other people's. From an early age, it was clear to him, he was a disappointment. Why couldn't he put a bit of effort into his schoolwork, why must he insist on coasting through life, superficial charm wouldn't take him far.

The first thing he did that impressed his parents was marry Catherine. He was twenty-two at the time and didn't know the adage about how you marry your mother. Even if he had known it, he wouldn't have seen it. When he looked at his bride, he saw mischievous green eyes, long auburn curls and a laugh that made him feel as if he was the funniest person in the whole world. However, underneath all that, Catherine was sensible, organised and inveterately cautious. She was a sheep in wolf's clothing.

As the years went by, Ed found these aspects of his wife's personality increasingly grating. His mother, however, was falling deeply in love, something that was only reinforced when Catherine produced a beautiful granddaughter and leaned on Liz heavily for advice. By the time Ed's dad died, it was inevitable that Catherine would be the person who'd support her mother-in-law through her grief, and she and Emily all but moved in with her for a few months.

Ed looked across at Emily, her pale eyelids closed against the salt-licked breeze. He suddenly wanted to reach out and stroke her cheek the way he used to do when she was asleep in her cot.

Maybe today would turn things around? When Emily woke up, he'd persuade her to have a swim in the sea with him. Then, when they were all wrapped up warm and snug afterwards, he'd get them fish and chips to eat on the beach. You can't beat fish and chips on the beach.

He was looking forward to seeing the wedding venues too. His role as father of the bride felt important. (Also, undeserved, but best not to dwell on that.)

A thought crashed into Ed's mind and made the breath catch in his throat. If Emily found a venue she liked, he'd need to put down a deposit. It was like the wedding dress situation all over again.

He closed his eyes and tried to be calmed by the rhythm of the waves. He had a few bets placed on the football and the horse racing today but, even if they all went his way, he couldn't win the sort of money you needed for the deposit on a fancy wedding venue.

His thoughts were interrupted by a thump as a ball thrown for a black Labrador landed right next to him. The dog retrieved its ball, allowing Ed a quick stroke. 'What am I going to do, boy?'

The dog didn't answer but Ed knew what he had to do. He reached for his phone.

Ed's online poker game ended seconds before Emily woke up. She sat up, blinking in the sun. 'How long was I asleep?'

'Err, about an hour.' Ed's heart was pounding against the wall of his chest. He'd been doing so well and won £650, but then he'd got cocky on his last bet and lost £200. What a bloody idiot he was.

'You okay?' Emily said. 'You look a bit pale.'

'Fine,' Ed said, forcing a smile. He still had £450 plus the £110.50 he'd started the day with and he still had this afternoon's bets. He should be able to cobble together a wedding venue deposit. Just.

Emily was ringing the vet for the third time in as many hours. Ed wanted to tell her to ease up a little – that the vet would be sure to call if anything was wrong – but he knew that wouldn't go down well. 'Apparently Pebbles is *being kept comfortable*,' Emily said, ending the call. 'There's a phrase that takes me back. Doctors and vets must all get a copy of the same script.'

'They'd tell you if there was anything to worry about,' Ed said. 'Want to go for a swim?'

Emily screwed up her face. 'It'll be really cold.'

'Yeah, but it'll be lovely once we're in. And think how smug we'll feel afterwards.'

Somewhat to his surprise, Emily stripped down to the swimming costume she'd only put on 'just in case'.

The water was cold, but Ed had trained himself years ago to get straight in, knowing that a few seconds of discomfort was offset by the rewards. 'C'mon,' he shouted to Emily, shaking water from his hair as his head broke the surface of the water.

'I need a minute,' Emily said, a pained look on her face as she took a couple of steps forward and then immediately retreated.

Ed considered sharing his technique for getting into cold water (essentially: just get on with it), but decided it was probably best to leave Emily to her own devices. The mood between them was fragile at best.

He dived back underwater, taking big, long strokes.

When Ed came up for air, Emily was standing with her arms raised, the water waist deep and anguish written all over her face.

'It's lovely once you're in,' Ed shouted before diving back under.

He re-emerged to the surface to see that Emily had finally got in. She was swimming like a dog with her head held high out of the water.

'Race you to the pier,' Ed said.

Emily grinned and rolled her eyes. 'You've got no chance, old man!'

And then the two of them were swimming side by side and Ed forgot all his troubles. He was just a guy swimming in the sea with his daughter.

The two of them were pretty evenly matched, but in the last second Emily pulled ahead, her youth clearly trumping her strange swimming style.

They ran back to their spot on the beach, shivering and laughing, with Emily making a mock fuss about her big victory.

'Fish and chips?' Ed said, as soon as they were dressed.

'I thought you'd never ask. Do you need some money?'

Ed thought about the sorry state of his finances. He wanted to treat his daughter to fish and chips though, especially after his failure to pay in the restaurant last night. 'Course not.' He trudged back up the beach, leaving Emily lolling on the towels. He passed a row of brightly coloured beach huts. They were tiny but he'd heard they went for outlandish sums of money. He should have invested in one years ago when they were as cheap as the proverbial chips. But then he should have done a lot of things.

The man in the fish and chip shop asked Ed if he was American.

'I'm a Broadstairs man through and through but I live out in the States now. Didn't think I had an accent though.'

'You've got an accent,' the man said, handing Ed two packages the size of newborn babies.

Ed raced back towards Emily, the heat from the packages seeping through and warming his cold hands. Everything was fine.

Chapter Forty-Five

For a short while when I was swimming in the sea with my dad, I forgot about everything.

But now it is all back.

I have been with Mark my whole adult life. I don't know how to function in the world without him by my side. At some point in the future, unless I want to die alone, that will have to include dating. The mere thought fills me with dread. I know nothing of Tinder or Hinge or Bumble except what I have picked up second hand. From what I can see it seems like one big smorgasbord of rejection and pain with the odd dick pic thrown in for good measure. I thought I was going to get through my whole life without being sent images of a random penis.

I stare at the couple who carried their baby's buggy slowly across the sand, suddenly furious at their smug togetherness. I hate the way he reaches out and brushes the hair out of her face, loathe her casually pouring two cups of tea out of a thermos and handing him one.

The woman gets a jar of baby food out of the cool bag and proceeds to spoon it into the baby's mouth. Both parents gaze adoringly as if the infant is doing something a whole lot more extraordinary than just opening its beak to receive orange mush.

I stare at the grey-green sea, my nerves and synapses remembering the searing cold: my muscles constricting, my toes and fingers starting to numb, the exhilaration as I swam myself warm.

'Was that yummy?' The mother's voice carries across the briny breeze.

I wonder if I will ever have a baby now? Whether I even want one that isn't Mark's? I used to be so sure of what was ahead.

I shake my head. Of course I still want a baby. My life isn't over. I can still do whatever I want to do.

Like travelling.

My brain replays the conversation I had with my father in Cici last night. I was furious when he suggested that it was Mark who had stopped me from travelling, but the truth is, it has always been Mark coming up with all the reasons why we shouldn't go. Am I actually okay to give up the idea of seeing Sydney harbour or Uluru or the freshwater lakes of Fraser Island? My dad has a point when he says teaching is a career you can come back to. Maybe I'm not stupid or childish or reckless to want to travel, and Mark just made me feel that way? Maybe he squashed my dream?

I give myself a mental shake. Of course, Mark didn't squash my dream. It is important to build a future here. And the two of us have always been on the same page about everything. Well, until he dumped me.

The baby has finished his meal and is now being carried towards the sea by his father. His mother follows close behind laden with inflatables and toys. She has more questions for the baby. 'Shall we take you to see the sea? Would you like that? Maybe you can dip your little toe toes?'

I am sick with nerves about tomorrow's meeting too. Am I going to casually drop in the Ofsted thing? And can I really lie to Clare about what happened with Tommy? Will I allow Natasha and the rest of my colleagues to believe the Cassidys are the perpetrators not the victims in all this?

Setting aside such moral questions, is a letter of complaint something that will go on my record forever? I picture myself being fired.

The headache I thought I'd got rid of with max-strength painkillers starts to pulse behind my eyes.

'I hope you're hungry?' my dad says, reappearing with two large paper packages and handing me one.

'Starving.' I unwrap my warm parcel to the waft of vinegar.

A large seagull has positioned itself near and is eyeing me hopefully.

I spear a chip with the doll-sized wooden fork.

'What sort of vibe are you wanting from a wedding venue?' Dad says. 'Bohemian? Classic? Glam?'

The piece of fish I am eating turns to sand in my throat. 'Erm—'

'I guess it's good not to have too many preconceived ideas.'

'Yeah.' Vinegar seeps into a paper cut on my finger, making it sting. Improbably, I feel tears rise.

'It was great the swimming, wasn't it? So important to do things like that. Shona reckons the ocean has the ability to trigger a psychological state of calm and contentment. She says it can literally wash away pain. I'm not sure about that, but I know I love it.'

If only the sea could wash away pain. If only it had been more than a temporary distraction.

The seagull moves a little closer and Dad shoos it away. 'One thing I do know for sure is that we should all live every day as if it's our last.'

214

'Oh, for goodness' sake. I *hate* it when people say that. If we all lived every day as if it was our last, no one would ever get a smear test or do their tax return or clean out their cupboards. It would all be about instant gratification rather than working for things. So much of what's wrong with the world today is people not caring enough about the future. We chop down rainforests, burn fossil fuels and pump raw sewage into our rivers and oceans.'

'Riiiight,' Dad says. 'You know what I mean, though?'

'No, I don't. It's a stupid, trite phrase that people trot out without thinking.' I wrap up my half-eaten fish and chips and cast them aside.

Dad opens his mouth to say something but then closes it again.

I lean back against my rucksack. Why did I get so snappy over nothing? I do think the old 'live every day as if it's your last' thing is BS, but that doesn't mean I had to jump down my father's throat like that. What the hell is wrong with me?

Chapter Forty-Six

Ed

To misquote Jane Austen, Ed thought, it's a truth universally acknowledged that every single woman says 'fine' when you ask her if something is wrong. Even if at the time she'd like to slowly club you to death with a blunt instrument.

Ed leaned back in his seat. Emily drove exactly like her mother used to – never going so much as half a mile above the speed limit, triple checking before moving out of every junction, being astounded when another driver was reckless enough to change lanes without indicating.

Ed looked out of the window as the countryside flashed past. The trees were a riot of orange, yellow, scarlet and russet – a last hurrah before they fluttered to the ground and left their branches bare and colourless.

Emily must still be miffed about the conversation on the beach. She'd clearly been furious, immediately casting aside her fish and chips (it was all Ed could do not to say he'd spent £22.50 on that lunch and every penny counted right now). For the life of him, he couldn't see why she'd been so upset by him saying you should live every day as if it's your last. It was the sort of thing

Shona would stitch on one of her needlepoint cushions. As innocuous as it was positive.

It was such a shame things had turned sour. The mood had been pretty good between them just beforehand. The swimming in particular was brilliant. For that brief time they were in the water together, it really was as if the sea had washed the pain away. As if the past and all Ed's mistakes no longer existed.

Hopefully, seeing the wedding venues would put things back on an even keel. Especially if he could put down a deposit on one. He surreptitiously glanced at his Betz account. He reckoned his horse in the 3.15 at Kempton was in with a great chance. His football bets looked good too.

Anxiety pulsed through Ed's body. He had to sort out his financial situation. No fifty-four-year-old man should have to resort to gambling to pay for his daughter's wedding. Or, for that matter, be at risk of losing their home.

If he could just scrape through the next few days unscathed, and somehow get that loan out of his mother, he was going to make sure his finances were more secure in the future. He'd find something new he could sell online. Although he'd had a couple of false starts with the watches and the fancy dress costumes, that had just been plain bad luck. He remained convinced reselling was an easy way to make money.

Maybe it would be better to give up on it though; get a 'proper' job instead? Even, God help him, if that meant his old telesales job at Spectrum? Sure, it would be soul-shrinking, particularly if puffed-up, micromanaging Brad was still there. Ed pictured him standing in a power pose guzzling disgusting-smelling protein shakes and barking, 'Let's do this, team!'

At least working at Spectrum would be a steady income though.

Ed shook the thought from his mind. He could definitely make money from reselling. Shona's mate was raking it in and, not to be unkind, but she was no Warren Buffett. It would be foolish for Ed to admit defeat and take some job he hated. He'd find the right thing to flog. He didn't care whether that was air fryers, jewellery, trainers – whatever.

Ed glanced across at Emily. Her mouth was set in a line and there was a deep furrow between her brows. She was either furiously concentrating or just furious.

'So,' Ed said, 'you must be excited about looking around these venues, right? It all gets very real when you've booked a venue.'

'What do you mean "gets very real"?'

Jeez! 'It's just an expression.'

Ed fidgeted in his seat. The radio was set to some dreary channel with endless rolling news punctuated by angry people arguing about that news. He'd like to switch it to some nice, upbeat music, but he didn't dare suggest such a bold move given the current mood.

'If we find a place you like, are you going to FaceTime Mark – give him a bit of a virtual tour?'

'He's in meetings most of the day,' Emily said, stopping at a junction.

'On a Sunday?'

'Yes, on a Sunday.'

There was a distinctly icy note to Emily's tone. Ed stared out of the window. They were driving through a sleepy little village full of whitewashed stone cottages. Occasionally, Ed wondered what his life would have been like if he'd stayed in England. It was weird the guy in the fish and chip place commenting on his American accent because back in Tampa his Britishness was still a constant source of surprise and delight. Over the years, it had helped him to secure everything from dates to a table in a fully booked restaurant.

Emily stopped to let an elderly woman cross the road. She was leaning heavily on a battered tartan shopping trolley that had red satin ribbons tied all up the handles. The studied cheerfulness of it all brought a lump to Ed's throat. He'd be old soon. And quite possibly alone.

Just before she reached the other side of the road, the woman stopped to raise a hand in a gesture of thanks, her scrunched paper-bag face breaking into a smile. Ed watched as she made her way haltingly towards the corner shop/post office, stopping briefly to pet a three-legged dog who was tied up outside next to the wizened-looking apples and brown, spotty bananas.

'Hey,' Ed said, turning back to realise that Emily was still sitting at the crossing.

'Sorry. I was in my own world there.'

A thought hit Ed like a thunderbolt: he couldn't remember Emily speaking to Mark the whole time he had been here. He knew Mark was working but surely that was odd? Ed hadn't spoken to Shona today but that was because she'd convinced herself he was cheating on her. Normally, when they were apart, they chatted at least a couple of times a day. 'Em?'

'Yeah?'

'Is everything all right between you and Mark?'

Chapter Forty-Seven

I grip the steering wheel tighter, panic coursing through my veins. 'What kind of question is that? Of course Mark and I are okay.' My father stays infuriatingly quiet, his eyes fixed on me. 'We're literally on our way to look at some wedding venues.' I fight to keep my voice even. 'Yesterday, we bought a wedding dress. Why would you ask me that?'

Dad holds his hands up. 'Okay, okay, forget I asked.'

I keep my eyes on the narrow country road, willing my heart rate to slow down. I've got away with it. For now. My dad keeps glancing over at me though. He knows something is wrong. He can be weirdly perceptive for someone whose emotional development arrested somewhere around the age of fourteen.

My mind cartwheels. 'If you must know I'm having a bit of a problem at work.' I really don't want to get into this, but I have to give my father something.

'Oh?'

'It's no big deal.' *Yeah, you keep telling yourself that, Emily.* I turn down the car heating. I was freezing when I first got out of the sea, but now I'm regretting piling on the layers. My skin is sticky and itchy from the salt water too. What possessed me to go in the sea when there was no chance of a shower afterwards? It's typical of one of my dad's suggestions – Mr bloody YOLO. 'You know the kid you bonded with so much on Friday?'

'Tommy?'

'Yeah. Well, the other day, I had to tell him off and now his overprotective mother is making a huge fuss on behalf of her little darling.'

'Hmm. Well, I guess she must be pretty stressed.'

'Because of Tommy?'

Dad shoots me a sideways glance. 'Because of the divorce.'

'Divorce?'

'Yeah,' Dad says, adjusting his seat belt. 'Tommy told me.'

A wave of shame washes over me. That's why Tommy always acts up. And if I'd been a bit nicer and more perceptive, he would have confided in me and not my father.

'What do you mean by a fuss?' Dad says.

'She's written a letter to the head. Accused me of bullying Tommy, no less.'

Dad lets out a low whistle. 'I see.' He scratches his neck. 'So what happened exactly?'

I take a deep breath. This is good practice for my conversation with Clare Wood tomorrow. 'He kept whistling in a lesson.' As I say the words, I am back in the classroom. I hear Tommy's loud tuneless whistling and the giggles of the kids around him. Feel the irritation fizzing around my body as I asked him to stop and he looked me straight in the eye and said, 'Stop what?' Before doing it again. And again. 'It was pretty annoying.'

'I'm sure.' Dad rakes his hands through his hair. 'So what did you do?'

'I just told him to stop.'

My dad's brow furrows. 'Right? So why a formal letter of complaint?'

'I don't know. Because his mother is a neurotic nightmare?' My voice goes up an octave. 'She once wrote an email to the school asking people to show understanding towards Tommy because they'd run out of croissants at breakfast so he wouldn't eat anything.'

'She sounds like a right pain.'

Dad is saying the right words but somehow his tone doesn't quite match them. I miss the turn-off and the satnav robotically nags me to turn around where possible. It feels like a metaphor for my whole life.

I execute an 83-point turn, aware that my father's eyes are still on me. '*What?*' I snap, swinging the car back in the direction we came from.

'I just don't get it.'

'What do you mean?'

'Why would the mother write a formal letter of complaint to the headteacher if all that happened is that the kid was whistling, and you asked him to stop?'

For Christ's sake! Can he see inside my head or something? 'Didn't you hear me when I said this is the same mother who emailed the school about croissants? *Croissants.*'

'Sure. Just this is different, isn't it?'

Nausea swirls in my belly, and I can feel a muscle start to twitch under my eye. If my dad isn't buying this, then there is no way Clare Wood is going to. I am also seriously shaken by the discovery that Tommy's parents are getting divorced. It put both his behaviour and mine in quite a different light.

Dad's phone pings as he pulls it out of his pocket. 'Yes!'

'What?'

'Nothing, nothing. Just some good news concerning... err, work.'

Something about the way he says this makes me think he's lying, but I don't care. All that matters is that whatever he saw on his phone has distracted him from interrogating me.

My relief is short-lived though.

'The whistling must have been very irritating when you were trying to teach a class? Is Tommy generally a bit of a naughty kid?'

I swing the car around a corner. 'Erm… well, yes, actually.'

'Really?' Dad says. 'He was good as gold for me.'

My fingers turn white on the steering wheel. 'He's often disruptive. The kind of kid who thinks it's hilarious to keep getting out of his seat every time I turn my back. Once he started barking too. Barking, for goodness' sake!'

Dad laughs.

'It's not funny.'

'Was he barking in response to things? Or just randomly?'

I roll my eyes. 'I'm not sure why that matters, but in response to things. "Tommy, please may I have your reading record." "Woof woof." "Tommy, please could you stay in your seat?" "Woof."'

Again, my father laughs. 'That is quite funny.'

'Yeah, not when you've got twenty-six kids you're trying to teach phonics.'

'I'm sure. Sounds as if Tommy is the class clown? And he often plays up?'

'Yes. But I don't like what you're insinuating.'

'I'm not insinuating anything. I'm just asking you to tell me a bit more about it.'

'There's nothing more to tell.'

'Okay.'

I turn up the volume on the radio. The presenter is droning on about a giant aquarium exploding. Apparently, it contained a million litres of water and 1,500 fish. I picture them all flopping around on the floor gasping for breath.

'Listen,' Dad says, 'if you did lose your cool with Tommy, well, obviously that's not ideal but neither is it the end of the world.'

I remember what Callum Reed's mum said to me in the Lidl biscuit aisle: *Tommy's an annoying little sod. I wouldn't blame you if you did shout at him.* I keep my eyes fixed on the road. 'Only five minutes away from Northcombe Hall now. I hope it's as nice as it looks in the photographs.'

Dad ignores my attempt to change the subject. 'It sounds as if Tommy was being pretty annoying and you're a human being. Human beings make mistakes.'

'I DID NOT LOSE MY COOL, OKAY?' The irony of me raising my voice to protest about how calm I stayed isn't lost on me.

Chapter Forty-Eight

Ed

'It's like having your very own stately home for the day.'

Yvette, the events coordinator, must have said that at least six times since Ed and Emily arrived.

It had been part of her greeting as they stepped out of the car onto the sweeping gravel drive. 'Welcome to Northcombe Hall. I can't wait to show you around. Having a wedding here is like having your very own stately home for the day.' It had been dropped into conversation again before they'd even reached the five-foot stone lions that flanked the steps up to the glossy black front door and mentioned in the library, the 'conservatoire' and the Princess Mary Drawing Room.

And now they were in the banqueting hall and here it was again.

Yeah, Ed felt like saying, we get it. There was no denying this was an impressive place though. With its deep red walls, stained-glass windows and abundance of dark wood, the banqueting hall had a Hogwarts Britishness. Shona would go mad for it.

Whether or not it was having the same effect on Emily was harder to tell. She'd barely said a word since they arrived. Her mind must be on the problems at school. Being the subject of

225

a formal letter of complaint would be worrying for anyone, but for a perfectionist like Emily it must be mortifying. Ed couldn't help but think there was something about the story that didn't add up. He couldn't imagine that parents, even neurotic ones, would write a formal letter of complaint to a headteacher or mention bullying just because a teacher had asked their child to stop whistling.

'We pride ourselves on our award-winning fine dining,' Yvette said. 'Chef uses premium quality, locally sourced produce including vegetables and herbs we grow in our own garden.'

Ed looked to Emily, expecting her to respond, but she just gave a cursory nod. It made him feel a bit sorry for Yvette really. She might be a little overzealous when it came to her point about having your own stately home, but there was no denying she was putting in lots of effort. 'It must be a lot of work looking after these gardens.'

'Oh, yes,' Yvette agreed. 'All eighteen acres of it.' Her fingers fluttered to her pearls. 'Do you have any questions about the options for how we set up the banqueting hall or the food itself?'

'Em?' Ed prompted.

Emily blinked as if she was emerging from a deep slumber. 'Umm…'

'Of course, you'll want to see sample menus,' Yvette said. 'But let's have a look at those over a cup of tea when we've finished our tour. And when you do see the menus, please bear in mind that Chef prides himself on working closely with every couple to make the unique menu that's just right for them. You'd be amazed at some of the requests he's managed to accommodate. *Amazed.*'

Ed's phone pinged and he saw it was a notification from Betz telling him he'd won £310 on the 3.15 at Kempton. And he'd had that message in the car about another win. Things were on the up.

He still thought it was a bit odd that Emily was choosing a venue without Mark. He knew these appointments got arranged way in advance but surely you'd reschedule if one of you was going to be away on business? Mind you, Ed could totally see that Mark would be happy to leave the decision to Emily. Not only was she the very epitome of a safe pair of hands but, sexist as it might sound, she probably cared more about all the little details than Mark did. You can pin a lot of blame on the patriarchy, but in Ed's experience it was women who made weddings such a fandango. When he'd married Catherine, he'd have been happy to nip down to the local registry office and then go to the Dog & Duck, but instead there had been lots of talk about colour schemes and flowers and where they could possibly sit Uncle Rick.

Ed followed Yvette and Emily down a long dark corridor with bottle-green walls hung with portrait after portrait of grim-faced folk from the past. Yvette was telling Emily that the old stable block had been converted into 'superbly appointed luxury accommodation'. There was enough room for the bridal couple and forty of their family and friends.

'That sounds good, doesn't it, Em?' Ed said. 'I like the idea of not having to get back anywhere on the night. We can keep the party going.'

'Yeah,' Emily said in a tone that sounded as if Ed had suggested all the wedding guests might like to stay on for late-night appointments with a dental hygienist.

'Exactly,' Yvette said. 'Here at Northcombe Hall we want you to feel as if the whole house is your own. And for some of our guests that's definitely partying into the wee small hours.' She let out a small, shrill laugh.

Ed suddenly felt a wave of sympathy towards Yvette. There was something nervy in her quick movements and rehearsed enthusiasm. He had noticed she wasn't wearing an engagement ring or a wedding ring, and couldn't help but feel it must be a bit odd to organise weddings for a living if you hadn't found love yourself. Of course, he was making a lot of assumptions and rather old-fashioned ones at that. Yvette might not believe in marriage.

'There's such a sense of history here,' Yvette said. 'The main house was built in the sixteenth century. In the 1920s, it was occupied by Her Royal Highness Princess Mary—'

'So it's fit for royalty,' Ed said.

'Quite,' Yvette said. 'And would you just look at that wonderful staircase?' She swooshed a bony arm through the air. 'Many of our brides choose it to make their grand entrance on the big day.'

'Very nice,' Ed said. 'I can picture you walking down those steps in that gorgeous dress we bought, can't you, Em?'

'Erm… well… I guess.'

Why was Emily being so weird? She obviously didn't like this place very much, but she could at least feign a bit of excitement for Yvette's sake.

'Shall we venture outside?' Yvette said. 'I can assure you it's every bit as impressive as the interior. As I mentioned earlier, the grounds are eighteen acres. We even have our own orchard. Such a beautiful spot for photographs, particularly as you're having a spring wedding. I mean, why have confetti when you can have blossom, eh?'

They stepped outside. The sun had disappeared behind the clouds and there was a chill in the air that made their swim in the sea feel as if it was another lifetime ago. They crunched across the gravel, passing a uniformed gardener on his hands and knees with what looked like a sieve. Surely he didn't sieve the whole mile of driveway?

'Many of our couples have photographs taken on the bridge,' Yvette said as they reached the lake.

'Hmm,' Emily said, sounding as if Yvette had talked about dredging the lake for dead bodies.

'It's stunning,' Ed said. 'Absolutely stunning.'

Yvette rewarded him with a beaming smile. 'Let me take you on to the orchard.'

As they walked across the immaculately manicured lawn, Ed thought ahead to the visit to his mother this evening, nervousness gnawing at his belly. Would seeing Emily and him together for the first time in years be enough to convince her that he had managed to repair some of the damage from the past? Would she finally forgive him if she believed Emily had? It would certainly help if Emily was in a better mood than the one she seemed to be in now.

'Many of our guests have pre-dinner drinks right here,' Yvette said. 'It's such a lovely view, particularly as the sun starts to go down.'

'Stunning,' Ed said. 'Absolutely stunning.' Jeez, he'd said exactly the same word to describe the bridge over the lake. He needed new superlatives.

Even if his mother was convinced by the rapprochement between him and Emily, it was still a leap to think she'd give him the loan. Ed had to keep believing it was possible, though.

'And this is the orchard,' Yvette said, clapping her hands together. 'Isn't it pretty?'

'Stunn— Gorgeous,' Ed said.

After they'd been shown more of the grounds, Yvette invited Ed and Emily into the library for a cup of tea.

'That's very kind,' Emily said. 'But we need to get going.'

'Oh,' Yvette said, her wan face falling. 'But I haven't shown you the sample menus yet. Or discussed our roster of suppliers for things like the cake and the flowers. At Northcombe Hall, we make sure we only work with the best of the best.'

'I can follow up with you afterwards,' Emily said.

'Oh,' Yvette said. 'Well, let me at least fetch you our brochure. There are all kinds of helpful details in that.'

She scuttled away, leaving Ed and Emily standing on what she had previously billed as the east terrace.

'Maybe we should have a quick cup of tea?' Ed said. 'Yvette looked a bit crushed when you said we had to head straight off.'

Emily shook her head. 'I'm not sure exactly how long it will take for us to drive to Melinsey Barn and I don't want to be late.'

'I'm sensing you're not very keen on this place?'

'It's all a bit formal and fusty.'

Ed nodded. 'I know what you mean. I keep expecting to see people walking around in period costume.'

'Yeah, it's not really the vibe I had in mind.'

'Even though it's like having your very own stately home for the day?'

Emily grinned and it was the first genuine smile Ed had seen from her in a couple of hours. 'Even though.' She gestured towards the imposing red-brick building. 'It's just not really Mark and me.'

Chapter Forty-Nine

Not really Mark and me. What was I talking about? There isn't a Mark and me.

This whole thing is insane. Who goes to look around wedding venues when there is no wedding?

My father and I crunch across the gravel. It has started to drizzle lightly.

'Look,' Dad says, pointing at the horizon. 'A rainbow.'

I have to hand it to my father, he maintains a childlike enthusiasm for life. Shame it's so often matched by childlike behaviour.

'Want me to drive?' he says. 'You said your insurance covers anyone you give your permission to, right?'

'Well, yes, bu—'

'C'mon. It will give you a break.'

'I'm fine.' I know his offer is nothing to do with giving me a break. He thinks I drive too slowly. Well, I think he drives too fast. That he is as reckless at the wheel as he is in life.

'So you thought Northcombe Hall was too stuffy and formal?' he says as we get into the car.

It was too weddingy. I turn the key in the ignition. 'I just wasn't feeling it.'

Northcombe Hall had been Mark's mother's suggestion. She'd

gone to a wedding there and loved it – such a sense of history, staff who couldn't do enough for you, the best food she'd ever had at a do. I wasn't that keen on the photos on the website but had agreed to look around just to keep my future mother-in-law happy. I suppose that's one problem I no longer have. Every cloud.

'You can pull out of the junction now,' Dad says.

'Don't be a backseat driver.' My father isn't listening though. He is glued to his phone as he has been for most of the afternoon. Like some sort of overgrown teenager.

I think about my mum. The great lie about grief is that time heals everything. It knocks the edge off the rawness of the pain, sure, but it doesn't heal it. When someone you love dies, you lose so many moments you should have had with them. Mum wasn't at my graduation, and she will never hold her grandchildren or see me walk down the aisle (neither will anyone else right now but that's another matter).

'Shit,' Dad mutters under his breath, still looking at his phone.

'What's the matter?'

'Nothing, nothing.'

God only knows what he's up to, but I don't have the time or energy to worry about it.

'Do you ever wish you'd dated a few other people?' Dad says, his eyes still fixed on his screen.

'Of course I don't,' I snap. 'Why would you even ask that?'

Dad shrugs. Clearly, he is now adopting teenage mannerisms to go with the phone addiction. 'Just to see what else is out there, I guess. Not that Mark isn't great—'

'Mark *is* great. And I hate this idea that being an adult means you have to sample every item from some kind of romantic buffet. That there's something inherently grown-up about clocking up numbers on the bedpost.' The truth is I have occasionally wondered if I should have dated at least a couple of other people. If, although it isn't something I mind now, it might be something I'll mind later in life. 'Not everyone is some kind of serial shagger like you.'

Dad laughs. 'I'll have you know I'm a reformed man.'

'Hmm. We're here.'

Melinsey Barn is a low-slung buttery-coloured stone building set in rolling meadows. It's the kind of place that instantly makes you picture brides with bare feet and fresh flowers in their hair.

Dad glances up from his phone. 'Oh, this has got a very different vibe.'

An exceptionally tall man carrying a small, scruffy-looking dog is making his way towards us. 'Emily and Mark?'

'This is my father, Ed,' I say firmly. 'Mark couldn't, err, be here today.' *Probably shagging someone else at this very moment.*

'Lovely to meet you both,' the man says. 'I'm Ralph.' He drops a kiss on the dog's small shaggy head. 'And this is Judy. She won't walk on wet grass. Bit of a diva.'

Dad and I laugh, decline offers of tea or something stronger and follow Ralph as he shows us into the large, light-filled barn where they hold their indoor wedding ceremonies.

'It's still set up from the wedding we had here yesterday,' Ralph says.

'Is that pampas grass in the vases?' Dad asks. 'Isn't that something that swingers use to alert like-minded folk?'

'*Dad!*'

'I don't think Lauren and Elliott were swingers,' Ralph says, laughing. 'But you never know.'

The scruffy little dog, who allowed herself to be put down when we came inside, is now sniffing around under each table.

'Judy,' Ralph says. 'No eating scraps you find on the floor.'

'It's a lovely sunny space,' Dad says.

'It is,' Ralph agrees. 'Although I have to confess, if the weather plays ball, I don't think it can compete with having the ceremony in our private woodland. Especially if you get married as the sun is going down. That's what Pete and I chose for our own wedding.'

'Sounds lovely,' Dad says. 'I can't place your accent, but I know you're not a Broadstairs man.'

'Guilty as charged,' Ralph says, laughing. 'I'm an Aussie. You guys been?'

Dad and I shake our heads and I squash down a pang that maybe there was something in my dad's comment about how someone can be a good person but not your person.

As we are about to step out into the courtyard, Judy appears at Ralph's feet and starts whimpering to be picked up.

'*Judy!*' Ralph coos, scooping her up. 'This is where we hold our barbies.' He grins. 'You can take the guy out of Australia… I don't mean your typical English number either.' He does a mock shudder. 'No sad charred sausages with supermarket white buns and vinegary coleslaw here. We do a proper Australian barbie. King prawns the size of Judy, steaks that lead vegetarians astray, fantastically good salads – the real deal.'

'Sounds great,' I say. I look around the pretty courtyard that's festooned with fairy lights.

'How many people are you having at the wedding?' Ralph says.

None. 'Umm, not sure.'

Dad glances up from his phone. 'Not like you not to have that nailed down, Em. I thought it would all be on a spreadsheet by now.'

I arrange my face in an approximation of a smile.

'Let me show you the woodlands,' Ralph says. 'Judy, are you

going to walk?' He attempts to put the dog down, but she raises her paws before they hit the ground to indicate her disapproval. 'Silly girl,' he says affectionately.

'It's all so pretty,' I say. 'But I worry that this bumpy path might be an issue for some of our older or less able guests.'

'Oh, don't worry about that,' Dad says, cutting in before Ralph has a chance to answer. 'I'll give them all piggy backs if I have to.'

Even though my 'concern' is entirely fake and merely something I said to avoid Ralph feeling as if we are wasting his time, I can't help but be irritated by my father's glibness. 'What, just like I shouldn't have been worried about Pebbles yesterday?'

My father has the good grace to look a bit sheepish.

'There's another way down that's accessible by car,' Ralph says. 'I'll show you it when we go and say hello to our chickens and goats.'

We reach an oak arbour nestled in the woods. Fairy lights hang in the canopy of trees and rough wooden benches encircle the space.

'This is gorgeous,' I say truthfully. Much as I like Ralph and his laid-back aura, I haven't been completely sold on Melinsey Barn up until now. If Northcombe Hall was too fusty, this is a bit too rustic for my taste. This woodland area is enchanting though.

'It really is,' Dad agrees. 'It's a place where you'd imagine fairies getting married.'

'Again, guilty as charged!' Ralph says, laughing.

Dad laughs too and then asks if we could please give him a minute because there is something he needs to sort out.

I watch as he moves about ten feet away and jabs frantically at his phone. Whatever is he up to and why is he acting as if he's a City trader on the verge of a mega deal?

'Your dad's lovely,' Ralph says, cutting across my thoughts. 'Lucky I'm so happily married otherwise I'd definitely be making a play for him.'

'Eww,' I say, laughing, 'that's my father you're talking about.' *My father who charms everyone apart from me.*

Ralph starts talking about the onsite accommodation. They have space for up to twenty-six people. There is an honesty bar and an open kitchen because you never know when you might need tequila, or milk and cookies at four a.m.

I nod and smile, but I'm not focused on what Ralph is saying. I'll be able to truthfully tell my dad that, although the woodland area is magical, and although I love Ralph and his diva dog, I wouldn't choose Melinsey Barn. But we still have another venue to see, and I know I'm going to have to make more effort to seem interested and engaged. My dad isn't stupid and will soon cotton on to something being wrong if I don't seem to be taking the venue hunting seriously. Especially since he has already been asking uncomfortable questions about me and Mark.

Chapter Fifty

Ed

Ed and Emily were ten minutes into their tour of the third wedding venue, and Ed was pretty sure his daughter was impressed. If the first place had been too stuffy and the second too rustic, this one seemed the perfect happy medium. A Georgian manor house set in twelve acres with its own lake, it was definitely special, and yet somehow there was a pleasing informality about it all. This wasn't a place where the 'gentlemen' would be required to wear a jacket and tie for dinner, but nor were you likely to find a goat sauntering around.

Emily was talking animatedly to Tom the events coordinator about the advantages of round tables over rectangular ones. Ed was just pleased to see her smiling. It was fair to say she hadn't exactly seemed like the joyful bride-to-be for most of this weekend. She must really be worried about all the stuff going on at work. Ed had tried to bring the subject up again on the drive here, but Emily had cut him off with a terse, 'I'd rather not talk about it.'

'And this is the orangery,' Tom said, showing them into a light-filled, double-height room with gorgeous 360-degree views. 'This is where we'd serve supper.'

Ed fished his phone out of his pocket. He'd won all but one of his afternoon's bets and was now just two hundred quid short of having enough for a deposit. Which meant his fate was in Arsenal's hands (feet?).

The game was thirteen minutes in and there hadn't been any goals yet, despite Arsenal being all over their North London rivals Spurs.

Saka shot but the ball hit the post and Ed let out an involuntary gasp.

'Dad,' Emily said as she caught a glance of his phone screen. 'I can't believe you're watching the football.'

I'm doing this for you. Ed forced a smile and put his phone back in his pocket.

'Let me show you some sample menus,' Tom said.

Ed scanned the page: sea bass with chilli and miso, slow-roasted shoulder of lamb with boulangère potatoes, hispi cabbage with butter beans and nduja. If Cici was a favourite restaurant of Emily and Mark's, then this should be right up their street.

Ed's phone thrummed in his pocket. It was sure to be a notification about the game. He was desperate to look at it, but he could hardly pull his phone out after being so recently remonstrated by his daughter.

Salvation was delivered in the form of Tom asking Emily if she'd like to meet the head chef?

'Sure,' Emily said. 'Dad?'

Ed said he'd leave that to her. 'You know I'd be happy with beans on toast!'

As soon as Emily and Tom were out of sight, Ed pulled out his phone. Arsenal had scored! It was all he could do not to whoop and cheer. His joy was short-lived, however, because there was going to be a VAR check. Ed waited, his eyes never straying from his screen.

Goal disallowed. For Christ's sake!

'You okay, Dad?' Emily said, reappearing with Tom.

'Fine. Fine.'

'I don't suppose you've started to think about things like flowers, cakes and photographers yet,' Tom said to Emily. 'But we work with a wide variety of companies, all of whom are dedicated to getting everything just the way you want it for your big day.'

'Great,' Emily said. 'And what about the accommodation?'

'Oh, it's amazing. You get the whole house to yourself, you see. Let me show you now where the bride and groom stay.'

Ed followed in Tom and Emily's wake as they walked across the springy lawn. The earlier rain had disappeared, and the late afternoon sunshine cast a dappled golden light. Ed was sure Emily had fallen for this place. Which meant he desperately needed Arsenal to win.

As if on cue, his phone buzzed and, as Emily and Tom seemed locked in conversation, he risked a peek. Sure enough, Arsenal had scored.

Tom opened the door to a huge bedroom complete with a freestanding claw-foot bath and doors out to its own private walled garden.

'Wow,' Emily said.

Ed had watched enough football games in his life to know that the other team could easily still equalise or even win. Which meant his stomach was in knots.

But, after seven long minutes, Arsenal scored another goal. Ed and Emily were being shown the Norman chapel at that point and Ed stood behind the pulpit feeling an uncharacteristic rush of religious gratitude. This was cemented less than sixty seconds later when Arsenal made it 3–0. As they were into the last minute of stoppage time, there was no chance of the other team making a comeback either. Even Spurs couldn't dive three times in a minute.

'Yes!' Ed said as the full-time whistle blew.

'Dad!' Emily said. 'What did I say to you about watching the football?' She turned back to Tom. 'It's gorgeous. Really gorgeous. Could you excuse me for a second, I need to nip to the loo? I'll leave you with my dad. You never know, he might even manage to put his phone away for a few minutes.'

Ed was left looking at Tom. 'So, my daughter is obviously pretty keen on this place.'

Tom nodded. He was clearly used to people falling hard for Holly House 'As I said to your daughter when she booked the viewing, we do currently have availability on that date, but slots are going fas—'

'Yeah,' Ed said, cutting him off. 'I'd like to put down a deposit.' For a second, he wondered if he should wait until Emily came back from the loo and ask her if that was what she wanted, but she'd made her feelings about the place pretty obvious. Mark hadn't seen it, of course, but again Emily had been clear on that: Mark trusts me completely.

'The deposit would be one thousand pounds,' Tom said, telling Ed what he'd already checked online.

A thousand pounds. It was a lot of money for anyone, let alone someone whose home was at risk of repossession. Ed shook the thought from his brain. His mother would give him the loan. And, if there was ever a time for another grand (no pun intended) gesture, it was now.

'No problem,' he said, reaching for his bank card and praying the bookies still paid up straight away like they did in the old days.

The bookies did and Tom was just handing back Ed's card and the booking confirmation when Emily reappeared.

'What's going on?' she asked.

'I just put down the deposit on this place,' Ed said.

Emily stared at him, seemingly lost for words, before bursting into tears.

Ed put his arm around her shaking shoulders. It was wonderful to see her overcome with joy like this.

Chapter Fifty-One

Liz

When Liz was at home, she never sat in the garden drinking a cup of tea. Every time she tried, she found herself seeing a job that needed doing and jumping up, not returning to her tea until it was cold. Here it was different – someone else was responsible for pulling weeds, tying ramblers, snipping and pruning.

She had always loved autumn. The soft, mellow light, the back-to-school feeling that never leaves you, the foggy mornings that so often give way to warm sunny days like today. And, of course, the riot of golds, reds and oranges – the trees' triumphant encore before their winter sleep. She closed her eyes and turned her face to the sun.

'Hello, there,' Judith said, appearing through the double doors.

'Hello. Isn't it a beautiful day? Not a cloud in the sky.'

'Perfect,' Judith agreed, sitting down.

'Would you like a cup of tea?' Liz said. 'And did you manage to find all the bits I asked you for?'

'No thanks to the tea – I had a huge cup just before coming out.' Judith handed Liz a carrier bag. 'I got the things you asked for. Are you sure it's a good idea to have John's Rolex here? It could get stolen.'

Liz hadn't actually considered that possibility. Still, the watch wasn't going to be here for very long. 'It'll be fine. I'll keep it with me at all times. Sleep with it under my pillow.' She laughed but couldn't help noticing Judith stayed stony-faced. 'How's Martin?'

Judith made a sound like a deflating balloon. 'Okay, I suppose. Things are a bit tense. We had a huge row yesterday over mashed potato. How ridiculous is that?'

Liz and Peter had yet to have a row and, while she was realistic enough to know they would, she was pretty sure it wouldn't be over potatoes.

Judith smoothed an invisible crease from her skirt. 'Sometimes I think we're only still together because we're too old to find anyone else.'

Liz reached out her good arm and placed her hand on Judith's. 'That's not true. On any level.'

They were interrupted by Bella and her clipboard. She wanted to know if she could put Liz's name down to watch the entertainment this evening? She'd booked a fabulous singer. He was called Sammy Bourne and he had an incredible voice. Not unkind to look at either.

Liz thanked Bella and said she'd think about it.

'God, that sounds deadly,' Judith said as soon as Bella was out of earshot. 'You definitely don't want to go to that.'

Liz had been thinking exactly the same thing herself and yet there was something in Judith's tone that rankled. She had never been great at being told what to do. 'I was wondering if you might help me have a look online for a dress to wear to Emily's wedding? I know it's still seven months away, but I don't want to leave it to the last minute.'

'Yes, of course. I always love a spot of shopping, as you know.

243

And totally agree you should get something sooner rather than later.'

Liz reached for her iPad. 'I don't want some "old lady" number, I want something glam. Especially since it'll be one of the first big occasions that Peter and I go to together.'

'Oh, will he be in England by then?'

'Oh, yes. He's hoping to be here in four or five weeks. As soon as his grandson is better, really. Where shall we try first for dresses? Good old John Lewis?'

'The Rolex?' Judith blurted out. 'You're not thinking of giving it to Peter, are you?'

Liz felt almost winded by the abruptness of the question. 'No.'

'Are you sure?'

'*Yes.*' Liz stifled the urge to add: not that it's any of your business.

'It's just—'

'Let's not do this again.'

Judith puffed out her cheeks. 'I'm worried he might not be who he says he is. Yo—'

Liz held up her left arm to stop the ugly words. 'Why do you keep saying things like this?'

'Sometimes they're not – these people you meet online.'

Anger bubbled in Liz's belly. 'Stop it. Please.'

'I've been reading up—'

'I said stop it. I told you I've googled Peter and everything he has ever said checks out.'

'Great, but you haven't met him in real life yet.'

Liz clenched her good fist. 'I'm perfectly well aware of that, thank you. And it's for reasons completely beyond either of our control. Also, we have had a video call.'

Judith looked visibly shocked. 'Really? I didn't realise that.'

Yeah, you don't know everything. So just shut up and leave me alone.

'I still wonder if you should be a little bit careful, though?'

Jeez, the woman is like a dog with a bone.

Judith rubbed her hands together as if she was washing them. 'I'll feel terrible if I don't say something and then this man turns out to be dodgy.'

If Liz was of a more dramatic disposition, she'd have sworn the sun suddenly disappeared behind a cloud. Why was Judith saying these vile things? She didn't even know Liz had lent Peter money (thank God).'*This man*, as you call him, is not dodgy. And to be completely honest with you, I resent the accusation. Do you really think it's so hard to believe someone could fall in love with me?'

'No, of course not. And Peter might very well be the real deal. It's just everything is moving so fast between the two of you.'

'So that makes him dodgy, does it?'

'No. It's just whenever I've got together with anyone, it's taken a while for things to develop. Martin and I didn't even start thinking about moving in together until we'd been dating for a couple of years.'

'Oh, so you and Martin are the benchmark now, are you?'

The words were cruel, and Judith looked suitably stung, but Liz didn't care. The second Judith mentioned Martin, Liz knew she was right when she'd concluded her friend was jealous. Fury washed through her body, and she bit the inside of her cheek to stop herself from saying all the things she wanted to. She was bitterly disappointed in Judith. She knew her marriage was going through a rocky patch – if indeed the word 'patch' could be used to talk about a thirty-year period – but couldn't she find it in herself to be happy for Liz?

The silence pulsed between them until eventually Judith spoke.

'Look,' she said, using the sort of voice one might use to address a toddler having a tantrum in the chocolate aisle. 'All I'm saying is it wouldn't hurt to be a little careful. That's…' She trailed off because Bella had reappeared pushing the wheelchair of one of the regulation haircut ladies.

'Bella,' Liz called out. 'I've been thinking about the entertainment this evening and I'd very much like to come.' She gave Judith a look: Don't you dare tell me what to do.

Chapter Fifty-Two

As I was still sobbing when we got to the car, I'd had no choice but to let my father drive. Ten minutes in, not only am I feeling decidedly travel sick, but there is also the very real risk that he might kill us both – something that at this moment doesn't feel like a wholly unpalatable option.

Since we left Holly House, Dad hasn't stopped talking about it. Do I think I'll go for the walled garden or the main lawn for the welcome drinks? What time will the ceremony be? Would we go for a bespoke cocktail; it's pretty cool to have your own cocktail, no?

I am desperate to change the subject but how can I without seeming wildly ungracious? My dad has just shelled out a considerable amount of money on a non-refundable deposit, and I know he's never exactly flush with cash.

It's amazing to me that my dad doesn't suspect I don't share his excitement at having booked a venue. For all his faults, he is normally good at picking up a mood. But he is clearly convinced my tears are happy ones.

Dad swings the car around a bend.

'You're going too fast,' I say.

'Nonsense, it's a sixty-mile-an-hour speed limit.'

'Yeah, that's a guide not a target.'

He laughs as if I'm trying to be funny. 'When are you going to tell Mark we booked the place? Are you going to do it on the phone or wait until you can tell him in person?'

I could be waiting a while. I choke back fresh tears. 'In person.'

'Yeah, better, that way you get to see his face.' He shifts the car into fourth gear. 'That dance floor was something, wasn't it? What are you thinking about in terms of music? The thing with weddings is that you're catering to such a diverse audience with such different tastes.'

'I – we – haven't thought much about the music.'

'Hmm, you know what you could do? Ask every guest to list three of their favourite "gotta hit the dance floor" tracks when they RSVP.'

'Yeah, maybe.' How has this fake wedding got so completely out of hand? I like to think of myself as a reasonably good person. I do a worthwhile job (don't Buddhists count teaching as one of the most noble professions?), vote the right way and have not one but two monthly standing orders to charity.

But am I really Good? I realised earlier that, apart from seeing her in hospital after her fall, this evening's visit to my grandma will be my first in five months. I frequently wish bad things on people who don't use headphones on public transport and, the other day, I saw a man begging outside Zara who didn't have any shoes and, while I gave him a tenner and it upset me, it didn't completely spoil my day. (To be fair, if you allowed yourself to get as upset as you should get every time you saw a homeless person, you wouldn't be able to live in London.)

'What did you think of Tom's suggestion about having some additional entertainment?' Dad says. 'The flame throwers could be fun.'

My integrity certainly doesn't seem that watertight under pressure. I am prepared to let my dad spend money he doesn't have on a wedding that isn't happening. Because of what, my pride? And I am ready to throw the Cassidy family under the bus; to let a five-year-old be seen as the liar when actually he is telling the truth.

'Oh, bugger,' Dad says, as we get stuck behind a tractor. 'Never mind, we'll be on the freeway again soon.'

'Motorway,' I say.

Dad grins. 'Motorway. How many bridesmaids are you having? What about flower girls and boys?'

Who is this man and what has he done with my father? 'Three bridesmaids and two flower boys. Grandma has no idea we're coming, right?' I add, desperate to change the subject.

'No. She doesn't even know I'm in England. I wanted it to be a surprise.'

'You're big on surprises suddenly.'

Dad laughs. 'Yeah, let's hope this is a nice one. I know she'll be happy to see you. Me? Well, we'll see. She'll be pleased to see us getting along though.'

'Why is that so important to you?'

Dad shrugs. 'She's not getting any younger.' He drums his fingers on the steering wheel. 'Annoying being stuck behind this tractor, isn't it?'

'Oh, I don't know. I'm quite enjoying the feeling I might live through the day.'

Dad laughs. 'My driving is not that bad. Oh, look at that, tractor guy is pulling over. Thank him for me as we go past, will you?'

I half-heartedly raise my hand.

Dad puts his foot on the accelerator so hard, I am flung

backwards. Truthfully, I'm surprised my battered old Mini can go this fast. 'Slow down.'

'Spoilsport!' Dad says, grinning. He does reduce his speed a little though. 'The thing with your grandma is she has never forgiven me for leaving you and your mum. Mind you, even before that, I was never her favourite person.'

I wonder if I'd be my mum's 'favourite' right now if she was still alive. Seems unlikely considering honesty and integrity were her non-negotiables. Goodness knows how she kept a job in customer services given her steadfast refusal to be anything less than scrupulously honest with customers. It wasn't uncommon for her to tell someone that strictly speaking something wasn't covered by the returns policy, but she thought it was only fair that she issued a refund. 'So it's about getting into Grandma's good books?'

'It's about a lot of things.'

'Hmm.' I've never thought my dad cared that much about his mum. It's one of the many things I have chalked up against him over the years – yet another opportunity to take the moral high ground. But now I wonder if I have been doing him a disservice? Maybe he has cared all along, or at least he does now and he's trying to make up for lost time. It's nice that he is so intent on his mum seeing the two of us reconciled. I decide there and then that I will make sure that the visit to Grandma is everything Dad wants it to be, not just for my grandma's sake but for my dad's. I owe him that much.

Shona's name flashes up on Dad's phone screen and he hits 'decline'. 'Can't talk while I'm driving,' he explains when I look at him quizzically.

I phone the vet to check on Pebbles. 'He's *still* fine,' the receptionist says, barely bothering to conceal her irritation.

'I loved that orangery,' Dad says, as I end the call.

And we are back to weddings. The man is obsessed.

'I can see myself walking you down the aisle of that Norman chapel too—' Dad checks himself. 'Sorry, you probably don't want me giving you away.'

'Don't be silly,' I say.

'What? You would want me to? Really?'

I take in my father's face, full of hope. 'When I get married, you can give me away.'

Chapter Fifty-Three

Ed

Ed was sitting in an aggressively over-lit, tired-looking motorway service station that smelled faintly of vomit. However, nothing could puncture his good mood. He was, to use a peculiar English expression that hadn't entered his consciousness for about a decade, cock-a-hoop.

It was hard to believe that Emily had asked him to give her away. It felt like a huge public statement that he was part of her life (and he'd be the first to concede he didn't really deserve to be).

It was also a good sign that his plan was going to work. Despite being an optimist at heart, Ed had doubted this many times. Now, though, it actually seemed possible that his mother would see he'd repaired his relationship with Emily and witness the genuine warmth between them. And surely if that was true, she'd give him the money?

Emily had insisted the coffees should be her treat and was now standing in the line (or queue, as Ed supposed he should think of it when in England). There weren't that many people waiting, but everything was moving incredibly slowly due to what seemed to be some sort of staff training. Each task was being minutely explained to the trainee: 'You put the toast in the toaster, then you get two packets of butter from the fridge. You get out a medium plate and a knife. Not a large plate…'

Did anyone really need that level of instruction? Ed thought of himself as a bit of a useless bugger, but even he knew toast went in the toaster and butter lived in the fridge.

A family got up from the table near the window and Ed decided to swoop in and take their spot. This may be a sectioned-off seating area of a grubby motorway café and not Chateau Marmont but there were still good and bad tables.

As he sat, Ed flashed a beaming smile at the couple in matching beige anoraks at the next table. He was slightly disconcerted that, despite him immediately pinning them in his mind as middle-aged, they were probably around his age. But then he supposed he was middle-aged. Even if that wasn't how he liked to think of himself.

Emily had been the one to suggest a stop for coffee and Ed was pretty sure it was because she could no longer stand his driving, but he didn't care. He was always up for a caffeine fix, and he was in too good a mood to fuss about getting a little behind schedule. It was also a cruel truth that his mother wasn't going anywhere.

A young lad in uniform approached and, without a word, started spritzing the table with some heavily scented cleaning spray. Normally Ed might be a little irritated the lad hadn't said a word and gave off such a sullen vibe, but today he smiled beatifically. He was full of bonhomie and love for his fellow man.

Ed's phone buzzed. Joanie requests FaceTime. Odd. Shona's sister hardly ever called him. He felt his stomach lurch – maybe Shona had had some kind of accident. 'Hello.'

'How could you?'

'Sorry?'

253

This one word seemed to make Joanie incandescent with rage. 'Don't you dare act the innocent with me, Ed. Shona's told me everything. About how you faked a migraine to get out of going to yoga with her when really you were with God knows who—'

'Joanie—'

'Don't you Joanie me. I know how men like you operate. Shona never should have got involved with you in the first place. You told her you cheated in the past, right? Well, she should never have ignored that red flag…'

Joanie's voice was now so loud, beige anorak couple were openly staring. The man had a forkful of chocolate cake hovering mid-air. Ed didn't care so much about what they thought, but he was worried about Emily overhearing all this. Luckily though, as he'd moved tables, she was just about far away enough not to be able to hear (thank you, thank you, family who were sitting by the window).

'Joanie,' Ed said, cutting across the stream of abuse coming in his direction. 'Let me speak. I'm not cheating on your sister. I never have and I never will.'

'Oh really?' Joanie said, wagging her carmine-tipped finger at Ed. 'Then where were you on Monday afternoon when you claimed to have a migraine and Lillian saw you strolling down Boulevard?'

'I went to get some migraine tablets.'

'Bullshit,' Joanie spat.

Ed briefly met the eye of the woman in the beige anorak and saw immediately that she was with Joanie in all this. Well, screw her and screw Joanie because he was innocent and the only person he had to convince of that was Shona. Ed was now starting to see that this might not be quite as easy as he'd hoped, but he refused to let anything shake his confidence. As soon as he got back to the States and saw Shona face to face, he'd be able to make her see he wasn't cheating. And, as long as his mother shelled out, Shona would never find out that her home had been on the brink of being repossessed. Ed had another ace up his sleeve too, because he'd decided he was going to propose. It's a cliché that you don't appreciate something until you're about to lose it, but it also happens to be true.

'If you had a migraine, there's no way you would have gone out in the sun,' Joanie said. 'Plus, I called Lillian, and she said you weren't even wearing sunglasses.'

Ed tipped his head back and closed his eyes. He'd realised as he was leaving the apartment block that his sunglasses weren't in his pocket, but by that time he was already running late for his appointment and the loan shark was not someone you kept waiting. What he wouldn't give now to be able to rewind time and run back up the stairs.

'ONCE A CHEAT, ALWAYS A CHEAT,' Joanie shouted, before ending the call.

Ed let out a huge sigh. And then he opened his eyes to see Emily standing in front of him carrying two cappuccinos and wearing an expression that could only be described as appalled.

Chapter Fifty-Four

Broken promises are very much my father's stock in trade, so his 'promise' that he isn't cheating on Shona shouldn't mean much. Especially since he also has a patchy record when it comes to fidelity. He had numerous liaisons when he was married to my mum and subsequent girlfriends have also discovered monogamy not to be his strong suit.

But as I pull into a parking space outside my grandma's care home, I decide I am going to let the subject go. My dad may well be telling the truth on this occasion. He does seem something of a changed man and it's impossible not to notice that he's potty about Shona. The woman has even got him drinking spirulina, for goodness' sake. No Englishman, even one who has moved to the States, does that unless it's for love.

My dad's relationship with Shona isn't my business and, yes, sisterhood and all that, but the first time I clapped eyes on Shona was yesterday on FaceTime. I'm not going to get sucked in. Dad and I are getting on better than we have in years, and I have plenty to contend with on my own plate.

'Not sure these are going to pass muster,' Dad says, nodding towards to the cellophane-clad bunch of chrysanthemums he picked up at the services.

I smile. My dad looks nervous, which I find touching. He obviously cares very much about this visit and making it a success. 'Yeah, Grandma's not really someone you give service station flowers to, is she? Especially ones that look a little droopy. But at least they're nice and bright.'

We sign the visitors' book and exchange pleasantries with the receptionist about the weather. Yes, it has been lovely for October and, yes, the sunshine does lift the mood.

Eastwood House is relatively nice as care homes go. It is certainly a lot less basic than the place Mark's grandad was in. Here the common areas have been designed to give off a hotel vibe, with large vases of faux flowers, deep carpets and fancy coffee machines. Money hasn't completely stamped out the bleakness though. A very elderly woman is shouting desperately for her mummy and a man with candy-floss-white hair sits staring out of the window with quiet desperation.

A carer called Anna shows us to my grandma's room. She is sitting in a wing-backed armchair, her back as straight as a ballet dancer's, watching the news. 'Well, this is a surprise!' she says, her face splitting into a big grin.

I have always found it disconcerting that my grandma's smile is exactly the same as my dad's. The two of them are different in almost every respect, but their full-beam smile is identical, and both can use it to melt a room.

'Anna,' Grandma says. 'Now I have visitors, please could you turn off the TV? It's all so depressing anyway, and I'm fed up with listening to that joker of a PM.'

'You look great, Grandma,' I say, kissing her. I gesture towards her hot pink top and red skirt. 'You're colour-blocking.'

She laughs. 'Is that what they call it nowadays? You know I've always liked strong colours.'

Dad bends down to give Grandma a kiss.

'What are you doing back in England?' she asks.

'I came to see you. Well, you and Emily.'

'Really?' Grandma says. 'Well, that's nice. Good job too – I'll be dead soon!' She chuckles and Dad and I both tell her not to say that but laugh along with her.

Dad hands Grandma the flowers. 'These are… bright,' she says. Her eyes twinkle. 'Anna, please could you pop them in water for me, and maybe bring us all a nice cup of tea?'

Anna smiles and tells Grandma she drinks way too much tea.

'Better that than gin,' Grandma shoots back. 'Use some of my Yorkshire teabags will you, please? None of that weak rubbish.'

'Do you have a phone charger I could borrow please, Mum?' Dad says. 'My battery is almost dead.'

'Yeah,' I say. 'Probably because you've been on your phone most of the day.'

Dad rummages around in the drawer. 'You've got Dad's watch in here.'

'Yes,' Grandma says. 'Nice to have something of his with me.' She grins. 'I must be getting sentimental in my old age. Anyway, tell me your news, both of you. Ed, when did you get back to England and how long are you here for?'

I'm grateful the spotlight isn't yet on me. Obviously, given the weekend's activities, I have no choice but to lie to my grandma about me and Mark, but it feels desperately uncomfortable, especially as my grandma is something of a moral compass.

The room is small and somewhat tired looking, but it overlooks the garden and is pleasant enough. Grandma has even brought a few framed photographs from home. I stare at one of her, me, Mark and Mum having lunch in the garden on a summer's day. It must have been taken by my grandpa. He was great at taking pictures before anyone really noticed and this one perfectly captures the carefree mood of the day. I remember clearly how happy I was. Mark and I had recently become a couple and had spent the night before planning a future of travel and adventure. As we sat in my grandparents' garden, surrounded by people I loved, soaking up the sunshine, eating a simple but perfect salad niçoise and drinking very cold rosé, I felt life couldn't get much better.

'What about you, Emily?' Grandma says, interrupting my thoughts. 'How are you and how's that handsome fiancé of yours?'

I force a smile. 'Good thanks. Mark's away this weekend – working. He sent his love.' God, I am becoming a regular little Pinocchio. But Mark would have sent his love if he'd known I was coming here. He adores my grandma. My guts twist. That's the thing about breaking up with someone you have been with for a long time – your lives are enmeshed and separating them is a painful and complex operation.

'Emily and I have had a great weekend planning the wedding,' Dad says. 'Today, we put a deposit down on a venue and yesterday we bought the dress. Emily looks absolutely gorgeous in it.'

'I bet,' Grandma says, beaming at me.

Yeah, shame I'll never wear it. I'm relieved when the wedding talk is curtailed by the arrival of Anna and the tea.

The chat continues amiably, and I try not to notice that my grandma's good hand shakes a little when she picks up her cup. I picture a younger version of the same hands pushing me around the living room in a cardboard box the two of us had fashioned into a racing car. I was five at the time, and I made Grandma do lap after lap, but she didn't once complain about being tired.

I look at her now. I know, notwithstanding the broken shoulder and slight shakiness, we are lucky. She has got to seventy-nine in good health and her mind is still sharp as a tack. She seems in good spirits too and, apart from some gentle teasing about how she is forever grateful that I take after my mum, not my dad (which he takes in good part), appears pleased to see both of us.

'How's the teaching going?' Grandma says.

My stomach knots. 'Fine. Good.'

Grandma gives me a slightly quizzical look but doesn't press the subject. She places her cup back on the side, sits back and smiles. 'It's lovely to see you both together.'

'Yeah,' Dad says. 'We've had a wonderful weekend, haven't we, Emily? One of the reasons I wanted to come over to England, apart from seeing you, of course, was to try to make amends with Emily. I'm very aware that I haven't always been the best father or been there for Emily when she has needed me.'

'I'll say,' Grandma adds with a little too much gusto.

'Have you heard of the 12-Step Program?' Dad says.

Grandma's face crumples. 'For drunks? You haven't got a booze problem now, have you, Edward? As well as everything else.'

The 'everything else' seems a little punchy to me but Dad appears unconcerned.

'No, I haven't got a drink problem, but my partner Shona used to, and the 12-Step Program changed her life. She's taught me a lot about it and how saying sorry isn't enough and it's all about making amends.'

Grandma makes a harumphing noise. 'Sounds a bit American to me.'

'Maybe,' Dad says evenly. 'But it's helped me to see things differently. And to realise how much it means to me to make things right with Emily.'

'Hmm,' Grandma says, fiddling with the silver locket she's wearing. 'Well, I'm all for that.'

I let out the breath I didn't realise I'd been holding. It's clearly desperately important to Dad to demonstrate to his mum that he's changed and, as a result, so has his relationship with me. Somewhere along the line, this has started to matter to me too. It feels like something positive I can do on a weekend where I have really started to doubt my own integrity. I might be faking a wedding and lying at work, but at least I am making my dad and my grandma happy. I want Dad to see that I appreciate him flying across the world to see me, that I'm grateful to him for throwing himself into wedding planning and doing everything in his power to show me this time he really has changed. I am a firm believer that everyone deserves a second chance (even though it's probably my father's tenth chance).

'It's nice you made the effort to come to England,' Grandma says to Dad. 'I expect I really put the willies up you when you phoned me wanting money and I said no.' She laughs.

I stare at my grandma, processing what I've just heard. I am sure my mouth must have literally dropped open, and I am sitting here like a gormless fool.

Which is apt really. Because I have most certainly been a fool.

I have to use every drop of willpower in my body not to tear into my father there and then. But there is no way I would do that to my grandma. Let her believe the reconciliation between Dad and me is real; let her think her useless no-good son has actually done the right thing for once in his miserable life.

I sit there drinking tea and making chit-chat while all the time my jaw is clenched, my fists balled and my heart racing. Yes, I've seen the photos of Auntie Jen's new puppy – a-dor-able. No, I didn't know Barry had had another knee op, poor thing he's really had a tough time of it recently.

How could I have been so monumentally, epically stupid? *Of course* this had all been about money. My father didn't fly 4,000 miles to see me and he doesn't give a monkey's arse about making things right between us. His 'making amends' is just as phoney as his 12-Step Program.

At the point I'm sure I am about to spontaneously combust, I stand up and tell my grandma I have to be getting back to London.

My father stands too.

'Dad's going to stay with you a bit longer,' I say. 'You know, because he's come all this way to see you.'

My father's mouth opens but then closes again when he sees the look I am giving him behind my grandma's back.

'If you just want to grab your jacket from my car,' I say to him.

Again, he looks at me confused and beseeching, but I shoot him back a 'smile' that brooks no argument.

I bend to kiss my grandma's soft, warm cheek. 'Bye, Grandma. Love you.'

She holds my hand with a surprisingly strong one-handed grip and tells me she loves me too. 'You're a good girl. Just like your mum.'

I blink back tears. I'm not a good girl or anything like my mum. Still, I'm not the worst person around here.

'What's going on?' Dad says, the second we are out of Grandma's earshot.

I don't dignify his question with an answer, instead continuing to march down the corridor. We will do this outside.

In the car park, the light has faded, and it has started to drizzle. 'Wha—'

I put my hand up to stop my father saying another word. I

have heard quite enough from him. 'Just stop with all your lies and your bullshit. I can't believe I actually thought you'd changed. The truth is you're the same lying, conniving bastard you've always been. You didn't come back to England because you wanted to make up with me or see Grandma. You don't give a damn about either of us—'

'That's not true. I—'

Again, I raise a hand to indicate he should keep quiet. We are standing on a bay marked 'ambulance' and the way I feel right now, I can barely trust myself not to put my father in the back of one.

'EVERYTHING YOU HAVE DONE SINCE YOU'VE BEEN HERE HAS BEEN TOTALLY FAKE,' I scream. 'JUST LIKE ALWAYS.'

A youngish couple emerge from the care home and stare at me, but I am way too angry to care, and not just with my moral vacuum of a father but with myself. How did I let this happen? Fool me once, as the old expression goes.

'Emily, listen.' Dad tries to put his hand on my arm, but I shake it off.

'I will not listen to you. Not now and not ever.' I open the boot of the car, take out my father's jacket and shove it roughly into his arms.

'How am I going to get home?' he says.

I look at him and shake my head. 'Figure it out.' And with that I get into the car, lock the doors, and drive out of the car park at a speed that is most unlike me.

Chapter Fifty-Five

Ed

Ed trudged along the care home corridor like a death row prisoner on his way to the chair. Emily's words rang in his ears.

He had no idea how he was going to convince her that, although in many ways he was guilty as charged, not everything about this visit had been fake. There was nothing pretend about how sorry he was for failing her so many times over the years. Nor was there a shred of phoniness in how much he'd loved being around her, or how made up he'd been at the thought of giving her away (yeah, kiss that one goodbye).

And, of course, it wasn't just his daughter Ed was in trouble with. With Shona not even taking his calls anymore, Ed had doghouses on two continents. And that was without Shona even knowing about the possibility of the condo being repossessed. Was his mother going to shell out? He bloody well hoped so.

His mother was not in her bedroom. Ed's mind flashed back guiltily to him telling the woman in the wedding dress shop Liz was dying. Had life imitated fiction? Was it possible his mother, in rude good health apart from her shoulder, had somehow dropped dead in the short time he's been outside being yelled at by Emily?

'Is that you, Ed?' came a voice from the en-suite bathroom. 'I've just nipped to the loo.'

Ed slumped in the armchair, closed his eyes and pressed his thumbs into the bridge of his nose.

He heard a ping and reflexively glanced over to see his mother's phone, which had lit up on the bedside table.

I adore you. That's all. Xxxx

Wow, he didn't even know his mother was dating. As far as he knew, she hadn't been out with anyone since his dad died. She'd always claimed she was happy on her own and could 'do without all the hassle'.

Are you free? For the rest of your life :)

'You're seeing someone?' Ed said, as Liz emerged from the bathroom.

'How do you kn—' Liz stopped. 'Have you been reading my messages?'

'Sorry,' Ed said. 'I didn't mean to. The phone pinged and I glanced over without really thinking. That's great news, though. Tell me all about him. What's his name? How did you meet? Is it serious?'

Liz grinned and suddenly she looked more like a seventeen-year-old than a seventy-nine-year-old.

The phone pinged again, and Ed glanced over.

Thanks again for helping me out, my darling. I'll pay you back very soon xx

'Wait,' Ed said. 'You're giving him money?'

Liz snatched her phone off the bedside table and stuffed it in her pocket. 'Stop reading my *private* messages.'

'But Mum—'

'I lent him a few hundred quid because he has a few cash-flow problems at the moment and he's paying his grandson's medical bills. Not that it's any of your business.'

'Right,' Ed said. 'Just a few hundred quid?'

'Like I said, Edward. It's none of your business.'

Ed puffed out his cheeks. 'How did you meet him? Please tell me it wasn't online?' The look on his mother's face answered his question for him. 'But you've met him in person, right?'

'I don't want to discuss this with you, Edward. I barely hear from you for months on end and then you turn up here and have the nerve to start cross-examining me about my life.'

Ed held up his palms. 'Okay, listen, Mum, I get it. I realise I'm not always the most solicitous of sons—'

Liz made a pfftt noise.

'But this isn't about me. I'm worried about you. There are lots of dodgy people on the internet.'

'Do you think I'm some kind of idiot? Or that it's so impossible that a man might genuinely have fallen in love with me?'

'No, of course not. I'm just looking out for you, okay? Are you honestly sure you've only given him a few hundred pounds?'

'*Yes.*'

Ed was almost certain his mother was lying. Like all inveterately honest people, she wasn't good at it. 'It's just he may not be who he says he is. He may be a scammer. The whole sick relative thing – it's textbook stuff.'

Liz laughed mirthlessly. 'Oh, is it now?'

She was about to say more when she was interrupted by the

arrival of a woman with a mass of dark curls and a clipboard. 'Ah, Liz, I came to see if you were ready for the entertainment, but I didn't realise you had a visitor.'

'That's all right,' Liz said. 'My son was just leaving.'

Ed would put money on his mother being scammed (not that he had any money to put on anything).

Of course, he couldn't be a hundred per cent certain. It was possible this bloke was a good guy and Liz had simply lent him a bit of cash to get him out of a bind. God knows, Ed had borrowed money off girlfriends enough times in his life and, whatever else he was or wasn't, he was no conman. But there was something about this situation, and his mother's defensiveness, that didn't smell right.

The tables had been moved aside in the dining room and there were rows of chairs facing the front.

Ed spied Liz sitting a few rows back next to a woman with jet-black curls.

'I thought you'd left?' Liz said.

'Not yet,' Ed said. 'We didn't get a chance to say a proper goodbye.'

His mother stared straight ahead.

'I'm Sonia,' said the woman with the black curls. 'Good you're not missing Sammy Bourne. He's a brilliant singer. Could give some of those famous fellas a run for their money. He's my second favourite of all the entertainment we have here. My first is when they bring the doggies in. I love them – especially Buddy the Jack Russell.'

A young, very good-looking man in an immaculate dinner suit walked in and greeted his audience before launching into 'That'll Be the Day'.

Ed watched him sway and croon. An hour ago, he might have

felt sorry for the guy. If it wasn't the pinnacle of a performer's ambitions to sing on a cruise ship, that still felt like a big step up from performing to an audience of fifteen people in a Broadstairs care home. Not to mention being unfavourably compared to a Jack Russell, who presumably did nothing more than allow you to feed him a Bonio or pat his head.

But now Ed felt his perceptions shifting. At least Sammy Bourne had a job. And quite possibly a home and a few successful personal relationships. Perhaps it was Sammy who ought to be feeling sorry for Ed?

'Mum,' Ed whispered. 'This guy – are you sure you only lent him a few hundred quid?'

Liz's head snapped round. 'Stop asking me that. I expect you only came to visit me because you reckoned you could get me to change my mind about that "loan".'

'Ooh,' Sonia said. '"Don't Know Much About History", I like this one.' She seemed utterly oblivious to the rising tension.

Ed rubbed his palms across his face. 'I came to visit you because I wanted to see you.'

'He reminds me of that Michael Bublé fellow,' Sonia said to no one in particular.

'Mum—'

Liz cut him off. 'I don't want to hear one more word from you about this relationship, Edward. I'm happier than I have been in years. Happier than I've ever been in my whole life, probably. And you have no business spoiling that for me.'

'I don't want to sp—'

Liz silenced him with a look. 'Not. Another. Word. And don't try to talk to me about giving you a "loan" either. That's a fait accompli.'

'*What?*'

'Fait accompli. An accomplished fact: done.'

'I know what it means, Mum.'

'As I told you on the phone, the answer is no.'

Ed feared there was a very real possibility he might vomit.

'I went to see Michael Bublé perform live once,' Sonia said. 'Very good he was. Such a talent. My friend Rose says…'

'Thank you, ladies and gentlemen,' Sammy said, responding to a weak flutter of applause. 'And now I'm going to do one of your favourites and mine. Ladies and gentlemen, "New York, New York".'

If Sammy was expecting this to bring the house down, he hadn't taken into account the house. That said, this did seem to be a popular number and several people in the audience started singing along.

Emboldened by this audience participation, Sammy stuck his microphone in Ed's face and invited him to join in with the chorus.

Ed had rarely felt less like Frank Sinatra in his life or, for that matter, like singing, but he had little choice but to play along.

'You've got a nice voice,' Sonia said when he finished.

'He sings on cruise ships,' Liz said.

'I haven't done that for twenty years, Mum.'

Liz waved away this triviality.

'My granddaughter Charity has a beautiful voice,' Sonia said. 'I expect she'll sing at Hope's wedding.'

'Stop looking so sour-faced,' Liz whispered to Ed. 'I honestly believe you'd have made much more of your life if you hadn't always been able to run back to Dad and me every time you needed money.'

'It's a bit late to think about your parenting style,' Ed hissed. 'I'm fifty-four.'

'Exactly. Old enough to stand on your own two feet.'

Ed didn't trust himself to speak, so just sat there staring ahead. Sammy had now launched into 'That's Amore'. Ed's mind flashed back to Denise performing the same number wearing a barely there nude-coloured dress as they cruised around the Caribbean. After the show, she and Ed had passionate sex on her dressing-room table. Happier times.

'Hope's wedding is next June,' Sonia said. 'They're going to have eighty people. I think that's just right. Not so small…'

Ed took a deep breath. 'Let's not fight, Mum. We don't get to see each other that often.'

'Whose fault is that?' Liz said.

Sammy was now down on one knee, holding the hand of a thick-set lady in surgical support stockings and singing directly to her.

Ed watched him, fascinated. Life was so random. Sammy had talent, charisma and good looks. In fact, there was little to separate him from people who performed to packed audiences at the London Palladium.

Had Ed ended up where he was now because of bad luck? Or was it down to his own actions? He quickly pushed the thought away, not wanting to examine it.

Sammy launched into 'Cry Me a River'.

'It'll be a lovely wedding,' Sonia said. 'Hope's always been good at organising things. Ever since she was…'

If Ed was going to get anywhere with his mother, he was going to have to be placatory. 'I completely understand what you're saying, Mum. You've helped me out loads over the years and you shouldn't have to still be doing it.' He pictured himself old and poor in a place that made this look like its residents were living the dream. The way he was going at the moment, he probably wouldn't even have any visitors.

He shook the thought from his brain. There was no time for self-pity. 'The thing is, Mum, I've had several months when I've been out of work. And then I started up a business and, while I know it's going to be a big success, there have been lots of start-up costs.' Ed pictured the huge piles of unusable fancy dress costumes littered around the condo. 'And I've had to take out a loan on the condo that Shona and I own. I need to make a repayment tomorrow, so I was wondering if there was any chance you could help me out one more time?'

Liz turned to look directly at Ed. 'You took out a loan on your home?'

'Yes. I had no choi—'

'That was silly,' Liz said without rancour.

Ed dug his nails into his palms. His mother was really making him work for this. 'Yes, I guess it was.'

Liz nodded. 'I'm afraid I don't have any money to give you, Edward. I've had a lot of expenses recently.'

'Expenses?'

'Yes, this place for one. It costs a pretty packet, I can tell you.' She scratched her neck. 'And I also gave a large donation to Cancer Research.'

'Cancer Research?'

'Yep.'

Ed slumped in his seat. There was so much more he wanted to say. Isn't charity supposed to begin at home? Is 'Cancer Research' actually this bloke? But his mother had made it very clear she was done talking. Just as she'd made it very plain there would be no loan.

Cry me a river indeed.

Ed got as far as the car park before he remembered he only had £20.50 to his name. Which wouldn't even cover the train fare.

He sat on a low wall, put his head into his hands and screamed.

'You all right there, mate?' said a guy in chef's whites, emerging from the shadows with a cigarette in hand.

'Fine,' Ed said, wondering how many more humiliations today had left to offer.

He would have to go back into the care home. Walk back into that dining room and, once again, get out his begging bowl with all those people looking on.

'Don't suppose I could cadge a fag, could I?' he said.

The chef nodded and proffered a packet of cigarettes.

'Thanks,' Ed said as the chef lit it for him.

He hadn't smoked in twenty years but God it felt good.

'I'm Gerry,' the chef said.

'Ed.'

'Nice to meet you, Ed. Bad day?'

'You could call it that.'

Gerry nodded. 'Life's a bitch.'

'Thanks for the fag,' Ed said as Gerry disappeared back into the care home. He stood finishing his cigarette and fighting the urge to cry.

Eventually, when he could put it off no longer, Ed trudged back into the care home. Sammy was high-kicking his way through 'New York, New York' and Sonia was still chattering away to no one in particular. 'You're back,' she said, seeing Ed.

'Yes,' Liz said. 'Why is that?'

'Umm,' Ed said, aware of several pairs of eyes on him. 'I was wondering if I could borrow a bit of cash for the train fare home. I think I left my wallet in Emily's car.'

'A likely story,' Liz said, sighing. 'I've got a bit of cash in my handbag. I'm not sure exactly how much there is — enough to pay the hairdresser who comes here on a Thursday and enough to give Judith if I need her to buy something for me.'

Sammy finished his song and, after muted applause, there was a moment of near silence.

'Anna,' Liz said, beckoning over the carer.

Ed wasn't sure if he was imagining it, but his mother's voice seemed particularly loud. 'Please could you take my son to my room and give him my handbag. He's after my cash as per usual.'

Yes, yes, that's me, the scrounging good-for-nothing ne'er do well. Hi, everyone.

Ed briefly met Sammy's eye. He was pretty sure he saw pity in his face.

Ed stood in his mother's bedroom, his father's watch in his sweaty palm.

He could still picture the Rolex on his father's wrist. It had been an out-of-character purchase for him. Most of his clothes were bought by Liz and the only label one was likely to find in them was Marks & Spencer. John had loved that watch though. Ed could remember him explaining that each movement was made up of hundreds of carefully manufactured components.

Until tonight, Ed had believed in his heart of hearts that his mother would give him the money. Sure, he'd had moments of panic, but that's all they were, moments, because deep down he'd been certain that, once he saw her face to face and explained his home was at stake, his mother would relent. Especially if she saw he'd made things right with Emily. (He hadn't, of course, but that was something he couldn't allow himself to think about now. The full force of that pain was on hold.)

He stared at his mother's dressing gown hanging limply on the back of the door. He'd been shocked that she was unmoved by the prospect of him losing his home. She was obviously giving money to this bloke she'd met on the internet, yet she wouldn't help him, her own flesh and blood. She was probably even planning to give this guy the Rolex.

Ed ran his fingers over the cool, smooth surface of the watch. It must be worth about ten grand and it felt heavy in his hand, not like those flimsy things he'd tried to flog – it had about as much in common with them as a kebab van had with a Michelin-starred restaurant.

He glanced at the closed door. Did they have CCTV in these places? No, they couldn't do. Otherwise, they would have footage of the residents being washed and dressed. That wouldn't be right at all.

When his mother asked Anna to take him to find her handbag, he'd jumped in, saying there was no need. He knew where the handbag was, he'd seen it earlier. Plus, he knew Anna must be tired – the shifts here were long. Why didn't she just sit tight and enjoy the entertainment? Anna looked hesitant but Liz stepped in. Ed was right. He was a bloke, but he wasn't completely useless. He could manage to find a handbag on his own. Anna should stay right here and enjoy 'You Make Me Feel So Young'. Sonia chimed in: wasn't Sammy something? The kid could easily be in the West End if you asked her.

Ed had made his way towards his mother's room, sweating furiously. He'd greeted a carer walking in the other direction with a little too much enthusiasm and nearly tripped over a cleaning cart.

Now he stared at the watch. Heard his dad explaining to him that each Rolex took about a year to make. That's why they were an investment – something that would retain or even gain value. John had put the watch on Ed's slim nine-year-old wrist and told him that one day it would be his.

Those words came back to Ed now. Loud and clear.

Chapter Fifty-Six

I pull up outside my block of flats and turn off the engine. I'm not ready to go inside yet though.

The drive home has done nothing to calm me down, as an unwitting pedestrian discovered when she walked into the road without looking. 'Are you trying to get yourself killed?' I screamed. The poor woman looked horrified. As well she might have done. I'm normally disgusted by road rage.

How can I have been so monumentally, epically stupid? Why did I imagine that this time, unlike all the others, my father had changed?

I cannot go into the flat, just me, my thoughts and a zillion reminders of both Mark and Pebbles.

Where am I going to go, though? I can't face a pub or a restaurant on my own, and the park will be shut by now. I decide I'll have a little walk. That will do me good – clear my head. It is drizzling a little but who cares? It isn't like there is anyone around to see me soggy and frizzy.

I pound along the pavement trying to make sense of everything that has happened. I know I shouldn't be surprised my father has let me down. He has done it my whole life. The man has the staying power of invisible ink.

I stop to stroke a cat that is staring at me from on top of a dustbin, but it scarpers as I get too close. It's as if Pebbles has deployed a representative in his stead.

My father's flakiness is who he is. Even as a little kid and before my parents split, I had got used to the idea that he was mercurial. He'd *promise* he'd be home to read me a story, *assure* me he wouldn't miss my school play for the world, say he'd *definitely* take me to football. Sometimes he would, sometimes he wouldn't.

My mother made excuses for him: You know what he's like. I would end up being angry with her.

The rain is getting heavier and more insistent now and I regret not bothering to get an umbrella from the flat. I didn't want to go in there though. Every inch of it reminds me of Mark – another bloke who has left me high and (not) dry.

I come to a Catholic church with its lights on. Can I go in for a bit, just until the rain eases off? Is that okay when I'm not religious or does it mean I'll go straight to hell?

A crack of thunder makes up my mind.

There is some sort of service going on, although there aren't many people here. I take a seat near the back and hope no one will notice me.

My friends Sarah and Anthony got married in a beautiful Catholic church that was almost as ornate as the Vatican itself. This one, a single-storey 1960s building, is much more spartan, with plain white walls and little artifice. It doesn't even have stained-glass windows.

Mum and Dad didn't take me to church as a child, apart from at Christmas. I have always been envious of people who have real, genuine faith. How different Mum's death would have been if I thought it was part of an ever-loving God's masterplan and not some cruel and random gene mutation.

The priest looks similar to my father. Like I want to be reminded of *him*.

I bet he is cheating on Shona. For a second, I think about contacting her on Messenger: *Don't believe his bullshit.* I check myself quickly though – just because my dad is a toerag doesn't mean I have to be too.

Maybe that ship has already sailed though? I've spent the whole weekend planning a fake wedding and tomorrow I'm planning to tell a bare-faced lie about what happened with Tommy Cassidy. All quite toeraggy.

I shove such thoughts firmly to the back of my mind. I'm not nearly as bad as my father. I scratch my arm. My skin is sticky and itchy from the salt water. How long ago that sea swim seems.

The service appears to have drawn to a close and, oh Lord, a stout-looking woman in magenta is making her way towards me with a purposeful look on her face.

'You're new here,' she says. 'Welcome.'

I squirm on the hard wooden pew. 'Er, thanks.'

'Do join us for a cup of tea in the vestry. We'd love to get to know you and tell you a little more about the St Anthony's family.'

My mind cartwheels. I simply can't fake any kind of religious curiosity this evening. I've told enough lies to last a lifetime. 'That's very kind of you but I have to run.'

'Oh, that's a pity.'

'Yeah, my dad is over visiting from the States and tonight is his last evening here.' Nothing I just said was a lie. And the woman isn't to know I have no intention of spending one more second with my father.

Chapter Fifty-Seven

Ed

Ed was on the train back to London. He was nursing one of the most unpleasant cups of coffee he'd ever had in his life. His stomach churned as he thought back over the last few hours and the choices he'd made.

A middle-aged woman opposite looked up from the book she was reading and smiled at him. Normally, on a longish journey such as this, he'd get chatting to everyone in the vicinity. By the time the train pulled into London, he'd know what his new-found train buddies did for a living and would have looked at photos of their kids or dogs. He'd have offered to show them around Florida if they ever visited. Today though, Ed just gave the woman the briefest of smiles.

He took a sip of his horrible coffee and watched a toddler being chased down the aisle by his weary-looking mother.

The toddler, whose thumb was jammed firmly in his mouth, stopped next to Ed and stared at him intently. For a second, Ed had the notion that the child could see into his soul.

'Hello,' he said as the child scrutinised him.

The child's mother caught up with him. 'Sorry,' she said.

'It's fine.' Ed thought it was sad that people felt the need to apologise for their kids when they were just being kids. If he had his time again, he'd never apologise for Emily. But then, if he had his time again, he'd do a lot of things differently.

The toddler and his mum moved on and Ed picked up his Styrofoam cup and then put it back down again without taking a sip. Things were bad enough without disgusting coffee.

His mind flashed back to him standing alone in his mother's room, his heart hammering as he opened the bedside cabinet and reached for the watch.

The train whooshed through the darkness of the countryside, the trees and bushes in silhouette.

Ed had stood there holding the watch for what felt like forever. He wouldn't even have to sell it to get himself out of the hole he was in, he could pawn it – maybe even get it back at a later date.

A young couple at the next table had started bickering. She was fed up with him expecting her to do all the heavy lifting when it came to Christmas. At the very least, he should buy the presents for his family. Fine, her partner spat back, although he didn't know why she was fussing about Christmas in October.

Ed had put the watch back in the drawer, shut it firmly and then walked out of the care home.

He was a lot of things. But he wasn't a thief.

Chapter Fifty-Eight

I am collecting my father's various belongings from where he has scattered them about the flat. I am also trying very hard not to think about the poster I saw at St Anthony's. (Or, for that matter, *everything*.)

I'd asked magenta lady if there was a toilet I could use before I left. Then, as I was following the directions, there right in front of me was a huge poster:

> *First take the log out of your own eye, and then you will see clearly to take the speck out of your brother's eye.*

It may as well have read: *Emily, you raging hypocrite.*

I shake the thought from my mind. I am nothing like my father. At least, my behaviour this weekend has been out of character.

I pick up my dad's anti-ageing moisturiser, which, inexplicably, is in the fruit bowl, and stuff it into the rucksack on top of the ridiculous yoga pants. He has always been a messy sod. I am a 'place for everything, everything in its place' type, just as my mum was. A recurring memory from my childhood is the three of us searching high and low for Dad's keys or wallet or jumper and my mother saying, 'Oh, Ed.' There was a world of frustration in those two little words.

The box containing the watch my father left for Mark is still on the coffee table. I stuff it into the rucksack.

My father's book, a thriller with the obligatory picture of a woman in a red coat on the cover, is lying on the coffee table next to an empty mug. Naturally the book's spine is cracked, the hallmark of a monster. I pick it up to put it in the rucksack and the bookmark falls out. I gasp because it's the one I gave him on Father's Day when I was about six or seven. My drawings have been printed on to the leather – a wobbly rainbow, some flowers and an oversized bumble bee with a short, chubby proboscis. On the back, there is a printed message in gold type:

Thank you for being the best daddy in the whole world. I love you, Emily xx

A lump rises in my throat. I stuff the bookmark back at a random page and place the book in the rucksack.

So many things about this weekend don't add up in my mind. My dad cried when he saw me in that wedding dress – were those fake tears, just for show? What about the dinner at Cici when he told me he knew he hadn't always been the best father? Was there even a scrap of meaning behind the words or were they just what he thought I wanted to hear? And what about the moment when I told him he could give me away? I would have sworn blind he wasn't a good enough actor to fake the look of sheer joy but maybe I underestimated him?

The poster is seared into my consciousness. It is as if it is right there now in front of my eyes with its annoying close-up photograph of a huge pile of logs and its casually devastating message. That will teach me to go to church. I've heard of Catholic guilt, but I didn't realise you could be afflicted by it quite so quickly. I'd only been in search of the toilet.

My phone bleeps. I have stopped thinking it's going to be Mark, moved from denial to anger. How can he do this to me – casually destroy the future we have been planning our whole adult lives. Maybe I should think about deleting his number? That's what you are supposed to do, isn't it? So you can't do the dreaded drunk dial or fire off a rambling, impulsive missive. *Yeah, too late.*

The message is from Rachel:

Hope you're not too nervous about tomorrow. Remember, we're all 100% behind you. Just tell Clare the truth and you'll be fine.

Yeah, are you sure about that, Rachel?

Maybe I *should* tell the truth tomorrow? As a teacher, I am always on at the kids about honesty, and didn't my father suggest that as the only way forward when I talked to him about the situation at school? Perhaps he is right?

No, of course he isn't. He is the very last person in the world I should be taking life advice from.

I head for the bathroom, averting my eyes when I pass Pebbles' basket, empty and accusatory.

Dad has left his wet towels on the bathroom floor. Gross. The vanity unit is littered with his various unguents. I scoop them haphazardly into the rucksack, not even stopping to check the lids are on tightly. He doesn't deserve me to worry about such things.

I stop as I come across a sausage-shaped piece of muslin packed with what appears to be dried herbs. It looks like the world's largest bouquet garni but then what is it doing in the bathroom? I stuff it into the rucksack.

Back in the living room, I notice my father's leather jacket hanging over the back of a chair. Like there aren't perfectly good coat hooks by the door. I pick up the jacket and am shoving it into the rucksack when something flutters out of the pocket – a business card. *Geraldine Hobbs, Design Director.*

Who the hell is Geraldine Hobbs? Shona's cheating allegations bubble to the surface of my consciousness.

Not my problem though. I zip up the rucksack and put it outside the door to my flat. My father will be here soon, I'm sure, and the last thing I want is to see him.

I close the door behind me, sink down to my haunches and put my head into my hands.

I *am* taking the log from my own eye. I am *not* a raging hypocrite. And I am *not* my father.

Chapter Fifty-Nine

Ed

Ed stepped off the train and made his way through the crowds in Paddington station.

If he'd taken the watch, he wouldn't have to worry about tomorrow's repayment on the condo. Now him keeping his home, and more importantly Shona, was up to the poker gods. The plan was to pull an all-nighter, play his heart out and place big bets (go big or have no home).

He manoeuvred his way around a rowdy crowd of teenagers who were laughing and clowning around. Oh, to be so ebullient. Not to mention young.

Ed's phone pinged and he fished it out of his pocket, hoping against hope it might be Emily. He knew he'd screwed up big time, and desperately wanted a chance to talk to her; an opportunity to explain that this visit hadn't just been about the money.

It wasn't Emily, of course. It was Jared, a bloke Ed used to work with on cruise ships many moons ago and hadn't spoken to for at least ten years. Aware that Emily's sofa bed was unlikely to be an option for tonight, Ed had messaged Jared and everyone else he could think of that lived in London. Any chance he could cadge a bed for the night – it would be lovely to catch up.

Been a long time, man! Would have loved to have seen you but I live in Leeds now. Another time! J

Ed let out a hefty sigh and dialled the number of the one person left. 'Uncle Rick,' he said, trying to sound considerably more enthusiastic than he felt. 'It's Ed.'

'Who?'

'Ed. Edward. Liz's son.'

'Oh, *you*.'

Uncle Rick had never liked Ed much, although to be fair it was hard to think of anyone he was actively keen on, unless you counted his long-suffering pug, Him.

Ed explained he needed a bed for the night. No point in peddling the 'nice to catch up' schtick here. Uncle Rick was hesitant, and Ed considered abandoning the mission, but the thought of kipping on a park bench was even less appealing than begging his misanthrope of an uncle.

'Well, I suppose I can put you up for one night,' Uncle Rick said eventually. 'Don't be expecting me to put the bunting out though. This is just out of pity.'

Terrific. Looking forward to seeing you too!

Ed trudged down the steps to the tube. Before going to Uncle Rick's, he had to stop off at Emily's to pick up his stuff. He was also hoping he might get a chance to talk to her. He wasn't feeling overly optimistic though. His exchange with her in the care home car park had led him to believe that the reception he'd get from her would make the one he'd got from Uncle Rick look gushing.

Ed stood in front of the ticket machine. He tapped the screen and was told that the fare was £6.70. Jeez, that was pricey. He scrabbled in his pocket and saw he had £25.90. The minimum bet for a poker game was £20 though.

A wave of misery washed over him. Give a guy a break.

He looked around the underground station, trying to decide if he could bring himself to ask anyone for eighty pence. The young couple exchanging a passionate kiss goodbye? The eyes-down woman with the bright red wheelie case? The scruffy-looking man with a sign...

Ed had been on the cusp of begging money from someone who was homeless. This was who he was now.

He looked back at the ticket machine as if the price would somehow magically have changed. And then he was hit by a flash of inspiration. Emily's was about an hour's walk from here. What's more, by some stroke of the luck that otherwise seemed to have deserted Ed, Uncle Rick was only fifteen minutes or so from her. Which meant that he could complete all this evening's journeys on foot.

Ed walked back up the steps, stopping to give a quid to the homeless man, who thanked him and told him to have a good night.

Yeah, doubtful.

Walking had lifted Ed's mood a little. It was good to feel the steady rhythm of his feet hitting the pavement, to be aware of the muscles in his legs stretching and working, his heart beating in his chest.

He'd forgotten just how beautiful London was at night. The famous landmarks lit up against the night sky, the welcoming glow of cosy-looking pubs, lights glittering across the Thames.

Ed was feeling more positive too. He was going to win back the money for tomorrow's repayment on the condo and he was going to win back Shona.

Emily was going to be a tougher nut to crack. He would find a way though. He'd do whatever it took.

He was also going to talk to her about this guy Liz had got

involved with. His mother clearly wasn't going to listen to him – and really who could blame her? – but Emily might well be able to talk some sense into her grandmother.

The maps app on Ed's phone directed him down a narrow side street. The cobbles made him think of the street Helen Yately Brides was on. Hard to believe that was only yesterday.

'Excuse me, mate, you got the time?' The young lad seemed to have appeared out of nowhere.

'Yeah, it's—'

Before Ed could utter another word, his phone was swiped from his hand.

'Wha—' Ed stopped before the word was out of his mouth, understanding dawning and cold fear flooding his belly.

'Empty your pockets.' The kid enunciated each word.

Ed stood there, his brain gelatinous.

'EMPTY YOUR POCKETS OR I'LL FUCK YOU UP.'

Ed glanced around wondering if there was any chance he could run.

Up ahead in the shadows were three other guys. Waiting. Nausea pumped through Ed's system. He needed twenty quid to play poker this evening. He fumbled in his jacket pocket, his fingers slick with sweat.

A memory crashed into his consciousness of him and Catherine talking to a teenage Emily about what to do if she was ever mugged: Hand over whatever they want. Nothing is worth putting yourself in danger for.

This was different though.

'I haven't got much,' he stammered, handing over a paltry stack of coins.

The kid grabbed his forearm and squeezed so hard it made him gasp. 'I SAID EMPTY YOUR POCKETS.'

There was no choice. With trembling hands, Ed reached into his right pocket and turned out the flimsy cotton lining. Then he turned out the left pocket, complete with two ten-pound notes.

He watched as the kid and his mates disappeared around the corner and then he sat on the edge of the kerb, his whole body trembling.

A burger wrapper skittered in the breeze, oddly graceful.

He was dazed. The whole thing had happened in a couple of minutes, if that.

The cold from the stone kerb seeped through his jeans, and he started to shiver.

He couldn't believe he'd lost all his money and his phone. He had no way of playing poker tonight, which meant he had no way of getting the money for tomorrow's repayment on the condo. He started to laugh hysterically. It wasn't long before the laughter turned to tears.

Chapter Sixty

Without the distraction of rounding up my father's scattered belongings, I am poleaxed by both everything that has happened and the emptiness of the flat.

I am deafened by the silence and mocked by unclothed hangers, hooks without coats and a bathroom devoid of any products except my own.

I don't even have Pebbles here to ignore me.

And whose fault is that?

Guilt gnaws at my belly. He could have died, for God's sake. Because of me.

I open my laptop and search for pet-proof bins. Why has it taken something like this to make me do this? I start comparing options. Pebbles will not just have a pet-proof bin, he'll have the best pet-proof bin that money can buy.

The lies my father has told this weekend are jostling for position in my mind. I am angry with him but also with myself for being suckered in by him. (Surprise: the leopard's spots are unchanged.)

But there's another reason to direct the anger inwards too – the one nailed by that ugly poster at St Anthony's with its curled-up edges. Am I really as different to my father as I like to think I am? I have also lied and lied. I've allowed my father to buy me a wedding dress, let him put down the deposit on a wedding venue. And, even if I tell myself he deserves no better, what kind of slippery moral slope is that? I have also lied at work. What if I am not the Good Person I like to think I am? As the old adage goes, it's not until people are under pressure that you see who they really are.

I settle on a pet-proof bin with over a thousand five-star reviews. It's stainless steel, so will show every fingerprint and drive me crazy, but as long as it's safe for Pebbles I don't care. I should have got one ages ago. Maybe as well as being less honest than I thought I was, I'm also less responsible? Like my father.

Wait, though. Doesn't everyone always tell me I'm like my mum? She herself used to call me a 'chip off the old block'. Just this afternoon, my grandma went on about how I remind her of Mum.

I look across the room at Pebbles' empty bed, suddenly noticing how old and shabby it is. I should have replaced it ages ago. I type *luxury cat beds* into Google.

The Sleepycatz luxury igloo bed is our softest and comfiest bed. Ideal for even the fussiest of felines!

I add it to my basket. I'll buy Pebbles some new toys as well. He has shown precious little interest in any plaything before now but maybe I've just never chosen the right ones? I want to make everything perfect for when he comes home tomorrow.

A memory pierces my consciousness, sharp and jagged. Me, aged seventeen, trying to make everything nice for when Mum came out of hospital. I cleaned the house from top to bottom, cooked Mum's favourite supper of fish pie and bought a huge bunch of hyacinths for her bedroom. But when she came home, she was so sick and tired that she didn't even comment on how clean the house was. She couldn't eat more than a couple of forkfuls of the fish pie and the hyacinths had to be moved downstairs because the smell was making her nauseous. And I was cross with her, actually cross. And I covered it up, of course I did, but *still*.

I add a catnip-filled mouse toy to my basket. Apparently, it will satisfy Pebbles' natural hunting instinct and offer physical and mental stimulation. I also add a teaser toy and a turkey drumstick that squeaks. I have always avoided squeaky toys in the past for fear they will drive me insane, but maybe that's selfish? Like my father.

I've thought about that day when Mum came home from the hospital so many times over the years. Tried to find a way to excuse myself. Told myself it wasn't really about the clean house or the fish pie or the flowers, it was because Mum's diagnosis had been so out of the blue and so devastating and I was in shock.

But she must have been in shock too. I remember her National Trust wall calendar. The entries, in Mum's small loopy handwriting, went from 'Coffee with Sue' or 'Pick up dry cleaning!' or 'Book group' to 'Chemo appointment' and 'Hospice visit' and 'Funeral director' with no warning. And she was still nice.

I start looking at cat towers. They're both ugly and pricey.

Sometimes my mum's niceness annoyed me. After she was diagnosed, she was so worried about letting people down at work she didn't tell them how ill she was, instead offering up her full month's notice. I thought she was being ridiculous. 'You've got weeks to live and you're spending them pacifying people who are disappointed with the performance of their steam mop, or don't think their twelve-hole mini-muffin tin is suitably non-stick.'

I add a cat tower to my basket.

My mum almost always pushed her own needs to the bottom of the list, from letting my father walk all over her, to saying she had no time for the drawing she loved (we found box after box of unopened charcoals in the loft after she died), to never visiting her best friend, who'd moved to the south of France ten years before she got ill. Even Mum regretted the latter, commenting in an uncharacteristic moment of self-pity that we always think we have all the time in the world.

Will I be saying the same one day about travelling?

Maybe I am like my mum? But that's not all good either?

The thought is as shocking to me as if someone has suddenly revealed the world to be flat. For me, things have always been binary: my mum equals good, my dad equals bad.

For all Dad's faults – and I could happily punch him in the face right now – he does have an enviable knack of squeezing the joy out of every day. He takes risks. He lives.

I shake the thoughts from my brain and pay for the Pebbles haul. Best to focus on the practical right now.

Chapter Sixty-One

Ed

E d stood outside Emily's block of flats. He took a deep breath and rang the buzzer.

'Your rucksack is outside the door to my flat,' Emily said, buzzing him in.

Not the best start but then what did he expect?

He climbed the stairs. It was some time since the mugging, but he was still shaking. Ridiculous really – he didn't have so much as a scratch on him and the whole thing had been over in less than a couple of minutes. It would take him a long time to forget the look in the kid's eyes though.

Tchaikovsky seeped from under the door of one of the other flats and Ed tried to imagine the people inside. People having a nice, normal Sunday evening. No muggings, no family show-downs, no drama.

His rucksack slumped alone in the hallway. Ed knocked on Emily's door.

Nothing.

He knocked again. 'Emily.'

Nothing.

He knocked harder. 'Emily, please.'

She threw open the door. Her eyes were red and puffy, and guilt stabbed at Ed's guts. He'd done this. Again.

'I don't want to see you,' she said.

'Just give me five minutes.'

'Why should I?'

The old Ed might have mentioned the mugging now; played the sympathy card. 'Because I'm asking you to. Because I have things I want to say to you.'

'Has it occurred to you I might not want to hear them?'

'*Please*. Just five minutes.'

Emily said nothing but wordlessly stepped aside.

In the living room, Ed waited for Emily to ask him to sit down, but when no such invitation was forthcoming he started to speak. 'I want you to know that I'm truly sorry—'

'You're always sorry, Dad.'

'I know. Listen, Grandma is not going to give me a penny.'

'Shame you've had such a wasted trip then, isn't it?'

Ed steeled himself to ignore the hostility. He deserved no less. 'The reason I'm telling you is because I want you to believe that I have nothing to gain financially.'

Emily stared at him, her face stony.

'This visit wasn't just about money, Emily. And I get that's hard for you to believe right now but it also happens to be the truth. I do want to make amends with you for all the times I've let you down in the past, I do want to do better, and I do want to be part of your life.'

'That's a lot of "I dos",' Emily said, laughing mirthlessly. 'By the way, who's Geraldine Hobbs?'

'*Who?*'

'Don't play the innocent with me. Her business card fell out of your jacket pocket. It made me think of Shona being convinced you're cheating on her.'

Suddenly Ed was able to place Geraldine Hobbs – the woman from the blackjack table. 'She's a woman I met on Thursday. She owns a design company, and she offered me mates' rates on wedding invitations and stationery for you.'

Emily screwed up her face. 'Right. And how exactly did you meet her?'

Ed hesitated. 'In a casino.'

'A *casino*?'

'Yes, I can expl—'

'So you're not sleeping with her?'

'No. Of course not. Listen, like I told you at the services, I'm not cheating on Sh—'

'You know what?' Emily said, cutting him off for the second time. 'I don't care. Let's get back to why you're here now. It isn't about tonight, is it? You're not trying to manipulate me into letting you stay over? Save yourself the price of a Travelodge?'

Ed shook his head. 'I'm staying at Uncle Rick's.'

Emily's eyebrows shot up. 'Uncle Rick's?'

'Yeah.' Ed ran his palm across his face. His mouth felt as though it had been wiped out with cotton wool. 'May I have some water please?'

Without saying a word, Emily went to the kitchen area, got a glass from the cupboard, half-filled it with water and slammed it down on the coffee table.

The water was lukewarm. Ed drank some and took a deep breath. 'Thank you for giving me a chance to talk to you now. I know you didn't have to after everything that's happened—'

'Which part, Dad? You turning up on my doorstep without

warning and pretending you were an alcoholic bravely getting through the 12-Step Progr—'

'I never sa—' Ed stopped himself. It didn't matter.

'You making up a big story about how you were desperate to make amends with me after all these years. Not just for my sake, but also for Grandma Liz's. So we could give her that tiny bit of joy and closure in the twilight of her years. You faking an interest in my wedding.' Her voice went up an octave. 'Which part of this visit would you say has been sub-optimal?'

Ed felt a muscle start to pulse under his eye. 'Shona told me this thing once about how, when she'd been very drunk one night, she got into a fight with her sister, and she punched a hole in her sister's living-room wall. Then, when she was in recovery, Shona told Joanie she was sorry, and Joanie said that was fine, but she had to fix the wall.'

'And how does this relate to us?'

'Our relationship before I left your mother was the wall – smooth and strong and flawless. And every time afterwards I let you down or didn't show up for you, I punched a hole in the wall. And then, instead of trying to fix things the right way, do you know what I did? I tried to paper over the holes.'

'*Oh, please.* Spare me the dodgy analogies.'

'Okay, how about this? I've been letting you down since you were eleven years of age. When I left your mum, I promised you it wouldn't make a difference to my relationship with you, but I broke that promise. I wasn't there for your first day of secondary school. I missed parents' evenings and sports days and school plays. I didn't know you'd had an operation to remove a burst appendix until two days afterwards. I came back when your mother was ill and tried to help out, but I left when the going got tough…' He swallowed hard. 'When you needed me most of all.'

He took a sip of the lukewarm water and cleared his throat. 'With your mum gone, I needed to step up more than ever, but I didn't. Since you've become an adult, we've become more and more distant. I know you're a teacher but, until I went to the Science Museum with you last Friday, I wouldn't have been able to tell you how old the kids you teach are. I barely know the man you're going to marry and, yesterday morning, when I made you a cup of tea, I had no idea of how strong you like it.' His voice cracked. 'A dad should know the exact Pantone reference of how his daughter likes her tea.'

They were both crying now, and Ed desperately wanted to put his arms around Emily, but everything in her body language forbade it.

'Why are you telling me all this?' she said.

Ed swiped his palm across his face. 'Because nothing I can do can change the past. I wish to God it could, but it can't. But what I can do is stop papering over the holes in the wall. I need to stop dodging the difficult conversations, own the damage I've inflicted and stop making excuses. I need to show you that I've changed, that I want to put the work in, and I will always show up for you from here on in.'

There was a long silence punctuated only by the thrum of the traffic outside and the whisper of the classical music from downstairs. Ed pictured the people settling down for their after-dinner coffee. It would be served in doll-sized, bone china cups and accompanied by foil-wrapped dark chocolate mints.

Eventually Emily spoke. 'It's all just words, Dad.'

He shook his head. 'No. I want to change. I want to fix the wall. Really fix it. I can't change the past, Em. I wish I could, but I can't. I can do things differently from now on, though.'

Emily's eyes filled with fresh tears and Ed wondered if he

dared reach out and hug her. They both stayed as frozen as if they were playing musical statues, though.

After what seemed like forever, Emily wiped her eyes with her sleeve and looked straight at Ed. 'It was a good speech, Dad, but I've heard a lot of good speeches from you. And, you know what, words are cheap.'

'Emi—'

She held up her palm to silence him. 'It's too little, too late.'

Chapter Sixty-Two

My dad asks if he can use the bathroom before leaving. I'm not sure if it's some sort of delaying tactic – who knows with my father? – but I can hardly say no.

I slump down on the sofa, overcome with exhaustion. Just over a week ago I still had a perfect life.

The buzzer rings and I wonder whether to ignore it. It will be some poor person trying to get me to sign up for a monthly standing order to their charity. Either that or Jehovah's Witnesses wanting to save my soul (too late).

'Em, it's me.'

Mark?

What the hell? I buzz him in, throw open the door to the flat and watch him coming up the stairs.

'Why didn't you use your keys?' I say. *Yeah, Emily, because that's the most important question right now.*

'I didn't want to—'

Mark is interrupted by my father emerging from the bathroom. For a second, I'd forgotten he was still here.

I am hit by a sudden and unwelcome realisation: my father has just come face to face with the man he thinks is still my fiancé. I am busted.

'Ed,' Mark says. 'I didn't know you were in England.'

'Yeah, just until tomorrow night.' Dad shakes Mark's hand. 'Good to see you, mate.'

How can he be so perky? A few minutes ago, he was in tears, but perhaps that was all fake?

'How was your business trip?' Dad says.

Mark's face crumples in confusion. 'Business tr—'

'Dad was just leaving,' I say, fighting the urge to physically push him out of the door.

'Emily and I have spent most of the weekend planning the wedding,' Dad says.

I stare at the floor, my face flaming and my heart racing. I can't bear to look at Mark. 'I'll call you, Dad.'

He takes the hint, scoops up his jacket and rucksack and shakes Mark's hand again. 'Good to see you.'

I follow my father out onto the landing, pulling the door to. 'I won't be calling you,' I hiss. I am furious he made me look an idiot in front of Mark – the tragic little soul who can't accept the wedding is off. Rationally, I know this isn't his fault, but that doesn't stop the white-hot anger pumping around my body.

'Everything okay with you and Mark?'

'Yes, of course it is. Just go, would you?'

He nods and I watch as he heads down the stairs. He looks old and tired and defeated, but I am damned if I am going to let myself feel sorry for him.

I take a deep breath and steel myself to go back into my flat and face the humiliation that lies on the other side of the door. I have no idea why Mark is here – maybe to discuss selling the flat – and now I have to cope with the shame of him knowing I have spent the weekend playing the part of bride-to-be.

'I can expl—'

'It's okay,' Mark says. 'I haven't been able to bring myself to tell my parents about the split yet either.'

My brain struggles to catch up. Mark not yet mentioning the break-up to his parents is a little different to what I have done. But I suppose he thinks 'we've spent all weekend planning the wedding' was my father's usual hyperbolic nonsense. He doesn't imagine for one second that we actually bought a wedding dress. Or walked around wedding venues with me feigning interest in where they suggested for photographs, what canapés were on offer and how they set up the room for the live band.

'May I sit down?' Mark says.

Why is he asking me if he can sit down in the flat he still half-owns? Have I really got away with what I've done? When did everything get so bloody weird?

We sit side by side on the sofa, my mind immediately serving me up a memory of the last time Mark sat in the same place.

'What's your dad doing in London?'

'Long story.' I don't want to talk about my father.

Mark reaches out and puts his hand on my arm. I can feel the heat of his skin through my shirt.

'Emily, I'm so sorry. I've had the worst week of my life. I've missed you so much. I don't know what I was thinking before. I love you. I've always loved you. I'll forget about the job in Manchester.'

Relief floods my body. Mark is saying all the things I have been desperate to hear.

'I know it's a huge ask, but I want to know if there's any way you can forgive me; pretend this never happened? I think I just got scared but that's crazy because the scariest thing of all is being without you. I'm not even sure I know how to do life without you. We've been together all our lives, haven't we? We grew up together. You're the Dec to my Ant.'

'That's true,' I say, through the tears.

Mark reaches out and pulls me closer towards him. He has big dark rings under his eyes. He has been suffering too. Not out shagging other women like I imagined.

'Please forgive me, Emily. Please say you'll still be my wife.'

I look into the face I know almost as well as my own. I see the sixteen-year-old version of Mark, shy and awkward as he leaned in to kiss me for the very first time; I see the Mark who held me while I sobbed after Mum died and the Mark who proposed to me in the Howarths' garden.

Less than an hour ago, I was reflecting on Mum's regrets about never getting to visit her best friend in France. I was vowing to myself that nothing was going to get in the way of my dream of going travelling. I heard my father telling me that someone can be a great person but not your person.

What the hell does my dad know about anything though?

I put my hand on Mark's warm cheek, stroke the scar he'd got falling off his bike when he was three. 'Of course I'll still marry you.'

Chapter Sixty-Three

Liz

Ed was lucky Liz's right arm was in a sling or she may well have thumped him.

Just turning up like that out of the blue, snooping on her *private* messages and then making all those snap judgements about Peter. Who he doesn't even know.

She paced up and down the tiny bedroom, too angry to sit, let alone read or watch TV.

She'd been thrilled when Emily and Ed arrived unexpectedly. Of course it was always delightful to see her granddaughter, but she'd been happy to see Ed too. It had been years since he'd last come to England and, although he'd blamed Covid restrictions, there were months before and after the pandemic where he hadn't made it over.

A woman Liz hadn't met before appeared in the doorway and said she was here to put her to bed. Like she was six.

'Already?' Liz said. 'It's early still.'

The woman's head went from side to side like one of those bobble-head toys. 'Nice to get cosy.'

Yeah, you mean it suits you to get us all tucked up in bed and out of the way so you can sit and gossip. 'I'm not really tired yet.'

The woman's head bobbled. 'You don't have to go to sleep.'

Thanks. Very big of you. 'Fine,' Liz said, forcing a smile. She didn't know why she was being difficult. At home, one of her biggest luxuries was to be in her PJs by eight o'clock.

Ed's words resurfaced unbidden. *He's not who he says he is. He's scamming you. This is textbook stuff.*

Who was more likely to be after Liz's money, though? Peter, who was a millionaire in his own right, albeit one with a few short-term cash-flow problems, or Ed, who had siphoned money off her all his life and, by his own admission, was now on the verge of having his flat repossessed?

'Horrible night,' Bobblehead said, pulling the curtains closed.

Judith hadn't gone as far as Ed, but she'd strayed into the same territory. How dare they both? Was it that hard to believe that Peter had genuinely fallen in love with her? Was she so old and so repulsive as to make that fantastical?

Did they think Liz was a fool? Again, how dare they? She had more sense than the pair of them put together. It was particularly galling to be on the receiving end of life advice from Ed, a man who had failed to hold down a single relationship or job in fifty-four years.

Bobblehead held up a pair of pyjamas in each hand. 'Which jim-jams?'

Jim-jams? Really? And that classic thing you do with children where you make them feel as if they have choices. 'The blue ones, please.'

Liz and Peter would show Ed and Judith just how wrong they were; they'd show the world. Liz knew in her gut that Peter was a good and decent man. The last few months with him had been wonderful. He had showered her with love and affection. She had never known anything quite like it. Her late husband had loved her, of course, but he was a man of few words. His way of showing he cared was always knowing when it was time to put the kettle on. Peter was unashamedly romantic. Sending her that huge bunch of white peonies, for example. It was about way more than flowers though. Peter made it clear that Liz was the epicentre of his universe – she was cherished and desirable, not old and invisible.

'Right,' Bobblehead said. 'Let's get you sitting on the edge of the bed, shall we?'

Liz hated the idea of Ed getting in Emily's ear about all this: Poor Grandma has been made a fool of. But Emily was a sensible girl. She wouldn't take her father's words at face value. She, more than anyone, knew he wasn't exactly Mr Reliable. And Liz would talk to Emily herself and explain that she and Peter were soul-mates just like Emily and Mark.

'Did you enjoy the entertainment earlier?' Bobblehead asked.

'Yes.'

'Voice of an angel.'

Liz winced inwardly at the cliché. Sammy did have a lovely voice though. Not that she'd been able to properly appreciate that. The whole thing had been completely spoiled for her by Ed.

It wasn't all soppy stuff with her and Peter, it was also a meeting of minds. He was one of the most knowledgeable, inquisitive, smart people she'd ever come across, and the two of them had talked about everything you can imagine, from politics to art to grief. Tears had rolled down Liz's cheeks as Peter talked so movingly about nursing his wife with terminal cancer. There was such tenderness in the way he described her final days. He didn't just talk about himself like a lot of men, though – he asked Liz question after question. As if she fascinated him.

'Ouch,' Liz said as Bobblehead yanked her jumper off.

'Sorry,' Bobblehead said, not sounding very sorry at all.

Peter was so witty too. Liz reckoned she'd laughed more in the last four months than she had in the last four years.

'There, all ready for bed,' Bobblehead said, her head moving so much it looked as if it might plop off and roll across the horrible green carpet.

'Thank you.' Liz got into bed.

'Oooh, looks as if someone is getting a phone call!'

Did this woman think she was simple? Liz snatched up her phone.

'Hi, my darling,' Peter said

Just the sound of his rich, honeyed voice with its flat Yorkshire vowels made Liz's clenched jaw soften and her whole body start to relax. 'Hello, my darling.' Was she imagining it or had Bobblehead's face registered palpable surprise? And what was she still doing in here, sticky-beaking? 'Thank you,' she said, pointedly.

Bobblehead disappeared and Liz sank back against the pillows. She was never going to take being in her own home, or good health, for granted again.

'How has your day been and how's your shoulder?'

'My shoulder is a little better, thank you. And, as for my day, well, Emily and Ed turned up unexpectedly.' For a second, Liz thought about saying more, but she could hardly tell poor Peter her son had accused him of being a scammer.

'How lovely,' Peter said. 'Did you even know Ed was in England?'

'Not a clue. I think he wanted to surprise me.' And extract money from me. 'How was your day? How's Michael?'

'It was good. I've just left the hospital. Michael is doing much better. I reckon I'll be able to come to England before too long. We'll be together at last.'

Liz's stomach flipped. *See,* she told Ed and Judith in her head. 'That will be wonderful.'

'It really will. I can't wait to hold you in my arms.' Peter laughed. 'Not that that's all I want to do to you, mind.'

Liz felt a smile spread across her face. 'By the way, I need your son's address so I can send you the watch. I'm going to ask Domenica if she'll take it to the post office for me tomorrow. She's the carer I trust most.'

'Probably best if you don't send it to Kevin's apartment. We're all at the hospital so much, it's more than likely there won't be anyone around when they try to deliver. I've got a parcel locker address for you.'

'Oh. Is that safe?'

'Of course. Have you got a pen?'

'Yeah.' A parcel locker sounded so hokey. And there was something else nibbling away at the edges of Liz's consciousness too. She wrote down the address.

'Thank you so much for helping me out again, my darling. The Murcia deal is all but complete now, so I'll soon be able to pay you back every single penny. And then I'm going to treat you to a wonderful holiday. I know how much you love to travel, and we can go anywhere you want to in the world – no expense spared. I think you'd like this place I stayed at once in the Maldives. Think white sands and crystal sea set against a lush green backdrop. All the villas are overwater ones, and you get your own private plunge pool and a butler to tend to your every need. The diving and snorkelling are out of this world…'

Liz let Peter talk, but she wasn't listening properly. Maybe she was being silly but there was just something that didn't feel right about sending the Rolex to a parcel locker. This was ten grand's worth of watch, for goodness' sake.

'…the food is incredible too. I've been lucky enough to eat all around the world, but, honestly, the food at La Roche is some of the best I've ever had. From what I remember, there are five different restaurants, including one that will grill you fresh seafood to order.'

'Lovely,' Liz said, as the thing that had been nibbling away at her clunked into place in her brain. 'I thought you said there was a concierge at your son's apartment block? You mentioned him the other day. He hailed a cab for you when we were chatting on the phone.'

Silence buzzed down the line. 'He's not always there.'

'Really? Isn't the whole point of a concierge that they are always around? That they're there to take parcels and stuff?'

Peter gave a small mirthless laugh that didn't sound like him at all. 'Jeez, Liz, yeah, I guess, but this one isn't, okay?' His voice softened. 'Listen, let's not fight about silly stuff. I'm exhausted and I know you must be.'

She was tired. It had been a long and emotional day. She was also dosed up on pretty strong painkillers. 'Yes. Sorry.'

Peter laughed – a proper one this time. 'You're forgiven, my darling. I told you before, you've got me wrapped around your little finger.'

The conversation continued for a few minutes after that. Peter chattered away about what a wonderful life they were going to have together and how it wasn't just things like fancy holidays he was looking forward to, but the normal stuff like the two of them sitting in the garden having a cup of tea or preparing a meal – 'I'll be your sous chef.' He was even excited about the prospect of them going to the supermarket together, for goodness' sake.

Liz made noises in all the right places, but she wasn't really listening to a word Peter was saying. Because she was tired, and she was on heavy-duty painkillers, but also something just wasn't right.

Chapter Sixty-Four

Ed

Ed was halfway down Emily's road when he reached for his phone and remembered he no longer had one. How was he going to get directions?

He briefly considered going back to Emily's, but she'd made it clear he was the last person she wanted to see right now. She couldn't get him out of the door quick enough and had barely given him a chance to say hello to Mark.

Well, what did you expect?

The lights from a convenience store loomed into view.

'Hi,' Ed said to the guy behind the counter, who was playing Candy Crush on his phone. 'I was wondering if you could give me directions to…' He suddenly couldn't recall the name of Rick's road. He *had* to remember it. If he didn't, he had nowhere to stay tonight. 'Bellevue Road,' he said, relief washing through his body.

'Don't know it.'

Ed's body sagged.

A tiny middle-aged woman emerged from behind the canned fruit. 'Take a right at the traffic lights on to Maple Street. Follow that for about a mile and turn left when you get to the garage. Bellevue Road is the third on the left.'

'Thank you,' Ed said. He went to pick up a bottle of water but remembered he didn't have a penny on him.

The temperature seemed to have dropped outside and he wished he had a warmer jacket. It was almost impossible to imagine that earlier that same day he and Emily had swum in the sea. Impossible for lots of reasons.

He was suddenly nervous about walking alone in the dark too. Streets that were almost identical to ones he had deemed beautiful earlier felt sinister, the quiet that was calm had become eerie. Ed's heart raced and his eyes darted back and forth.

As he turned off the main drag, he became aware of footsteps behind him. He crossed the road and so did the footsteps. Ed's mouth went dry. It couldn't happen twice in one night, surely?

He couldn't fight the rising panic though and, without thinking, found himself breaking into a run.

After what seemed like forever, he reached the low-slung, red-brick block where Rick lived. Ed doubted he had ever in his life been so keen to see his uncle.

'You took your time,' Rick said by way of a greeting. 'Thought you weren't coming.'

He showed Ed into a small dark living room that was dominated by a huge sagging couch. A true-crime documentary blasted from the TV and a plate with the congealed remnants of what looked like stew sat on a side table next to a half-drunk cup of tea.

Ed's stomach rumbled and he realised he hadn't eaten anything since the fish and chips at lunchtime.

'You look older,' Rick said.

Ed swiped his palm over his face. He'd like to attribute his uncle's tactlessness to him being eighty-two, but the truth was he'd always been that way.

'You're in here,' Rick said, leading him towards a box room with a single bed pushed into its corner. A wonky clothes horse covered in chewing-gum-coloured Y-fronts and brown and beige socks blocked the path from the door to the bed and there was no blind at the window.

Still, it was a lot better – not to mention safer – than sleeping on the streets.

The whole flat smelled of damp dog and Ed suddenly realised he hadn't seen the pug. 'How's Him?'

'Dead.'

'I'm sorry,' Ed said.

Rick shrugged his shoulders. 'Happens.'

Ed felt a wave of sympathy. The dog had been smelly and yappy and had bitten several children, but his uncle had loved him – well, as much as he loved anything. Without Him, Rick must be very lonely.

Just like you'll be when you're old.

'Bathroom's down there on the right,' Rick said. 'Shower doesn't work.' He turned and headed back into the living room where he planted himself on the couch.

Ed sat down next to him. 'I went to see Mum earlier.' He suddenly realised he hadn't managed to talk to Emily about his worries about Liz being scammed before she'd bundled him out of the door. He'd message her about it tomorrow.

The mention of his sister hadn't dragged Rick's eyes from the mug shots of serial killers on the TV.

'She seemed well,' Ed said.

Rick made a sort of grunting noise, although what it was supposed to convey was anyone's guess.

'Please may I use your cell… your mobile?' Ed said. It was obvious that neither a cup of tea nor conversation were going to be forthcoming, so he may as well retreat to his room. It had been a long and emotional day.

And he still had one more soul-destroying task ahead.

Ed lay on the lumpy single bed holding Uncle Rick's mobile phone. It had taken him a long time to convince the older man you can call America without it costing anything.

Now he just had to make himself dial the number.

Shona picked up almost immediately, her face registering shock when she saw it was Ed. 'I don't want to talk to you right now.'

Ed's mind flashed back to Emily saying exactly the same thing. 'Please don't hang up.'

'Why the hell not?' Shona said. 'Are you going to tell me some more lies? Refuse to say what you were doing on Monday afternoon or explain why you're jumpy as a jitterbug recently or why you're avoiding having sex with me. But then claim you're not a cheat.'

'Shona, I'm not cheating on you.' He saw her hand move towards the red button. 'Wait! Please, I can explain everything. That's why I called.'

Shona stayed on the line. 'Well, go on then, I'm waiting.'

Ed took a deep breath. He knew he had to do this. If he didn't tell Shona the truth about their financial situation now, then tomorrow she'd find it out from the bank. Ed had to make sure that didn't happen. He owed her that much at least. 'So here's the th—'

'Wait,' Shona said. 'Whose cell are you calling me from and where in the hell are you? It doesn't look like Emily's place. Are you with some woman now? Are you cheating on me while you're in England? I swear to God if you are, Edward, I'm going to ask Mary-Anne to cast a bad spell on you. She might be a white witch, but she can do bad spells as well, y'know. Oh, and I'm

312

also going to shoot you right in the nuts the minute you set your cheatin' ass back here.'

'Shona,' Ed said. 'I'm staying at my Uncle Rick's.'

'I don't believe you.'

Ed heaved himself off the bed, walked into the living room and turned the phone to face Rick on the sofa.

'Doesn't mean you weren't cheating before,' Shona said.

'You're making a video call?' Rick said. 'Don't tell me that doesn't cost anything.'

'It's called FaceTime,' Ed said to his uncle. 'And I promise you it's free.'

'Since when have your promises meant anything?' Rick muttered.

Ed shut himself back in the bedroom. He stared at the contents of his rucksack spewed across the bed. Emily had packed the watches he'd left for her and Mark. The message was clear: we don't want your presents or your presence. He looked at Shona and took a deep breath. 'Okay, before I say anything else, I want you to know that I love you. You're the best thing that's ever happened to me. Really.'

'Sounds like the kind of stuff a guy comes out with right before they tell you they've been cheating on you.'

Ed sighed. 'I'm not cheating on you. But you're right, I've been jumpy and distracted lately, and you are right that I didn't miss yoga because of a migraine last Monday.'

Shona started to cry, and Ed felt as if his heart might cleave in two. How many more people he cared about was he going to destroy?

'I've got myself into a bit of debt,' he said. 'Because of being out of work for a while and then the reselling business. The watches weren't quite what I'd hoped they'd be, and the fancy dress costumes can't be sold in the US—'

'What?' Shona said. 'You told me you had a big order for them.'

'I know. I'm sorry. The truth is the costumes don't meet safety standards for fire retardancy. Some bulls—' He stopped himself. No more excuses. 'I should have checked it all out before I bought them. Anyway, that's why I've been distracted and weird recently. Why I haven't always been in the mood to have sex.'

'How does that explain you lying to me on Monday afternoon?'

'I went to visit a loan shark.'

'A loan shark?' Shona said, her voice cracking. 'Oh, Ed. Everyone knows those fellas are bad news. You shouldn't have done that. You should have talked to me. I don't have the money to give you, we both know that, but together we could have worked something out.'

Ed felt sick. Shona was good and she loved him, and he absolutely should have told her the truth.

'Maybe we could even have borrowed a bit more against the mortgage?' she said.

The nausea tightened its grip.

'I have done that.' He could hardly bear to look at Shona. Her face was a mask of shock. 'The next repayment is due tomorrow, but I don't have the money to pay it. I thought I'd be able to get it in time, but I can't. I'm so sorry.'

'What happens if you don't make the payment tomorrow?' Shona said, her voice so small as to nearly be inaudible.

It was cold and damp in the box room, but Ed had started to sweat. He looked at the woman he loved and saw she was desperately trying to cling on to some shred of hope – some iota of belief in him and his ability to fix this.

'We lose the condo.'

Chapter Sixty-Five

Mark has gone back to his mate Josh's to collect his things (apparently, he thought it was too presumptuous to turn up with his suitcase earlier).

He nearly didn't make it out of the door. We started kissing and Mark said perhaps he could leave the stuff until tomorrow. He could wear these clothes to work, right? But the mention of work made me remember I had yet to write up my notes for tomorrow's meeting with Clare Wood so, using every ounce of willpower in my body, I pushed Mark away and told him we would pick up where we'd left off later.

Now I am sitting at the table staring at a blank page. Can I go through with this?

I have to.

I pick up my pen and start writing:

Monday 16/10: Phonics lesson.
Tommy Cassidy began to whistle.
Asked him to stop but he whistled repeatedly.

So far, so truthful.

Restated the request for TC to stop, which he eventually complied with.

Why, Emily, why did he comply? I push such thoughts from my head.

Wednesday 18/10: Mrs Cassidy asked to see me after school. She asserted...

I stop, my pen hovering above the notepad. It is hard not to think I am writing a script and not notes.

...She asserted Tommy said I had shouted at him. I assured her this was not the case

I sigh. Think about my dad saying that if I had shouted at Tommy, that was okay. I am a human being and human beings make mistakes. I should just be honest about what had happened.

But what does my father know about teaching? Or holding down a job? Or anything?

I shut my notebook and stand up. Hopefully, all the problems at work will soon be behind me and, in the meantime, I should focus on enjoying being back with Mark. I replay his words in my head: *I've missed you. I love you. The scariest thing is the thought of being without you.*

It is amazing. The best news.

Mark and I can carry on with our lives. I need never go on Hinge or Tinder or get sent dick pics. I won't have to see photos of Mark with someone else on social media and wonder if I have to 'like' said photos.

The vast majority of people don't even know we split up. I can wear the wedding dress that is hanging in my wardrobe next door. We can use Holly House as the venue (I know Mark will love it as much as I do).

The only reason I'm not ecstatic right now is because it hasn't sunk in yet. Also, what with all the awful stuff with my dad, today had been *a lot*. This looming meeting doesn't help either – as impossible to ignore as toothache.

I need to do something to calm me while I wait for Mark to come back. Reading. That's the answer. I pick up a thriller whose blurb promises it to be a twisty and engrossing story of betrayal.

I put it back on the shelf. I have had quite enough betrayal of late.

I pick up a book with a lilac cover. There's an illustration of a man and a woman standing at opposite ends of the title. A quote on the front describes the story as 'Heartwarming and uplifting'. Another says it is 'laugh out loud funny and deliciously romantic'. I read the first few paragraphs and then shove the book back on the shelf.

My fingers land on the *Insider's Guide to Australia*. I put it in Mark's stocking a couple of Christmases ago.

I read the intro.

Australia is the ultimate backpackers' destination, offering everything from natural wonders of the world to beautiful beaches (11,000 of them!) to shimmering cities. Our comprehensive guide tells you everything you need to know with itinerary suggestions, insider tips and off-the-beaten track treasures.

I flick through to a photograph of the Great Barrier Reef, majestic even on the page. I imagine snorkelling in its warm, turquoise waters and seeing myriad colourful creatures peeping out from vivid corals.

A few pages on is a picture of Uluru at sunset. It is breath-taking, its red landscape in the fading light otherworldly.

I come to a picture of Hyams Beach, which apparently has the world's whitest sand. I can almost feel it slipping between my toes.

I turn to the Queensland chapter and read about watching tiny turtles hatching from their eggs and scampering into the sea.

I can feel my heart thudding against the wall of my chest. I want to go to Australia and experience all these things for myself. I want to see kangaroos and emus and quokkas (deadly spiders, sharks and snakes not so much, but fear isn't a good reason not to do something). I want to see Sydney Opera House and the gigantic waterfalls of Kakadu and drive along the Great Ocean Road. I want to eat Vegemite and Tim Tams and shrimp the size of my hand.

I *want*.

And not when I retire either. Now.

The trouble is, I know Mark doesn't feel the same. The book I'm holding in my hands is unthumbed. It received a polite but muted response when Mark unwrapped it and has sat untouched on the bookshelf gathering dust ever since.

A fat tear rolls off my nose and lands with a splash on the Twelve Apostles rock formations. I wipe it away with my sleeve.

I hear my dad telling me that someone can be a great person but not your person.

Eurgh, once again I am considering life advice from *him*. Perhaps I am losing my mind?

Mark bounds up the stairs two at a time and I feel as if my heart is literally ripping apart inside my chest.

'I just grabbed the bits I need for the time being,' he says, putting his small holdall down on the floor. 'I'll get the rest of my stuff in the week. Right now, I was in a hurry to get back to you, though.'

He leans in to kiss me and I pull back. 'We need to talk.' It's an accident that I've used exactly the same words he had just over a week ago and I wince as I hear them come out of my mouth.

Mark's face is a mask of confusion and pain, and it is all I can do not to reach out and stroke it. To tell him not to look so worried.

I can't do that though.

We sit down on the sofa, which I make a mental note to throw in a skip at the earliest possible opportunity.

'When you talked about wanting me back you said the scariest thing in the world was the thought of being without me.'

'Yeah?'

'Well, that's exactly how I feel about you. We've been together for so long, we don't know how to be apart. We're scared by the thought of having to date new people, to learn how to live without the other person by our side, to be alone—'

'What are you saying?' Mark obviously wants me to get to the point, to avoid prolonging the agony.

I stare at the floor. 'I'm saying fear is a crappy reason for us to be together.'

'What are you talking about? I love you.'

A lump rises in my throat. 'I know you do. And I love you too. But I still think the main reason we're getting back together is because we're too frightened of the alternative. Also, I think we want different things. I want to travel, not "maybe someday" or even when we retire – but now.'

'You didn't mention that an hour ago.'

'I know. I'm sorry. I didn't want it to be true.'

There is a long silence, which Mark breaks. 'Okay, we'll travel. If that's what you want, we'll do it. We can go wherever you like. We'll quit our jobs, rent the flat and go.'

'But is that what you want?'

Mark doesn't answer for a beat too long.

'I don't want you to travel because it's what I want,' I say.

Mark shakes his head, clearly struggling to take in what is happening. Again, I fight the urge to reach out to him – to make all the pain go away for us both. I am finding out the hard way that being the one doing the dumping is every bit as hard as being the dumpee.

'So that's it then?' Mark says eventually, his voice cracking. 'I go back to Josh's and you book a one-way ticket to God knows where.' He rakes his hand through his hair. 'How the hell did this happen to us, Emily?'

'I don't know,' I say, stifling a sob. 'I think someone can be a good person but not be your person.'

I have cried all the tears. I lie awake staring at Mark's side of the bed. He could be here now, holding me. I have always felt safe in his arms.

I know I have done the right thing though. It hurts like hell, but it is best for the both of us.

I also know that tomorrow morning I am going to go into that meeting with Clare Wood and tell her that I did shout at Tommy Cassidy. That Tommy and not me has been telling the truth and that, as neurotic and overprotective his parents might be, on this occasion they happen to be right.

The thought of this makes me feel sick. I don't think I'll lose my job, but I'll certainly lose my reputation as a 'perfect' teacher, not to mention the trust of the colleagues who have come forward to support me.

It is what I have to do, though. My father was right about that too.

Monday

Chapter Sixty-Six

Ed

Ed woke up in the lumpy single bed and there was one beautiful nanosecond when he didn't remember anything that had happened yesterday. But then the memories crashed into his consciousness and with them a sea of faces.

Emily's twisted with disgust at all the lies he'd told her.

His mother furious that he dared suggest this boyfriend might not be what he seemed.

Shona's naked disappointment and hurt.

And, of course, the mugger's cold, dead eyes. The unlovely icing on the unlovely cake.

Ed sat up, the synthetic sheets sparking against the movement of his body. He rubbed his stiff neck. He'd slept terribly. Not only had he been tortured by his own mind but, whenever he had managed to drift off into a fitful sleep, Rick had woken him making yet another trip to the bathroom. Ed, whose own bladder was already not what it once was, had listened to the tortuous sound of his uncle squeezing out a few pathetic drops of pee, before flushing and shuffling back to his bedroom, only for the same routine to begin again after what seemed like just minutes. It was an unhappy glimpse of the future.

Ed walked into the kitchen and manoeuvred his way around the sagging clothes horse.

Rick was standing in the dingy, narrow kitchen staring out of the small window and watching a jogger with a disgusted look on his face.

'You're up early,' Ed said.

'I never sleep well.'

'Shall I put the kettle on and make us both a nice cup of tea?'

'If you like. There's some bread over there if you want toast.'

Ed felt a surge of relief. By some stroke of luck, he'd bought a return train ticket back to Heathrow for tomorrow and it had been safely in his rucksack at Emily's when he'd got mugged. What he didn't have was a penny to buy anything to eat or drink, and his flight wasn't until 8.15 in the evening.

After breakfast, which, despite Ed's best efforts, wasn't exactly a chatty affair, he told Rick he'd be out of his hair soon but wondered if he might borrow his phone one more time and also his computer.

Rick looked anything but certain that was okay but handed over his mobile and logged Ed into the ancient-looking PC.

Back in the poky box room, Ed thought of his daughter. He knew she was nervous about her meeting with the headteacher this morning. At least Mark was back now. Perhaps at this very moment he was reassuring her that she could do this, and he was by her side and there to support her no matter what.

Ed keyed in his mother's mobile number, which came up on his uncle's phone as 'Liz, sister'. As if there were a huge number of Lizes in Rick's life.

He listened to the ringtone, fighting the urge to hang up. He was still angry with her but he didn't feel good about the note they'd left things on last night, He'd barely said goodbye.

The phone rang and rang. It wasn't like his mother not to answer. He'd have to try her again later. He wondered vaguely if, when he did speak to her, he should make another attempt at talking to her about the new boyfriend. Despite his mother's vehement defence of the guy, Ed was convinced something didn't smell right.

He went back into the living room where Rick was installed on the sofa watching another true crime documentary. Ed wondered if that was what he did all day every day. His uncle's life terrified him: the dinky bottles of milk, half loaf and ready meals for one, the single cup and plate on the drainer, the clothes line with just his washing. Ed suddenly remembered something his mother said to him when he first left Catherine, 'You remind me of my bloody brother. Life gave you every card it has to offer, and yet you treat happiness as if it is something to be squandered.' At the time, Ed instantly dismissed it – he was nothing like Uncle Rick and his mother was just angry and spiteful. But now, her words floated up to haunt him. He thought about a photograph he'd seen once of Rick in his Oxford days. He was sitting in a punt surrounded by other young attractive people. The sun was shining, and the smiles were bright. According to Liz, a few years later Rick's fiancée left him for his best friend. Ed couldn't get his head around the idea of someone's life being irrevocably changed by such a common or garden catastrophe. He couldn't fathom the difference between him and his uncle not being as big as he liked to think. Best not to dwell on that now though. 'I'm just going to use the computer. Won't be long.'

Rick grunted.

Ed pulled up the recruitment company's website. Last night on the phone to Shona, he'd told her he remembered what she'd told him about 'fixing the wall', that he knew that when he told her he was sorry those were just words, and that he was going to show her he was prepared to do the work.

He skimmed the list of jobs, hoping against hope there would be something new.

He asked himself for the umpteenth time if this was a mistake. Maybe he could make the reselling business work? Sure, he'd had a couple of false starts, but Shona's mate was making good money flogging crystals.

In sunshine-filled, glamorous, monied Los Angeles lurked one of the most notorious serial killers in American history. Witness this shocking story of violence and depravity...

How could Rick watch this stuff? Like his life wasn't depressing enough.

Ed scrolled down to the telesales job at Spectrum. The job he'd walked out on, telling his protein-shake-guzzling, micromanaging, business-talk cliché spewer of a manager Brad that he'd rather 'eat raw sewage than be in the same office as him one more day'.

Would Brad even take him back after that? Ed reckoned he would. His sales figures had always been good, and Brad cared about the numbers above all else. It wasn't just that though – Ed returning with his tail between his legs would give Brad more joy than bench pressing 140 kilos. He'd act gracious, adopt a power pose and give Ed a poor man's TED Talk about redemption and second chances.

Ed started to fill out the application.

Crimes so horrible that seasoned police officers needed treatment for PTSD...

Maybe there was another way? Ed could retrain for something. Find a job he actually enjoyed, something that made him want to leap out of bed in the mornings. What though? He was fifty-four – hardly a sought-after candidate for NASA.

The blood spatter pattern showed...

He could write a novel. Everyone said he told a great story. He'd set it on a cruise ship. The main character would be a handsome Elvis tribute act who seduced all of the beautiful women. One day, there would be a murder on board.

Hope coursed through Ed's veins. His novel would shoot up the bestseller lists, be turned into a miniseries for Netflix. He'd win literary prizes and journalists would interview Shona and Emily and Liz about how proud they were of him.

Charlene was a model student. She was a cheerleader and popular with her peers...

The only problem was that a novel would take a while and Ed needed money now. Plus, who was he kidding, he found it hard pinning himself to his chair long enough to write a few emails so 90,000 words was going to be a stretch.

Ed finished the application and his finger hovered over the send button. If he wanted to have another go at making a reselling business work, he could do that on the side. In the meantime, though, he needed a steady income. A monthly pay cheque that would hit his account no matter what.

Neighbours said he'd always seemed like a normal guy. He kept himself to himself, but he was polite and friendly when you saw him on the street...

Ed pressed send.

When it came to trying to repair the damage he'd done to his relationship with Shona, he had to do the work.

Literally.

Chapter Sixty-Seven

I put the cat carrier down in the sitting room and open the door to the sorry sight that is Pebbles. He has a large surgical dressing on his abdomen and wears a cone and an expression of disgust.

'I'm so sorry, Pebbles,' I say, sitting down on the floor next to him.

I glance at my phone. Only a couple of hours until my meeting with Clare Wood. My stomach churns just thinking about it, but I know I am doing the right thing. How can I possibly teach kids the value of honesty and then lie myself?

I'd been worried about leaving Pebbles alone, but the vet assured me it was fine as long as he is wearing the cone and can't get outside. All I have to do is keep an eye on the wound, administer his painkillers and give him lots of love. I resisted the urge to tell the vet Pebbles does not welcome my love.

'I hope Mark is okay,' I say.

Pebbles doesn't reply.

'And Dad.' The words surprise me as they come out of my mouth. 'I was really hard on him yesterday. I mean, don't get me wrong, he deserved a lot of it. But it's difficult to not feel a bit of a hypocrite, especially since seeing that bloody poster in St Anthony's.'

Pebbles doesn't pass comment.

'When I was little, Dad used to play with me for hours on end. I can still see him drinking a pretend cup of tea, his little finger extended. Telling Jemima the rag doll to eat nicely and Horace the hippo to sit up straight.'

I reach out to stroke Pebbles behind his ears, but he moves his head away.

'Mum often had to work on Saturdays and, although I would have felt bad to admit it, I loved those days when it was just me and Dad. We'd stay in our pyjamas until lunchtime, eating Coco Pops and watching daft kids' TV. In the afternoons, we'd go to the park and play cricket. I can still hear the ball thwack thwacking against the plastic bat. Dad would buy me an ice lolly, tell me to look over there, and then take a bite. Daddy, I'd say crossly, and he'd look all innocent and tell me it must have been a pigeon and to look at that one over there with strawberry Mivvi around his beak.'

Pebbles stares at me.

'On one of our Saturdays, he took me to the horse racing. It probably wasn't the most suitable activity for a nine-year-old, but I loved it, especially when Dad asked me to make his bets for him. Somehow, I chose the winning horse. God the pair of us screamed as it crossed the finishing line. On the way home, we stopped at McDonalds – where Mum would never let us go – and had celebratory burgers and fries.'

Pebbles puts his head to one side.

'I've lost so many important people. Dad, Mum, Mark. And now Dad again.' My voice cracks. 'When I was little, I used to wait to hear his key in the lock. I loved that he was so fun to be around, that he could always make me laugh and that everywhere you went with him people acted as charmed as if he was a celebrity. My dad was my absolute favourite person in the world.'

I feel something touch my leg. I look down to see Pebbles' paw.

The air is thick with the smell of overpriced coffee and freshly baked cinnamon buns. Clare picked them up from the expensive bakery on the high street – said they were a little something to make up for having to come in at half term.

I mumble a thank you.

'Please sit down,' Clare says.

The sun is streaming through the window, casting a literal spotlight on me as well as the metaphorical one. My lips are sticking to my teeth, and I take a sip of coffee, which burns my tongue.

'I do hope you weren't worrying about this all weekend?' Clare says.

'Umm—'

She swats her hand through the air. 'Oh, Emily, what a silly thing for me to say – of course you've been worrying.'

'A bit,' I admit. 'Also, I don't think my observed lesson in front of the Ofsted inspectors went that well. I hope I haven't adversely affected the school's rating.'

Clare pulls off a small chunk of cinnamon bun and pops it in her mouth. 'Actually, I chatted to the inspectors about your lesson, and they said you met all the criteria for EYFS and they were impressed.'

'Oh.' *Oh.*

Clare takes a sip of coffee. 'You're way too hard on yourself.'

I feel a small glow of pride. I didn't mess up my observed lesson.

'So about the letter from Mrs Cassidy.' Clare says, immediately puncturing that bubble.

I look at the scratched laminate flooring. My colleagues always tease me about being Clare's golden girl – the teacher who is a teacher's pet. It's a role I am reluctant to relinquish. It would be so easy to let everyone think Tommy's mother is making a fuss about nothing. There is no proof one way or the other. This is a simple case of 'he said, she said', and one where the 'she' has the distinct upper hand. 'Umm… I did raise my voice to Tommy. He kept whistling and it was very annoying, and I told him to "stop that now".' I swallow hard. 'Then I shouted.'

Normally, even when you are shut away in Clare's office, you hear the hubbub of a busy school – children laughing and playing, the bell going, a recorder being played with scant attention to a tune. But with it being half term there is nothing but deathly silence when Clare doesn't say anything. 'I see,' she says, after what seems like forever.

I can't bear to look at her. I have always liked the older woman, but I know that, for all her outward affableness, there is a quiet steeliness about her that only a fool would underestimate. She reminds me a little of my mum.

'And why didn't you tell me that on Friday?' Clare says.

'I… I… '

'Or be honest about it with Rachel and Natasha, both of whom have been advocating very hard on your behalf?'

I wish the dark wood laminate would swallow me up. 'I suppose I was ashamed,' I stammer eventually.

'I see.'

Again, the silence stretches between us. 'I'm sorry,' I blurt out finally.

Clare nods. 'I can forgive you raising your voice, Emily. Children can push our buttons and none of us are perfect. But I must admit to being rather disappointed that you lied about it. Not just to Mrs Cassidy but then subsequently to your colleagues and to me. You have made things so much worse than they needed to be.'

'I know.' I bite my lip and swallow back tears. 'Mrs Cassidy said she thinks I have a problem with Tommy and that I bully him but that's not true.'

'I'm glad to hear that.'

Not 'I know you don't' or 'of course you don't'. 'What will happen now?'

'You'll apologise to Mrs Cassidy and to Tommy and then I'll talk to Mrs Cassidy and let her know that, while I am disappointed in how you handled this particular situation, I am confident it does not indicate a wider issue. I will also reassure her that I will personally be keeping an eye on things from now on.'

I nod.

'Right, well, I'd better get on,' Clare says, standing up.

I rise, my legs gelatinous beneath me. 'I'm so sorry.'

Clare gives me a tight smile and then goes back at her computer.

I walk along the deserted school corridor feeling wretched. It would have been less awful if Clare had torn a strip off me, but the naked shock and quiet disappointment were far, far worse. Still, it is over now.

'Emily,' come voices behind me. I spin around to see Rachel and Natasha. 'What are you two doing here?'

'We wanted to be here when you came out of the meeting with Clare,' Rachel says.

'Yeah,' Natasha adds. 'A bit of moral support. I hope you gave her your side of the story?'

Chapter Sixty-Eight

Liz

With a shaking hand, Liz keyed in the number she'd found on the website. She wasn't quite sure what she was hoping to achieve but, if the number was real and his assistant Alba Perez was real, then surely she was making too much of the whole parcel locker thing?

'Casas Marga, Alba Perez.'

Liz swallowed hard. She'd achieved what she'd set out to and could just hang up. 'Do you speak English?'

'A little.'

'My name is Catherine Nicholls.' Sweat prickled Liz's armpits. Whatever had possessed her to use her late daughter-in-law's maiden name? Come to that, whatever had possessed her to make this call? 'I'm interested in one of the apartments on your website. The new-build apartments by the golf course.'

'Very nice.'

'Hmm, yes. Well, I was just wondering if you could tell me a little more about them.'

What was the point in this? She was being ridiculous. Letting other people get in her head.

'Really, you must to speak to Señor Curran about that. But he is not here at the moment.'

Of course he isn't. He's in America. Just as he told you.

'If I am taking your number I will ask him to telephone with you when he comes to office. He should be here any minute.'

Liz's blood turned to ice. It was probably just a language thing though. Alba's English, while five million per cent better than Liz's Spanish, wasn't great. 'You'll ask him to call me from America?'

'America?'

The hesitation in Alba's voice brought Liz up short. Of course this fictitious woman she was playing would have no idea Peter was in America. 'Señor Curran and I spoke before about these apartments. A few weeks ago. He explained then he had to go to America to visit his grandson in hospital.'

Silence buzzed down the line until eventually Alba spoke. 'I am being sorry, Señora, but I think you have made mistake. Señor Curran is not in America.'

Liz's mouth filled with saliva as she squashed down a powerful wave of nausea. 'Er, okay… thank you. Bye.'

'Wait please, Señora Nicholls. I did not get your telephone number.'

Liz choked back tears. 'It's okay. I'll call another time.'

'Okay, as you wish. Goodb—'

'Wait,' Liz said, gripping her phone so hard her knuckles turned white. 'Señor Curran. What does he look like?'

'I'm sorry, Señora Nicholls. I must not understand.'

'What does he look like? I know it's a stupid question but—'

'I must go.' Alba clearly thought Liz was nuts. As well she might do. 'I wish you good day, Señora Nicholls.'

'Please,' Liz said.

Alba hesitated and Liz could almost hear a shrug. 'He is not tall and not short. He has English skin and eyes blue.'

A perfect description of Peter. There must be some innocent explanation for the confusion about America. Maybe Peter didn't want potential clients to know he wasn't in the office?

'He is – I don't know the English word – *calvo.*'

Liz racked her brains for her schoolgirl Spanish trying to remember what 'calvo' meant.

'Goodbye, Senora.'

Poor Alba, no wonder she was desperate to get this lunatic off the phone.

Liz put down the phone, her heart racing. She knew the word 'calvo' but she couldn't for the life of her make it pop into her brain.

Wait, she could use the internet. It wasn't like the old days – everything was online. She put 'calvo' into Google Translate.

Bald.

Liz had been taken for a fool (there's no fool like an old fool).

She was pathetic, deluded, stupid.

She took off her sunglasses and dabbed furiously at her eyes with an already soggy scrunched-up tissue. She'd been at the bus stop for nearly an hour but couldn't find it in herself to care.

It had caused consternation in the care home when she'd said she was going for a walk. 'Where?' Domenica said.

'I don't know,' Liz replied. 'Just for a walk.' She was lying, though – she knew exactly where she was going. What she had to do. There were no other choices now.

Domenica must have mentioned the 'walk' to the manager because she appeared in Liz's room a few minutes later on the pretext of saying good morning. Like that was something she made a habit of.

'I just feel like a walk,' Liz said.

'But your shoulder—'

'Yes, far as I know you walk with your legs, not your shoulders.'

The manager sucked her teeth. She couldn't stop Liz though. Liz wasn't one of the dementia people behind the double set of key-coded doors. She wasn't even a permanent resident.

A bus trundled into view and Liz stuck out her good arm. On board, it smelled of stale sweat and cheap perfume. There were hardly any other passengers. Just a middle-aged man in an ill-advised football shirt and a harassed-looking woman with twin girls of about five.

Liz took a seat near the front. Ed and Judith had been right about Peter. Well, the man who called himself Peter – that probably wasn't even his real name. He'd never been in love with Liz. All his beautiful words and promises meant nothing. There was no happily ever after. No future.

Liz could hear the mother hissing at the kids not to stare. She knew without turning around that she was the focus of their attentions. She may be wearing sunglasses, but they did nothing to disguise her shaking shoulders or the small hiccupy sounds that kept escaping from her mouth. If she'd had the energy, she'd have told the woman not to worry, that she couldn't possibly feel any more shame. She was no less humiliated than the women they used to tar and feather and cart through the streets.

This was worse than when her husband had died. Then, people had sent cards and flowers and left casseroles on the doorstep. What would they do now? Laugh at her, probably. Poor old thing. Can you imagine being taken in like that? She must have been lonely.

Liz had been lonely. She saw that now, even if she'd be less ashamed to admit to having chlamydia or a secret penchant for torturing kittens.

To be lonely was the ultimate failure as a human being. From the minute we start to walk and talk, it's drummed into us that our worth is determined by the number of people we have around us and the connections we make.

Liz's phone vibrated in her pocket. Even before she looked, she knew it would be 'Peter'.

Good morning, my darling. How are you doing today? Xx

Can't believe we're going to be together soon. Counting the minutes xxx

Love you to the moon and back xxx

Bastard! How could anybody be so cruel? Liz had given him over £45,000 (fool!) – all her savings plus twenty grand she'd got taking out an equity release deal on her home (the home she and John had worked all their lives for). But the money wasn't the worst part. What really hurt was that Liz, who prided herself on being sensible and level-headed, had believed in him and in them. She had swallowed all his lies. She had loved 'Peter' with every fibre of her being. Now, her confidence was shattered, and her heart broken. He had destroyed her.

The bus came to a stop and the man in the football shirt stood up, his eyes stopping on Liz. Hadn't he heard the woman who said it was rude to stare?

It was another beautiful day outside and Liz squashed the idea that the bright sunshine and blue skies were mocking her somehow – underlining the fact that her misery didn't matter and neither did she.

The vibrations of the bus and the twisty country roads were making her feel slightly nauseous. Her shoulder was starting to hurt too. She was due a painkiller about now.

But Liz would need more than a couple of tablets to make her feel better.

She stared out of the window. She had one more bus journey after this one and then a short cab ride. Then it would be over.

Chapter Sixty-Nine

Ed

Rick was watching another true-crime documentary. Truly, Ed feared for his soul.

A prominent family who seemed to think they were above the law, until the death of college student Mary Beth Parker in a freak boating accident...

'Uncle Rick, I was wondering if I might be able to borrow your mobile one more time?'

The older man's eyes didn't stray from the TV. He grunted in a way that sounded vaguely affirmative. Ed would have felt he'd outstayed his welcome, but that would presuppose a welcome in the first place.

...crime scene experts described the scene as one of the most gruesome they've ever seen...

Ed picked up the mobile and headed back to the box room. He sat on the edge of the lumpy bed and pressed 'Liz, sister'. The phone rang and rang.

He ended the call and stared out of the smeary window. A red-faced woman was trying to coax a rigid toddler to sit in a buggy.

A prickle of worry nudged at the edges of Ed's mind. His

mother usually answered the phone. She could be doing anything, though – another care home activity, perhaps? Also, what exactly did he think was the problem here? If anything had happened to his mum, the care home would surely have called? And, apart from her shoulder, she'd been in perfectly good health yesterday.

Ed thought about this new bloke in her life. An image flashed into his mind of a masked man sneaking into the care home in the dead of night and bundling Liz into the back of a car, bound and gagged.

Ridiculous! He'd been watching too many of Rick's true-crime documentaries.

He stared at his uncle's chewing-gum-coloured Y-fronts. He guessed he could just give the care home a quick call.

'Eastwood House. Sandy speaking. Can I help you?'

Ed explained that he had been trying to get hold of his mother on her mobile, but she wasn't answering.

'Liz has gone out.'

'Gone out?'

'Yes. For a walk.'

'A walk?' Ed wasn't sure why he kept parroting everything the woman said. 'How long has she been gone?'

'Hmm, I'd say she left just before nine.'

'That's nearly two hours ago.'

'Hmm,' the woman said. 'So it is. I've been ever so busy this morning.'

'Right, I'll call back later.'

'Want to leave a message?'

'No thanks.' Ed pressed the red button. His mother was allowed to go for a long walk. There was no cause for alarm.

Chapter Seventy

'Still no answer from Grandma,' I say.

'She'll be fine,' Dad says in a way that sounds as if he is trying to convince himself.

We are in the car on our way to Broadstairs, exact destination tbc. Hopefully, Grandma will be back in the care home by the time we arrive, slightly bemused and irritated by us turning up: *I went for a walk. It's a free country, isn't it?*

I watch as the hedgerows speed past. I let Dad drive and, if that isn't a sign I am in a hurry to get to my grandma, I don't know what is.

I came out of my meeting with Clare Wood to see I had five missed calls from Uncle Rick's number and a message from my dad explaining it was him and that he'd lost his phone but needed to speak to me as soon as possible. I was already on the verge of tears and felt a stab of unspecific panic. I told myself it was probably just my dad doing his whole 'mea culpa' bullshit again, though, and wouldn't have even called him back if he hadn't phoned me again.

'What's that's smell?' I say, wrinkling my nose.

'Ah, sorry, I think it's me. Well, my clothes. Uncle Rick's whole house smells of dog. Which is extra cruel as Him is dead now.'

'Him is dead? Poor Uncle Rick.' I crank open the car window. 'So tell me again what you know about this new bloke in Grandma's life.'

Dad puffs out his cheeks. 'Not much. That they met online, and she seems completely smitten. She's adamant she's only lent him a few hundred quid—'

'Yeah, well, that's how it starts.'

Dad flicks on the indicators and moves into the fast lane. 'I know. Apparently, he has a grandson in the States who's in hospital following a serious car crash.'

'Eeek,' I say, shaking my head. 'The whole sick relative thing. How long has it been going on and why hasn't Grandma mentioned him at all?'

'I don't know. She got very cagey when I tried to talk to her about it.'

I stare out of the car window. One of my favourite things to do as a little girl was go to stay with my grandparents. What was that silly game Grandma and I played called – the one where we threw sticks into the rushing river to see whose would emerge first from under the bridge? Pooh Sticks.

I check my mobile for the umpteenth time. I sent Grandma a message asking her to give me a ring, but it has been ignored along with all my calls. I also tried phoning her landline number just in case she'd gone home, but there was no answer there. 'Maybe I'll give her friend Judith a ring? Grandma might be with her?'

'Good idea.'

Judith picks up straight away. Grandma isn't with her, and Judith hasn't heard from her today. She last saw her yesterday afternoon at the care home. 'You've got me worried now.'

'I'm sure there's no reason to worry,' I say, ignoring the sick feeling in the pit of my stomach. 'I'm just wondering if you've met this new guy Grandma is seeing?'

Silence buzzes down the line. Judith is clearly weighing up how much the friendship code allows her to say. 'I haven't. In fact, she hasn't either.'

My stomach drops. 'I see.'

'He lives in Spain. Apparently, he runs a very successful business as a property developer. He was going to come to England to see Liz shortly before she fell and broke her shoulder, but then his grandson in America was involved in a car accident.'

'Right. And do you know anything more about him? Did Grandma ever say anything to you about giving him money?'

Judith hesitates. 'She says he's got plenty of money of his own – that he's very successful. All I know for sure is that Liz is potty about him. I mean "potty" too – I've never seen her so love-struck. And, by the sounds of it, he feels the same way. They've talked about him moving back to England – he's originally from Yorkshire – and the two of them making a life together. It's all gone incredibly quickly. In fact, only yesterday I told her she should be a bit careful.'

'And how did that go down?'

'Like a cup of cold sick,' Judith says. 'God, I hope he's not taking advantage of her. I feel so responsible – it was me who cajoled her into going on the dating apps in the first place, you see.'

'I'm sure it's fine,' I say, feeling sure of no such thing. 'Listen, give me a call back if you hear from her, okay? And try not to worry.' I end the call.

'I really don't like the sound of this bloke,' Dad says.

'Me neither.' I glance at the satnav and see that we are thirty-two minutes away from Broadstairs. 'What's our plan when we get there?'

'Let's try the house first. We know she's not loving being in the care home, so it makes sense she would have gone back home.'

'Except she can't look after herself with her broken shoulder and she knows that. That's why she booked herself into the care home in the first place.'

'I know,' Dad says. 'But maybe she has just popped home for a bit. To check on the place or collect mail or whatever.'

'Then why wouldn't she have said that? Why pretend she was going for a walk?'

'I don't know,' Dad admits. 'But you know what she's like about people knowing her business. She's probably sitting in the garden with a cup of tea right now, completely oblivious to all the worry she has caused.'

'Probably. She could have switched her phone on to airplane mode by mistake. Mark did that once and I was almost on the phone to the police by the time he realised.' The mention of Mark makes my chest hurt. I wonder how he is doing right now. I can't afford to think about that, though. One drama at a time.

'How did your meeting with the headteacher go?' Dad says.

I shudder inwardly at the memory of Clare Wood's face. The naked disappointment. She'd been devastatingly clear in her assessment: *I can forgive the initial mistake, Emily, but you've made it a lot worse by lying about it. To so many people, as well.* 'Fine.'

'Sure?'

'Yes, of course I'm sure.' I scratch at a patch of eczema on the inside of my elbow.

Dad takes the exit off the motorway. 'Listen, about yesterday evening, I really meant the things I said. I am genuinely sorry I lied to you—'

I cut him off. I have told plenty of lies myself but now is not the time. 'Let's just focus on Grandma for now. I'm going to give the care home another call. I know I asked them to call me the second Grandma got back but I don't trust that Sandy woman. She sounded bored by me.'

'Eastwood House. Sandy speaking. Can I help you?'

'It's Emily Baxter. I called before about my grandmother, Liz.'

'She's still not back.'

My stomach drops. Grandma left the care home nearly three hours earlier. That is a hell of a long time for a seventy-nine-year-old woman with a broken shoulder to be on a walk.

'Ask to speak to one of the people who saw her this morning,' Dad says.

I pass on this request, which meets with an audible sigh from Sandy. Eventually a woman who introduces herself as Domenica comes to the phone.

'I'm just wondering if my grandma said anything to you about where she was going?' I ask.

'Only that she was going for a walk.'

'Right. It's just it's been a while now.'

'I know,' Domenica says. 'And, I don't want to worry you, but this morning she seemed not quite herself. She was quiet and her eyes were red and puffy. Sonia – she's one of the other ladies here – said she could hardly get a word out of her at breakfast, and she didn't touch her porridge.'

I thank Domenica for her time and end the call. 'Drive faster,' I say to Dad.

Chapter Seventy-One

Liz

Liz was standing on the bridge where she and Emily used to play Pooh Sticks, tears streaming down her cheeks.

It had taken her an eternity to get here. The wait for the second bus hadn't been as long as for the first one, but the bus seemed to travel at the speed of a milk float and stop at nearly every stop. Liz had had to take a taxi for the last bit of the journey. The cab driver had asked her how she was going to get herself back. Did she want him to pick her up at a prearranged time? Liz said she did not.

She stared down at the rushing water, listened to the babble and burble that would normally soothe her.

Sobs racked her body. Ed and Emily had both tried to call her multiple times. She didn't want them to be worried about her, but she couldn't face talking to either of them. What could she possibly say?

Sunlight shimmered across the water. Liz wished it was colder. It would be quicker that way.

It was impossible to stand on this bridge and not picture Emily. Her small, heart-shaped face lit up with excitement as the two of them ran from one side of the bridge to the other looking to see whose stick would 'swim' faster.

Reflexively, Liz found herself looking around for a stick. She found one and threw it into the river. 'I love you, Emily.'

She wiped her eyes and nose with her sleeve. Normally, she'd abhor such street urchin behaviour. Not today, though.

She trudged along the riverbank, inhaling the musty mulchy scent. Her thin-soled shoes squelched in the mud. She was surprised that it was so muddy given the recent fine weather. It was good though. It played into her story.

She stopped when she found the perfect spot. A place where the riverbank looked steep and slippery.

She fished her phone out of her pocket. More missed calls from Emily and more messages from 'Peter'.

You okay, sweetheart? Bit worried because I haven't heard from you all morning xxx

Please let me know you're okay, my darling. Going out of my mind here. Love you to the moon and back xxxx

Fresh sobs convulsed Liz's chest. He didn't love her to the moon and back. He didn't love her to the end of the street.

She had three messages she wanted to send. None of them were to 'Peter'. When she'd been sitting on the bus, she'd thought of all the things she was going to say to him but, in the end, she'd realised there was nothing to say. He'd won and she'd lost and it was as simple as that. He didn't deserve a single word more from her.

She sat down on the ground, the damp from the scrubby grass seeping through her thin trousers. She'd thought carefully about what she was wearing, refusing the skirt that Domenica had pulled out of the wardrobe. She'd been humiliated enough without the world seeing her knickers.

The messages needed to be worded very carefully. They had to be loving but not sound like a goodbye. What was about to happen was going to be an accident.

Would he hear about it somehow? Would he care? (Of course he wouldn't care. *Fool.*)

She tapped out a message to Judith.

So sorry about yesterday. I think the pain is making me a crabby old thing. Please forgive me. You have been a wonderful friend to me over the years.

She paused. Did the last line sound melodramatic? This had to seem like a normal message, albeit an affectionate one. She deleted the last line and wrote:

Thanks for looking out for me as always. You were right and I'll be careful. xx

That was good. She saved it as a draft. Now, Ed.

Sorry I missed your calls – switched my phone off by mistake. More importantly, sorry about our row yesterday. It was lovely to see you and Emily. Love you, Mum. Xx

That last line might be a bit of a giveaway – she didn't often tell Ed she loved him nowadays. Maybe she should have done a lot more of that.

She left it and saved the message as a draft, shivering a little against the breeze. It was good that she was already slightly cold. Her fingers hovered over her phone as she thought about what to write to Emily, her darling girl.

Sorry I missed your calls – switched my phone off by mistake. So lovely to see you yesterday. Forgive an old lady getting a bit sentimental, but I wanted to tell you how immensely proud of you I am. You deserve all the good things in life, and I only hope Mark realises what a lucky man he is!

Liz's breath caught in her throat. She wasn't going to be at Emily's wedding.

It didn't matter. This was the only way.

Love you, Grandma. Xx

Liz stood up, looked at the sky. She had never been a religious woman, but she felt as if she ought to say some sort of prayer. She walked towards the water.

Chapter Seventy-Two

Ed

Ed fetched a thick blanket from his mum's bedroom. She was still shivering despite them having got her out of her wet trousers and it being an unseasonably warm day. She hadn't stopped crying either. It broke Ed's heart to see her like this. He'd always thought of her as a tough old bird but, of course, we all have our breaking point.

He and Emily had agreed to bring her to the house for a bit because they were desperate to get her inside and she refused to go either back to the care home or anywhere public. Emily had suggested they stop off at a supermarket for a few provisions and was now downstairs force-feeding her grandmother hot, sweet tea.

'Here we go,' Ed said, gently tucking the blanket around his mother's legs.

He sat down and rubbed his palms across his face. He couldn't stop picturing the moment they'd found Liz, sobbing as she dipped her legs into the water like a child about to go for a paddle. She told them she'd dropped her phone in the river and was going in to try to retrieve it. Ed and Emily had exchanged glances. Quite apart from the fact that Liz hadn't so much as rolled up her trousers, they knew she was way too sensible to do something like that. She'd spent both their childhoods warning them of the dangers of open water, saying even strong swimmers could struggle with currents and the shock of water that was so much colder than you'd think.

'That bastard isn't worth you being so upset, Mum,' Ed said. 'He's not worth anything.'

Emily shot Ed a look: not now. When had she got to be so much wiser than him? Somewhere around the age of twelve, he reckoned.

'I'm sorry,' Liz said for the hundredth time since they'd found her at the edge of the river.

'Don't say sorry,' Ed and Emily said in unison.

Ed's hands trembled as he picked up his mug of tea. 'We'll find the bastard. Go to the police.'

'And have more people know what a fool I am?'

'We can't let him get away with it,' Ed said.

Emily nodded, 'Dad's right, I'm afraid. Quite apart from what he's done to you, and probably others, this is a real person's identity he's stolen.'

'Oh God,' Liz said. 'I hadn't even properly processed that.'

'You're in shock. Have a bit more of your tea.' Emily held the mug to Liz's lips as if she were a baby.

'We had a video call,' Liz said, her voice cracking. 'I don't understand—'

'These people are very clever,' Ed said. 'Which is why you mustn't blame yourself.'

'Exactly.' Emily squeezed her grandma's good hand.

'I wonder if the photos are him?' Liz said. 'Or whether that's another innocent person who's been dragged into all this?'

'Who knows?' Emily said. 'But the police will find out.'

351

Liz sighed. 'Isn't your flight today, Ed? I don't want to make you miss it.'

'It's fine. It's not until eight fifteen this evening. And I don't care if I do miss it. I need to know you're okay.' Was that even true? He did want his mother to be okay, but today was also the day the bank was foreclosing on the condo, so he kind of thought he ought to be with Shona too. Wherever he was, he was letting someone down.

'Do you know what I thought this morning?' Liz said. 'That I feel even worse now than I did when John died. Isn't that shameful? That I let this… this… hologram of a person upset me more than the death of a man I loved for thirty years.' A sob came out of her mouth. 'But it's the humiliation, you see – everyone knowing that I'm an old fool. That's what I can't live with.'

Ed got up and squeezed himself onto the sofa on the other side of his mother to Emily. He took her small bird-like hand in his. 'Mum, you know the old adage: we're all fools for love.'

Liz gave him a watery smile. 'But how can I love him? We've never even met. He's not real.'

'He was real to you,' Emily said, gently. 'And you're anything but a fool. You're one of the smartest people I know.'

The three of them lapsed into silence.

'I was going to give him John's Rolex,' Liz said.

Shame washed through Ed's body as he remembered how he'd thought about taking the watch himself. Started to justify it to himself in his own mind.

He peeled off his jumper.

'How did you get that bruise?' Liz said.

Ed thought about making up a story. There had been quite enough drama, after all. He was done lying, though. 'I was mugged. Yesterday evening.'

'Are you okay?' Emily and Liz said in unison. 'Were you hurt?'

Ed was almost undone by this flash of kindness he knew he didn't deserve. He felt a lump rise in his throat. 'I'm fine.'

'Why didn't you tell me you were mugged?' Emily said. 'When you came to the flat last night.'

'I didn't want to play the sympathy card.'

'But you love the sympathy card,' Emily said.

'I'm trying to change,' Ed said.

Emily looked at him, her expression unreadable.

'I hate the idea of going to the police,' Liz said. 'I know I have to but it's horrible. They're going to think I'm such an idiot.'

Ed took her hand. 'No, they won't. And Emily and I will be right there by your side.'

Chapter Seventy-Three

Liz

What had changed *everything* for Liz was the love her son and granddaughter had surrounded her with. She wasn't alone after all.

Of course, love wouldn't pay her debts or keep her in this house – the house she'd lived in since she was a young bride. It wouldn't inure her to the humiliation of knowing people were laughing at her and it wouldn't stop her beating herself up about what an idiot she'd been. That would go with her to the grave. But, with her family by her side, she could face another day.

The three of them had moved to the kitchen. Emily was slicing a white farmhouse loaf into thick wedges. 'Have you got yourself into debt, Grandma? It's just I've got some money saved up for the wedding.'

The breath caught in Liz's throat. The thought that Emily would hand over her wedding fund, or that she would take that. 'I don't need to borrow any money.' She hesitated, not wanting to say more, but she was sick of lies and half-truths. 'I am in a little bit of debt. For the first time in my life. I've given him just over forty-five thousand pounds. All of my savings and twenty thousand pounds I got from an equity release deal on the house.'

'Bastard,' Ed said.

'I'll be okay financially if I sell the house,' Liz said. 'It's probably a good idea for me to move somewhere smaller anyway.' It was the first time she'd admitted this to herself, but it was true. She wasn't getting any younger and breaking her shoulder had given her a glimpse of the not-so-distant future. It was deeply humbling, she now knew to go from being a physically active person to someone who needs help to get dressed and can't take a shower on their own.

'What about before you sell the house?' Ed said. 'Do you have enough money to get by?'

Liz nodded. 'I've got my state pension. I won't live like royalty, but I won't starve. The care home is pricey, but luckily they demanded their fees upfront. I'm covered for the next three weeks and I'm sure I'll be out of this cast by then and able to look after myself.'

'Are you okay about going back to the care home?' Ed said. 'I know you don't like it much.'

'It's fine,' Liz said. 'I don't like it because it makes me feel old. It's not that bad, though, and guess what, I am old.'

'Shona always says you're only as old as you feel,' Ed said.

'Pfftt,' Liz said. 'What nonsense.' She took a sip of her tea. 'You love Shona very much?'

Ed nodded. 'I do.'

'Dad,' Emily said. 'I have to ask—'

'Am I cheating on her?' Ed said, finishing her sentence. 'No, I'm not. I can see why you might think I am, but I'm not.'

'Thank goodness for that,' Liz said. 'Do you know how many conversations I had with "Peter" about cheating? How we both thought it was something a relationship could never fully recover from. At the time, I thought it was yet another example of how our values aligned, but now I realise he was just telling me the things I wanted to hear. What an idiot I am.'

'You're not an idiot,' Emily said.

'These people are very clever at manipulating people,' Ed added. 'You're not the first and you won't be the last.'

'I really believed he was the love of my life,' Liz said, a fat tear plopping onto the scrubbed wood table. 'My soulmate.'

'I'm sorry,' Emily said, kneeling down beside her.

Liz squeezed her granddaughter's hand. It seemed impossible to imagine that less than a month ago she'd been in this kitchen batch-cooking special meals for the freezer in preparation for 'Peter's' arrival. She'd even asked him what his favourite dinners were. *Fool.*

'How's your shoulder?' Emily asked.

'Not too bad,' Liz lied. 'But I could probably do with a couple of ibuprofen.'

'I'll fetch them,' Ed said, getting up.

'You'll need to eat with ibuprofen,' Emily said, putting two slices of bread into the toaster.

Liz wondered what messages 'Peter' was sending to the phone that was lying at the bottom of the river. Tomorrow morning, he would set off to the parcel locker ready to make his collection. After that, who knew? Moving on to his next victim, most probably.

Emily set down a plate of toast and some butter and Ed came back with the ibuprofen.

Liz watched as Emily buttered her toast and Ed doled out her ibuprofen. It felt wrong to be babied by people she'd looked after as actual babies.

She looked around the kitchen. She'd imagined her and 'Peter' sharing candlelit suppers in here. Chatting and laughing into the night before going upstairs to bed. She'd even put away a photograph of her and John that had been on her bedside table. She felt guilty about that now. But then she felt guilty about a lot of things.

Chapter Seventy-Four

I have so many happy memories in this house. I took my first steps in the garden right next to Grandpa John's treasured vegetable patch. It is a family gag that, if I'd tumbled into his runner bean canes, my grandfather wouldn't have been nearly so delighted by my achievement.

The thought of my grandma losing this place because of that bastard makes my stomach hurt. I can't imagine new people in this kitchen. Will they keep the dark green Aga, will they have a huge wooden table or a Welsh dresser that groans with mismatched blue and white china? Will they understand that this is the perfect country kitchen and nothing must change?

Of course, the house isn't the most important thing. For all its memories, it is just bricks and mortar. What really hurts is seeing what all this has done to my grandma. There is no way that story about her going into the river to try to retrieve her phone is true, and I shudder to think what would have happened if I hadn't suddenly thought to look for her where we used to play Pooh Sticks.

I reach my hand out across the table and squeeze Grandma's good hand. 'Can I get you anything? More tea?'

She shakes her head.

'Dad?'

'I'm fine thanks, love.'

'God, I feel ashamed,' Grandma says. 'To get to my great age and be so... so... gullible. That bastard must have thought all his Christmases had come together when he found me.'

'Don't be so hard on yourself,' Dad says. 'These people are very clever and know exactly how to reel you in.'

'He's right,' I say.

'Anyway,' Dad says. 'You definitely don't scoop the prize for Most Shameful Family Member. That's got to go to me. I've lied to Emily, lied to you and lied to Shona. Oh, and let's not forget, Shona is going to lose her home because of me. Pretty unedifying.'

'You must have had a terrible upbringing,' Grandma says, smiling. 'I still reckon it's a tie, though. I was prepared to fall out with you over this man. And my best friend of sixty years. It's as if I was in a cult. Thank God for you, Emily, it seems you're the only one in the family with any sense.'

Anxiety bubbles in my stomach.

'Yeah,' Dad says, grinning at me. 'My perfect little girl.'

'I'm not perfect,' I blurt out. 'Very far from it.'

'Well, of course not, my darling,' Dad says. 'We're all human. But you're as—'

I shake my head. 'You don't understand. I've been lying my head off for days. Mark and I aren't getting married.'

'*What?*' Dad and Grandma say in unison.

I stare at a whorl on the surface of the table. 'We broke up about a week ago. Oh, and then we were engaged again last night but only for about an hour.'

'Sorry, but I'm not sure I understand,' Dad says.

I nod. 'It's complicated. But the point is, when you turned up on my doorstep on Tuesday night, I lied to you. Mark wasn't away on business; we'd split up.'

'So when we bought the wedding dress?' Dad says.

'I knew I wasn't getting married.'

'And when we went to look around all those wedding venues?' Dad says.

'I knew I wasn't getting married.'

'But what happened with you and Mark?' Grandma says.

'He dumped me.'

'Well, then he's an idiot,' Dad says. 'I still don't understand though. Why did you lie to me?'

My eyes fill with tears. 'I wanted you to think I'd done okay even though you'd walked out on me and Mum. That my life was perfect. That I was perfect.'

'Oh, Em,' Dad says softly.

I look up. I can hardly bear the pain in my father's eyes. My grandma has started crying again too. Maybe I shouldn't have dumped this on her today? I am so sick of all the lying though. 'I'm sorry, Grandma. I know you love Mark.'

'Pfftt,' she says. 'I love you more, you silly girl. Are you okay?'

'You know, I kind of am. Sad but okay if that makes sense?' I look at my dad. 'Someone once told me a person can be a good person but not your person.'

Dad smiles. 'Look at me with the life advice.'

I smile back. 'You were right about a couple of things actually. I did shout at Tommy. I told the headteacher that this morning.'

'How did she take it?' Dad says.

I shrug. 'She was okay about me making a mistake in the first place. Not so okay about me lying to everyone about it.'

'I don't know about any of this,' Grandma says. 'Should I be worried?'

'Absolutely not,' Dad says.

I smile. Sometimes it is rather nice to be around someone who makes you feel as if nothing is insurmountable. 'It'll be fine, Grandma.'

'Good,' she says. 'And I think I could do with another cup of tea now.'

'I'll make it,' Dad says, getting up.

I watch as he fills the kettle and puts fresh teabags into the teapot. A memory rises up of him in the kitchen of our old house before he left Mum. He didn't do much cooking but breakfasts were his speciality. I smile as I think of the silly French accent he used to adopt as he 'took Mademoiselle's order'.

'You were also right about me wanting to go travelling, Dad.'

He puts down three steaming mugs of tea. 'So many instances of me being right!' he says, winking.

I smile and roll my eyes. 'Don't get ahead of yourself. You know what they say about stopped clocks.'

'Perhaps I can set up a life coaching business?'

'You've done stranger jobs,' I say. 'But, yeah, the travelling. That was probably the biggest thing with me and Mark. I'd told myself I wasn't that bothered about going, but really that's because it wasn't his dream.'

'You've always wanted to see the world,' Grandma says. 'Do you remember when you were little and you used to beg me to show you photos from my trip with Judith? You never got bored of hearing those stories.'

'I do remember,' I say. 'And very soon I'm going to have stories of my own because I'm going to go to Australia. Not right now, but when the school year ends.'

'That's fantastic news,' Dad says.

'You'll have a wonderful time,' Grandma agrees.

'Yeah, I'm going to use the money I've set aside for the wedding to help fund it.' Thinking about the wedding again makes guilt stab at my guts. My lies have cost my dad a lot of money this weekend – money he could clearly do with. 'Dad, I know the deposit you put down on Holly House is non-refundable, so I'd like to pay you back for it.'

'You'll do no such thing,' he says.

'I must,' I say. 'Especially as you've got financial problems at the moment.'

'He's always got financial problems,' Grandma says.

Dad laughs. 'Thanks, Mum. Listen, Emily, the truth is the deposit on Holly House is neither here nor there when it comes to the mess I've got myself into. Shona and I will still lose the condo. So, I won't be taking a penny off you.'

'Are you sure?' I say. 'Well, at least, I can take the dress back and send that money to you.'

Dad shakes his head. 'Why don't you use that money to buy your ticket to Australia? That will make me feel like a proper dad.'

'But it's not exactly as if you're flush with cash at the moment?' I say.

'I know,' he says. 'Which is why I'm going to get a job as soon as I get back to the States. A real job I stick at no matter what. I've applied for my old job at Spectrum, actually.'

'Didn't you hate it there?' I say.

'He hates every job,' Grandma says.

Dad laughs. 'Again, thanks, Mum. And, yes, I did hate it, but I hate the thought of losing Shona much, much more.'

Grandma reaches out and squeezes his arm. 'Sounds as if you're growing up.'

'Can I ask you something?' Dad says to me. 'You know earlier you said you wanted me to think you were perfect? You do realise that all human beings are flawed and imperfect, right? That people are messy. We screw up, act out, cause hurt.'

'Some of us more than others,' I say, smiling.

'Ha, touché. But my point is, we don't have to be faultless to be worthy of love.'

'Thank God,' Grandma says.

I raise my mug aloft. 'Here's to being perfectly imperfect. And loving each other no matter what.'

Ten Months Later

Chapter Seventy-Five

Icing sugar sand, palm trees gently swaying in the soft breeze and clear turquoise water – if there is a nicer place in the world to tie the knot, I'm not sure I can think of it.

Dad, Grandma and I walk side by side towards the flower-laden gazebo, our bare feet sinking into the soft sand.

'I can't believe you're getting married,' I say to my dad.

'Because you can't believe she'll have me?'

I smile. 'Yeah, pretty much. She must love you. Y'know, despite all logic and reason telling her otherwise.'

It is impossible for me to be at a wedding without thinking about my own cancelled one but, while I inevitably feel a pang of sadness and the knowledge that Mark is someone I will always have a lot of love for, I know I did the right thing. Mark and I have managed to stay on good terms, and he is even looking after Pebbles while I'm away. (Pebbles, it goes without saying, remains cantankerous.)

'Thank you for being here,' Dad says to me and Grandma for the umpteenth time.

'Of course,' I say. 'Although, you do know you completely messed up all my plans.'

Dad laughs. I was supposed to be a couple of months into

my solo trip around Australia right now and, when Dad first told me about the wedding, I imagined I wouldn't make any kind of appearance, except maybe on FaceTime. But within a week I'd changed my plans. I've spent July and August travelling around the States, with my grandma joining me for the last couple of weeks. I'll fly to Australia next weekend. 'Are you sure?' Dad said, when I told him. 'I'm sure,' I replied.

'I'm so proud of you both,' Grandma says now. A small smile springs to her lips and her eyes twinkle. 'I mean, Emily, obviously, I've always been proud of you, but you too, Edward.'

Dad raises his eyebrows. 'You're *proud* of me? Have you been drinking?'

Grandma gives him a mock punch on the arm. 'I'm trying to have a moment here. You've achieved a lot recently. Making an effort to be the dad Emily deserves – a high bar – working on things with Shona, sticking at that job.'

'Yeah,' I say. 'I can't believe you're still at Spectrum.'

'Me neither!' Dad says, laughing.

'Also,' Grandma says. 'I need to thank you both for helping to pull me out of the dark hole I was in.'

My mind flashes back to that awful day when Dad and I found her by the river. She has come so far since then, even setting up an online support group called *Mending Hearts*. We've talked about it a lot, how she started it to help others but how it has helped her more than she could possibly imagine by showing her that being taken in by a romance scammer doesn't make you stupid or weak. I cried when she said that to me because I can't think of anyone less stupid or weak.

'Do you still think about him?' I say to her now.

She shakes her head. 'I try not to. Well, except when I want to enjoy the thought of him rotting away in jail.'

We reach the gazebo. The altar (if it is even called an altar when it's a non-religious ceremony) is covered with satin ribbons. They are to be part of the hand-fasting ceremony and their colours, according to Shona, have been chosen to honour Mother Nature. The shaman will use them to complete the symbolic tying together of Dad and Shona's hands.

The wedding is quintessentially Shona. As well as the hand-fasting, guests will be asked to form a circle as the spirits of the East, West, North and South are called upon to bless the union. Later, after a vegan wedding feast, we will all be gifted rose quartz crystals as a symbol of unconditional love and harmony.

'I can't believe Rick sent you a card,' Grandma says to Dad. 'I mean, I know the message was just "All the best, Uncle Rick", but still.'

'I know,' Dad says. 'And he got it here in time.'

'It was a kind thing you did for him with the dog,' I say. A few months after he'd been in London, Dad called one of his exes who works at Battersea Dogs & Cats Home and found out they were currently looking after a very old and very grumpy pug. He then phoned Uncle Rick and asked him if he could possibly offer this dog a home. Apparently, Rick was resistant at first, but Dad pushed the point, saying no one else wanted this dog so he was its only chance. Three days later, Uncle Rick turned up at Battersea ready to take home the pug he renamed Her.

'Oh, my goodness,' I say, pointing towards the ocean. 'Dolphins.'

'Yeah,' Dad says. 'I arranged them specially. The hand-fasting and the shaman and the spirits blessing the union are all Shona, but the frolicking dolphins are down to me. They've been a nightmare to train.'

I laugh and roll my eyes. 'Always taking credit!'

'Yeah,' Grandma says, grinning. 'Next thing we know he'll be saying the lovely weather is all down to him. Y'know, nothing to do with us being in the "Sunshine State".'

The travelling has been everything I expected it to be and more. I have loved the last couple of weeks with my grandma, but I also relished the five weeks before that when I was on my own. It was nice being able to please myself and decide without compromise what my next adventure was going to be. Plus, I quickly learned I could easily find company if I wanted it. I got better at talking to strangers – ironic for someone who spends much of their professional life telling children never to do this – and realised an opening gambit doesn't have to be spectacularly clever or witty. A question about where someone is from or a comment about the weather (I am British, after all) does just fine.

'My goodness,' Grandma says. 'The dolphins are really putting on a show for us. I reckon there must be a whole pod.'

Dad winks. 'Well, you know I don't do things by halves.'

Not everything about travelling alone has been easy, of course. In the first week, I got horrible food poisoning and sat crying on the dirty bathroom floor of the hostel as I tried to decipher the small print of my medical insurance. It was my dad who saved the day. I FaceTimed him, fully expecting him not to pick up, and sobbed incoherently about how I had never been so ill in my life and there was a sign in the bathroom that said 'Not drinking water' but it would be okay, wouldn't it? It had to be because there was no way I could get down to the kitchen. Within minutes of hanging up, someone brought me a big bottle of water and some rehydration salts and, not long after that, a doctor arrived.

There have been other less dramatic moments that have been testing too. Sometimes the sheer responsibility of having to organise everything myself – itinerary, tickets, places to stay – has been overwhelming, and single supplements are surely the work of the devil.

'Do you think Shona is going to stand you up?' Grandma says, grinning.

Dad gives her a mock punch on the arm. 'Of course not. Who'd turn down this? Anyway, it's the bride's prerogative to be late.'

I am looking forward to teaching again when I go back to England. For me, although I might joke about the views where I eat my lunch now being more inspiring than a dingy staffroom, travelling was never about escaping my job. When Grandma and I were hiking in Yosemite, I got chatting to an American teacher and burbled with excitement as I told her I was planning lessons around failure. I want to encourage the kids to talk about mistakes they've made, from failing to play nicely with their siblings to not getting their spellings right or not being able to do a forward roll. I want to teach them they don't need to be perfect.

'Here's Shona now,' Dad says.

I look up to see her making her way across the sand in a surprisingly traditional wedding dress. Even at a distance, I can see the huge grin across her face.

'What a lucky man I am,' Dad says. He squeezes my arm. 'On so many counts. Thank you for being my best woman.'

I feel a lump rise in my throat. 'Yeah,' I say, winking at him. 'You might want to hear my speech before thanking me!'

Dad laughs.

I reach out and adjust the white rose that is pinned to the lapel of his white linen suit. 'There you go – perfect.'

Acknowledgements

I am so lucky to have so many brilliant people around me.

Thank you to my fantastic agent Ger Nichol for always being in my corner. You are everything I could possibly ask for and more.

Thank you all at Bedford Square Publishers. I couldn't have a better home for my books. I'm especially indebted to my brilliant editor Carolyn Mays who has shaped this book into being a much better one than it was when it first hit her inbox. I also owe a huge and heartfelt thank you to Laura Fletcher, Jamie Hodder-Williams, Polly Halsey, Anastasia Boama-Aboagye and Hollie McDevitt.

Cover designer Henry Steadman deserves a special shout out, not only for another brilliant cover but for not losing patience at my painstaking explanations of *exactly* what expression Pebbles would wear. Thanks too to Kay Gale and Jacqui Lewis for copy editing and proofreading – otherwise known as sparing my blushes.

There are lots of bad things about social media, but I am forever grateful to it for bringing the D20 authors into my life. A great many of them have become proper mates and, while it feels almost impossible to pick out just a few names, Frances

Quinn is a heartbeat away from needing her name on the cover and Gillian Harvey, Louise Fein. Eleni Kyriaciou and Charlotte Levin have also helped keep me (mostly) on track.

Social media has also brought good things in the shape of Book Twitter (it will never be Book X) and I want to say thank you to all the brilliant book reviewers, book bloggers and booksellers. Your love of books is inspiring.

Inspiring is the perfect word to describe both Sophie Hannah and Anstey Harris, amazing authors and purveyors of much good advice.

Thank you to my family who put up with me constantly stealing their stories and saying 'shush, I'm writing.' Top of that list, and top of all my lists, are my lovely sons Charlie and Max Gill. Nothing would mean anything without the two of you. The rest of my family are pretty awesome too: Jenny Crichton-Stuart, Kit Crichton-Stuart, Harry Crichton-Stuart, Freddie Crichton-Stuart, Toby Green, Lex Green, Saskia Green and Jo Dangerfield. And, of course, my brilliant brother and sister Patrick Crichton-Stuart and Sophie Crichton-Stuart to whom this book is dedicated. (I'm afraid that does mean you'll have to read it, Patrick).

I can't talk about my family without mentioning my Mum and Dad. I miss you both every single day.

Thank you to my friends, who feel like family. (That's supposed to be a compliment, for the record). Hedy-Anne Freedman, Debra Davies, Caroline Donn, Sara Nair, Brian Davies, Steve Clinton, Sally Bargman, Frani Heyns, Nicky Peters, Georgina Heyward, John O'Sullivan, Gemma Champ, Carol Deacon, Katia Hadidian and Alex Judge.

Finally, the biggest thank you of all to my readers. There are a huge number of books out there and the fact you've picked up one of mine is an honour. I hope you've enjoyed it.

About the Author

Photo Credit: Stuart Gill

Nicola Gill lives in London with her husband and two sons. At the age of five, when all of the other little girls wanted to be ballet dancers, she decided she wanted to be an author. Her ballet teacher was very relieved. When she's not at her desk, you can usually find Nicola reading, cooking up vast vats of food for friends and family or watching box sets. Occasionally she even leaves the house...

www.nicolagill.com

𝕏 **@Nicola_J_Gill**

🅞 **@NicolaGillAuthor**

Bedford Square Publishers

Bedford Square Publishers is an independent publisher of fiction and non-fiction, founded in 2022 in the historic streets of Bedford Square London and the sea mist shrouded green of Bedford Square Brighton.

Our goal is to discover irresistible stories and voices that illuminate our world.

We are passionate about connecting our authors to readers across the globe and our independence allows us to do this in original and nimble ways.

The team at Bedford Square Publishers has years of experience and we aim to use that knowledge and creative insight, alongside evolving technology, to reach the right readers for our books. From the ones who read a lot, to the ones who don't consider themselves readers, we aim to find those who will love our books and talk about them as much as we do.

We are hunting for vital new voices from all backgrounds – with books that take the reader to new places and transform perceptions of the world we live in.

Follow us on social media for the latest Bedford Square Publishers news.

@bedsqpublishers
facebook.com/bedfordsq.publishers/
@bedfordsq.publishers

https://bedfordsquarepublishers.co.uk/